SPANISH FLY

Also by Will Ferguson

SPANISH FLY

A NOVEL

WILL FERGUSON

VIKING
CANADA

VIKING CANADA

Published by the Penguin Group

Penguin Group (Canada), 90 Eglinton Avenue East, Suite 700, Toronto, Ontario, Canada
M4P 2Y3 (a division of Pearson Canada Inc.)

Penguin Group (USA) Inc., 375 Hudson Street, New York, New York 10014, U.S.A.
Penguin Books Ltd, 80 Strand, London WC2R 0RL, England
Penguin Ireland, 25 St Stephen's Green, Dublin 2, Ireland (a division of Penguin Books Ltd)
Penguin Group (Australia), 250 Camberwell Road, Camberwell, Victoria 3124, Australia
(a division of Pearson Australia Group Pty Ltd)
Penguin Books India Pvt Ltd, 11 Community Centre, Panchsheel Park, New Delhi – 110 017,
India
Penguin Group (NZ), 67 Apollo Drive, Rosedale, North Shore 0745, Auckland,
New Zealand (a division of Pearson New Zealand Ltd)
Penguin Books (South Africa) (Pty) Ltd, 24 Sturdee Avenue, Rosebank, Johannesburg 2196,
South Africa

Penguin Books Ltd, Registered Offices: 80 Strand, London WC2R 0RL, England

First published 2007

1 2 3 4 5 6 7 8 9 10 (RRD)

Copyright © Will Ferguson, 2007

Photograph on page 389: Getty Images/Archive Films

*Publisher's note: This book is a work of fiction. Names, characters, places and incidents
either are the product of the author's imagination or are used fictitiously, and any
resemblance to actual persons living or dead, events, or locales is entirely coincidental.*

Manufactured in the U.S.A.

ISBN-13: 978-0-670-06684-1
ISBN-10: 0-670-06684-2

Library and Archives Canada Cataloguing in Publication data available upon request.

Visit the Penguin Group (Canada) website at **www.penguin.ca**

Special and corporate bulk purchase rates available; please see
www.penguin.ca/corporatesales or call 1-800-810-3104, ext. 477 or 474

Part One

A Carnival
in the Desert

ONE

I think sometimes Columbus was wrong. Maybe the world *is* flat.

You've got Heaven and you've got Hell, and somewhere in between, the plains of West Texas. In the kiln-baked emptiness out here, there's hardly a hint of Earth's curvature in evidence.

And there's me, Jack McGreary, riding shotgun in a Nash Ambassador sedan as it skims across the landscape, chasing the chrome torpedo of the car's hood ornament like we were traveling in the slipstream of a bullet.

There were three of us in that car: Virgil, at the wheel. Miss Rose, stretched out in the back. And me, on the lam from a life I'd long ago outgrown.

I'd only known Virgil and Miss Rose for a couple of hours, but that was plenty. I'd met them back in town, in an alleyway beside the dry goods store. When Virgil introduced me to Rose, she eyed me over like she was examining a quarter horse.

"You're a big one, aren't you. How old are you, boy?"

"Nineteen," I said. "Just turned."

"Nineteen?" She laughed. "Hell, I don't even remember nineteen."

The Nash Ambassador was a joyous ride. I'd seen advertisements for them; now I was in one. Four-door 1939 limited, sat six with a fold-out sleeper in the back. Rear-wheel drive, 105-horsepower, valve-in-head engine. Twin ignition system. Shatterproof glass. Flow-through ventilation with patented Weather-Eye climate control. Body stream-lined like one of those luxury passenger trains, the kind they used to show on promotional posters, curving through the Rocky Mountains or leaping gracefully over bridges—before the rail companies started tossing vagrants off of boxcars, that is. Sleek and smooth, the Ambassador, and full of innovational wonders. Virgil hit fifty without the slightest hiccup.

Rose sat with her legs up, dress billowing. Hair blowing every which way. Asleep—or pretending to be. I angled the side mirror and watched her awhile. Even with her eyes closed in a full face of wind, she kept trying to tuck back a loose strand of hair behind her ear.

Virgil had good taste, no doubt about it. In cars, and suits too. He was looking mighty dapper in his shimmery silk and Errol Flynn mustache. Made me feel awkward enough in overalls that were salt-crusted from the mine and poorly patched.

"This particular swindle?" said Virgil as we rolled into the next town on the map. "Easy as pie."

We'd crossed over into Yoakum County. Gattonville, the sign said. Looked like a smaller version of Paradise Flats, where I'm from. Not much to Gattonville. You could spit across it if the wind was in your favor. A few ragtag stores. Faded goods in the windows. Awnings in need of repair. An adobe church in the main square with a bell that lacked a clapper, moving on dry air. That bell creaked, back and forth, without a dong, a ding, or a "How d'you do?" Entire town was built out of compressed dust, it seemed.

"Two-handed games are hard to play," said Virgil. "And a lot of plum opportunities have gone to waste solely on account of Rose and me not being able to swing them on our own. Oftentimes you'll need a roper, a switch, and a getaway. That makes three right there. Which is where you come in. Rose will make the drop, I'll do the swoop, you get us out."

Rose had stirred as soon as we stopped moving. She leaned forward, tapped out a cigarette. "Treasury scam?"

Virgil nodded. We were hunkered down in the Nash now, parked in an alleyway across from Gattonville's sorry excuse for a downtown. We were waiting, though I wasn't sure for what.

Rose crushed out her third cigarette in as many minutes, said, "Can we do this, Virg?"

He nodded. "Anytime you're ready, doll."

Rose pulled out a stack of clean twenty-dollar bills. She read the serial numbers to Virgil, who jotted them down in a small notebook, each number on a separate page.

Rose got out of the car and walked across the street to the first store in front of us: a grocer's. We saw her look back through the screen door just as it closed, like she was being followed. Which was the whole entire point, according to Virgil, to appear as furtive and memorable as possible.

How it plays out is this: Rose goes in, skulks around the store, eyes darting, and makes a smallish purchase with a crisp twenty-dollar bill. Something under a dollar. Grabs her change in a hurry and beats it out of there.

Virgil then storms in, having assumed the gruff confidence of a U.S. Treasury man. "Did a lady come in here?" he asks the clerk. Virgil flashes a badge. He'd shown me the badge back in the car. It looked real, because it was. If you peered closer you might see the words DEPT. OF FISH & WILDLIFE—Virgil won it in a game of faro, he said—but who stares that closely at a badge? "Yey tall. Blond curls, blue dress?"

"Just in!" they'd say, remembering her clearly.

"Did she pass a bill?" Virgil asks. "One with the following serial number—" and he reads it from his notebook.

The clerk would pull Rose's twenty from his till and his mouth would flop open. The very same number! Well, that clinched it.

"She left not five minutes ago," the clerk'd say. "Maybe you can catch her."

"We have men waiting for her on the road outta town. My friend, you've just had an encounter with Bonnie Parker's cousin."

"Her cousin?"

"Connie. Notorious counterfeiter. Been flooding the area with these." Virgil would pull on a pair of cotton gloves and carefully extract the (perfectly legal) tender from the clerk's grasp, hold it to the light and mutter, "Bogus, all right." Then, steadying his gaze on the clerk, "You do know that accepting counterfeit money is a federal offense."

The clerk would gulp down that news, but Virgil would always decide to go easy on 'em.

"I can see you're an honest man," he'd say. "And there is a possible reward in this for you ..."

There you had it.

Fear, followed by greed. A powerful one-two combination. Virgil would write up a receipt for the supposedly bogus bill—law required the immediate confiscation of counterfeits, after all—and he'd walk out, twenty dollars in hand, making the change Rose had received earlier pure profit.

By this time, Rose was several doors down. She tended to get in and out quicker than did Virgil.

Having reclaimed the twenty, Virgil would step back outside, flip his notebook over to the next serial number, and enter the next shop.

My job consisted of one thing: starting the car. As it turned out, I couldn't even manage that.

Twenty minutes down and almost eighty dollars in the clear, Virgil and Rose hopped in. "Let's go!"

But in my sweaty-palmed panic, when I pulled the choke I flooded the engine. *Damn.* I pushed the choke back in, turned the key, and stood on the throttle. I was trying to get a good rush of air, blow the spark plugs clear. The engine sputtered; a poof of black smoke appeared from under the hood. Close enough. I slammed the Nash into gear. The engine sputtered a second time, the car lurched forward, then stalled. I tried again, hitting the throttle harder this time. More smoke. The Nash lunged forward again. Died, and this time for good.

Virgil hit the dash with both hands. "Well, that's just swell!"

He got out, slammed the door. And didn't the last clerk of the day appear, puffing and red-faced with radio-fed junior G-man fantasies urging him onward.

And didn't that clerk spot Virgil beside the Nash, and didn't that clerk holler, "Mister! There she is! In the car!"

These are the moments as test a man. I stumbled out from the driver's side, heart thumping, fists already balled, expecting a donnybrook right there in the lane.

But a strange sort of calm came over Virgil. He turned, slowly, like a matador might.

He smiled. Called out to the clerk in the friendliest of tones. "Sir," he said. "Would you be so kind? The government of these United States requires your assistance."

Virgil grabbed me by the collar and yanked up hard, even though I was a head taller than him, at least, and he had to go up on his tiptoes to do it.

"Sir, I have just nabbed Connie Parker and her young whelp here. You take this boy back to your store, don't let nobody see. Other members of Parker's hardened gang of criminals may be hiding nearby. Once I get this boy's mother out of the car, I'll join you. We'll need to take a state-ment—for the citation of bravery that's sure to follow. You just make sure Junior here doesn't escape." (Virgil, I later learned, had left a trail of citations for bravery across the greater Southwest. "I'm something of a philanthropist that way," he liked to say.)

With pudgy virility now well stoked, the clerk marched me back to his hardware store, arm on elbow, whispering, "Don't try nothing funny," like he was a tough guy in an Edward G. Robinson picture.

The thought occurred to me that Virgil and Miss Rose might very well leave me there to turn on the wind. From the length of the wait that followed, I imagined they were discussing that very possibility. But the door finally did open, with Virgil giving Rose a theatrical shove through. Her head was hanging down and her hands were out front with Virgil's jacket tossed over them, as if concealing handcuffs. Virgil flipped the sign over to CLOSED.

"Connie Parker?" asked the clerk, wide-eyed at meeting someone famous. (Nonexistent, true, but still famous.) "*The* Connie Parker?"

Rose said nothing. Kept her gaze downward cast.

"You did a fine job," said Virgil to my chubby captor. "Outstanding. There'll be a reward in this for sure. *Local man helps capture notorious criminal gang,* can see it now. I'll run these two down to the police station. You sit tight by the phone for a call from headquarters."

"Won't move an inch," the clerk vowed. Then, as we were turning to leave, our friend added, "Didn't you need to check the till too? See if there's any fingerprints need dusting?"

Virgil stopped. Turned. A strange twitch came to his lips, like a man suppressing, oh, I don't know, a smile perhaps. He smoothed down his mustache, which didn't need smoothing, and said, "Sir, that is a most excellent suggestion. You have the makings of a G-man, I do believe."

"Really?" said the clerk, as he opened his register wide for the plundering.

"I'll have to take the entire drawer," said Virgil. "Dust it for, ah, evidence. And whatnot."

Virgil wrote a receipt for that as well.

The clerk handed the drawer from the register over to Virgil, the money neatly stacked and sorted for our ready convenience. The man then leaned behind the counter and pulled out another drawer. This one, empty.

"I'll get my float from the safe," he said. "No never mind."

This caught Virgil's interest as well. "Where do you buy those?" he asked, referring to the replacement drawer.

"Office supply station, up in Silver."

"They fit any register?" asked Virgil.

"They do. Clean as a whistle. It's standardized. Makes no matter who the manufacturer is."

"So," I said as we walked back to the car, "just as well I flooded the Nash. Right?"

Virgil muttered something. It took him a good half hour to get the Ambassador running again, and once we were out of Gattonville, Rose was put in the driver's seat. I was now cast as the shifty one who'd skulk through the stores, dropping twenties, while Rose waited—with the motor running. Virgil told me to look nervous, which wasn't difficult. My hands were shaking the entire time, and though I found I could hold down my fears, that tremor in my hands never seemed to die. We hit the next three towns, one after another, with me doing the drop and Virgil racing in afterwards, scaring the clerks with threats of persecution and then enticing them with promises of rewards. He would replace their till drawer with the last one we'd taken. The till he gave them was always stacked with money; we couldn't count on every clerk being as numskulled as that first one, and replacing one till with another filled just as readily with cash hardly seemed suspicious. Virgil would write his receipts, and the clerks would figure they had nothing to lose.

Rose and Virgil had a suitcase stuffed with counterfeit bills, you see. Along with a satchel full of blank paper, pale green and cut to size.

"You never want to pass queer money," Virgil said. We'd pulled over to the side of the road, and he was preparing our latest till for the next switch. "Not if you can help it. I bought this lot for forty dollars, keep it primarily for emergencies and the occasional pigeon drop."

Pigeon drop?

"When you set up passersby with a Mish roll—"

Mish roll?

"A single high bill wrapped around blanks or cut newspaper. Name comes from 'Michigan,' where it was perfected. Myself, I prefer a 'live Mish.'"

A live Mish?

"A stack of actual one-dollar bills sandwiched between counterfeit hundreds. Jesus, kid, you've got a lot to learn. A live Mish looks more authentic than newsprint or green paper. It's hard to catch, at least in transactions that occur at night. Problem is, forged bills are childishly easy to spot in the light of day. Colors are never quite right, nor is the feel of the paper. The Treasury Department uses cotton weave, deep ink, expensive plates. Almost impossible to duplicate. If forgery were easy, there'd be no need for swindles."

We headed back on the road, Virgil at the wheel, the Ambassador's patented Weather-Eye humming, the air flowing over us, and Rose stretched out in the back again.

We stopped at every town we passed, each one smaller than the next. The game had taken a new and unexpected turn, and our haul soared. Where it would have taken us an entire street to harvest eighty dollars, we were now getting more than that in every till we exchanged. Each time we emptied our latest drawer of money we'd stack it with blanks, then put a single twenty, ten, five, and one on top. All counterfeits, except for the dollar. Obvious, too, if you held any of them up for scrutiny, if you crinkled them even a bit. But when they were sitting pretty atop a U.S. Treasury Department till?

"No one'll blink," said Virgil. "Won't even take a second look."

He added further insurance, though, just to be safe.

"The bills are marked," he'd tell the clerk. "So don't handle any of it until we send our man in to dust 'em." (Virgil didn't say with what or why, but that didn't matter. It would keep the clerk's hands out of the till long enough for us to put some serious distance between ourselves and whatever town we'd just hit.) "And remember," Virgil would say, dangling that string before their kitty-cat gaze, "a mighty reward is coming your way. So make sure you wait for our man to arrive."

A reward! And a mighty one at that! Their eyes would shine with undisguised *avarice*. That's from A, in the dictionary. "An excessive desire for wealth." Not a desire for wealth, which is natural born, but an *excessive* desire.

"People who're that greedy and that stupid deserve to be taken," said Virgil as we blew away from our last till exchange of the day, the sun sweeping red behind us and the lights from the next town flickering in the distance. "They have it coming," he said.

"Sure," said Rose, sleepyheaded in the backseat. "Blame the mark." Then, more to herself than anything, she said, "I can't believe you told that clerk in Gattonville I was Jack's mother."

"What did you want me to say?" asked Virgil. "That you were his moll? I was thinking on my feet, that's all."

She looked out the window at the sagebrush rolling by. West Texas, hammered flat. And only the mesas of the Richardson Range in the far distance to remind you of a horizon. "Can't believe you told him that," she said.

"Come on, Rose. You ain't that old."

"Has nothing to do with my age," she said, still looking out of the window. "You shouldn't have said I was his mother."

Two

It's hard to know, isn't it? Where things begin. Why we end up taking one path and not another. With me, I think maybe it started when I got arrested. That was out east, in Louisiana. All part of the plan, and it worked wonderfully well, but I do feel perhaps that's when everything started to go awry.

Say a pair of friends are playing cards and one catches the other cheating, so he goes home, gets a gun, loads it, comes back, puts a bullet clean through the other fellow's chest. Well, when did that murder occur, exactly? What was the moment of no return? Was it when the bullet left the barrel? Or when it hit that man? Was it when the man's heart stopped beating? Was it when his friend pulled the trigger, or when he failed to talk said friend out of shooting him? Maybe if he'd pleaded his case just a little more effectively. Had wept just a little more. Or was it when his friend first left the card table, went home to get a gun? Maybe it goes back further still, to the roots of their friendship, to how they were bred, what they were taught, whether they were raised rich or poor, God-fearing or scientific. When was the clock set to ticking? When did that second man's life really end?

Or take something bigger. A railroad disaster, say. When things go off the tracks like that, it can be tricky trying to pinpoint the specific cause of the derailment. You might trace the catastrophe back to a signalman, asleep at the switch. But *why* was he asleep? Was he up through the night on account of his neighbor's dog baying at the moon? And if so, are the train wreck and the destruction that followed the dog's fault? Or is it the moon's? And who put that moon to spinning, anyway? Yes sir, you could pull at the threads of a thing forever and never succeed in unraveling the truth.

In my case, maybe it went back further than Louisiana. Further than Virgil and Miss Rose. I think maybe in my case it started with the dust.

THEY CALLED THEM "black blizzards," on account of how they'd pile up like rain clouds and blot out the sun. Some rumbled with thunder, others were eerily silent. All were as dry as boneyards. When they rolled over us, it was as though a winding sheet had been pulled across the land.

That was topsoil climbing into the sky, those were farms drying up, blowing away. One farm for every mile of dust, that's what they said. The dirt left behind might be ashen gray or wax-paper yellow. Oily brown if it came from Kansas, thick black from East Texas, a reddish copper color if it was from the hills of Oklahoma. Each storm had its own color and each color had its own smell. The red sands were peppery and burned your nostrils when you breathed them in. The darker browns held a greasy aroma that left you feeling sick in your stomach. The yellow storms smelled of rancid meat. One black blizzard, it stretched all the way from the Texas panhandle to the Canadian border, darkening skies as far away as Albany, so you do the calculations. The heart of a continent, a space so big it's hard to imagine. Emptied out. The wind started to pick up on Armistice Day and just kept blowing, lifting years of homesteading and hard work clean off the land. That was back in '33. Six years later, and they were saying we'd "turned a corner." By my count, that was the fourth corner we'd turned. If prosperity was at hand, none of it had reached down here yet.

It was a fearful and wondrous thing, watching a dust storm roll in. The horizon grew black, then blacker still, became an inky line drawn along the edge of the Earth. The sky began to churn like the hoofprint clouds of an approaching army, drawing nearer and nearer until—in a rush of wind, the very air seemed to solidify and was set in motion, burning your throat and eyes, stinging at you till it felt like you were naked in nettles. And there was Crazy Eli, eyes wild, flailing away in the worst of it, raving on about Judgment Day and the end of the world, shouting into the bone-scour of a sandpaper wind. "Punishment!" he'd cry, though I never did figure out for what.

Houses rocked on it, groaning from the assault. The sand sifted in. Grit got between your teeth and in your eyes. Into your ears. You learned to lie still at night; turning only kicked up the dust from the blankets. You learned to sleep with a washcloth over your face and to not dream of suffocation. When you woke you'd find an outline on your pillow, like a jigsaw puzzle with a piece missing. There were some months the storms rolled in every two or three days. The ponds turned to sludge, the sludge turned to clay. And hadn't the Pharaoh's dream come to pass, the lean years eating the fat? It was the Sunday services I suffered through come to life.

Biblical, is what it was. Animals died by the score, Noah in reverse: creatures big and small walking backwards out of the ark and into a lack of water, walking backwards into ribs and hanging hides and the eye-mucus-swarming of flies. They died of a terminal thirst. Died licking at their own shadows.

The contours kept shifting: high dunes in some fields, down to hardpan in others, as the winds peeled back layers of history, laid it bare. Half-forgotten Indian camps reemerged, along with arrowheads and Spanish stirrups, teepee rings and buffalo bones. It was as if the years spent breaking the land, the years of homesteading and sod turning, had never occurred; that it had all been a dream. Over in Dalhart they were organizing a Last Man's Club, with each member taking a pledge never to abandon the plains—even though it was clear to many that the plains had already abandoned them.

They say the dust storms ate entire towns, that some simply disappeared beneath the drifts and dunes. They say men died in it, drowned, swallowing dust, trying to breathe. Don't know if those stories are factually true, but I do know I've seen people fleeing the darkness, kerchiefs over their mouths as though escaping a mustard gas attack. Scurrying home, stuffing sheets and old rags into every crack they can find, putting gummed paper around windows and doorways, trying to keep the dust at bay as best they could. It snaked in anyway, leaving ripples across the floor in fingerprint patterns.

I was nine years old when the stock market crashed. They were calling it Black Thursday and then it was Black Monday and then Black Tuesday, then Black October, and then they were speaking in years.

Funny thing is, early on, before the drought hit, the problem had been too great a yield. After the Crash, bumper-crop harvests threatened to drive prices even further down. Grain was already rotting in the silos—"abundant decay," as they called it—so the Department of Agriculture was forced to set fire to thousands upon thousands of acres, destroying great swaths of wheat and cotton, beets and tobacco and other such, in a last-ditch attempt at preventing an oversupply. The fields burned. Flames cast a red glow against the sky, as though someone had wandered off and left the gates to the Underworld open. It's a sight you don't soon forget, a landscape burning like that.

In the South, farmers were ordered to plow their cotton under, but Southern mules were trained to walk *between* rows. They wouldn't run a plow straight through, refused to trample any crops underfoot. Had to be whipped into doing it.

Bumper yields and fields on fire: it seems so long ago. The drought years are upon us now, and grasshoppers have laid ruin to what little was left. Dry storms and stifling heat. Hoppers and bleached bones. We once lived in America's Bread Basket; now we're at the bottom of the Dust Bowl—southernmost reach of it, in fact. "Where the sediment settles," as we say. Our idea of an outing around here is three gasps of fresh air between one storm and the next. "This New Sahara" is what they're calling it in the papers.

I remember when I was ten, maybe eleven, getting caught in the yard when the grasshoppers hit—and them swirling around, everywhere, pelting me from all sides, and me in tears calling for my mother, knowing she would appear and save me if I just cried loud enough.

To the west of our town lay the mesas and sunsets of a Newer Mexico, and to the south, the salt fields, cracked and crusted. Life was always to the north. That was where the wide fields of the Great Plains opened up like an embrace. Was a time, they say, when a man couldn't throw a handful of seeds out the window without swimming through crops, lush and full, come morning. I have vague notions of green fields, but that's so far back at this point it hardly seems true.

People are buying tripe and soup bones now, maybe a cut of pork fat if fortune sends a few extra coins their way. Men tramping for work till their feet bleed, till they have to line their soles with cardboard and folded-up newspapers, have to stuff cotton in the heels, just to dampen the pain. Evicted, foreclosed, turfed out. Living on cabbage soup and hardtack in canvas tents and tin-can hovels, in shantytowns made of packing boxes and old crates not much bigger—or much better—than chicken coops. Kerosene lamps for light, coal stoves and charcoal buckets for warmth, and hope as rare as roast.

Over in Arkansas, fifty men were caught fighting over a barrel of garbage out back of a restaurant. Even in our local church, where every manner of calamity is seen as the mysterious application of Providence to human affairs, the despair is there, and when the ragged women rise to ask, voices wavering, "What can we do? Please tell us. What can we do?" the only answer they get is "Plant corn and pray."

Corn was just about the only thing that would grow, kernels so hard you had to soak them in well water a week before they'd cook right. Me, I've always been too big for my size. I outgrew my classmates, outgrew my clothes, damn near outgrew the corn. Outgrew my overalls several times over, till I ended up looking like a woeful version of Li'l Abner. My overalls needed patching but my Da didn't sew—not manly, he said, though truth be told he couldn't thread a needle if the fate of the Free World hinged upon his doing so. I taught myself how to mend, and soon could patch up near about anything, from canvas to corduroy. I have big hands, but agile fingers. "You'll make some woman a fine wife" is how Da put it.

Now, my Da—I call him Fayther, but not to his face, him being of fiery Scots breeding and inclined to find the insult in anything—he's a McGreary out of St. Kilda, small granite islands on the far side of nowhere. (Beyond the Outer Hebrides, if you can imagine such a thing.) St. Kilda was the farthest outpost of the British Isles. After that, you fell off the map. "Only five surnames in the history of St. Kilda," my Da liked to boast, "and McGreary was one of them," though why this should be a point of pride eluded me. Seems like that must have involved a goodly number of cousins marrying cousins, and, far as I knew, that sort of thing was still frowned upon.

My Da came to the New World via Cape Breton. That's an island too, up north somewhere. A whole shipload of McGrearys were brought in to work the Cape Breton coal fields, but a cave-in at Dominion Mines buried five of my Da's brothers (three in the early tellings, but the number grew over the years), and Da fled this accumulation of ghosts. He followed a seam of coal south into the U.S., through the Appalachians, then worked his way westward on the Rock Island Railroad, stoking fire on the regional runs. Memphis. Little Rock. Oklahoma City. And then south again into the borderlands of Texas.

He fell in love with my mother from the back of a freight train.

He was catching a ride to camp on the caboose, hanging from the rear, the wind playing on him like a "cat on a string," as he said. The train was crossing the open country north of Sweetwater when it clattered past a homestead and he saw my mother, bent in a beet field, red hair blowing back. That's all he had, just a glimpse of red hair, but it was enough. He jumped off at the next water tower and walked back along the tracks, twenty miles or more, stopping at every farm he came upon. "I'm looking for the girl with the red hair," he said. And he found her. And they were married. "Things were simpler back then," he said.

Later on, my Da would ascribe his success in courting my mother to charm and persistence on his part. I always suspected it had more to do with her not wanting to ruin the ending of such a fine story. A man walks twenty miles along the tracks to find you? How could you *not* marry him?

My mother was of Finnish stock. Came from cold waters and blue forests to this: flatlands and tinned fish. She spoke of snow as though it were something magical. "It melts in your hand when you try to hold it," she said.

"And gives you shivers and a snot nose, as well," my Da would add.

Pride in surnames aside, when my father spoke about St. Kilda the words always turned sour in his mouth. With Da everything was either "shite" or "askew," and the islands that had tossed him into the world, they were very much askew. "Glad to get out of there," he said. "Needed room to breathe. They should shut St. Kilda down. Nothing but crofts and wet coughs. Oughta empty it out and lock the door. Drag them into modernity, kicking and screaming if necessary."

Fayther always said the best thing he ever did was leave, but when word came that they had indeed closed down St. Kilda—had forced the last of the toothless ones off the island, leaving only empty farms and feral goats behind—I do believe my Da was sad, sorry to see the source of so much of his scorn come to an end. It was sort of like shadowboxing a memory after that.

Fayther found work with Southern Pacific, on the Berton Line southeast from Tucumcari, and he settled with my mother here in the Flats, as our town is locally known. ("Paradise Flats," officially.) Da worked his way up to line foreman and then set about building his young wife a proper home. A regular mansion, it was, with high gables and drawing-room vistas, a wide-sweeping staircase and oak paneling throughout. A parlor and a piano to go with it. A veranda, with a garden out back and a pond to catch the moon. At night he would take my mother down to the property, show her where the house would be, how it would fit together. He'd show her where the sun porch would be located, and where the nursery. He'd point into midair, and together they would admire the power of his imaginings, the scale of his architectural dreams.

Then the economy crashed, and my mother died, and that house never did get built. My Da only ever managed to lay the foundation. I pass by it sometimes, on the way to Main Street.

The only really clear recollection I have of my mother is of her sitting beside the radio, beautiful, cheeks wet with weeping, and her mouthing the word "No" again and again because Rudolph Valentino had just died. The other memories I have are faded and curled in at the corners, like photographs of a photograph, like memories *of* a memory, not the memory itself. But that moment, with her crying for Valentino, that one

I see directly. I can hear her softest sobs. I can smell the rainwater and sunlight in her dress, fresh from the line. Funny, isn't it? How smell is the last thing to fade.

Somewhere between Valentino dying and the grasshoppers arriving, my mother passed on to a better place. The year she got sick was the year Lindbergh made his solo hop across the Atlantic. There were celebrations and tickertape parades everywhere. The crowds on the newsreels were cheering loud and silent, and then the movies were talking, and then they were in color.

One actor, Jackie Cooper, a boy about my age, he became famous for crying on cue. It was a terrific knack. Later on, I found out the director would get Jackie to weep by telling him they were going to shoot his dog; if Jackie still wouldn't cry, they'd take that dog away and the prop man would fire a shot in the air, out of sight. As Jackie bawled the cameras would roll, catching every blubber, every tear. What a cruel thing to do. But truth be told, I was jealous of Jackie Cooper. I figured he was just about the luckiest boy on earth, because afterwards *they always brought his dog back to him.*

My Da bought a handsome new RCA radio console a few years ago. Cost him sixty-nine dollars and fifty cents. Six-tube, complete with radiotrons and an Airplane dial for a full 360. Walnut veneer cabinet, ornate borders, elegant legs, and a cloth grille: that radio was just about the nicest piece of furniture we owned.

And every Tuesday at nine o'clock Da would tune in to the Ben Bernie music show, and I'd have to wait it out till Bernie got through that long, sleepy farewell of his, the one that dragged on forever. If I got restless and tried to search the airwaves for *The Green Hornet* or *The Lone Ranger,* my Da would snap, "This was your mother's program. Show some respect."

And so, Ben Bernie would whisper on, in his phony accent and purring voice, "Goodnight, goodbye, pleasant dreams and cheerio … from your bandmaster and all the lads in the orchestra … Think of us until next time, when you may want to tune in again … Adieu, my friends, and keep this old Maestro in your hearts … May good fortune and happiness, success and good health, attend you wherever you may be ... Au revoir, a fond cheerio, a bit of tweet-tweet and God bless."

She liked long goodbyes and she cried when strangers died. Not much to hang a picture on.

"Your mother missed the worst of the dust storms," Da said. "And she wasn't here when the grasshoppers came, so we can take some blessing in that."

I suppose.

My mother was laid to rest under a stand of elm trees, deep in a side pocket of shade. That was good as well, Da said, "what with her being from colder climes and tired of the heat."

Some nights my Da and I would walk down to inspect the foundations of his unbuilt home, overgrown now, the indent in the earth hardly visible, the grass as dry as straw, crunching underfoot, with even the poison ivy turning in on itself. And my Da would explain how he'd decided to rejig this wall or lower that ceiling, and how he still wasn't sure about the central foyer, and how maybe he needed to add a window, just so, to catch the morning sun. We would stand there, the two of us, admiring air. Sometimes, he'd suddenly sob and throw his arm around my shoulder, pull me in tight, hold me as though I were trying to get away. He wouldn't look at me or say anything, just stare straight ahead as he held me, and all it did was make me uncomfortable. I learned to keep my distance when we went to look at the house.

My mother had been taken to the New World as a child, with only the memory of melting snow to cool her. With Da, it was different. He chose to go. Left St. Kilda on his own accord. Left Glasgow, in turn. London, too. Landed in Canada, still on British soil and with his employment prearranged, but he left that too.

"I had to," he said. "How could I not? To be that close and *not* go in? Couldn't live with myself if I hadn't tried."

Sometimes it seemed like the rest of the world was just a waiting room for America. And what happens if you finally get there, only to fail? What then?

THREE

When they paraded Lindbergh along Broadway, it felt like the confetti would never end. Ten years later and the Hindenburg goes down in New Jersey, crashing to earth in a fearsome ball of fire, bodies dropping, bodies running. We heard it live over the radio, the announcer's voice cracking, not with static, and watched it on the newsreels, with the skeleton frame revealed, the burning zeppelin impaling itself on the mooring mast. They played that reel again and again, and we leaned forward, as though this time it might not happen, as though maybe this time no one would fall.

From Lindbergh's solo hop in '27 to the Hindenburg crash in '37, it was a heck of a swan dive. Those years seemed to mark the heart of what people have been calling a "low-down, dirty decade." Not entirely fair, that. We still had eleven months to go, so who knew but the Thirties might yet turn around? Might still end in butterflies and rainbows.

But that's not how I'd lay the wager.

It's been a difficult time for navigators. Take Miss Earhart, vanishing into the emptiness like that. They're saying there's still hope of her turning up alive, the queen of a distant jungle isle, perhaps, or the flower-festooned bride of a Samoan chieftain. But there's hope and there's false hope, and you need to distinguish between the two. Some folks think maybe Miss Earhart was captured by Hirohito, that the Japanese Empire is making plans for a larger war and our Amelia stumbled upon their dastardly machinations, like a heroine in a movie serial. *The Perils of Pauline* projected onto a larger world. But sometimes people just disappear and there's nothing you can do about it—and no point in sending out a search party.

Sometimes people simply *evaporate,* like creeks and ponds do—or bank accounts. Down here in the Glorious Free Southwest, eight hundred banks went bankrupt, the depositors left with nothing but pale promises and sand in their pockets. When the panic hit, bank managers invented holidays just to keep their doors closed, just to stop the mobs from running the vaults. In Nevada, one "holiday" lasted twelve days. People started hoarding hard currency, taking so much out of circulation that several cities—Atlanta, Richmond, Knoxville—began printing monetary notes of their own. Postal stamps, telephone slugs, Mexican pesos in the south, Canadian dollars in the north: anything that could be used in lieu of real money was.

In Paradise Flats most of our prouder financial institutions were boarded up, and those were some fine buildings left standing vacant, their false fronts lined up along Stoffer Drive with the dome of City Hall beside them. Only Co-Op Mortgage & Loans and United Financial survived, and even then, just barely.

Worse than the banks toppling were the automobile companies that collapsed. I kept a list. It was taped over my bed in yellowing paper, and penciled in. I wasn't sure why I ran a tally like I did, except that I suspected someday it would be important to know what we'd lost. It was a roll call to break your heart. Pierce-Arrow. Peerless. Elcar. Stutz. Detroit Electric. Kissel Motors. Marmon luxury sedans. Auburn. Stearns-Knight. All those beautiful Pierce-Arrows that would never be built. Velour upholstery, special levers to summon the chauffeur. Now, a bank you could lose, but a sky-blue Arrow? Or what of the Peerless Automobile Company? They used to make luxury sedans, now they were selling beer. Drowning different sorrows, I suppose. And just last year, hadn't REO stopped making automobiles as well. When that last REO rolled off the assembly line, it was like a book closing before you'd read the final chapter. And it's the final chapter of a life that tells you the most about it, isn't it? It also meant I'd never be able to ride around town in a brand-new, polished-red REO Flying Cloud of my own. Maybe it was the name that doomed them—flying clouds didn't conjure up images of summer skies and picnics anymore. A cloud was something you ran from.

Now my Da, he hung on. Southern Pacific Rail cut his pay and increased his hours, but he hung on. "I'm thankful I have wages to be cut," he said. It was sad, but the farmers had brought it on themselves, according to Fayther, "plowing their land into chalk like that." With the air of a man who knows something you don't, he'd say, "We'll be fine, Jack. You'll see."

Yes, my Da stood fast, stayed true, and when the men on the branch lines arranged a sit-down protest, he stood bravely to one side and allowed the railroad's hired bulls to wade in, clubs swinging. They put that strike down well and good, but if Da was thinking he'd won a spot in Heaven for that he was sadly mistaken. Even as he was counting out his bonus, the storms were getting darker.

My Da ignored all portents and omens, though. He even traded up; a couple of years back. Decided it was time to turn in our Model A, with its four-cylinder coughing fits and bone-rattle ride. He'd thought about getting one of the new V8s, but he was tired of stalling on steep hills, as Fords had a habit of doing. I was sixteen at that point, and aching for something better. "Have you seen the new Dictator?" I asked him. "That's one beautiful automobile, Da. Think of it." And I'd paint a picture of a cream-colored Studebaker Dictator sedan, with its sleek hood and a grille that curves up, graceful as a wave about to crest, parting the air with its goose-in-a-teardrop hood ornament. Stylish, that's what it was. The sort of automobile you'd expect to see leading a parade. The Studebaker Dictator had what the advertisements called "panache," yet it wasn't crazily expensive. No sir. It's not like I was asking for a Duesenberg J or anything. Heck, even a Hupmobile would have been fine. At least a Hupmobile was sporty.

"I'm not driving to work in no Hupmobile," Fayther said. "The men look up to me, dignity is required."

We ended up with a De Soto instead. An Airflow, just about the clunkiest car ever made. It's like De Soto's engineers got together and said, "Gentlemen, let us design as unstylish an automobile as is possible to build." Bug-faced grille and blunt snout, with those strange sad-eyed headlights and its low-riding rear, like pants needing a heft up. Lumpy and bulbous, the Airflow was. I died a little riding home in it. And not long after, didn't Studebaker go and discontinue the entire Dictator line, relying instead on its Presidential series with their automatic chokes and vacuum brakes and all-steel bodies: more expensive than the Dictator, Presidents were, and well beyond my Da's price range.

So.

A De Soto it was. And a De Soto it remained, marooned out back beside the toolshed with a dune of sand angled shin-deep against the driver's side. We couldn't afford to run it. Not anymore.

You see, what happened was, Southern Pacific shut down the Berton Line—and that changed everything. There was no warning, no nothing. The doors were closed and notices posted. And that was that. Might as well have pulled the tracks themselves up from the ground, like sutures out of an arm. Those rail closures tore right through the supply towns and service sidings from here all the way to Silver City. Brakemen, switchmen, roundhouse workers, section heads: the whole lot of them. They showed up for work one day to padlocks and dark windows. Sandbagged, that's what they were, those men, and too dumbfounded for anger. They just walked away, silent as a prayer, without pay or a word as to why.

Fayther came home, said, "Get your jacket, son, and bring a hankie, wind's picking up."

We walked past the shanties and silos to the Southern Pacific branch office, under a sky of dry tobacco. Went around back, and Fayther broke a pane of glass with his elbow. He reached in, fumbled a bit, then jimmied the door open. I was told to whistle if I saw someone coming, but with the powder that was caked like paste in the corners of my mouth, and me spitting sand, I wasn't sure I could manage it. Fayther was right. The wind was picking up. I held that hankie tight over my mouth and tried not to look like a desperado.

Footsteps, crunching glass, and Fayther reappeared. He was carrying several ledger books, bound in green leather and the size of family Bibles. The two of us, my Da and me, we walked back, grim and silent, into the thickening storm. Dust billowed across the road, and as he strode on ahead of me, the distance between us grew and grew until I lost him in a sea of gray.

Back at home, I asked him, "Why not raid the office for something worth stealing?"

"Because I am a man of substance," he said, "and I will not be reduced to common thievery."

That night he made a bonfire, even though it was summer and still warm.

FOUR

Perhaps it came from losing my mother earlier than is natural. Or maybe from always being a head taller than everyone else, or from having a strikebreaker for a Da, but Paradise never cared much for the McGrearys, and I have to say the feeling was mutual.

Truth was, my Da was pitied more than he was resented. There were some who mumbled about thuggery indulged and payoffs unproven, but others looked upon his downfall with more charity. I remember one fine lady in a black bonnet, watching Da pass by and then whispering to a friend, as Da pretended not to hear, "He never got over it, did he? Losing everything he had like that." I thought she was talking about my mother, but it might have been the house. Then, as I passed, "The spitting image," and it was my turn to pretend.

I don't see much of my mother in me. My face is McGreary all the way through, my hair a dark and muddy brown. But in the right light it catches faint traces of red. When I see a glimpse of this in a mirror it's like the afterglow of my mother, somewhere inside me.

The topsoil continued to snake away with every wind, wisp by wisp. And even the corn had begun to fail: stalks the color of old straw, bleached dry by the sun, the silk crumbling in your hands. When you did manage to pry open a cob, nothing but shriveled teeth inside. Could soak those forever and they'd never grow soft.

We'd been eating ragweed, lately, my Da and me. Eating it stewed in a cast-iron pot of Finnish ancestry. Milkweed, too. Scottish thistle. "Road harvest" is what they called it, and I'd be bent over a fence on the way to a school I hated attending, stomach in spasms like someone was punching me hard in the gut. Bent over and retching, throwing it back, the weeds and stewed greens coming up on a bile so sour it scalded the throat like hot tea, made your jaw ache and your eyes water.

For some, it was just a matter of confidence. Billboards proclaimed FORWARD AMERICA! NOTHING CAN STOP U.S.! But the enemy was invisible and impossible to corner. An adversary that congealed out of the dust and melted away with every punch thrown, immune to ballots and bullets. And every night, America huddled around the radio as if it were a Boy Scout campfire, listening as it crackled and popped with slogans and speeches aimed at rousing us from our dreary slumber: "Let's beat Old Man Depression once and for all! A roof over every head, food in every pantry, fuel on every fire. Can we do it? Of course we can! We just need to dig deep enough. Yes, Mr. and Mrs. John K. American, this means you—and you—and YOU!" To hear them tell it, we had only to roll up our sleeves, spit in our palms, and, lo and behold, our woes would melt away.

But in Paradise Flats, the down-and-outers still congregated past the railyards, in their shantytown sorrows, living on handouts and table-scraps. And didn't that tar paper sizzle in the heat?

Desperate people will cling to the faintest rumors of hope. So when a couple of smooth-talkers blew in, rented some rooms, and started throwing around promises of honest work, a line soon formed, down the street and two men deep. Prospective employees were told to bring a "sizable" cash deposit towards their work-related training—which would be reimbursed on their first day on the job. *On the job!* Words to murk the mind, those. The men were herded into a room, told to strip down to their skivvies and place their personal belongings in wicker baskets, as provided. They were then moved to another room and told to wait until their names were called, one by one, for medical examination. Only healthy men would be hired, but boy, weren't they looking for everything! Drywallers and roofers, lathe operators, painters, hangers, day laborers, clerks and accountants, builders and bricklayers—anything you could think of, and at livable wages, too. The men in that room, they waited and waited, perspiring in the heat. And when finally they screwed up the nerve to investigate, they discovered they were locked in. They started shouting, broke down the door. Realized they'd been cleaned out. And not just of their cash deposits, already paid. Every dollar in their wallets, every nickel, every penny. Watches, wedding bands in some cases, all of their clothes, even their shoes. And lacking trousers, they could hardly give chase. With their dignity and money taken, and them left standing in their underwear, any wonder some couldn't go home? Couldn't face their wives, their families?

One of those men? The very next day? He jumped off the East Coulee Bridge. The river was dry, of course, so he didn't drown, but that trestle is high enough it didn't matter. When they found him, he'd stripped down to his underwear again—though I don't know why. Left his clothes up top, neatly folded, maybe so his family could sell them. Or maybe he just wanted the humiliation to be complete.

No, sir. Not a lot of cause for cheer around here. The last true outpouring of joy had been when Prohibition ended. I was thirteen at the time, and happy enough to stop drinking our locally brewed rotgut. The celebrations spilled out into wind-whipped streets, people defying the dust to shout loud and slap backs. They fired shotguns into the air and toasted each other blind. The only folks that mourned the passing of Prohibition were Anti-Saloon League die-hards and the moonshine men themselves—who could no longer charge ten dollars a jar for rubbing alcohol flavored with licorice. Everyone else was happy, and our artfully named "cordial and beverage shoppes" could finally come clean as the taverns and taprooms they'd always been. Speakeasies and back-door dodges closed as the drinking of alcoholic beverages became a sitting pastime, not a standing one. Men no longer had to crowd the counter, on their feet and ready to bolt at a moment's notice. Drinking became respectable, even, with women involved and meals served along-side. In this parched land of ours, through the long years of dust and mirage, it was the booze that got us through, I figured: the homebrew and bathtub gin, or the now legally sold, quenching a thirst that was always there, that we couldn't seem to shake ourselves free of.

The president of these United States, right there in our living rooms through the marvel of radio, he himself called upon the country to put

Prohibition aside, saying it was a great experiment, "noble in motive," that had failed. With the soup kitchens and breadlines growing, and Southern Pacific throwing men from moving trains, some folks were thinking maybe America itself was an experiment that had failed. Noble in motive, but spun out of air, like all that money that wasn't there.

Or maybe it was Crazy Eli who was right. Maybe it really was the End of Days, a judgment in gray. At dance marathons you'd see couples pursuing the pettiest of prize money, turning slow circles, propping each other up, shell-shocked and past the point of exhaustion, heads heavy on shoulders, eyes staring into nothingness. Around and around the dance floor. They said one girl, she died on her feet and it was hours before anyone noticed.

That's how it felt, those times we were living through. Like a dance that never seemed to end.

FIVE

Here's the thing about Paradise Flats. It's a town settled entirely by suckers. Part of our heritage. You can see it in the name of the "Tedstof Hotel" or in the Tedstate Access Road, which are variations on the town's original name.

It started when a pair of prospectors followed a vein of silver south from the hills. It soon petered out, though, and with the good sites already staked along the Boracho they laid claim instead on White Mud Creek. They were hoping some of the silver might have washed down. They raked the clay a bit, turned some muck, even got down to bedrock, but found nothing.

Enterprising men, they figured, hey, why should a lack of silver stop them?

So they sent a request to the regional assayers office, said they'd found a whole shelf of sedimentary ore. An inspector arrived to pace off their claims. Then came the tricky part. By regulation, the inspector could spot-check any section he liked. Halfway up one bank, he turns and says, "We'll dig here, ten feet, both ways."

"Sure thing," says the pair of prospectors. And then don't a rattlesnake appear—almost as though flung from behind a bush by a crouching confederate—and don't that first prospector shout "Step back!" and don't he blast that snake with his shotgun, both barrels. "Whew! Close call," he says to the inspector. Then: "Carry on, sir." And wasn't that buckshot loaded with silver filings. The first scoop alone contained enough to launch a bonanza.

A wave of miners soon arrived, and those first two were waiting for them. Land was thick with nuggets, they told 'em. And it was true. It was true because they had salted the lots, had melted down some old silverware, then blackened the lumps with coal oil and plugged them along the creekside at profitable intervals. As more miners swarmed in, and as more lots needed salting, the two fellows started to get lazy. They began chopping up silver dollars rather than melting down spoons. They'd then pound the pieces into lumps. Scheme might still have worked too if one of those "nuggets" hadn't turned up with TED STATES OF still visible. And that was that.

They hanged those two men, our town founders, vigilante-style. "Honest justice," they call it down here. By then a few sheds and some tawdry lean-tos had been erected, and even a canvas tent saloon. The settlement became known as Tedstof, in honor of its unofficial founding, although Mrs. Mabel, our local historian, her of the expansive bosom and pinched face, disagrees with this story in its entirety. She says the name came from an early pioneer, a stalwart by the name of Ted Stoffer who first broke the virgin sod and cleared the land of Indians and other such nuisances. Fine story, hers, and one to stir the blood, were it not for the fact you could sift through the land holdings and civic records all day and never find a mention of anyone named Stoffer, Ted or otherwise, going right back to the first deeds that were issued—as was discovered to the embarrassment of some and the merriment of others when the town council decided to raise a statue to our "true founding father." In search of Mr. Stoffer's particulars, and a likeness if possible, the review committee came to the conclusion that the stalwart pioneer existed only in the imagination. "Town was founded by a silver dollar," one of the local wags liked to say. "Should erect a statue to that coin instead."

It wasn't silver, though, but salt that gave our town its first official designation, as taken from geological surveys marking the area as Salt Flats #217. This in turn became the Salt Flats Improvement District and then, simply, the townsite of Salt Flats.

It was only when Southern Pacific announced a trunk line that the Flats really boomed. Land speculators had been staking out towns on the routes they hoped the railroad might take. Normally, a rail line would breed towns. In this case, it was the opposite. Speculators were banking on the towns calling forth a railroad. A dozen such sites were staked out across the plains, all duly registered, all with grandiose names like "Central City," "Metropolis Valley," "Gateway Center," "Grandville," or "Rapid City." You can see some of these names on older maps even now.

These same speculators, deciding that the name "Salt Flats" was not as enticing a label as might be presented to future would-be investors, petitioned to have the name changed. Deciding the aforementioned cluster of lean-tos and shacks would be better represented by the title "Paradise City," they sent a telegraph to the central land office: *By 5 to 1 vote Town Council unanimous STOP change city name to Paradise STOP.* Their request was processed, but the wording of it hadn't been entirely clear, which is how the settlement of Salt Flats became Paradise Flats.

A boomtown launched by silver and salt, and by right-of-way land speculators and their victims.

It was from these first proud investors, these nobly duped, that Paradise Flats grew. A good deal of the town's population is descended from those founding suckers, and even now there were vacant lots in Paradise Flats that once went for $5,000 available for $50—without any takers.

Same game was still being played. I remember when the Hoover Dam was going up, how everyone said the desert was going to bloom. The sand swindlers swept in, selling huge tracts of Arizona and Nevada on the promise of "proposed lakes," "proposed country clubs," "proposed canals," and "proposed aeroports." You can propose anything you like. That's the beauty of it. "Proposed," "projected," "planned," "contemplated." Slap that in front of a scheme and you can conjure up what you wish. You can "propose" a railroad to the moon or "contemplate" an opera house; don't mean it's going to happen.

The Great Florida Land Boom of the 1920s? Same thing. And like any feeding frenzy, it brought out the sharks. We'd seen it before, people becoming the proud owners, sight unseen, of forty acres—all of it vertical. The swindlers figured, if you could sell the side of a cliff to someone, you could as easily sell land that was mostly underwater.

"Great development potential" is how they put it. "America's tropical paradise." All true, so long as you defined "potential" as "impossible" and "tropical" as "malarial." As for it being "paradise itself," well, with the gators, the skeeters, and the quicksand, I suppose your entry into Heaven might very well be hastened. That much was true. Florida land dealers would slap up a huge sign reading MILLION-DOLLAR HOTEL COMING SOON! to help sell the surrounding lots at an inflated fee. Again, all true enough as long as you defined "coming soon!" as "never."

The naming of a place was important. Have a swab of land with a muddy creek running through it? Why not christen the creek the Riviera or "Le Grand Canal" and peddle your property as the future site of a "New Venice"? I'd read about this sort of thing. I admired the panache involved in it. One fella down in Orlando, he sold the town dump. Said the soil was "rich in nutrients." Another pair of fellows, they specialized in sunken treasure. They'd stake out a swampy bit of coastline and then "discover" a map, maybe even unearth a few doubloons, and the rush would be on. In one inlet, they must have sunk half a dozen Spanish galleons at least.

Turned out they weren't the only ones with dreams of Spanish gold.

Six

When you're big, people decide you must be good at sports. They want you to take up boxing or football or to help settle a score with welchers. They congratulate you on your size, as though it's something you've achieved. But if you knock down a smaller man, I don't see how that's cause for boasting. It's purely mathematical: weight X set against a lesser weight of Y. What's to celebrate?

On community sports days, they always put me in the outfield, shouting "Go deep, Jack, you should be able to throw a ball from the back fence clear past home plate." Well, I can throw hard enough, that part's true, but there's no telling where that ball will land once I let go, so the opposing team's home runs pile up and my teammates exchange looks on the bench when it's my turn at bat.

One day, I was deep in the field, trying to care, when a sudden dust squall blew in. Home plate dissolved into it. I heard a crack! and the ball appeared out of the dust over my head … and just as quickly disappeared back into it. I knew I'd be out there ages, and even if I did find that ball everyone would be miserable at me. So I just walked away, and that was the last I ever gave a damn about baseball. Far as I know, they're still out there waiting for me to finish the play.

I've wanted to be somewhere else for as long as I've been aware that somewhere else existed. It's like the feeling that comes over you when you're listening to the radio. Wanting to escape *through it,* knowing you can't. Radio expands you, it truly does, connects you to that world out there, beyond the edge of town. Makes you feel larger. Smaller, too. That's the feeling that comes upon you when you tune the dials and cut through the crackling static to pick up distant voices, clear as if they're in the next room. Voices from faraway. Franklin Delano's latest, or maybe Mr. Amos and Mr. Andy, those colored fellows from Harlem in New York City. Always so joyfully fun up there, with hijinks and laughter and "oh wah, wahs." Oftentimes I dreamed about living in Harlem, and how sweet life must be. Couldn't be any worse than Paradise Flats. My Da said that Amos 'n' Andy were just regular boys in blackface, but I knew that wasn't the case. Why would you need to wear blackface if you were on the radio? And why pretend to be laughing, when you weren't?

When Fayther tired of hijinks, he'd set the dials to something dismal like *Captain Tim Healy's Stamp Club*—and you don't know the meaning of boredom till you've listened to stamp collecting over the radio. It was as bad as Edgar Bergen and Charlie McCarthy. Whose idea was it to put a ventriloquist on the radio? Didn't make a lick of sense. The radio is a marvel, to be sure, but you have to wonder. I mean, a ventriloquist. On the radio?

"I think I saw his lips move," I said one night. Da just glowered.

Whether it was Ivory Soap or Cream of Wheat, Ovaltine or Spic-and-Span, every show was sponsored by a product that would either warm our bellies or wash us clean. Even *Jack Armstrong, All-American Boy!* was sponsored by Wheaties. Some of the radicals in town, they said in America everything's for sale. But that's not true. In America, everything is *sponsored.* And that's fine with me. I suspect the dreariness of this world would eventually overtake us were it not for the purity of Ivory Soap or the calming effects of Lucky Strike cigarettes. *"Take our advice and you'll look nice, Your face will feel as cool as ice, with Colgate Rapid Shaving Cream!"* True, I had to make do with Da's straight razor and a dry shave, but still, that jingle for Colgate Rapid Shaving Cream was catchy and cheerful, like finding unexpected coins in your pocket. I often walked to town singing one of those perfect little ditties that did so much to lift the dust: *"Laugh awhile, let a song be your style, use Fitch Shampoo! Don't despair, use your head, save your hair, use Fitch Shampoo!"*

I was rubbing my scalp with lye soap every night, but still, a fellow could dream, couldn't he?

One evening, after the *Lux Radio Theater* broadcast had ended and Kate Smith had sung "God Bless America," and after Mutual of Omaha had switched over to hymns and Fayther had had his fill, he called me over, soft and solemn as any parson, and said to me, "Jack, my boy, there's something you need to know. Something important. But you must take a vow—one of abject and utter secrecy."

I didn't have a surplus of friends, so it was with limited risk that I agreed to keep silent on whatever it was he was about to reveal. With great care, Fayther slid open the bottom drawer of the kitchen dresser and removed the Finnish dinnerware inside—the dinnerware with the pale blue borders. He then lifted the corner of the oilskin beneath. Hidden under it was a sheaf of pages. One by one, he took them out and placed them on the table: certificates, filled with flourishes and stamps and regal-looking seals and names signed in bold, confident swirls.

Fayther tapped a finger on the insignia in the corner of one such certificate. "Know what that is?" he said, voice reverent, almost whispering. "That, Jack, is the family crest of Sir Francis Drake."

Judging by the pause that followed, I was expected to say something. "Is it?" I said.

"Oh yes." Eyes shining. "Official family crest. And these—*these,*" he fanned the certificates out for me to admire, "represent the McGreary family fortune." Now he really was whispering. "We're rich, son. Richer'n you can dream."

Well, I can dream pretty big, but in this case my Da had indeed out-dreamed me. Never would I have imagined that we were on the brink of such fortune, such "unfathomable riches" as Fayther said—and had been for years, apparently, without me knowing so.

Da explained the whole thing. Sir Francis Drake had been an admiral under Elizabeth I, and he'd hoarded a fortune in Spaniard gold over the course of a career spent buccaneering. When Drake died in 1596, this mountain of wealth was left to his only son, a boy born both out of wedlock and out of favor with the Queen. The royal court refused to honor Drake's will and confiscated the entire estate—illegally, and with a cackle of cruel laughter, I imagine. And now, these hundreds of years later, hadn't some sharp fellow out of Iowa tracked down the only remaining descendant of the Drake family line, and weren't they even now challenging the British courts for this vast fortune. A fortune now worth not millions but *billions*. They needed money, though, to mount their case, to wrestle free the inheritance from the greedy English bankers and their ilk. And boy, weren't those Limey bastards digging in for a fight! Who could blame them? Paid out, the Drake estate might very well bring down the entire Bank of England.

And so the Francis Drake Association was formed, with chapters across the Midwest and into the South. Thousands of investors—what the association called "subscribers" and "donators"—now had a claim on the prize. Only thing they had to do was sign a vow of secrecy on pain of being disinherited.

Fayther placed a finger on the side of his nose. "Not a word," he said. "Not to anyone."

The silence that followed was painful. I didn't want to bring it up, but it had to be said. "We're not Drakes, Da. We're McGrearys. Crofters out of St. Kilda." It was about as far from being a Drake or duke as one could hope for. Our claiming that gold made about as much sense as blackface on radio.

Those fancy certificates Fayther had laid out before me—fair dripping with pomp, they were—had been issued in numerations of a hundred dollars: a stack of 200s, several 300s, and more than a few 500s. One especially ornate certificate was for 1,000. And that's when it all crashed in: the truth, my chest. There'd been rumors, you see. Tales told about my Da, about how he'd been skimming the payroll, doctoring the books. Bleeding the Berton Line dry, word was, and if the company hadn't gone tits to the wind, and if those ledgers hadn't gone missing, they'd have caught him for sure. The Depression saved my father from three-square and twenty at the penitentiary. That's what was whispered. I never paid heed, though, because I knew just how poor we were. I'd seen what little money we had, had watched it trickle away, and even at nineteen I knew wealthy embezzlers weren't given to living on dandelions and root weed. But now I saw where the lost money had gone: into fancy papers and equally fanciful promises. It was another belly blow, worse than any road harvest.

"We aren't Drakes, Da. It's not ours to claim. How can we—how can we lay ownership to any part of it?"

He brushed the reality of this away with one hand, like how you might a fly that's annoying your face. "Doesn't matter, son. That's the beauty of it. Used to be limited to the Drake family and their descendants—"

"You said there was only one surviving member of the—"

"But they opened 'er up, Jack. Opened 'er up! Any soul wants to, they can invest in the Drake Inheritance, just so long as they sign a stipulation of secrecy. And when the estate is settled—"

"If—"

"*When.* When that happens, we will reap a great and just reward. They're going to pay out $500 on every dollar invested. You understand what that means, Jack? Can you do the math?"

"I can do the math."

"That's a 500 percent return!"

"No," I said. "That's 50,000 percent."

He blinked at this.

"One dollar paid for every dollar given," I said, "that would be a 100 percent return. So $500 would be a 50,000 percent return on investment."

"Oh," he said. "Well, then. Even better. Splendid!"

Splendid didn't begin to describe it.

He smiled at me. "Remarkable, don't you think?"

Remarkable? Yes. Unbelievable, even.

"Jack, right here, in front of us, we've got"—he scooped up the certificates and waved them at me—"upwards of four million dollars! And let me tell you, when I went to the investors' meeting—up in Silver City, all on the hush-hush—I drove a hard deal. They resisted, at first. But I wore 'em down, son. Wore 'em down till they agreed to let me invest double the maximum initial allotment. Double!"

My face was burning. "That was mighty generous of them," I said. "Allowing you to give them your money like that."

"And how!" he chirped, eyes shining bright with what might very well have been tears of joy.

That was an inheritance I was looking at, all right. But it wasn't Sir Francis Drake's, it was my own. I am worth four million, I thought. On paper. Felt again like I'd been punched in the stomach. Stranger still, and sadder, too, was realizing that my Da had no more lessons to teach me. I had nothing left to learn from him, except perhaps in a negative capacity.

And maybe that was the true inheritance in all of this.

SEVEN

Having cast me as his beneficiary, Da could now speak freely—and at length if you let him—about our family's immense and imminent wealth. Hardly a night went by he didn't spread those certificates out for me to admire. He'd then march me down to that crumbling foundation of his, lost in dry grass, and with his hands waving he'd once again start sculpting the air.

"Think what we can do with that money. We'll expand the veranda, add a second sunroom off the first. Mahogany trim. Maybe even a turret!" By the time Fayther was done, his imaginary house would have grown another imaginary floor. That made five, by my count.

My Da didn't need a bottle to get hoary-eyed, he just needed the vision of a ship filled with gold, coming in, sails wide and catching the wind.

There were times I would have preferred if Da *was* a drunkard. Would have made it easier, having something specific on which to blame his unraveling. He was getting harder and harder to talk to. Often, I'd wake to find him at the kitchen table in his undershirt, the Drake certificates carefully arranged, his eyes to the window like he was waiting for something. He had no work to go to, true, but a man needs his sleep.

"It's late," I'd say.

"See that," he'd whisper, peering through the window, the sun scarcely up.

"See what?" I'd say.

"A shadow," he'd reply, voice hoarse, as though he'd spent the night shouting at something. "*There*. See? It's on the move."

But there was nothing. Just wind and sky and dust.

So I'd boil an egg and we'd split it, him eating the yolk, me the white, and he would whisper, "We're rich, son. You know that, don't you?" and I'd say, "Yes, Da. I do," and then I'd brew a pot of barley tea and we'd look together for something that wasn't there.

By the time I left for school Da was usually buried deep in newsprint. Like as not I'd find him still hunched over the kitchen table when I got home, our local paper spread before him. He frowned his way through them as though the editorials in the *Greater Paradise Times-Tribune* contained the cipher to a conspiracy. I'd read the commentaries, knew how they dissected the latest New Deal committees with a surgeon's certainty and examined the events in Europe like they were moves in a distant game of checkers, always managing to explain how they would affect the price of salt in Dacob County. Larger towns might have a morning and afternoon edition of the papers, but in Paradise Flats we made do with only the one print-run daily. It came out in the evening, after everything was over. "Ought to call it the *olds*," my Da grumbled. "Hardly nothing new in it." Caused him no end of vexation, the events of our day. He would argue with the paper, or me if I had the misfortune of wandering within range. "Look at that? Will ya?"

The newspaper also had a Word Jumble, which I solved on an egg timer, and several columns of dwindling feedlot prices—which I took a mathematical interest in. I'd see how quickly I could tally the numbers in my head and then divide them into order of depreciation. Sometimes I'd try skipping every fourth number, say, and take it from there. Always did have a knack for sums, even back in grade school when I dumbfounded the teachers by adding any number they threw at me by 98 or 99, in my head, instantly. What's 57 plus 98? One hundred fifty-five. It was a trick I figured out, adding 100 and then subtracting either a one or a two. See? Easy. Doesn't take a genius.

Radio programs and newspaper hog prices aside, there wasn't much in the way of diversionary activities in our house. We only owned two books. Mind you, what those books lacked in number they made up in heft: King James and Webster's own. A Bible and a dictionary, both of them leather-bound and heavy with words. Both up high on the mantel, light from the window casting pale upon them.

It wasn't always so. I remembered an entire wall of books, floor to ceiling, in the hallway near the kitchen. My Da sold most of them for a penny a pound. Others were broken apart and used to feed the stove, and some had their pages stacked neatly inside the outhouse. Fayther hadn't even had the decency to tear them horizontally, so you might read a line or two first. Instead, just vertical strips of random words I couldn't connect no matter how hard I tried. The Bible and the dictionary, though. Those were sacred. We wouldn't want Daniel Webster haunting our toilet or John the Baptist stabbing an accusatory finger at us while we were doing our business. Sometimes, in the evenings, I would lug the Webster's down and slide the heavy pages over, idly and without purpose, till one day, while my Da listened to Captain Healy describe a particularly fascinating batch of stamps—which Da didn't even collect—I decided I'd read our dictionary all the way through, A to Z.

"*Aardvark:* noun: from the Afrikaans *aard,* meaning 'earth,' and *vark,* meaning 'pig.' A large burrowing mammal that feeds on ants and larval termites. *Abalone:* noun: a large edible sea mollusk with spiral shell ..."

But I never got past A that first evening, and I'll tell you why.

I was skimming my hand along the pages, filing certain words away in my brain, as you do for easy access later—*a capella, addendum, aegis, alchemy*—when one of them caught me cold. It was the kind of word that'll worm its way into you, if you let it.

amoral

Definition seemed clear enough: neither moral nor immoral; outside the bounds of normal judgment.

I was going to carry on, working my way towards B, when I stopped. Flipped back. How can anything ever be "beyond the realm of judgment"? I tried, but I couldn't see it.

Say you tricked a fellow, walked away from a fixed bet with his money in your hand. Now, was he gullible? Or was he trusting? It depended on whether you felt inclined in his favor. Words always carried a judgment, it seemed to me. If you approved of someone, you'd say they were innocent. If you didn't, they were naive. Same meaning; different verdict. "Childish" and "childlike": same thing. You could see it in the way a lady would look in a mirror, consider herself thin, when everyone else was thinking "skinny." Or vice versa. Or how a man would think stout, when everyone else thought "short."

Now, that pendulum between approving and disapproving, how did you stop it midway? Could you? "Amoral" suggested the possibility that something could be completely neutral.

A lion taking down a gazelle on the African plains. That was neither good nor bad, you might say. It was simply "amoral." But was it? Seemed to me, you always ended up siding with the gazelle. Or the lion. Couldn't remain neutral, even if you tried.

The thing about "amoral" was it couldn't be even the least bit bad. Not a smidgen. If it was, that'd tilt it towards immoral. Can't be the least bit helpful or good, either, because then you'd be talking moral. Even weather patterns. How could you view a drought or a rainfall as neutral? Especially if God or the Devil was behind it? And maybe that's what "amoral" was getting at. That neither Lord nor Lucifer was hiding behind the curtain, that we were all of us on our own, making it up as we went along.

When a word like that gets a hold of you, you can't be rid of it. It was like Owen's dog next door, the time it got caught in thick clay, tried to shake itself free of the mud. That dog shook itself till it went dizzy in the head.

Here was something I'd never have admitted in church. All that talk of damnation and eternal punishment? It's not so bad. I always figured, as long as good existed somewhere in the world, even hellfire would be bearable. Because there'd still be hope. Hope—not for you, what with final judgment passed—but hope in general, as would come from knowing, even as you were being raked across the embers, that good still existed, out there somewhere.

But if this world of ours was amoral at heart, then none of that really mattered. And if that was the case, we'd already arrived in Hell, only we just didn't know it. Maybe Hell was in the not telling you about it.

I pushed my chair back, staggered away from the dictionary. Felt my heart start to race.

I felt clammy and scared—and a little bit thrilled, I do confess—like when you see a dead tree crack in a high wind. The feeling soon passed, but my face stayed warm from the rush of it. Like I had brushed up against something larger than me in the dark.

"Going out," I said, leaving my Da to his invisible stamps and imaginary gold.

I took the long way into town, along the tracks, to avoid passing that jeezly hole in the ground, the one marking the location of the "McGreary mansion," as one fellow called it, right to my face, smile simmering. I had considered knocking him down, but him being a man of the cloth, I wasn't sure how that would factor in, come Judgment. He was a Baptist, but still. I'm sure there's a commandment somewhere that covers that.

EIGHT

I did my best to avoid "amoral."

Started in on Webster's again the next day, only in reverse this time, beginning at Z and working my way backwards, from *zealots* to *yowl* to *xenophobia.* I skimmed over a lot of it, picking out only those terms that snagged my fancy. No need to read up on *turpentine,* say, but *torpor,* now that was a good one. Some ideas you can't even express till you've pinned them down with a word. Torpor was what the streets of Paradise Flats reeked of, something I couldn't quite describe before. The McGreary mansion, choked with weeds? That was torpor, too.

The dandelions had overrun my father's imaginings, were growing and blowing across the parlor and the piano, dandelions with deep tuberous roots, sucking hard at any moisture they could find, dandelions that never seemed to be yellow, but went directly from green to gray. And all the while our phantom wealth grew in an exponential fashion. News of the Drake estate continued at a feverish rate. The original will had been found! The appeals had been settled! At one point a ship full of gold was actually on its way. By the time the rumor ran its course, a mob had formed at a dock in Galveston, only to be greeted by a crew of puzzled Welsh fishermen.

Forewarned that resistance would grow as success drew nearer, the Drake investors felt a certain twisted satisfaction when the U.S. government labeled their association "one enormous, insidious swindle." The feds made it illegal to buy or sell further shares in the Drake estate, but that just spurred the investors on. Great wheels were turning. Every trade deal the government announced, every restructuring, every event—all pointed to the coming settlement of Drake's lost wealth. Even the Depression itself, to hear the Francis Drake Association tell it, had been triggered by a panic over the massive payout about to be made. The slightest fluctuation in the British pound? Evidence of secret maneuvers; they were adjusting monetary value in anticipation of a settlement. Roosevelt's New Deal? An economic rejigging designed to soften the impact of the coming windfall. Mussolini's march into Abyssinia? A cover-up, to remove damning evidence in Ethiopia. There were portents everywhere.

Even with their ringleader—the fellow from Iowa that Fayther referred to as "Oscar," like the two of them were on first-name terms— even with him locked up in Leavenworth, the money continued to flood in. The fact that Oscar had been tried, convicted, and sentenced? That was just proof the entire thing was true. The governments of the world were trying to block the Drake claimants from their rightful due. Subscribers held mass rallies, took courses on how to manage their certain wealth. Fayther went to one such gathering, six thousand strong, he duly reported, up in Sioux City. He came back with more certificates to squirrel away under the oilskin. Had more space to stack them now, because our dinnerware was gone.

"They're conspiring against us, the forces of international finance," he'd say, eyes wild. "But I won't flinch. A McGreary never backs down."

Really? A McGreary never a won a fight I know of.

This talk of Drake gold and world cunning had grown fairy-tale fanciful. So I checked. Took me all of twenty minutes.

I stopped in to see Bertie Tomilson, the red-faced barrister above Sukanen's Dry Goods & Grocer's, the one in the office down the hall from Pinchbeck the Watchmaker. Bertie rolled himself up out of his chair, harrumphed his way over to a bookcase, ran a finger along the spines, pulled out *Volume 17: British Common Law*, turned to "wills, and the probate thereof."

"Statute of limitations," he said, reading aloud. "Established under King James I. It limits the reopening of a disputed will and testament to within thirty years of the initial settlement." He closed the book.

It would seem our local branch of the Francis Drake Association was a bit late in pressing their claims, having missed the cutoff by 313 years. Turns out as well, Drake had no son, bastardly or otherwise. He'd died childless and had left his inheritance, modest as it was, to his wife and his brother. They haggled over the split and eventually settled. Finding this out was as easy as opening the encyclopedia at the very same barrister's.

"Much appreciated," I said, as I dug out a wad of crumpled bills. "Regarding your fee …"

Truth told, those bills had been cleanly folded when I filched them from the pantry. I had crumpled them up just before I went in, to play on his pity.

I needn't have bothered. Bertie just smiled. "No charge," he said. "When the truth comes out and your father sues the Drake Association, I want your case—on commission."

I smiled back. Seemed appropriate somehow, paying him with imaginary money from a future imaginary lawsuit.

I took the knowledge I'd gained back to Fayther, and do you think he thanked me for it?

"Shite for brains, that's you! What the *feck* were you thinking? You can't go blabbing about it like that. Didn't I sign a vow of secrecy? Didn't I? Word gets out, everyone'll want in and our share will be reduced."

"There is no fortune, Da," I said. "Can't you see that?"

"Fine! You get nothing, then! Nothing. Y'hear! Not one thin dime. You're cut off entirely!"

It's not every day a father disinherits his son of four million dollars, but somehow I thought I'd manage. I pulled my cap on, and I left.

My Da saw himself as a sharp fellow, and sharp fellows don't get swindled. So. Either he wasn't as sharp as he thought he was, which was a hard thing to face, or he hadn't actually *been* swindled. Easier instead to decide that the governments of the world were conspiring against you than admit to yourself you'd been played for a fool. It was why Henrietta down the street with the bruises on her face could convince herself Useless Joe really loved her. And why Useless Joe could believe she brought it on herself. Otherwise he'd be a monster and she'd be a patsy, and, well, better not to face some things, wasn't it?

Now Plato, he said, "In the land of the blind, the one-eyed man is king." Those words were carved in red sandstone over the main arch at City Hall. *The one-eyed man is king.* But that's not the case, is it? In the land of the blind, the one-eyed man is not a king—he's a heretic, and he needs to be stopped. The one-eyed man tells you that the numbers don't add up and the one-eyed man is shouted down. Better not to let them know you can see at all. Better to slip in amidst the mob, turning partial vision to your advantage while avoiding kindling and the stake.

When I got outside Sukanen's Dry Goods & Grocer's, I unfolded the certificate, the one I had slipped free of Fayther's stashed pile. I walked in, brash as I could muster, slapped the paper down in front of the clerk and tapped the insignia in the corner.

"Know what that is?" I asked.

Nine

You wonder about the ripple effect of things.

The Francis Drake Association stole thousands of dollars from Fayther. I stole a hundred. The clerk lost ten. That's what they call "trickle down."

Could go the other way, though. A dollar here, a dollar there, in the hands of the right man, a dollar to someone on the down-and-out? Who knows but it just might be enough to turn someone's life around. Maybe all that was needed was that one single bill to shift things his way. If you drove clean across America, stopping at every breadline and soup kitchen you passed, giving one dollar to one man in every town, who knew the collective effect? Might build, like a wave. Might turn back the tide itself.

And diamonds might fall from the sky.

The clerk at Sukanen's traded me $10 for a $100 certificate, and I loaded up on corn muffins, coffee, baking soda biscuits, lard, molasses, dried plums and pinto beans, some canned goods and some apples and a goodly slab of sow belly. Filled two big sacks with Francis Drake's bounty. I was in desperate straits, I'd explained, had a father who wasn't working and needed caring for (all true up to that point). And there was the clerk, almost in tears, like he was doing something good, all the while raking in what he thought was a $90 profit on my misery. (In actual fact, a $49,990 profit, if the claims had been true; that's a $100 certificate to be redeemed at $500 per, minus the $10 he spotted me in goods. Though you'd have to know what the store had paid wholesale for the supplies to work out the exact amount. Either way, those were some expensive bags of groceries I hauled home.)

Did I feel a twinge of guilt over taking merchandise under such circumstances? I did not. It put food in the pantry and real coffee in our cups for the first time in a long while. Da never asked where the coffee came from and he never seemed to count his certificates. So he never noticed when that first one went missing, or the next.

Here's a hard kernel to chew: I don't see how it matters that Da and I were on the brink of ruin. What I did—taking that certificate, trading it for food—was wrong. Or it wasn't. It wouldn't matter if I was a millionaire or a hobo, the act itself is the same. Steal an apple, you steal an apple. Don't see how it matters whose tree it is, or whether you already have a bushel at home. The apples I swapped the certificate for at Sukanen's? Stolen, same as if I'd grabbed them and run.

But you know something? Those apples tasted sweeter for it, sweeter by far than if I'd paid for them honestly. And that was a lesson they don't teach you in Sunday school.

I was back again getting groceries not a week later, on a Tuesday afternoon, having cut out early from school. I purchased another $10 gunnysack of goods with a $50,000 claim on Drake gold, my fourth such exchange and the last, I feared, as my Da was sure to notice the missing certificates soon. At Sukanen's store they had daisies for sale, in from a government greenhouse in Silver City, and though they cost almost as much as a side of bacon, I bought the largest bouquet they had. I went home, dropped off the groceries, pocketed an apple, and then walked those daisies out to where the elm trees stand at the edge of town. I placed the flowers, then sat back under an elm and hoped that Valentino was sweeping her into his arms down through eternity—as he will, if God has any human decency.

Would have eaten that apple right there, had the wind not lifted a fine dust from the fields, spawning little twisters and sending brier weeds tumbling across. It was the wind that harried me back to town. I cut past City Hall and then ducked inside the granite-shaded interior of the library to get out of it. Maybe if I'd ducked into the fabric shop or the consignment store that day, things might have turned out differently. I might never have left Paradise Flats. Might have grown old there and, if not happy, at least calm. But I chose the library, and that was when things did go askew, well and truly—though I didn't know it at the time.

Our library was a civic landmark. When the branch line first came through, Paradise Flats seemed destined for a modest sort of greatness. Population peaked. Our fine City Hall went up with its dome and sandstone motto. Then came the twin spires of the papists, an Anglican to match, and a Lutheran seminary soon after. First National Bank appeared with its Greek columns, and Second National with its Roman. And on Main, overlooking our newly renamed Ted Stoffer Memorial Park (originally "Tedstof Park") and its stone fountain (now dry) and reflecting pond (same), stands our magnificent library, the regional equivalent of a Taj Mahal.

The city hall, the seminary, the library: topped in green copper, all of them. Source of abiding pride, those rooftops. There'd been talk at the turn of the century of renaming Paradise Flats "the Emerald City," something which still turned up now and then, most notably in the masthead of the *Greater Paradise Times-Tribune*: SERVING DACOB COUNTY AND THE EMERALD CITY. Remnants of history were everywhere, like bones in an ash pile.

The Paradise Flats Library had ladders on wheels and great high walls that were lined with acres of leather-bound volumes, all part of the original 1894 endowment. Last batch of books was purchased in 1928, something the *Times-Tribune* often lamented. Nonetheless, the library's inventory provoked something akin to reverence in many, envy in others. A college out East made a sizable offer on the entire collection. The town held out for more money, but nothing came of it, so we were stuck with all these books.

I might not have stayed long that afternoon, might have finished my apple and been on my way, but Mrs. Mabel, librarian and local history marm, her of "Ted Stoffer" fame, was not at her usual scowling post behind the front desk. Mrs. Mabel's preserves were locally famous, as were her pickle-weaned features, mouth permanently pursed like she was sucking seeds from between her teeth. She tried to keep us away from the books most days, but that day I managed to creep past the blockade without getting caught. I spotted Mrs. Mabel in a far corner helping Dr. Boltzhurst with something. Boltzhurst, with his tuft of hair up top like a radish ready for pulling, was a doctor of veterinary medicine; he made sure your animals died a little slower than they normally would. Dr. Boltzhurst was best known for the long letters he sent to the *Times-Tribune* and the even longer denunciations he wrote later, after the paper had inevitably chopped off a paragraph so his letter would fit the margins. He signed his epistles "Stefan B." as though no one knew his first name. Dr. Boltzhurst's letters to the editor were thick with scientific analysis of the country's economic crisis. "It needn't take bloodshed to bring this Depressed state to an end, only the concentrated application of rational principles. Instead of rule by bureaucracy, we need rule by *technocracy*, using a methodology that would employ the synthetic integration of physical sciences and social phenomena. Wages and prices, for example, could be set based on units of energy—ergs and joules—rather than on the outdated monetary theories that caused this crisis."

Next to the good doctor stood Father Augustus, papist propagator of the Blessed Virgin and known to imbibe communion wine after Sunday mass (at least, that was how we Calvinists told it). His name was the only grand thing about Father Augustus. He managed to be both large and fussy at the same time. With Mrs. Mabel at their side, the doctor and the priest were hunched over some book or another, arguing away, so I slipped in un-scowled at.

The interior of the library had a coolness, like the balm you spread on a burn. With the clammy heat and sheer itchiness of the outside world gone, I wandered among the stacks, the books looming above, handsome-backed. Knocked you on your heels a bit, seeing an entire landscape of books vertical like that. And strange to think that pretty much every word in them was contained in my Da's dictionary back home. You can pull any book you want out of a dictionary, like a magician pulling flowers from a wand.

There were books on everything in that library: astronomy and sailing and music, things I had no immediate use for, but was happier for them existing. Books on world faiths, too, with blue-skinned deities and round-bellied Buddhas. I found that reassuring as well, knowing that other gods were walking this world. Odd to think that what was so absolutely right in Paradise Flats was just as absolutely wrong somewhere else. Made you wonder if there was any standard of measurement at all.

I finished my apple and hid the core behind a copy of the King James. I had the texts of several competing gods open in front of me when Mrs. Mabel appeared, clearing her throat and asking if there was something she could help me with. It was like she caught me trying to sneak into the Palace for a noon screening. I don't know why she was so ticked; it wasn't like I was ripping the pages out or anything.

"What exactly *are* you looking for?" she wanted to know.

I turned. Stared her in the eye. "Won't know till I find it, will I?" And then, just for spite, I asked, "Got any books on gambling? Or how to mix moonshine?"

She didn't dignify that with a response. She just turned and swept back to her post behind the information desk.

Turns out, I did find a book on gambling, though not of the sort I was inquiring on. Our local racetrack had shut down, but the bookies in town were still doing a brisk business on the wire, and I figured maybe on getting some tips I could parlay into something bigger. I knew that the odds were always stacked against you and that luck didn't exist, but if there was some mathematical way of getting around that ...

The book I found was in the cart marked RETURNS. It was titled *Contemplations on Pascal's Wager,* which I took to be a guide for betting. Nope. Nothing doing. The book was about gambling, all right, but not of the pony or greyhound kind. It was about gambling on good and evil, on right and wrong. I found it a fascinating read, even if it wouldn't help me play the ponies. Pascal, you see, was a Frenchman who figured he'd worked out a way of outsmarting God. Or more accurately, I guess, of outsmarting his own doubts.

Pascal had applied the principles of gambling to matters of faith. The way he figured it, either God exists or He doesn't. It was like the flip of a coin. But which way to lay the wager? Well, if you believe in God and God exists, you win "infinite rewards" when you go to the Great

Beyond. If God *doesn't* exist and you *don't* believe in Him, well, that's fine, too. Nothing ventured, nothing gained.

Now. Suppose you bet on the wrong horse entirely. You say "God doesn't exist," but He does. Or you believe God is real, but He isn't.

Well, aside from living your life under false pretenses, and all the church-going and fear-stoking you have to endure, if you believe in God and he *doesn't* exist, Pascal figures this is no great loss. "If you gain, you gain all; if you lose, you lose nothing." But if you *don't* believe in Him, and it turns out you were wrong? Well, then you've got some serious justifying to do.

Eternal hellfire versus infinite rewards. Seems like an obvious choice, no? I mean, how could you cast your bet otherwise than in God's favor?

And yet ...

TEN

It was the library that did me in. No doubt about it. Had I stuck with the Palace I'd have been fine. The Palace was one of four cinemas we had in Paradise Flats. Like in every other Dust Bowl town, our banks were boarded up, but our movie theaters were going great guns. Radio was private. Movies were public. But both lightened the burden, both bedazzled and distracted. I liked the movies. Went as often as I could. Movies didn't ask hard questions the way books did. The library was full of dead ends and quicksand. Grasping at ideas was like trying to catch reflections off a bubble. With a fish hook. Could drive you mad.

But not at the Palace, with its name outlined in prima donna lights, and not at the movies. No sir. A projector advances film at twenty-four frames every second. That meant, in a single second, twenty-four images flashed past. To stop those images from bleeding into each other a shutter blocked the lens while the film was moving forward. As each image was projected, rapid-fire, onto the screen, the shutter stayed closed the same length of time it stayed open: *open, closed, open, closed, open, closed.* The images flashed. Your mind stitched it together, smoothed it out, made the separate frames blend together and appear to take flight. The illusion of movement. But here was the kicker. It also meant that, over the course of a two-hour movie, one hour was totally pitch-black. It was spliced together so fine you'd never notice, true, but that didn't change the fact that you'd just spent an hour sitting in darkness. Without realizing it.

What did I learn from the movies?

That darkness can be spliced. That cigarette smoke makes a fine filter. (Women look softer through a haze.) Spencer Tracy in *Captains*

Courageous taught me about being a man. Claudette Colbert in *Cleopatra* taught me about women. And from Boris Karloff and Bela Lugosi I learned there are two kinds of monsters in this world. Karloff as Frankenstein. Lugosi as Dracula. The first one overpowers you by sheer force, crushes you with brute strength. The other eats away at you from within. They represent two basic ways to die. A tornado or a plane crash, that would be Frankenstein. A disease that spreads slowly, taints your blood and turns it black? That would be Dracula.

I was ten or eleven when I saw the first of those horror films, and I remember thinking "Dracula got my mother."

Some monsters appear out of the dust, like the Mummy. Some can take bullet after bullet and never die. Some knock down the door, force their way through. Others have to be invited in. And that's the scariest part, isn't it? Not having an alibi when the darkness comes calling and you were the one who invited it in.

ELEVEN

Never did finish high school. I stopped going at some point, and no one seemed to care. Just as well; I was hardly there anyway and was failing at everything.

I was lucky enough to find work, night shift at Consolidated Salt. They were looking for strong backs, and I fit that particular bill. The first shipload of McGrearys had come over looking for something better, and there was me working in a salt mine. From black coal to salt rock—a lateral move at best, that one, and with no ship of Drake gold in sight.

The pay was spotty and the hours were long. I worked with Chicanos mainly, as a leveler when the boxcars pulled in, or as a dragger when needed. My hands became well calloused, and I tasted the salt in everything, be it ice water or brown sugar and tea. I was thirsty all the time, it seemed, and my eyes never got used to the sting of it. But it was honest work and I had friends now, or something to that effect, men as bone-tired as I was. Fellow "saltines." We got three dollars a day for a ten-hour shift, news of the Fair Labor Standards Act not having yet reached Paradise Flats.

There wouldn't be need of any more $50,000 bags of groceries; food and assorted goods came from the company store. Management kept a running tally, deducting what we owed from our paychecks. I did the math; I knew the game they were playing. They didn't even pay us in proper U.S. tender. No sir. We were given company scrip, what we called "chickenfeed": thin aluminum coins with holes punched through. The scrip was worth sixty cents on the dollar and could only be used at the company store, where the prices were set higher than at non-company shops. Only way to get hard currency was to sell our scrip to men with families at fifty cents to the dollar, which we oftentimes did.

Still, I wasn't complaining. In Kentucky, there were coal miners supporting families on twelve-hour shifts and four-dollar weeks, living barefoot in broken-backed shanties, sleeping six on a horsehair mattress. In some of those camps there were children who hadn't tasted milk since they'd been weaned. So I wasn't complaining, even as I went deeper and deeper into debt. Filled the belly just the same, on credit or on cash. And on the long walk home in the early morning, at that hour of day when only the wind is awake and the sky is a softer shade of blue, I'd think to myself, "I'll be all right."

I haunted Harry's Pool Hall, playing the Chicanos from the mine for pennies and beer. Afternoons, though, I often found myself drifting towards the library. I'd end up in among the stacks, with half a dozen books splayed open in front of me and Mrs. Mabel frowning fiercely all the while. She never did learn to accept my presence. I might have been frowned right out of the place if it hadn't been for the appearance of a flowered dress and a page-boy haircut.

That would be Rebecca. Mrs. Mabel's reed of a daughter.

She had been a grade or two behind me, so we knew each other only just. I hadn't seen her for some time, me out of school and all, and maybe it came from spending my nights at the mine surrounded by the sour smell of male sweat, but when Becky floated in that day, it was like a long drink of cool water.

The two of us were wary, at first. Her acting like I wasn't quite there, me like I knew what I was looking for in those books.

Rebecca started to come in every day after school to help her Ma stock the shelves, to stamp and sort cards. I started timing my visits to coincide with hers, early enough so it wasn't suspect. Twenty minutes, half an hour. I could get through several books before she arrived—running my fingers quickly down the page, reading as fast as my hand moved. It was something that had caused me no end of grief at school when the teachers refused to believe I'd finished the assigned reading in the time it took the others to open their text. It was a knack that came in handy now, because once Rebecca appeared, well, hell. The words on the page swam in front of my eyes. And if she swished her dress casually, just in passing, or cast a glance back over her shoulder at me—wasn't it all I could do just to remember my name?

I'd learned from watching *Cleopatra* that women were temptresses, and that suited me just fine. Problem was, Paradise Flats seemed to have a shortage of temptresses on hand. Even barn dancing was considered morally risky on account of all those bare limbs touching each other during the do-si-dos and the alaman lefts. Chaperones hung over us like dark clouds, trying to spoil the fun that came when—sort of accidentally— your hand butterflied across a girl's blouse as she passed. When a girl was keen on you, you'd know it by the way she arched her back just enough so that you could fan your hand across her so smoothly only she and you would know what was happening. As the circle flung you apart and then drew you in, moving her back towards you, you could see her face grow pink in anticipation as she came nearer and nearer, ready for another pass.

My entire experience with women consisted of those dances and one hurried round of pushing, trousers around my ankles, with a girl from the farms who had arched her back more than most one night. Thin, she was, and she held her breath the whole time, while I moved on top of her. I scarcely saw her face. I remembered her shoving me away when I got too hurried, and me casting my seed on the ground like Onan had, but that was about it. She had whispered "Don't tell no one, y'hear." But there was no one I could tell. She didn't have a name, and so had none to ruin.

Now Miss Rebecca, her eyes were of the deepest green—deep enough to get lost in, as they say. She moved around the library with a swish here and a turn there, till one day she passed the table I was at and said, "Read a lot."

"That I do," I said, but she was already gone, having wafted away without waiting for a reply.

Over the next few days I got it into my head to ask Rebecca out, someplace green to match her eyes, someplace where the ground wasn't parched so. But that would require a car. And nice as it would've been driving up to her house in a stylish new Dictator, that wasn't going to happen. I'd have to get the De Soto running again.

How hard could it be? The principles involved were straightforward enough: ignition, lubrication, piston, valve. The motor was just a mechanism for converting up-and-down motion into round-and-round, really. Follow the drive train back far enough, I figured, and you should be able to find the problem. The chain of cause-and-effect was simple with cars. I liked that. No need to ask *why* the motor broke. Just find the problem, fix it, and move on. Women were another matter entirely.

The latch on the De Soto creaked, rust on rust, and when I lifted the hood, up came a sort of moan. The inside—was empty. The entire motor, gone. And me shovel-smacked at the sight of it. That De Soto was a shell, no better now than the trucks farmers were pulling around with mules, what they first called "Hoover wagons" and then "Roosevelt buggies."

Damn it all to hell.

I stormed inside, found Da beside the window watching the horizon. It'd been a while since the last big dust storm. The wind was always there, sometimes as soft as talc, other times sharp as salt, but the black blizzards seemed to have pulled back. Yet there was my Da, peering out like he was waiting for a darker evil to enter the world.

"Can you explain to me," I said, "why the De Soto's got no guts?"

He said nothing.

"Where's the motor, Da?"

"Empty," he said, though I wasn't sure he was talking about the car.

"I know it's empty. I want to know why."

Well, that shook him out of it, me challenging him like that. He snapped his eyes onto me, said, "Think I don't know you've been stealing? Ferreting away certificates. Hoping to cash in after I cut you off. You mind your lip, boy. You're not so big I still can't take you."

I left, slamming the screen door hard as I could. The wind popped it back open, so I swung again. Harder. And just as hard, the wind slapped that door back at me.

I thought of Crazy Eli, how they found his body baking in the desert, thought of him and how he used to flail about in the dust storms. Maybe Eli was crazy, and maybe he lost whatever war he thought he was fighting, but at least he went down swinging. I had to give him that.

TWELVE

I was back at the library the next day, still caked in a crust of salt from my shift at the mine and determined to give myself an advantage of some sort. Couldn't ask Rebecca to go for a ride with me unless she wanted to be dragged down State Street in a broken De Soto on a team of mules. And I didn't imagine that sort of thing was conducive to romance.

No, I would have to arm myself with knowledge. Study my way into an understanding of her. I pulled a book on human anatomy from the shelf, to find out how everything worked. I found *female reproductive systems* and opened the pages. Dr. Boltzhurst walked past, nodding his approval. "Scientific interest. Good to see."

The book wasn't any great help, though. A bit off-putting, actually. Truth be told, my interest in Rebecca didn't run much deeper than the epidermal level, and the full-color prints in this text, with the parts labeled like a frog in mid-dissection, weren't quite what I was looking for. Knew more about Rebecca than I probably should have, too, after that. I didn't imagine any girl would want a fellow reciting odes to her Fallopians.

I yanked open the card catalog again, thumbed my way through "love." Perhaps romance was an art, not a science. And boy, didn't I find just what I was looking for. *The Art of Love*. Title said it all.

I tracked that book down and brought it to my table. It was a leather-bound volume, illustrated—as the title page read—with "sensual art deco depictions of love and seduction." Mostly of the clinging robes and lute-plucking variety, as it turned out, but no matter. I wasn't looking for pictures, though I must say, a couple of those partially clad nudes did distract my attention.

The Art of Love, or "Ars Amatoria," was translated from Latin, apparently, and had been written by someone named Ovid, a poet out of
Rome almost two thousand years ago. That surprised me, people
wrestling with "the art of love and seduction" even back then, around the
same time as Our Lord was being heralded into this world on angel
wings and trumpets. From the preface, it would seem the "sexual frankness" of this Ovid got him banished by the Roman Emperor. That was
just what I needed: frankness.

I leafed through it. Ovid had included chapters on "Where to Find
Her" and "How to Win Her Heart," with headings that gave advice: "At
Dinner, Be Bold," "First, Win Her Maid," "Be Wary of Your Friends."

Rebecca didn't have a maid, far as I knew, and I didn't have any friends
worth worrying over. I could hardly afford a dinner, let alone a "feast
worthy of Bacchus," as Ovid had recommended I lay before her. My
paycheck was whittled down enough already, and I still didn't know which
fork was for what. Even if I'd taught myself that, a fine dinner at one of
our better hotels—with the weight of those bedrooms hanging over us like
that, no less—would have required $200,000 in Drake gold to pay for it.

I say unto you, women contain a multitude of moods and their
hearts are as varied as their faces. Different hearts require different
methods, and a wise man adapts: now a gentle wave washing over,
now a solid and unbendable oak, now a lion, now a dove, now a
rooting boar. Some fish require spearing, some are caught by line and
hook, others by billowing nets. Just as older prey can spot a snare
farther off and must be approached from behind, so too, those more
experienced in love require a different take than do virgin maids.

I was assuming Rebecca was a virgin maid, her being from a church-
going family, so I skipped the passages on seducing other men's wives.
The key to conquering virgins, it would seem, was persistence:

Is anything harder than stone? Softer than water? Yet the softest
water can shape and wear thin the hardest of stones. Stay steadfast.

Such matters must proceed by step. Yield not to impatience and you will soon have that which you desire—if she wishes.

It was that last "if she wishes" that gnawed me down. How to know what it was she wished? Would *she* even know? Most of all, though, said Ovid, "compliment, compliment, compliment her."

Birds would sooner cease singing, or a hound turn from a hare, than a woman would ever refuse flattering words.

That was two thousand years ago, but I was hoping it was still true today. The key was to say pretty things about Rebecca. But what? Ovid had the answer to that, too. The man was sharp.

Find reason for light conversation, and engage her in trivial talk. The topic at hand is not important, but that you agree with her. When the steeds enter the stadium at the start of the chariot races, ask which horses she favors and then exclaim that those too are your favorites as well. Agree on the small matters and she will agree on the large.

As I said, our local racetrack had long since closed down, and I doubted Rebecca would want to play the ponies over the wire, but the advice still stood. Find what she liked, and agree.

By subtle flatteries, you may steal yourself into her heart. Never cease in praising the beauty of her face, the tapered elegance of her fingers, the dainty nature of her feet. The coldest beauty is warmed by praise, and even the most innocent of girls longs to be complimented and found fair; even the most untouched of virgins wants to be told that their bodily form is pleasing to the eye.

Elegant fingers. Dainty feet. I made note of that.

Seduce her with promises. Promises entice the heart. Swear by all the gods you care to name that your word is true and your vows of love heartfelt. Jove himself looks down from on high and laughs with delight at lovers' perfidies. For often did he swear by the Styx that he would remain faithful to Juno, only to break his vows on a whim. His example should give us the courage we need. As women learn to deceive themselves, so too will you learn to deceive the deceivers.

I was at the library the entire day, with only taffy for lunch, and was so caught up with the revelation of it all I didn't hear Rebecca come in until she passed directly behind me.

"Whatever are you reading?" she asked.

The chapter I had open in front of me featured a full-color illustration of half-naked lovers tangled up. My face burned, but Rebecca had once again wafted away before I could stammer any sort of reply. She looked back, though, to smile a small scold at me, and I took it as a good sign.

When her Ma went to the basement, I moved myself close enough to Rebecca to catch the smell of Noxzema coming off her. She looked up at me, but didn't say a word. She was waiting for me to begin.

"You have nice feet," I said, and cursed myself the moment I said it.

"Feet?"

"They're very dainty. And your hands. They're—elegant. And your eyes ..."

She nodded. Slowly.

"They're green," I said.

"Um, I still have a lot of books that need sorting," she said, but couldn't resist looking down at her hands first, holding them out to see what was so elegant.

I would have cut my losses and run, but the aroma of her Noxzema was intoxicating, and before my head could stop me, I blurted out, "You could be the next Scarlett O'Hara, you know that?"

Scarlett O'Hara was the biggest thing on people's minds those days. Who would be cast as Scarlett? The filming had started—I heard they'd burnt Atlanta down good and well already—but no one had yet stepped into the lead role alongside Mr. Gable. Some had bet on Tallulah Bankhead. Some on Bette Davis. Others, Joan Crawford. Factions were forming, and the search had reached a fever frenzy. So why not Rebecca?

She balked at this. Then smiled. She tilted her head ever so slightly, as though she were about to turn away, but she kept her eyes on mine. I recognized that look; it was what they called "coy." It could be separated into two elements: tilting down while looking up. Conflicting signals, those. They said "I'm going" and "come closer" at the same time. Had a powerful effect on a boy.

"Scarlett O'Hara?" she said. "You really think so?"

"I know so. I have an uncle out of Hollywood, he's a scout for the studios, and green eyes are what they're looking for. Said so himself." All of which was a lie, of course, up to and including "I have an uncle." Worth it, though, to see her blush like that. I do believe Ovid would have been proud.

But then her Ma came hippoing down the hall and Rebecca quickly moved away. And even though Becky and I stayed a respectable distance from each other, Mrs. Mabel had clearly picked up on something percolating below the surface. She kept a tighter watch on the two of us after that, and I was forced to communicate by other means. Rebecca would sort the books and shelve them, and I would give her something to sort. I'd pull out glossy art books and leave them open to paintings of nude women rising from the sea on a half-shell or of men ravishing Sabine wives, so that Rebecca would have no choice but to see them before she closed the books and put them back on the cart.

She replied with a copy of *Moral Fortitude: A Young Man's Guide to Restraint*, published by the American Christian Association, tossed lightly on my table as she passed by, a half smile at play.

Over time, she would throw glances my way more and more often, and would swish her dress like she didn't care I was watching as her mother looked on disapprovingly. And you know something? The more disapproving her mother became, the more that dress swished.

That was something they didn't teach you in Sunday school either.

Thirteen

The time had come to move the ratchet forward another notch, and Ovid had the goods on that as well. I was advised on arranging an accidental meeting.

> Contrive to cross paths as if by happenstance, at the market or in the alley, or even better, at the Shrine of Adonis, or the Memphite temple of the linen-clad heifer.

Not having a Memphite temple to the linen-clad heifer in Paradise Flats, the nearest thing would have been Sunday services. But Rebecca being a Methodist and me being not, such a happenstance would have been hard to contrive. True, it looked like the Methodists were going to reunite after more than a hundred years apart, and they may very well have been in a conciliatory frame of mind, but I didn't know if that extended to other faiths. Shrines to Adonis, Paradise Flats might not have. But alleyways, we had tons of. Still, I'd have to plan my ambush carefully, to make it look like chance and good fortune.

"The capture of skittish girls requires great skill," Ovid had warned. It was tricky, like trying to thread a needle in the dark. You had to be gentle: "As doves flee before an eagle, as a lamb quails at the sight of a wolf," so too would a lady flee if you came thundering in like a bull off its tether. At the same time, when it came to that first Lord Almighty kiss, Ovid said, "When the moment finally comes, it is not the time to hesitate. Take what isn't given. She may fight it, may pull away and denounce you as 'wicked,' but in struggling free from your embrace will find her desire. And once you've hooked the fish, do not let it escape. Press home your advantage, don't pull back."

I took my advice from Ovid, my inspiration from Crazy Eli. If I was going to go down, I would go down swinging.

I planned to intersect Rebecca on her approach to the library, having charted the path she took, and I caught up with her in the alley behind Sukanen's.

"Becky," I said, calling out, and she stopped.

She turned, like she'd been expecting me all along.

I was worried she was going to ask me about upcoming movie auditions, but she never did. With my patched-up trousers and salt-burned face, she must have known I had no Hollywood in me. She was just happy I'd cared enough to lie, I suppose.

We walked along the alleyway, and she talked about her classmates and the teachers she disliked and why, and common acquaintances and the movies she preferred and how they had overcharged her at the malt counter and how that wasn't right, with me agreeing to everything she said.

When it came to the radio, Becky favored continuing sagas over quiz shows, musicals over detective programs, and by gum, so did I! She tuned in regularly to *Woman in White* about a nurse in love with a young doctor, and *Young Dr. Malone* about a doctor in love with a young nurse. And *Young Widder Brown,* about a different nurse in love with a different doctor, both of them young.

"Dr. Anthony," she explained, "has the deepest, richest voice you can imagine."

I wasn't sure how she kept young Dr. Malone separate from young Dr. Anthony, but I didn't ask.

"I'm saving up," I told her. "Going to medical school to become a doctor—a young doctor. One who believes in doing good, helping the unfortunate."

I figured that was what she wanted to hear. Just as the coy look she gave in return was what she figured I wanted to see. Chin down, eyes up. Small smile. The sort of look you might practice in a mirror.

She said, "Why do you have to go telling stories? You're too rough for medicine, you know that."

That threw me back, and not a little. I would have stammered something wounded; but then I noticed. The look she was giving me had shifted ever so slightly. What was once fifty percent "go away" and fifty percent "come nearer" was now, by my estimation, at least sixty-eight percent the latter. So I lunged at her, the way a dog might chase a car, not knowing what he'll do with it if he catches it. I tried to kiss her full on the lips, but Rebecca pushed me back with a great shove. She flattened down her dress and gave me a jeezly stern look. "I ought to slap your mouth, Mr. McGreary."

Turned on her heel, she did, and marched away, head high. I was crushed by the thought that I had lost the entire deal. But then didn't she cast one last glance my way before turning the corner. So fleeting I couldn't read it proper, especially with my eyes clouded and my head pounding like that. I could scarcely hear my own thoughts. Looking back on it now, maybe that was the real attraction, to get your heart beating so loud it relieved you of having to think.

I was off work the next day for the Sabbath, and I lay awake wondering how I might have played that hand with Rebecca better. I ended up reading the dictionary by moonlight, trying to fill my mind with other clutter. Didn't help, though. I was fast approaching "amoral" from the other direction when I hit upon another word to stop me dead:

aphrodisiac

Noun: "food or drug known to heighten sexual desire." *Known to heighten sexual desire!* Now this was what I was looking for! It was worth reading a dictionary ten times over just for that. Examples listed included oysters, freshwater mussels, and Spanish Fly. Oysters and mussels were out of the question in the Dry Belt, so Spanish Fly it would have to be.

My elation had a short span of life, though. I went back to the library first thing Monday morning, was right there when Mrs. Mabel unlocked the door. I hurried past her scowling face to the medical books and tracked down an entry. First thing I found out? Spanish Fly was not a fly at all, it was a beetle.

> *Lytta vesicatoria* (from the Greek *lytta,* meaning "rage," and Latin *vesica,* meaning "blister"). The "blister beetle," as Spanish Fly is more properly known, contains high levels of the chemical cantharidin, which it excretes in concentrated form when threatened. Taken internally in powdered form, Spanish Fly causes irritation of the urinary tract, inflammation of the genitals, high fever, nervous agitation, excessive salivation, seizures, vomiting, diarrhea, urinary discharge, and possible priapism. Used in animal husbandry to incite mating among livestock, Spanish Fly is dangerous and potentially lethal when consumed by humans.

I could feel my chest deflate. I didn't want to irritate anyone's urinary tract, let alone poison them. But then something else caught my eye: "Any aphrodisiac effect ascribed to Spanish Fly is primarily of a placebo nature."

Placebo, I knew, meant "triggered by the imagination." I'd read about it in Webster's under P. So on to other medical texts I went. Placebos, it turned out, had a measurable physical effect. A doctor gives you sugar pills, tells you it will make you feel better, and it does *because you think it.* Now, you'd figure this would have completely undermined all medical and scientific certainty, but no. The fact that people could *will* themselves sick and then *will* themselves better again didn't seem to ruffle physicians in the least, even though science is supposed to be based on the notion that thinking something doesn't make it so.

With the placebo effect, there'd be no need for urinary irritation. With the placebo effect, if you gave someone an aspirin and told them it was Spanish Fly, it would still have the desired result. Problem was, for a placebo to work, the person had to *know* they'd taken it—and they had to *want* it to work. I couldn't think of a way to pull either of these off smoothly with Rebecca. No matter how I played out the scenario in my mind, it always ended with her delivering that promised slap to my mouth, and maybe even a dictionary to the head.

So I went home for lunch. Mulled it over. How to obtain oysters out here on the edge of a desert? And how to convince Rebecca to eat one? Maybe on a dare? I was back at the library that afternoon, trying to track down alternatives to oysters, when in comes Rebecca, stewing mad. She cast a cold look my way and then stomped across to OVERDUES.

I went closer, preparing to whisper an apology for acting not half a gentleman the other day, given how overpowered with passion I had been and all, was going to explain how the scent of Noxzema had clouded my mind, when she looked straight at me, no coy element whatsoever.

"Where were you?" she said. "I waited. An hour."

"You waited?"

"In the alley. Out behind Sukanen's. Like a fool."

"You waited?" I couldn't help myself. I started to beam, a big grin which she must have taken for mockery. She glared at me all the harder.

"Should have slapped you when I had the chance," she said. And off she went. I went back to the library a few more afternoons, but there were no more glances cast slyly my way, no more swishes of dress or looks that were coy.

And me with nothing to show for it.

FOURTEEN

"You need a plan, is what you need." That was Jorge Gaos, one of the fellows I worked the night shift with down at the mine.

We were inside Harry's Pool Hall, and Jorge was commiserating over my Rebecca predicament. With Becky giving me the icebox treatment, I was spending more time at pool and less at the library.

"You need a plan," Jorge insisted.

"I had a plan."

"A better plan."

Jorge lined up his shot. Missed. He'd spun it too far to the right. I had seen that coming, but hadn't said anything. We were playing for pennies, and I was one penny shy of a jar of beer.

"Puta!" said Jorge, stepping back to chalk his stick. "Tell her that you are mad with desire. You can't live unless she grants you one more kiss. Weep, tear your shirt if you have to, beat your chest, tell her your life is in her hands."

"I don't know," I said. "Not much of a chest-beating fellow."

He shrugged. "Well. Take her somewhere nice, then, and buy her a present."

"Can't afford to." I took my shot, dropped a ball clean in the far pocket.

"Can't afford not to," he said.

I looked up from the table. "I don't have the money for something expensive."

"Who said expensive? You have five dollars, you don't buy five-dollar pearls. You buy … a hair clip, say. The best hair clip money can get. You give her a *five-dollar* hair clip. Now that's going to impress her! Got to spend your money deep, not wide."

True enough. Except I didn't even have five dollars to spend, not on pearls or on hair clips.

"Ten ball, corner pocket," I said, tapping the corner in question with my cue as I circled around to set up the shot.

Jorge laughed. "What?"

"Ten ball, corner pocket."

He laughed, louder now. A great big Chicano laugh. "That corner?"

"That corner."

"*That* ten ball?"

"See any other ten balls on the table?"

"How?"

I pointed with my cue. "Twelve ball off the side, *here*, across and then behind for the split. Should peel the ten ball off, and in."

"You're going to put the ten ball in the corner pocket?"

"I'm going to put the ten ball in the corner pocket."

"No, you're not."

"Yes. I am. Wanna wager? Five dollars says I will. Five dollars or a hair clip of equal value."

"I got no five dollars to blow on a sucker bet." He turned to the room. "Hey, *compadres*! He's going to use magic, make a ball change direction halfway! Who wants to see that?"

Everyone, as it turned out. It wasn't exactly a wager. More of a feat. The crowd threw in two bits apiece to see it. Tally came to three and a quarter. Not quite a hair clip, but close enough.

I sank the ball.

It wasn't as hard as it looked, just a matter of geometry. You take the table as a plane, then work backwards from the pocket. All you have to do is match the angles going in and coming out. If it's 45 degrees from the pocket, then half on the next, so, 22.5 degrees. Start with a knife-sharp 11 degrees, slight side-spin to compensate for the warp in the middle of the table—I ran my hand along the felt; there was a bit of a swell, to the left—and, well, hell, long as you hit that first one hard enough and clean, the billiard balls don't have a choice but to go in. All you need is a straight line on a plane. Let cause-and-effect take care of the rest.

Jorge cheered when that ten ball sank, hands raised as though by being my barker he'd had a stake in my success. The crowd laughed. Someone shouted, "How'd you do that?"

"Magic," I said.

On one point, Jorge and Ovid agreed: You had to take a girl somewhere nice. But where Jorge favored a spot that was private and remote, the desert, say, or the top of a mesa, the better to proclaim one's love at full voice, Ovid took a different tack.

Back at home, I went over the notes I'd culled from *The Art of Love*. The mistake many first-time lovers made, Ovid said, was to start somewhere overly intimate. You ran the danger of drowning in uncomfortable silences. Plus, physical contact was difficult to arrange "accidentally." Instead, advised Ovid, start with someplace crowded. The Coliseum, for example, or the Theater—"a place arranged most fruitfully for your needs."

> Press your thigh against her own, as you must in such cramped quarters, jostled from every side. Take seats in the very heart of the throng. Complain of the crowds even as you crowd against her. And do not let her sit in the Theater row without you, at any time. If she should rise from her seat, so must you. If she should sit, so must you. Be attentive at all times, and if her robe should trail too near the ground, lift it for her. The reward for your kindness will be a glimpse of her legs.

I wanted more than a glimpse, I knew that. So did Ovid.

> Casually at first, and then with intent, let fingers brush thigh, foot touch foot. In the heated crowd, use a light fan to raise a breeze for her, and in doing so be allowed a caress without risking the touch.

And finally, this:

If, perchance, a fleck of dust should settle on her gown, flick it off with your fingers. And if no fleck of dust should settle, flick it off anyway!

Clearly, I needed to work at this step-by-step. Theaters we had, but a single movie wouldn't do it, so I decided to use a weekly serial to draw Rebecca in. That meant Saturdays, either the matinee or the evening show. Whether it was *Mandrake the Magician* or *Secret Agent X-9*, serials ran after the cartoons and before the main feature, always ending with the heroine dangling from a cliff or on a wagon pulled by stampeding horses—that were heading for a cliff. The idea was to keep moviegoers hanging on as well.

Most serials ran ten to twelve installments, at about twenty minutes each, which allowed me to chart out a plan. First week, brush against Becky as if by accident. Second week, as if by not. Third week, hand on knee at a key moment, quickly withdrawn. Then hand on knee, key moment, slow withdrawal. And so on, so forth, through to a chaste kiss on Week Nine and a deep one on Week Ten—followed by a promise to meet later that same night for full consummation. The picture got a little murky around step eight, granted, but at least I had a plan in place. I wasn't going into this blind.

I looked for a movie that had been condemned by the Legion of Decency, one deemed corruptible to youths, but none was playing, alas. *Gunga Din* was showing at the Roxboro with Douglas Fairbanks Jr. I'd seen it twice already, and knew it had several key moments during which Rebecca might gasp and grab hold of me. But did I really want her hearing someone say, "You're a better man than I am!"? And anyway, the serial playing alongside it was a *Zorro* that was already halfway through its run. So *Gunga Din* was out. The Rio was playing a Shirley Temple dance-and-prance, but although Becky loved musicals, and I had said the same, I couldn't stand watching people break into song as though life was just the prelude to a dance number. Same with the Busby Berkeley flick playing at the Varscona-Lux in stereophonic sound.

That left *Drums Along the Mohawk*, starring Henry Fonda. He was handsome, but not too handsome, and he never grabbed a top hat and cane and started tap-tap-tapping. It was playing at the Palace and was a nickel cheaper on Saturdays—meaning I could buy both my ticket and Becky's for fifty cents, and only need an extra dime to cover her soda. Even better, the Palace had a brand-new serial, *Scouts to the Rescue!*, that was just starting up. Matinees were cheaper still, but that would have expelled us into the glare of day afterwards. I wanted to leave the theater at dusk, with pockets of dark to steer her towards.

There was one more piece of the plan to put into place. For that, I went down to Cyrus Tweed's Antiques & Emporium, the one on Main, filled rafter to floor with family heirlooms confiscated for nonpayment and other such property as had been repossessed. Tweed's was a repository of riches, one that drew collectors in from all parts, some as far away as Utah.

Cyrus himself was one whisper away from becoming a legend, having invested in stocks with gay abandon during the Twenties before selling them off on September 3, 1929. That was the day the shares on Wall Street hit an all-time high. If you'd forgotten that, Cyrus Tweed was always pleased to remind you of it. Like so many stock speculators, he had invested heavily, and on margin, in such paragons of American industry as Bethlehem Steel and the Youngstown Sheet & Tube Company (before they started shooting strikers). Mr. Tweed had purchased stock in Allied Chemical and Columbian Carbon, in Western Electric and the U.S. Steel Corporation, in American Tobacco and Monsanto Chemicals, and in John D. Rockefeller's Standard Oil Company. His shares were small, but his portfolio was diversified, as they say. He even held a few U.S.-backed promissories to overseas governments.

But ol' Tweed, he cashed out his foreign bonds just before they collapsed and sold off his stocks on that highwater day. He'd placed his money in a strongbox and was trying to decide whether to reinvest in commodities or in oil, or maybe in banking. And wouldn't you know it, while he was mulling it over the entire house of cards came crashing down with Tweed left standing in the wreckage, a wealthy man.

Wealthier still because so many others had fallen. Anyone had a hair clip worth five dollars, it would be Tweed.

He was all Adam's apple and beak, Tweed was. Eyed me the entire way as I approached the counter. Silverware. Coin collections. Oak dressers and towering grandfather clocks. Surfaces dull with dust, mirrors catching angles in every direction. There were even some sewing dummies, both big-busted and small, standing discreetly to one side.

"I'm looking for a hair clip."

"A hair clip?"

"The most expensive one you have."

Long pause. Then, creaking in his Ichabod way, he slid off his chair, made his way down the counter.

"Part of a set," he said. "Don't make a lot of sense buying just the clip."

He pulled out a rose-red wooden box, opened it. A brush, a comb, a mirror, a hair clip, all in a tortoiseshell lacquer and artfully arranged.

"Hate to break it up like that," he said.

"Maybe this is only the start," I said. "Maybe I'll be back. Buy them all, piece by piece."

"A present?"

I nodded.

"You're McGreary's boy, aren't you?"

I nodded.

"Well, I know it's not for your mother. So it must be one of our local floozies, some girl you've got designs on. I'll let you have it, four dollars, fifty cents."

My pride and face were burning from the references he'd made. "I'll give you five," I said, staring him hard in the eye.

"Five? Price was—"

"I would like a five-dollar hair clip, Mr. Tweed. Not a four-dollar one. Not four-fifty. Five."

Didn't that raise an eyebrow.

He smiled, teeth fanning out like a bad deck of cards. "Five it is," he said.

I paid him with the money I'd won at Harry's, along with some shards of my check the company store had managed to miss.

He said it was a pleasure doing business. I was on my way out when I saw it, stacked high in the corner of one display case: a full set of Finnish dinnerware. Pale blue, it was, and priced at one dollar a plate.

I stood, looking at them, the hair clip held tight in my hand. I stood there for what seemed a long, long time. I·stared at that stack of plates, stared at it until it disappeared.

Then I left, bell jingling as the door closed behind me.

FIFTEEN

Saturday night at the Palace. The place was packed.

Couples and families, rich and poor, stumbles of farm boys, giggles of girls: crowding in to watch the same spectacle. Must have been how the chariot races and Coliseum shows were for Ovid. Becky and me squeezed through to sit in center row, our legs pressing up against each other every time someone scrunched past. Filaments of cigarette smoke. Catcalls and their replies echoing over our heads. No awkward silences were possible in a din like this.

I'd passed Jorge and some of the other saltines on the way in. He'd caught my eye, made a quick assessment of Rebecca, the way you might size up a chassis, and had given me his personal thumbs-up seal of approval. But Ovid had warned "Beware your friends," so I ignored him, pretended like I hadn't seen the "why-don't-you-ask-me-over-and-introduce-us" grin he was wearing.

The Palace was muggy with bodies. The owners of the theater had installed Manufactured Weather—they boasted of it on the marquee outside—but they rarely turned the conditioning on until the place was so stuffy that people were practically fainting; even then, it was usually only on Prosperity Nights, when families crammed in for a movie-sweepstakes chance at winning a hamper of food or maybe a hundred-dollar, one-time jackpot extravaganza. That night, with no one toppling over and no prescreening giveaway scheduled, we were left to stew in our own juices. Humidity was breathing down our necks like a dog that wouldn't leave, and I fanned Rebecca with a program as we waited for the lights to go down. She murmured, and pulled open the top of her blouse a bit. "Thank you kindly," she said. I kept it going, fanning the air as she shut her eyes and let the breeze play over her. Ovid was no chump, I can tell you that.

Rebecca's hair was pulled back and held with a tortoiseshell clip. It was some kind of beautiful, that clip. She'd said so herself when I'd given it to her, by way of apology for having left her stranded behind Sukanen's that day.

She'd turned the clip in her hand, seen it catch a gleam here and there. "Must have been expensive," she said.

"Cost me five dollars," I said.

"Really?"

"I'd swear on the Good Book. You can ask Tweed himself if you'd like."

"Why, this must just about be the most expensive hair clip I've ever seen," she said.

"Must be," I said.

After that, how could she have said no to an invitation to the Palace? It would have ruined the story, like turning down a man who'd walked twenty miles of track for a glimpse of red hair. And so. There we were, the two of, as the lights dimmed, our legs touching, lightly, thigh to knee.

Would've been fine, I do believe, if it hadn't been for that newsreel.

The cartoon hilarity had finished, Rebecca laughing lovely at every pratfall, and then the serial ran, ending with the heroine tied to a chair in a house that was teetering on the edge of a cliff (same cliff Pauline had been hanging from in the last run; you had to wonder why they kept building houses in such inappropriate locations). The room grew darker and darker. Rebecca moved closer. And then soldiers appeared, scissor-marching across the screen. Eagle flags snapped and swastikas uncurled and a little man with a Charlie Chaplin mustache began shrieking like a schoolmarm in a hissy fit. Would've been even more comical, if it weren't for the army arranged in endless ranks before him. It was footage from the Congress at Nuremberg the year before, the cries of *"Sieg Heil, Sieg Heil, Sieg Heil"* echoing again and again. Here it was, a year later, and the soldiers of the Reichland were goose-stepping into Prague. The armies of that House-of-Mirrors Chaplin had now gobbled up an entire country in the name of the Fatherland: "Czechoslovakia is no more." The *March of Time* announcer spoke solemnly about "the gathering clouds of war." The mob at the Paradise Palace Movie Theater, throwing popcorn and laughing, hardly seemed to notice. But I did.

I had seen those same uniforms in other newsreels, breaking glass in the Jewish quarters. Cracking bones. Burning books. Throwing heavy scrolls onto bonfires. I had watched Jewish churches going up in flames, on a night of fallen crystal. Just a warm-up, was what they were saying. A warm-up for something bigger. Something more ... ambitious. Those boots marching across the screen, they seemed to be getting nearer with every drum-beat step. Sometimes, at night, if you caught the wind just right, you could almost hear them moving across the plains.

The previous Hallow's Eve, when the radios had broadcast an invasion from Mars, people had taken to the streets, thinking it was true, the end of the world. They were terrified of death rays and liquid nerve gas and mass extermination. But no one in America was running for the exits now, and that seemed odd. You didn't need to look to the Red Planet for the threat of an invading force. It was right there in front of us, in flags that snapped and boots that fell in unison. When Germany had annexed Austria they hadn't needed Martian death rays to do it. All they needed was Chamberlain, waving that sheet of paper like it was a flag of surrender, cooing about the friendship pact he'd signed with Herr Adolf and speaking large about how it would bring peace for our time.

And then this. Into Prague. And on to the Danzig. I didn't know where the Danzig was, but the announcer spoke of it and Moravia and seaports on the Baltic in the same low voice. I kept smelling something burning.

"You don't smell that?" I whispered to Becky.

"Someone lit a match," she said. "That's all."

Phosphorus has an acid sting. Tobacco, a sweetness. This was something different.

That was when I noticed her hand. How it had touched my knee, as if by accident, and how it had lain there, as if by not. Turns out, I wasn't the only one with tactics in play.

I shifted closer, moved my hand over and held hers, impossibly soft, in my own. We sat there, the two of us, watching Henry Fonda as Rebecca traced figure eights and small circles and other such patterns on the palm of my hand and the calluses she found there. It was all jumbled up, the smell of Noxzema, the warmth of her hand, the taste of books burning, the sight of soldiers scissor-marching across borders, the echoing cry of *"Sieg Heil, Sieg Heil, Sieg Heil!"*

Sixteen

I walked Rebecca home along Parson's Lane, past empty warehouses and rooms with shutters drawn. She had to be back before it got too dark, but "too dark" is a slippery term. We lingered at a point of her choosing, under the Baptist steeple and just out of sight from her family's house on the hill.

"Had a wonderful time tonight," she said, as young ladies were trained to do.

"Was a pleasure," I replied.

We were sinking into silence, but I didn't know what to talk about. She was on the brink of turning and continuing on her way, and once she stepped out, into the light of the streetlamp, I'd be lost. So, with a boldness born of desperation, I reached over and flicked the front of her blouse, lightly, with my fingers.

"A bit of dust," I said.

She looked at me and a smile surfaced. "That's some eyesight you have," she said. "Picking up a piece of dust in the dark like that."

I was hooped. Caught cold, and just about to say how it had been an unusually *large* fleck of dust, and one that had managed to catch the only sliver of moonlight available, when she stepped in closer. "You know what I think?" she said. "I think you wanted to touch my blouse."

Things were getting worse by the heartbeat, and I had started stammering something dumb and even more desperate, when, damn, if she didn't step closer still. She began to undo the buttons on her front. "Five minutes," she said. "And you have to stay over the brassiere." She then squared her chest like a soldier awaiting inspection.

It didn't take me long to work my hand beneath the brassiere as well, her protestations so faint they seemed more a formality than anything. I kneaded her into a soft frenzy, and she pushed in closer, harder, backing me against the wall, kissing my neck again and again until my chest ached from the not breathing of it.

After a while I found if I turned my hand sideways I could slide it all the way up, between her legs to the warmth at the very top, even as she clamped her thighs tightly together to block my advance. Strangely enough, her actions also kept my hand from withdrawing. *"Now, who's got who?"* I asked myself.

I moved my hand back and forth. I could feel the soft cleft hiding behind her undergarment, and the more I rubbed, the warmer it got, and the warmer it got, the more I rubbed. I twisted my hand around, wedging her thighs open, caught that pocket of warmth in my palm, pressed up so hard I almost lifted her off her feet, until finally she pushed me away, falling back, breathing hard. She looked flustered, but her eyes were smiling. "Whatever am I doing with a boy like you?" she asked, then skipped off laughing, into the light of the streetlamp and the lane leading home.

That pocket of warmth had me. I could feel it glowing in the palm of my hand long after I had drifted home and toppled backwards into bed. "Thank you, Ovid!" I said, staring at the ceiling with a grin so wide I couldn't get rid of it.

The evening had certainly increased my interest in classical philosophy, I can assure you.

And then my Da stuck his head in and ruined everything.

"Quick," he said. "Come."

I followed him out to the kitchen table, where I could see stacks of Drake certificates arranged by denomination. The newspaper lay open to a map of Nazi Germany.

He pointed to the window. "There," he said. "In the far distance. Flashes of light."

"Rain?" I said.

He shook his head. "Dry lightning. It doesn't bode well."

"Da," I said. "It's nothing, just static electricity building up from—"

"Do you realize," he said, eyes wild, "how lucky you are? The wealth that is yours as birthright?"

I took this to mean I'd been written back into his will. But he was talking about something else.

"Not Drake. No. It's more than that, it's—*see?* There. Again. Closer now." Another silent flash of light.

"Listen, Da. I'm tired. I'm working swing shift on the dragger tomorrow, and—"

"Here, look," and he smoothed the newspaper out with his hand. I could see the ink from the map on his fingers. "You see this? You could do it, Jack. I'm too old, but you could do it."

Not this. Not now.

"When you've been blessed like we have, son, you owe it to the world. If I were a younger man, I'd join the fight. I'd stand tall, show old Adolph what the Scots are made of."

That was how he saw the world, my Da: lost treasures and individual heroics. As though one man standing firm could do anything against an army. Throw your hero in front of a 15-ton Daimler-Benz Panzer III tank and let's see how far he gets.

"Have you seen what they're building in Germany?" I asked him. "The cleanness of it? The modernity?"

But he was lost in his map. "Here—and here. That's where it'll start."

After I saw my first Buck Rogers movie serial as a kid, I rushed right out and joined up. Became an Official Buck Rogers Solar Scout, which mainly involved buying cans of Cocomalt and sending in the labels. The future sure was shiny, though. And *Flash Gordon?* That was even better. A brighter tomorrow, of gizmos and zero gravity, a world that shimmered, without dust storms or soup lines or emptiness. I couldn't wait for the surface sheen of a Flash Gordon future to arrive.

And wasn't Germany that most modern of countries: the Flash Gordon of nations? Hadn't *Time* magazine named Adolph "Man of the Year"? Wasn't my Studebaker dream car named in honor of Mussolini and the rest of them, those who had brought order to the confusion? Hadn't Lindbergh himself received the Iron Cross of the Order of the

German Eagle from Field Marshal Goering? Hadn't the American Nazi Party held its rally in Madison Square Garden, with brown shirts and storm troopers, hundreds strong, in front of a mob of twenty thousand, *just last month?* Wasn't this the World of Tomorrow today?

The American Dream was rusting from the inside out, crumbling into dust as surely as fields on the turn of a plow. And the Francos and Mussolinis of this world had already claimed the future, were already on the move.

What did we answer with? Tom Mix and his Wonder Horse Tony, riding the range and rounding up strays, drinking sarsaparilla and shooting pistols out of rustlers' hands. Embarrassing, is what it was. Ah, but we also had The Shadow and maybe that was our redemption. The Shadow had learned the secrets of invisibility. He could cloud men's minds. *Who knew what evil lurked in the hearts of men?* The Shadow knew. And always that same message at the end: "As you sow, so shall you reap." You could tell they'd added that just to keep the censor boards happy. The real story wasn't in the moral at the end, but in the darkness along the way. That was the real secret, wasn't it? About America. We liked to think of ourselves as Tom Mix, but deep down? Inside, where it counts? We're The Shadow.

I always was more attracted to shadows than to the chirpy sunshine of Tom Mix. (And honestly, now, who names a horse—a *wonder horse*—Tony? Lightning, maybe. Or Thunderhoof. Blazer, even. But Tony? A kid at school, he was named Tony, and he had spots on his face and bifocals you could crack a walnut on.) Kids could become members of the Tom Mix Range Rider Club, too, but after the Buck Rogers fiasco, I didn't much feel like being a joiner anymore.

My Da didn't see it that way. "You could do it, Jack," he'd say. "Go north. Join the British Army in Canada. Fight."

"Fight?" I said. "For what? Listen, Da. If the Boche ever invades Paradise Flats, I will happily take up arms against them. But till then, I don't see how I'm responsible for what happens to people on the other side of the world. Don't see how I owe them anything—least of all my life."

The conversation always ended the same, with him *shite*-ing me away, complaining that his son had gone askew. "Don't be such a girl's blouse," he'd say. "Don't be such a Percy pants." That night Fayther settled back, watching the window like it was a movie about to start.

"Can you smell that?" he said. "Something's burning."

Seventeen

It wasn't as though Rebecca and I had started keeping company. Not formally, at least. It was all stealth and secrecy, which was how she preferred things. Didn't even need the pretense of a movie serial after the first couple of times; we'd just meet in the evenings behind the steeple instead. I would juggle shifts with the Chicanos, promising them one and a half hours for every one of mine. Becky would back me against the wall and I would pull her in towards me.

I never could manage to get past the cotton barrier of her undergarments, though. I would try to loop a heavy thumb under the elastic, pull it aside, maybe worm my way in, but every time I did she would stop me, cold, hand on my wrist, and say no.

The Germans had marched on Lithuania and taken the city of Memel in Eastern Prussia. I couldn't even conquer Rebecca. We selected our rendezvous times in notes passed back and forth at the library, tucked inside books. "Tonight?" "Can't. Choir." "After?" "Maybe."

If only I could figure out how to cloud her senses that extra bit, not a whole lot, just the width of a single layer of cotton. The Shadow used his powers to fight crime. I could think of better uses.

Becky hadn't shown up at the library for several days, not since our last flurry of messages. I assumed this was a matter of illness or house chores, but I couldn't rightly check without raising her mother's bovine suspicions.

Meanwhile, I was taking another stab at Pascal. I couldn't let it go, this notion that there was an amoral way of getting into God's good books. I was reading again about Mr. Pascal's Wager when Dr. Boltzhurst came in, a derby crammed tight on his head. Father Augustus had arrived already, and he greeted Boltzhurst like he was a general returning fresh from the frontier—"Hail! Brave doctor! What say you of enemy incursions?" The two of them set to yammering so loud I had to move down the table.

Pascal had said the odds favored God. There was even a chart explaining how easy it was to choose your wager. The world's simplest racing form:

BETTING CORRECTLY:
God exists. You believe. *Result:* Infinite reward.
God does not exist. You do not believe in God. *Result:* Even draw.
(That is, no reward. No punishment.)

BETTING WRONG:
God doesn't exist. You believe anyway. *Result:* Another even draw.
God does exist. But you don't believe in Him. *Result:* Eternal punishment.

I wasn't so sure, especially the part about it making no never mind if you believed in something that didn't exist. Seemed to me you lost a lot of yourself in doing that, but Pascal hurries over that part of the equation. What he really wanted to stress was the *worst* possible outcome: you don't believe in God, but He *does* exist—and all you've succeeded in doing is raising His holy dander and bringing forth a vengeful and mighty justice. Hellfire and whatnot.

So.

If you were a betting man, Pascal figured the only reasonable thing to do was to bet on God: the potential payout was so huge, the potential loss so great. "Wager, then, that He is." Carrot and stick. Greed and fear, both in play. Choose the right horse, and you'd be drinking champagne with dead movie stars and laughing your way through eternity in no time. (The Mormons would be getting unfermented grape juice.) Bet wrong, though, and you'd be facing consequences enough to curl a Baptist's toes.

A couple of things troubled me about this.

Pascal put the odds of God existing at fifty-fifty, going by the coin toss he referred to at the start. But it seemed to me the actual odds mattered not a whit, not when the payoff was one of infinite reward. Whether the odds in favor of God were fifty percent or a measly two-in-ten-thousand made no difference. Any number multiplied by infinity equals infinity. Two multiplied by infinite value *equals* infinite value, just as surely as does fifty, or ninety-nine and nine-tenths of one percent for that matter. The probability of God's existence shouldn't enter into it, because it didn't affect the reward—not when you were talking infinite delights. It was like going to a horse race where every single horse paid out the same, regardless of its track record or the amount you bet. A nag or a champion, one dollar played or ten thousand: the payout was exactly the same. Based on the thinnest, tiniest possibility of God being real, you should still bet on God, because the payoff was infinite.

As I saw it, the problem with Pascal's Wager was not in the mathematics of it, but the morality. Or, the lack of. It avoided the really tough questions, this wager of his. Not, should you lay your money this way or that, betting on harps and eternal happiness versus pitchforks and slow-turning rotisseries. The real question was, does God exist—*and does it matter?* And even if the Old Guy was real, did He *deserve* our faith in Him? That was a question needed facing. Dracula didn't scour the world for victims on his own dime. God let him in. You couldn't blame Dracula for being Dracula. The dark Count required a stake through the heart, just the same, but it was the one who created him that needed to answer for it. A being capable of creating Dracula, maybe that's who we should have been arming ourselves with garlic against, no?

I wasn't so sure you could *decide* to believe in something, anyway, let alone God. Faith didn't seem like something you chose. Maybe this world of ours was a testing ground, a way of proving our readiness, our worth. Maybe it was an arena for the wrestling of lions. And if that was the case, it seemed to me that honest doubt was more honorable than a bookie's faith in playing the odds.

Boil it down to bones, and Pascal's Wager was just an appeal to our own self-interest. Which was fine, self-interest being a rational frame of mind, I figured. But how dumb would God have to be, for being tricked that easily? If anyone could look deep into your heart, see the cold calculations you've made, God could. And what then? This was a fellow turned a woman into salt *just for looking over her shoulder.*

God was a betting man, if the Bible was anything to go by. Look at what he did to poor Job, over a minor wager with the Devil. He was a sore loser, too. He would rather flood the world or let his only son be nailed to a board than change men's hearts on His own. No. I didn't fancy God would much enjoy being played for a fool. Especially by a Frenchman.

Dr. Boltzhurst was still talking loudly. Mrs. Mabel never hushed *him*. He was back from an emergency call to the meat packers, it appeared (or the *abattoir,* a beautiful word that should describe a ladies' parlor, with lace curtains and perfume, rather than a place of entrails and carved flesh). Dr. Boltzhurst had apparently been charged with keeping the sicker livestock alive long enough to be disposed of properly. You couldn't slaughter a dead cow, after all. Boltzhurst was the sort of man who could start an argument in an empty room, and he was now complaining at length about the lack of scientific rigor in today's meat-packing facilities. The priest, tiring of this topic, shifted the attention onto me. He peered down the table at the book I was reading.

"I see our young visitor is perusing Pascal." He was pleased by the sight of it, the way some are pleased at bears on unicycles.

I tried to ignore him, but he dragged the doctor with him down to my end of the table and pressed the conversation onto me like an unwanted handshake. I was in an irritable mood, Rebecca having still not shown herself, and the warmth in my hand having started to fade. Last thing I needed was a padre peering over my shoulder. Couldn't snub the good Father, though, him being a Man of God, even if he was a papist and not to be trusted.

"Enjoying Monsieur Pascal?" he asked.

I nodded.

"Able to follow the subtleties of his argument?"

I nodded.

"And what's the verdict?"

"Has its flaws," I said.

The priest smiled in that benign fashion parsons have, practiced in a mirror, I suspect. "Perhaps that is true," the Father admitted. "But Pascal's conclusions are sound, nonetheless. We must choose God."

"Because it's the better bet?"

"No, my son. We must choose God because it's the better story." The better story, mind. He then leaned back, convinced of his own cleverness, something he seemed to mistake for wisdom.

I couldn't imagine anything so—I tried to come up with a nicer word than "silly"—so *naive*. "Choose the better story?" I said. "The better story? That's just Pascal's Wager all over again." And it was. A watered-down, weaker-kneed version of it. "It's—it's naive," I said.

That set him back.

"Naive?"

"Why not believe in fairies, as well?" I asked. "After all, that too would be 'the better story.' Silly way to choose a faith, it seems. And sad."

"You're a thoughtful young man," Father Augustus said. "But do be careful not to let thinking sabotage you. Remember, Pascal isn't trying to prove God exists. He is seeking only to draw in stray lambs, to bring them closer to God."

"Lambs?"

"Gone astray. Those plagued by doubts, those for whom divine truth has perhaps not shone as clearly as it might. Mr. Pascal wants only that they consider the possibility of God."

"Which God?"

"Which God? *The* God."

"That's the problem, though, isn't it, Father? It's not a two-horse race." I had read up on some of the world's religions over many afternoons at the library, had seen the fine *array* on offer. "In laying down your bet, Father, you'd have hundreds of ponies to pick from. There's the Hindoos, and the Muhammadans. Anabaptists and Mormons. There's the peyote Indians, and their god. You'd have to worship Coyote, too, just to be safe. There's the Persians. The Turks. The Africans. The Eskimos and the jungle tribes of Madagascar. Even the craziest man in a padded cell, thinking the Lord speaks to him through a crack in his tooth, he might be right. Odds are terrifically small, of course, almost infinitesimal, but the odds don't matter, do they? Not when the payoff is infinite. Or what of faiths that have long since died out? Odin and Thor, all those Scandinavian gods in children's bedtime stories, the kind that mothers read to their little ones at night. No one believes in those stories. Not anymore. But that doesn't mean they aren't true. Maybe we turned our back on the truth long ago. Maybe it was Zeus or Odin all along."

"Now, just a second—"

"Seems to me, Father, you'd have to bet on the whole entire works. Build a temple to this god and that, cover every possibility. And even that wouldn't help. What about the whole 'No other God than me'? Well, now you'd be in big trouble, wouldn't you? It seems to me that gods are often exclusionary in nature. What will the God of the Muhammadans think if we show up, saying, 'Oh yes! I believed in you all along—but I bet on the Hindoos, too, just in case. No hard feelings, right?' Think of the thunderclap would follow that. There's probably a deeper layer of Hell specially for people who try to hedge their bets. I saw a picture of this one god? She had a thousand arms and was dancing on human skulls. How do you explain your strategic choice of beliefs to a god like that? Do you place a bet on her as well?"

"Young man, Pascal is not talking about lunatics or people who worship coyotes," said Father Augustus, his voice growing louder. "He is talking about the one true faith."

"Yes, Father. But *which* one true faith? There are so many of them."

He was angry now. Cheeks splotchy. "The faith of Abraham and Isaac—"

"Jewish?"

"Let me finish! The faith of Abraham and Isaac and Our Lord Jesus Christ, Everlasting. *That* is the faith of which Pascal speaks. Not Hindoos or heathens."

"I see. So it wasn't an honest wager after all. Entire bet was rigged, right from the start. They call that 'fixing a race,' Father, and I do believe it's illegal."

Dr. Boltzhurst was wearing an entertained smile. "He's got you, Father."

The priest took a deep breath. Forced a smile. Said to me, "Imagine you find a watch in the desert—"

But I cut him off. I'd read Deacon Paley, knew what was coming. It was no better than Pascal's Wager, or that watered-down version of it the good Father had tried to pass off earlier.

"True enough, Father," I said. "I find a watch in the desert, I assume someone made it. I also want to know, 'Why'd he discard it?' Is it broken? Maybe he lost it. Maybe it was stolen. And even then, it doesn't tell us anything about *who* designed it. Doesn't say if it was a Hindoo or a drunkard or a committee of archangels. Doesn't tell us if it was one god, or many. The watchmaker might very well be a bad person. Or a sloppy craftsman. We don't even know if the original watchmaker is still alive. Maybe he died a long, long time ago. Finding a watch, that doesn't tell us very much, now, does it?"

Dr. Boltzhurst cut in, quick. "Exactly right, son. It is reason, not blind faith, that—"

"Blind?" said the priest.

"Father, I'm simply saying—"

"The only thing blind is a faith in idols. Science can't—"

"A different realm, Father."

"A dangerous realm!"

"It is logic and the scientific method that will—"

"Logic can just as easily lead men astray!"

They bickered at each other, forgetting about me, which was just as well. I was considering tiptoeing out when Mrs. Mabel came swooping down. She cast a look my way. "Gentlemen, is this boy causing you trouble? I can ask him to leave, if you'd like."

"No, no," they both protested, not wanting me to go while my soul was still up for grabs.

"I didn't mean offense, Father," I said, not sure myself if I meant it.

He smiled. Trained to forgive, he was, and not quite ready to surrender. "God has a plan for all of us, son." He laid a hand on my shoulder, squeezed. His eyes were shining like my Da's after a late-night binge of Drake dreams. "You must have faith—faith in a grander design, in a larger purpose. You are a soul in turmoil, I can see that. Only God can assuage your fears."

I shrugged his hand off my shoulder. "I would join your flock, Father. If you can answer me one question."

The smile spread. "Of course, my son. Anything."

"Your church, like the others in town. It has a lightning rod on top, right?"

He nodded.

"Why?"

As quickly as his smile had waxed, it waned. Father Augustus made not even a pretense of smiling anymore. He was looking at me like there was some trick involved that he couldn't quite figure out.

I should've ended it there. Bid them good health and been on my way. But they wouldn't let me. To Father Augustus, I was a one-eyed man. To Dr. Boltzhurst, I was a trophy.

"Admit it!" the good doctor chortled. "The lad has bested you." He leaned in, uncomfortably close, smiled and said, "Tell me, son, have you ever heard of technocracy?"

The priest threw his gaze heavenward. "Here we go. This again."

"Technocracy is part of a movement—a movement towards logical certainty. One aimed at a purely scientific understanding. It's a way of ridding the world of mumbo jumbo."

"Mumbo jumbo?" sputtered Father Augustus.

"No disrespect intended," the doctor said, though I don't know how else you could have taken that. "*All* religion is mumbo jumbo," he said, clarifying the matter. "Not just yours. Technocracy," the doctor turned back to me. "Seeks to unify the sciences. To clarify ambiguities. It's a modern way of thinking. What we need is a unified science, a sort of encyclopedia that will bring all branches of knowledge together."

"Such a book already exists," cried the priest. "It's called the Bible!"

The doctor ignored him. Kept his attention focused on me. "We must apply scientific rigor to our thinking. We can't rely on fables and Bible stories. All that stuff—ethics, morality—all of it. It's not an expression of facts, but feelings. Doesn't describe how the world really is. Just our response to it."

What cannot be measured is not scientific. And what is not scientific is meaningless. I think he was quoting from his own letters to the editor.

All fine and good, but it seemed to me the things that were measurable were often the very things that weren't worth measuring. I wanted to say this to the good doctor. I wanted to say, Sure enough, it'd be simpler if life was a clockwork that could be reduced to mechanics, but it isn't. You could ask yourself why someone had to die, and the easy answer was that this microscopic germ triggered this response that led to this disease. But it didn't answer *why* they had to die. There was a bigger "why" lurking behind every problem. And it was the bigger why that always got you in the end.

I could figure out how to sink an eight ball. I could figure out a way around a blocked dragger-lift at the salt mines. What was harder to figure was a way around Rebecca's undergarments. And that was something I suspect Galileo never tested. Science describes the world well enough. It works wonders with billiard balls and dams and internal combustion engines—results speak for themselves. But billiard balls and dams aren't what keep us awake at night, are they?

I knew where Boltzhurst's technocracy was leading us. "You're the one writes those letters, right?" I said. "The ones speak so highly of National Socialism?"

The doctor smiled modestly at being recognized. "That's right," he said. "You've seen them?"

"I sure have," I said. "My Da uses them to stuff the cracks in the shit-house door. Says they work a marvel."

And that was the end of that.

Neither of them spoke to me again, which suited me just fine. I stayed at my table, watching the door for Rebecca's arrival, but she never appeared.

To a man with a hammer, everything looks like a nail. That was a saying out of St. Kilda, and it struck me as true enough. While I read and waited, and waited and read, the doctor and the priest continued their debate, arguing loudly over which end would best suit which means, and who was deluded and who was not, the two of them hammering away at nails they themselves had placed there.

And all the while, the jackboots continued to grow closer and closer.

Eighteen

I was working regular shifts at the mine now, sundown to sunrise—from "can't see to can see," as they said—and was late at the gates several times on account of hanging on at the library till the very last moment, hoping for Rebecca. And one day, wouldn't you know, I'm coming out of the open pit at the end of my shift, skin stuccoed with salt crystals, eyebrows so crusted they had a crunch to them—and there was Becky, waiting at the gate, eyes raw with crying, and she handed me her five-dollar hair clip, folded my hand over it, said, her mouth full of sad, "I can't see you anymore, Jack McGreary," and she turned, and turning, ran, trailing sobs behind her.

I would have pursued her—should have. But my workboots and spirit were weighted down with ground salt and weariness. A ten-hour shift and I could scarcely react, let alone give chase.

"I can't see you anymore." When she said that, I'd nodded, like I understood. And I did. My Dad had a De Soto. I worked in the mine. Hell, *I* wouldn't want to be with me. It was a long walk home that day.

I dreamed of rescuing Becky, but I wasn't sure from what. I'd read that in Charlemagne's time a courtier once carried his love backwards through the snow to cover his tracks, leaving only a single set of footprints leading *away* from the site of their lovemaking. I'd never seen snow; I imagined it was like salt, only softer. Down here, in the Flats, the only option would have been to walk backwards across the plains instead, with Rebecca in my arms, into the heat.

I never went back to the library after that, not wanting to give Mrs. Mabel the satisfaction of barring my way. For a while I waited across the street, under an awning, for Becky to show, but she never did.

I went to the Palace, the matinees and evening shows, hoping for a glimpse of her. She never showed there, either, and I sat in the inter-spliced darkness alone and watched *The March of Time* newsreels, the maps spreading ink across Europe. An ocean away, General Franco had captured Madrid, had ushered in "a new era of order." In Italy, Mussolini was massing his troops across from Albania.

Da said the Day of Reckoning was at hand.

"It's coming, son. The cards have been dealt. You can do it. Go north. Join the British Army."

But try as I might, I couldn't see how I owed anyone anything. Only battle worth fighting was one that would get me past that thin layer of cotton, and that was one it seemed I'd already lost. Or had I?

"Got the squirrel fever, eh, *amigo*?"

That was Jorge Gaos again, down at Harry's Pool Hall.

"Women," he said. A one-word summation of problem and solution, cause and effect, wrapped up with a question mark for a bow. *Women?*

"Don't know what to do," I said.

We were betting on an understanding of elementary physics. Or rather, on Jorge's lack of. He wouldn't play pool for pennies anymore; he always lost. Instead we were betting on what seemed an easy feat: that Jorge couldn't knock down a cigarette with a cue ball.

I'd stood one of Jorge's cigarettes up on its end—carefully and unlit, to spare the fat man behind the counter fretting over his felt—and then placed three billiards balls around it. One in front, two behind, making a snug fit. All Jorge had to do was scatter them with a cue ball and knock over the cigarette, and I'd buy the next round. I had no money, but that wasn't cause for concern. It wasn't a bet I planned on losing.

This was something I'd noticed whenever it was my turn to break. How the force from the cue ball *split,* getting redirected onto the two behind it. As long as the billiard balls that encircled the cigarette were in tight contact, the impact would always be transferred *around* the ciga-rette, no matter how hard the balls were slammed. In fact, the harder the better. Jorge and the other fellows who took me up on the bet could blast that cue ball with every patch of manhood they could muster, and it still wouldn't knock the cigarette over. Just simple physics, really. And sure enough, I'd won my fourth round already.

Then I sweetened the pot. I looked around the table, said, "A dollar from each of you that I can do it. I'll give you ten-to-one."

Four of Jorge's friends slapped down a bill. I didn't have any forty dollars, but it didn't matter. I set it up, fired the cue ball, toppled the cigarette.

"How did you—I know, I know," said Jorge. "Magic."

That, and the fact that this time around I'd left the tiniest of gaps between the front ball and one of the balls behind it. So thin you could hardly notice, but just enough to prevent the force of impact from being redirected completely around the cigarette.

I gathered up my winnings. Not much, but it was a start. I didn't know how I would win Rebecca back, but I knew money would be part of the formula. It always was.

"Want my advice?" said Jorge. "Take her someplace fun. Don't have a big heart-to-heart. Someplace … carefree."

"The carnival," one of his cohorts chimed in.

Jorge considered this, frowned his approval. "Sure. Carnival's in town. Take her to the midway. Make her laugh and smile, swing her through the lights till she forgets there was ever a problem, till she promises to be with you—only you."

"Can't," I said. "Her Mama's got her locked up."

"Well then, you're going to have to give her something nice, my friend. Something big."

Another five-dollar hair clip? She'd already returned the first one. And anyway, I owed the company store. If it weren't for the spare change and odd bill I managed to shake free from Jorge and the other Chicanos, I'd barely have enough for shoes. "Can't afford to buy her anything good," I said. "Even something small."

"Buy?" said Jorge. "Who said anything about buy? Not buy. Win. Look at the arms on you. You could blast a baseball through a steel can. They have booths. Games of strength and skill." (*Strens an' skeel*, in

Jorge's words.) "Go to the carnival. Find the biggest flash, hanging from the biggest rafter, and then win it for her. 'Win a prize. Win her heart!'"

This was what you call a "logical fallacy." It was a confusion of terms. A false parallel: winning a prize was not the same "win" used with a girl's heart. I knew that. I'd been reading up on logic before I cornered Pascal. Jorge's battle cry was built on a fallacy. I knew that, but I didn't care. There are times a fallacy is all you've got.

Nineteen

Never did throw any baseballs, and I'll tell you why. It was rigged. Entire thing, right from the get-go.

The plan I'd worked out with Jorge? The one with me toppling tin cans at the carnival and then sending Becky a secret note asking her to meet me in the alleyway behind Sukanen's, romantic moonlight falling across us, me laden with gifts I'd won to lay at her feet like roses, and her flinging herself into my arms at the sight of it. That plan? It went up like Lindbergh, came down like Hindenburg.

The carnival had staked its lot on the edge of town, where the setting sun turned the baked clay blood-red and the low-lying hills rolled away in sagebrush and long shadows. Out there, on the edge of that deeper emptiness, the Robbins Bros. Ltd. had built a caravan of lights and bells.

The midway was loud with noise and ricochets, and rich in distractions, with oom-pa-pa organs and electric lamps strung in lines like fireflies hung out to dry. Generators wheezing. The crowds surging through, and everywhere the air dripping thick with the smells of caramel corn and candied apples, of butter and beer malt. I bought a five-cent swirl of spun sugar on a paper cone, a pink cloud that dissolved into a sweet and transitory grit when you tried to bite into it. "Like eating air!" one girl marveled, pulling off fleecy fingers-full as she passed by, and me with no one to share the air with.

In the noisy disarray of that carnival, it didn't take long for patterns to emerge. It seemed slapdash, but a certain ruthless logic was at work. The midway formed a wide lane, booths on both sides and tables running down the middle. You could go either direction on entering, but everyone turned right. Probably came from driving on that side of the road, or from the majority being right-handed. Any lefties entering would probably just follow the surge. Now, being *ambidextrous,* I can write easily enough with either hand. Not something I learned. Just a knack. It's the way my brain is wired.

I tried going down the left side of the midway, in my ambidextrous way, but quickly found I was walking against the crowd, so I turned back. Began again. It started off with family fare: a fish pond and donkey ride, a merry-go-round with its rigor-mortis horses and brass rings. Then came the games of lesser skill: tossing pennies, throwing darts. As you moved farther in, the stakes crept up. Blackjack and roulette wheels appeared, and the customers there were better dressed. Stand back awhile and you'd see twenty-dollar bills changing hands—though the flow of cash seemed decidedly one way. I recognized business owners from town, a banker, one of our judges, too. They'd start with satisfied smiles, certain they could outsmart the uncouth carnies who stood before them—and would stagger away, not ten minutes later, with pockets emptied and crests well fallen. Same way Pascal thought he could outsmart God, I suppose. And who knew, but maybe God was just the biggest carnie on the lot; we kept placing our bets, growing ever more fretful as, slowly, we realized the game is fixed. The judge at the blackjack table, the granny at church, cut from the same cloth, perhaps.

They even had a Hall of Mirrors, smudged and clouded and angled every which way. I walked through a maze of my own reflections. It must have been a right headache packing those mirrors with padding for the hauling, hardly worth the nickel admission they charged. Which made me suspect the true reason behind it was to disorient you, throw your mind off its game.

Centerpiece of the midway attractions was the Death Car. It drew the biggest and most enthused crowds. The words "9:14 AM. MAY 23, 1934, GIBLAND, LOUISIANA" were painted high in lurid red letters—like it mattered when they died, or where. Gruesome photographs of Bonnie Parker and Clyde Barrow, slumped against each other, were on display outside, but you had to pay to go past the curtain. I paid my twenty cents, went inside.

Shameful waste of a car. A tan-gray Desert Sand Ford V8 coupe. Fine ride, and here it was riddled through with punctures. All told, 107 bullets hit that vehicle. Was some ambush, that one. Entire car pocked with bullet holes, and the crowd pushed in for a decent gawk, kept back by velvet ropes. "So ends a life of crime!" said the Death Car showman, his strawboater pushed back on his head, face sticky from the heat. "The Ballad of Bonnie and Clyde ended in a mighty barrage of justice!"

There were three other Genuine Bonnie & Clyde Death Cars touring the Southwest at that time, I was told, but the consensus seemed to be that the Robbins Bros. Genuine Death Car was of a superior quality. "Much better than the Death Car we seen in Santa Fe last year, isn't it, honey?" said one matron, clearly a fan of midway attractions. "Cleaner bullet holes." Her husband agreed. Yes. Of all the Genuine and Authenticated Death Cars out there, this one had a finer attention to detail. "Hell," he said. "One I saw in Topeka last year was *brown,* not tan. Got to get their facts right."

It played across my mind, me kicking open the screen door of Rebecca's hilltop home, firing bullets in the air, grabbing her by the hand, pulling her free, the two of us escaping Paradise, driving hard into Mexico, the law in pursuit and her hanging onto me saying, "I'd rather die with you than live apart!" Wasn't going to happen, though. I could picture Becky's Ma standing there, fists on hips, saying, "She's not going anywhere. Least of all with you! And who's going to clean up that mess you shot in the ceiling? Huh?" Becky wasn't the outlaw kind, I feared, and all I'd succeed in doing was looking more the flop than usual.

Out past the Death Car, at the farthest back stretch of the carnival, the lights were fewer and the booths set farther back. This was the corner with the freaks and burlesque shows, the live art tableaus featuring young ladies who recreated famous works of art, most of them involving nudity it would seem, French painters being particularly popular because of their tendency to have undraped ladies lounging beside picnic baskets.

The Tattooed Man was next, and beyond him the Snake Skin Woman, "Captured in the darkest jungles of Amazonia!" The Penny

Peep Show and the Ballet of Venus. Here a fellow could enter a booth simply by swinging wide as he walked by. Here a fellow could slip in easily without being spotted, almost like he'd wandered in by accident.

Drawn as I was to the darker corners, and still aching for more of the female form, I paid a hefty fifty-five cents to see a performance by Miss Isabella, "Queen of the Parisian Can-Can, Empress of the Hurdy Gurdy, Tutored in the Geisha Arts of the Orient." (That's France, Germany, and Japan in one throw. A regular globetrotter, our Isabella.) The illustration out front was lusty enough: a row of ruffle-skirted ladies, kicking high with the same perfect unison you'd see in goose-stepping armies. Inside, amid the wet stench of hay and sweat, there was only Isabella, a bosomy woman heavy on the makeup, who showed us her bloomers to organ music in a half-hearted dance with a single, sad shout of "Oo-la-la!" She then slipped out through a side curtain and the men started lining up, waiting their turn for a private showing with "the Princess of Gay Paree," "the Maid of Munich," "the Concubine of the Jade Emperor" at four dollars a visit. Seemed awfully steep for a closer view of bloomers, the likes of which could be peeked at for free down at Co-Op Ladies Wear.

Back outside, I spotted the Snake Skin Woman sitting on a crate between shows, pulling long on a cigarette. She reminded me a lot of the lady down the street from us, the one with the bad case of eczema. The Snake Skin Woman's looked a lot worse and a great deal itchier, but no one seemed to have left disappointed. A bit like the placebo effect, I suppose. If you'd decided you were going to see a Snake Skin Woman, captured in the jungles of deepest Amazonia, then by God, you were going to see a Snake Skin Woman who was captured in the jungles of deepest Amazonia. Never mind that the painting above the entrance showed a shapely lady, naked as a jaybird, captured in a net by big game hunters, her one bosom almost showing, while the lady I saw out back was just a sorrowful woman with haggard features and bad skin.

"carnival usa!" read the banners above the midway, pulled tight as a bow by the wind. Coming from that dark corner, back down the left side, the brighter lights were almost a relief, made you want to shed your money quickly as you sought the exit.

Time to win back Rebecca's heart.

The midway was ripe with prizes. They hung like grapes from every rafter in every booth of every game: stuffed animals of all shapes and stripes, Kewpie dolls with their deformed and bulbous heads, and higher up, on the shelves behind, stately radios and modern gramophones. A regular horn o' plenty, it was. And all of it just a nickel and a lucky throw away.

The patter of carnival barkers was woven through everything: the smells, the sounds, even the pure blaze of arc lights. "Step up! One and all, three balls, and all fall. Win big. Win often. Come one, come all."

The barkers peeled off players from the crowd the way coyotes will take down the slower-witted rabbits first. They played on the vanity of men. "Say! There's a strong arm! Three throws for a nickel. Five for a dime!" Or tried to provoke anger, "Don't have it in you? No? Didn't think so. Takes a real fella to win at this." Or played on unspoken affections, "A pretty girl like that? She deserves a prize! C'mon, win her one so we c'n all be happy."

Couples on promenade were drawn in with regularity, the poor doomed boys trying their best, the girls all aflutter at being wagered over. Workmen in coveralls were called for tests of strength. "Pound a nail, win a prize! Standard two-by-four. Standard nail. One blow. Winner takes all. Let's see who's the toughest among you." Skinny boys, intimidated by nails and the driving of, were corralled instead towards coin-toss games, where they could pretend that pitching a penny at paper cups was the equivalent of swinging a sledgehammer and ringing a bell.

Clearly, they had me pegged as a nail pounder, a bell ringer, a mouth breather. It was all strength, the games the carnies waved me towards with their frantic friendliness, only to sneer when I didn't stop. "Lot lice," they'd say as I passed on the offer.

The barkers targeted couples depending on how close the two love-birds were walking. Side-by-side and shy, the quieter booths would snag them. Beanbag tosses. Name that tune. Catch the paper flowers in a net. That sort of thing. Hand-in-hand couples, though, got threatening chal-lenges thrown at the boy's feet. "If you aren't man enough to knock down tin cans, what good are you?" Arm-in-arm couples, walking with dreamy slow steps, they were grabbed by the more expensive booths, usually by targeting the girl. "He still buys you pretty stuff, don't he? A sweet thing like you. Surely you're worth a dollar spin, Miss? Or does he take you for granted?" Panicked, the boy would have no choice but to play a round of tabletop steeplechase. Anything less would hardly have been love now.

"Games of chance! Games of science! Games of skill! Tests of strength! Tests of character! This is life, folks, played out right here in front of you. All the world's a stage, and everyone's a winner!"

The carnies were a wild, uncombed crew. Many had bent noses and cauliflower ears, souvenirs from less than gracious losers, I guessed. Most were missing teeth. One was missing an eye. Another a finger. I wondered if you gathered up the spare parts you might not be able to assemble another carnie from the pieces. Wouldn't need to worry much over a heart, though, not from the looks of it. They were hard souls, and I imagined you'd have to be, suckering money from strangers who were armed with hammers and baseballs.

Just past the String Pull and the Peach Basket Toss was the booth I'd come searching for. The one Jorge had recommended, the Milk Can Pitch.

Knock down the cans. Win a prize.

Win a prize. Win her heart.

There were three large metal milk cans to knock over: two on bottom, one on top. I watched for a while and almost took a chance on it. Might very well have put down some coin, even though no one else was winning. When a customer complained, the carnie reset the stack and knocked them down himself, easy-peasy. "All technique," he'd say. "Can't throw too hard, can't throw too soft. Have to throw just right." And the sucker would go at it again, from this angle, then that, but he always left with at least one can standing.

It was when the carnie was setting up for another demonstration that I noticed the muscles in his forearm. How they tensed more with one milk can than the others. Even a large milk can should be easy to heft when it's empty, but one of them clearly wasn't. That's when I figured it out. One of the milk cans was weighted. Maybe a lead bottom, or a sandbag packed in. When the carnie wanted to demonstrate how easy it was, he put the weighted one *on top*. When a sucker was throwing, he'd put the weighted one on the bottom.

At another booth, the Alley Oop!, people were pitching beans onto a numbered grid, trying to add up combinations of points for big, big prizes. They always came close but never quite managed it.

"Say, you look like a sharp fellow!" the carnie grinned when he saw me lingering. "One free pass. No risk. Bit of razzle."

I looked over the Alley Oop! point–prize grid and the combination of numbers needed to win. It was mathematically impossible, and I said as much. The carnie's smile shifted. Away. It had never really been there. Not in his eyes. "Beat it, kid," he said, and he went back to calling in others. "Throw a bean, win a prize! It's that simple, folks." When I still hadn't left, he said, low and from the side of his mouth, "You heard me. Scram."

They didn't take suckers for all their money, not right away. I noted that. They built up to it, letting them win a few to draw in a crowd. With a mob behind you and a girl beside, well, any man turns a fool. A fella will keep throwing that softball till it becomes a grim downward death spiral. I saw men empty their entire wallets over the course of a single game, and then walk away, quiet.

Even the kiddie games were rigged. At the fish pond, they'd send a hundred wooden fish tumbling around a stream of water, all numbered, face-up so everyone could see it was legit. Kids would fish these out with hoops and find out what they'd won. The largest prizes were assigned to numbers that had a certain characteristic: 9, 16, 18, 66, 89, and 98. Those were the big-ticket items: the hobbyhorses and dollhouses. But every one of those numbers reads differently upside down. And 6, 91, 81, 99, 68, and 86, wouldn't you know, were low-end giveaways, tin whistles and pinwheels, costing maybe a penny per and not worth the dime it took to play. Even when the players won, they lost.

So who were the fellows prancing up and down the midway carrying those huge stuffed animals? They were other carnies. You'd see some thin fellow parading with a girl on one arm and a giant giraffe on the other, and later you'd see the very same fellow back behind the Texas Tornado or the Huckly Buckly, the Hoopla Stand or the Screw Ball. You'd come across his girl ripping tickets at a freak show or covered in caramel behind the candied apple concession stand.

I noticed something else, too: how the carnies would pat the good-natured players on the back, the ones who'd lost but laughed it off and never beefed. There'd be white chalk on the carnies' hands, and if you followed the ones who'd been marked this way, sure enough, they got extra attention. Sometimes barkers would leap out to personally steer them towards a table, cajolery and glad-handing all round. "Hi, friend!" Seemed there was a secret language being spoken in that smudge of chalk and the message it sent.

I had almost given up.

I watched the Ring-and-Bottle Toss absent-mindedly, saw that the angle was all but impossible. You weren't allowed to lean in past a certain line, though when the carnie demonstrated he was always behind the counter, giving him the proper trajectory. The only way to win was to throw the ring up so high it came down almost straight, but the stuffed animals hung lower here than at other booths, cutting any chance of that.

Then I thought, Maybe there's another way.

I stepped up closer to the Ring-and-Bottle, took another look. What if you threw the rings *straight*, on a horizontal spin, the way you might toss a hat? If a ring hit the *side* of a bottle it might flip up and over.

The toss was only three feet or so, and I could draw the lines in my mind. I looked at the prizes on offer, but wasn't sure enough on what Becky would like. Kewpie dolls? Too childish. French perfume? Too womanly. They had magnifying glasses. Did she like to magnify? I knew she liked the radio—and they did indeed have a radio on display, but it would take some doing to win that. In the end, I decided to go for a stuffed animal. I'd win her a bear. Biggest one I could.

I put down a quarter, and the carnie behind the counter handed me my rings. I missed every one. It was tricky, getting the spin right. The rings just *tinked* off the bottle glass, one by one, and the carnie grinned, almost laughing, and said, "Never seen someone throw at the *sides* of the bottle. Object is to get them over the top!" He turned, mugging to a crowd that wasn't there.

The trick, I realized now, was to aim just below the lip of the bottle. That way the rim would keep the hoop in place for the fraction of a second it required to flip over. I paid another quarter. It worked a charm. *Bam-bam-bam-bam-bam*—five in a row, over, up, and down, before the carnie could do a damn thing to stop me.

Five rings on the same bottle. That was the top prize. And top prize was one of those stately RCA radios they had on such prominent display.

"I do believe you owe me a radio," I said.

The carnie was thrown back by this, but recovered quick enough. "Sorry, pal. Can't do it."

"I won," I said. "I won that radio."

"This here radio? Just a demo." He flipped over the tag that read FIRST PRIZE! and there on the back, in small faded letters, were the words: *For display purposes only.*

"Y'see, to claim your prize, you need to go to Sioux City, to our Western Regional office, fill in a form, in triplicate, have it notarized, pay the shipping and handling, in advance, of course. Here—" he moved the stuffed animals piled on the counter to one side and revealed a long list of Terms & Conditions listed below. "See? Them's the rules."

"Fine," I said. "Give me a bear instead. The big one, with the Teddy Roosevelt glasses."

He smiled, and his smile spoke of someone who has every angle covered. "Can't do that, either," he said. "Wouldn't be honest, rewarding such fine sportsmanship such as yours with a prize of lesser value. Against regulations. First prize is the radio. So you scoot up to Sioux City—have to register within twenty-four hours to be valid." He checked his watch. "Better hurry. Plus there's a skill-testing question required for the—"

"Just give me the bear," I said.

"Can't."

"Give me the bear. Or I'll take it."

That shifted everything. "Move along, hayseed," he said.

Two more carnies appeared from nowhere, as if condensing out of thin air. They stood on either side of him, arms crossed. "Problem?" one of them asked. His was a jaw made for jutting.

"No," said the ring-toss man. "He was just leaving."

I figured I could relieve my friend of his four front teeth by the time the other two got to me, but that wouldn't bring me Becky's bear. Nothing chivalrous in getting beaten up by carnies, either, so I didn't imagine bruised ribs and a puffed-shut eye would have got me into Becky's favor.

The larger of the carnies, staring hard, said, "You got five seconds, kid. Beat it."

I stepped back, which they mistook for the beginning of a retreat. Their shoulders relaxed. But I didn't leave. Instead, I eyed the prizes—and then looked at the crowds flowing by. I said, "Let's swap."

"Swap?" Didn't that crack them up. "Swap?" they laughed. "What you got to swap for, boy? Those raggedy overalls? Don't your momma know how to patch a pair of denim right? Sheesh, boy, looks like a one-eyed dog sewed that. What you going to swap for?"

Had I been in more of a fighting mood, I'd have suggested a straight-up trade: his teeth for my bear. But I had something more valuable than fists at my disposal. I had knowledge.

"That bear," I said. "In exchange for silence."

"Silence?"

"You give me the bear—the one with the Teddy Roosevelt glasses—and I won't walk through this midway whispering to everyone I pass how to win at ring toss. Throw me out, I'll hang around the entrance instead, spreading the gospel. Soon enough you'll have folks swarming through here, cleaning you out. It'll be a regular run on the bank. You'll have to shut down your booth, I imagine. Silence," I said. "That's got to be worth more than a bear with Teddy Roosevelt glasses."

The disdain they had plied my way earlier was gone, replaced by looks of cold hate. An unsettling sight, but forced to choose, I'll take hate over disdain any day of the week.

He pulled down the bear, tossed it over. It was even bigger when you held it.

"A pleasure doing business," I said.

Then, unexpectedly, the carnie slapped me hard on the back, said "No hard feelings, then?" He slapped the bear, too. I heard a pop but didn't connect the two until later. "Enjoy your winnings," he said, and then turned back to the midway crowds. "Step right up! Toss a ring, win a prize! It's just that easy!"

Strange thing was, the carnies stopped waving me over after that. They'd start to speak, then quickly turn their attention onto someone else. Only later did I notice red chalk on my shoulder. And by then I had other concerns.

The bear was bleeding. Badly. Trailing sawdust from a breach in the seams. While I was hefting it around by the head, it was emptying out from the rear. By the time I realized it, the bear was half-empty, hanging limp like a deflated windsock.

I stormed back. A different boy was manning the booth, but I found the carnie and his buddies out back, drinking bottled beer and talking big.

"You again!" they said, chortling at my arrival like it was a private joke.

"You broke my bear," I said.

"Prove it."

I stepped into their circle of lamplight. "I want another bear. And I'm not leaving without it."

An older carnie cut in, blocking my way. "Whoa now, sonny. Calm down," he said. "Only having some fun. You come back tomorrow, talk to Mr. Jones—he's the operational manager—he'll give you full redress for your grievances. We'll even get you that radio. Won't need to go to Sioux City or any of it."

"You give me your word?" I asked.

"As a man," he said.

Well, hell. You have to take a man at his word.

"You swear to God?" I asked.

"To God Almighty," he replied.

Up like Linden, down like Hinden. That's how it went. Oh, I came back, all right. Next day. First thing. With the skin of that deflated bear tucked under my arm, folded nicely, only to find the entire carnival had decamped. Gone, and only desert beyond. Nothing left but tatters of posters and a few torn ticket stubs pinwheeling away on the wind. I walked amid wagon tracks and litter. Hard to imagine a carnival had been there. Just so much spun sugar, I suppose.

And yet ... though they'd picked my pocket, I missed the lights. The ding and swirl of it. And for the brief tawdry moment that they'd set up camp there, I have to say, the desert was better for it, and was emptier for its having passed.

Maybe that's where it started, with the sawdust.

If only they hadn't poked a hole in that bear.

Twenty

You see, here's what happened.

I decided to stuff the bear with candies instead—peppermint twists and licorice, sweethearts and cherry rock, sugar cones and molasses caramels—and then present it to Rebecca. "Sweets for the sweet," that sort of thing. A teddy bear filled with candy? I figured you can't get much more romantic than that.

Would take a lot of money to fill a bear that big, even at a penny a peppermint. So I went down to Cyrus Tweed's, looking to shake a few dollars free.

When I entered the Emporium, they were moving things around. Don't know how they managed to fit so much into that place. It was like one of those Chinese puzzles. In the clutter of other people's lives, my mother's dinnerware had now disappeared behind a towering wardrobe, so at least I didn't have to face that, seeing those plates stacked up at a dollar per.

A team of men in work clothes and cloth caps were wrestling another great wardrobe into place as Tweed stood behind the counter, guiding them in. *"Easy … easy … stop!"*

"You," said Tweed, when he saw me. "Come for the hairbrush?" He turned to the men. "Here's McGreary's boy back for more of his hard-nosed deal-making."

The men took this as a chance to rest, wiping foreheads with forearms, their chests heaving in the heat.

"Bickered me *up* to a price, didn't you, boy?"

"I have something you want," I said.

"Do you now?"

"An engraving," I said. "Recently came into my possession."

"An engraving," he said, interest flickering like a candle in a tin can. "What sort of engraving?"

"Copper," I said. "In raised relief. A miniature of President Lincoln."

"I'd have to see it to—"

"Registered with the U.S. Treasury," I said. "Fully authenticated."

He rubbed his bony jaw. Threw a look to the workmen, as if to say, Watch me strip this fool boy clean. "I'd have to assess it for flaws, ascertain its value—"

"You can buy it or not," I said. "But I want a five-dollar finder's fee. Up front. Non-refundable. You can deduct that from the price should you decide to purchase."

"Boy drives a hard bargain," Tweed said with a laugh. He rang up NO SALE on the register, slid a five-dollar bill from the till. "I got witnesses," he warned.

So do I, I thought. *So do I.* I took his money.

"Now let me see this piece of yours." He wedged a jeweler's lens into one eye to better make his assessment.

And didn't that lens pop back out when I slid a penny across the counter at him. "There you go," I said. "Copper. In miniature. President Lincoln. As issued by the U.S. Treasury."

The workers roared their approval.

Tweed was in an instant rage. "You give me back that five spot!"

"Deal's a deal," I said, holding the bill tight in my fist.

He lunged over the counter at me. I stepped back, out of range.

"I will have my money," he screeched. "If I have to twist it out of your hand."

This whooped the workers even more. "Don't be a drip, Tweed! Boy cheated you fair and square!"

Tweed was a man with long strands of hair combed forward over an egglike head. Those strands were flying wild now. "I'm calling the police," he said, snatching the phone from its cradle. "Operator!" he yelled. "Urgent!"

But he was drowned out by laughter. "Cops are gonna hoot you out of town, Tweed," one of the workers said. "Your pride's gotta be worth more than five dollars. Boy outsmarted you. Take it like a man."

Tweed slammed down the receiver. His face was rhubarb red; his lips were pale.

"A pleasure doing business," I said, and I left, letting that door jingle a little bit harder than necessary on the way out.

I'd often wondered how the U.S. Mint could afford to issue pennies. Must have cost more than a cent to produce one, so all they were doing was spinning themselves further into debt. As luck would have it, I'd been able to use this to my advantage. *Boy cheated you fair and square.* That's what they'd said. And they were right.

Even better, I had succeeded where Fayther had failed. At five dollars to the penny, I had indeed finagled a 50,000 percent return on my investment.

Twenty-one

If I hadn't been blown into the library that day, hadn't been beguiled by Pascal or captivated by the greenness of Rebecca's eyes, if I hadn't won that bear and lost the sawdust, if I hadn't sold a penny for five dollars, I wouldn't have found myself at Kane's Drug Store & Candy Shoppe, mulling over treats at the hokey-pokey counter when a stranger in a fedora came through.

Hadn't been for that, I might still be in Paradise Flats, married to Rebecca maybe and working a dragger-line at the mines, buying back my mother's dinnerware one plate at a time.

But no. I was at the Kane's candy counter that day, trying to calculate the volume of the bearskin I needed to fill and the treats required to do this. Caramel popcorn took up more volume but wasn't near as romantic as chocolate kisses or cinnamon bonbons.

The door to the shop jingled like an echo of my exit from Tweed's not ten minutes earlier, and in came a man overdressed for the heat but smiling anyway. He was wearing a light gray Chesterfield overcoat with velvet collar and half-boots, bluchers as they are known. A natty dresser, with his felt fedora perched at just the right angle, sharp crease down the crown and the brim rolled smartly at the back. All the clothes I didn't have, there on display.

He was a small man, hair well-slicked, with a thin Errol Flynn mustache, neatly trimmed, and he moved with a certain lightness—an airiness—like one of those birds that can skip across slough water without getting its feet wet. He picked up a pair of Baby Ruth candy bars, smiled wide at the proprietor.

"A fine establishment you have here," he said, his voice slathered with honey. "Just about the finest drugstore in town, I reckon. Was over at Bryce's earlier, wasn't half so nice as this."

Mr. Kane, puffed up and puffy-faced, was more than pleased by these complimentary salutations. "Thank you, sir. Kind words indeed. What would you like?"

The stranger leaned in on one elbow. "What would I like? Just a few acres, a woman who loves me," he said, and then he grinned. Mr. Kane laughed. "But failing that," said the man, "these candy bars will have to do."

The man pulled out a ten-dollar bill. "Hope this won't break the bank."

"Not at all," said Kane, providing change for a ten having now been defined as a point of pride.

The Baby Ruths cost ten cents each. Mr. Kane gave back eighty cents in coins and nine dollars in bills. As it was handed over, the man frowned. Pushed back his fedora a bit. "That's a lot of change to be lugging around. Hang on."

Holding his change in one hand, the man rummaged deep in his pocket with the other. "Must have enough coins here somewhere ... Here we go." He dug up some coins, handed them over along with the other loose bills and change he'd received. "That should be ten."

Mr. Kane gave him back his ten-dollar bill in exchange.

"You better count that," said the man. "Make sure it's all there."

"Oops. You're a nickel short," said Mr. Kane.

"A nickel? Hang on." The man checked his other pocket, came up with a five-cent piece. "Here. I'll tell you what. I owe you a nickel, right?" He handed it over. "That makes ten dollars. And here—here's ten more." He handed back his original ten-spot. "That makes twenty. If you give me a twenty-dollar bill, we'll be even. It'll save me carrying a bunch of ones, and it won't clean you out of spare change."

"Sounds good," said Mr. Kane. He handed over a twenty-dollar bill.

Now that wasn't right, and I said so, cutting in on their conversation. "Excuse me, mister?"

The man turned, looked my way. "Yes?"

He had eyes so black you couldn't see the pupils. It was like staring into a pair of dark marbles. Hard to read.

"You made a mistake," I said. "When you gave back your change and Mr. Kane returned your ten-dollar bill, the transaction was complete. Or at least, it was as soon as you gave him that last nickel. But then, along with the nickel, you handed him *back* the ten and asked for twenty in return. That's an overpayment on his part."

The stranger smiled. "The man counted his money, son. It was twenty dollars, even. Isn't that right?"

Mr. Kane nodded. "Yup. Twenty dollars, right here."

"Yes, but ten of that was Mr. Kane's to begin with—"

"Don't pay him any mind," Kane said to the man. "Just some lug who don't know from nothing about this sort of thing. Works at the mine, you can smell the sweat and poverty all the way from here."

"But—"

"Run along, boy. Don't be bothering this gentleman."

The stranger looked at me, his smile tighter now. He touched his brim, bid us both good day, and strolled off.

I followed him out, forgetting entirely about my bearskin-and-candy plan. Was it an honest mistake, his having pocketed twenty dollars off a ten-dollar bill?

I had my doubts.

Outside in the dust-dry glare of day, wind was kicking up a milky haze. A truck lumbered by one way. A team of mules lumbered by the other. A couple of stray dogs loped past, weak from the heat.

I tugged my frayed cap down, tighter against the wind, and watched the man in the fedora as he crossed the street, heading for Thorpe's Hardwares. He came out a few minutes later with a paper bag—nails, probably—tossed it into a trash bin and then entered the Dutch bakery next door. Came out eating a sticky bun. Next was the shoe repair shop, and shoelaces. Then Felix the Sausage Maker and a link tossed to the strays on the street. Then the Ladies' Auxiliary Fabric Store, and ribbons. He would stop now and then to move coins from his overcoat pocket to his left-side trousers, jiggling them in deep. He'd throw something in his right pocket too; I assumed it was the nickel he would always seem to find.

I followed along the other side of the street as he worked his way down, and I did the math. Eight stores on this side, five on the other. Only four were boarded up, which was an improvement of sorts. No doubt about it, Paradise Flats was trying to work its way out of the pit, and our friend there was more'n happy to run a sieve through, catch what he could. At Kane's Candy he'd walked out with $9.80 more than he'd come in with. Using that as a guide, he'd have an extra $127.40 in his pockets by the time he got to the end of the block.

Not bad for a stroll down Main Street.

He even hit the *Times-Tribune,* coming out with a paper under one arm, whistling.

He stopped. Looked across, directly at me. Didn't say anything. He just stood there, watching me watching him. He tossed the paper, slid a cigarette case from his breast pocket, tapped one, lit it, and looked at me again. He took only a few draws before putting it out with a turn of his foot. When he moved, I moved. When he stopped, I stopped. And when he went into a store, I stood and waited.

I suppose I could've warned them, the shopkeepers he was targeting. I could've burst in, shouting, "There's a shyster heading your way!" in much the same manner as Tom Mix warning townsfolk of rustlers. But I never was a Tom Mix sort of soul.

You see, I knew all about those shops.

I knew how the Johansson Bros. Butchery Block had a fan angled towards the scales, how it added an ounce or two of weighted air onto every purchase. How the pneumatic cashier tubes at Norton's Department Store had thin tapered ends where smaller coins would get lodged deep inside when the canisters were sent down, and how most people took their pennies and nickels without noticing the dimes that had gone missing. I knew how Norton's raised its prices just so they could drop them back down again under the claim NOW ON SALE! Or how the Farm Center offered specialized blends of nitrates and fertilizer guaranteed to increase yields UP TO 200%! Or how Sukanen's Dry Goods bannered its windows with promises of ALL ITEMS UP TO 50% OFF! Of course, "up to" includes zero. Good luck collecting on a refund when your scraggly bed of lettuce failed to make any gains or when all you could find on sale at fifty percent off was a tub of ten-cent pinwheels. Yes sir. All the five-cent pinwheels you could hope for.

Just past Sukanen's, a car was waiting with its motor running. A 1939 Nash Ambassador sedan, by the looks of it. A swell automobile, that one. Even in the shade it shone like a blade: a polished navy blue so dark it almost looked black, like a night sky emptied of stars. It was glowing.

Behind the wheel was a lady, her face made partially transparent by the shadows reflected on the windshield. She was wearing a cloche, one of those bell-shaped hats women wore tight over their heads, like a helmet, with one of those oversized silk flowers pinned on one side.

Across the street, the man in the fedora ambled over to the Nash Ambassador, leaned in low by the driver-side window, spoke to the lady, and then passed her something—a fold of bills, I imagined. Then, casting a glance my way, he whispered to her and she snapped her eyes forward, straight at me. She didn't smile. Didn't nod. Just stared. Hard.

He spoke with her a few moments more, then he stepped to one side. Ran his thumb slowly along his mustache, once either way, and then looked again in my direction, like he was waiting to see what I would do.

When I did nothing, he continued on his way. Into Maggie the Milliner's. The Apex Tobacconist's. Co-Op Ladies Wear. (Came out carrying a kerchief on that one.) He reached the end of the block and then cut back across, towards Cyrus Tweed's Antiques & Emporium, at the end of the street.

I sat on the bench out front and watched him stroll towards me. He touched his hat to me as he passed, and was just about to enter when I blurted out, "He's good for fifty," surprising the both of us.

The man in the fedora stopped. Stepped back. "Pardon?"

"Tweed," I said. "Don't let the dust in there fool you. He's just about the richest man around here. Cash register's stuffed full of money. He's good for fifty. At least."

The man tilted his head to one side and looked at me—looked at me as though he knew me from someplace, like he'd seen me before. Like I was *familiar* to him. He nodded, thoughtfully.

"Obliged," he said, and then slipped inside.

He came out not ten minutes later, carrying a rosewood walking stick. Walked over to where I was sitting, tucked a couple of bills into the chest pocket of my overalls.

"What's this?" I asked.

"Your cut," he said.

Part Two

JITTERBUG

TWENTY-TWO

I know.

I should not have taken that money. But in some manner, I really did believe I'd earned it. After paying me my commission, the man in the fedora took a couple of steps, then turned and looked at me. He came back, said, with genuine puzzlement, "What are you doing here? In a town like this? Haven't you figured out yet that you can *leave?*"

He held out his hand. "The name's Virgil," he said. "Virgil Ray."

It was, I said, a pleasure making his acquaintance. I told him my name as well.

"Jack, is it? Good. Good name. Anonymous. Easy to lose." He said: "Walk with me."

And I did.

It's funny, Mr. Ray seemed to amble so slow and loosely, yet I had to scurry to keep up. He was moving faster than he seemed, down the sidewalk and then back across Main. In the alleyway beside Sukanen's the dark blue Nash was waiting still, with the motor running. The lady behind the wheel had the window down and a cigarette going. She had removed her hat, and her hair was damp and curling in the heat.

"Rosalind, honey," he said. "I'd like you to meet someone."

The lady in the Nash looked at me.

Pale eyes. Didn't blink. Like she was calling a bluff I hadn't yet made. Deep lines on either side of her mouth, from worry and wind, I imagined, and hair the color of straw. She tucked a loose strand behind one ear. Said nothing. Just let the smoke trickle out from between her lips.

A handsome woman, to be sure, and I tugged my cap in her direction. "A pleasure, Mrs. Ray," I said, and she snorted.

"Scheible," she said. "*Miss*. I haven't been a Mrs. in a very long time."

"Miss Scheible," I said. "Nice to meet you."

"Rosalind. You can call me Rose. And who are you?"

When I told her my name, a smile appeared, small and serrated. "My, my. Jack Armstrong, all-American boy." She pulled deep on her cigarette. "Eat your Wheaties, do you?"

"Every day," I said.

"Well, Wheaties. I suppose you're looking for a ride to someplace else, otherwise Virgil wouldn't have brought you over to meet me." She leaned her head out the window, gave me a slow once-over, starting with my shoes and working her way up. Lingered on my overalls and the sewing I'd done. When she looked back up at me, her expression had shifted. Not softened, exactly. Just shifted. "Where's your Mama? Run off?"

"No. Not that."

"Oh … Sorry to hear. Been long?"

"Ages," I said. "I'm over it."

Virgil clamped a hand on my shoulder. "Jack here's got change-raising down like a natural."

She tucked that same loose strand of hair behind her ear. "Is that a fact?" she said.

Virgil spotted me thirty-six dollars to buy back my mother's dinnerware before we left. Fayther was still in bed—he stayed up all night now, watching the horizon, and slept all day—so I stacked the plates and saucers, the cups, the creamer and sugar bowl, back into our cupboard, weighing down the oilskin and the Drake certificates beneath. Left a note for Da: "I found these at Tweed's. Must have been sold to Cyrus by accident, as I'm sure you wouldn't do such a thing knowingly. I'll be gone for some while. Found work that doesn't involve salt."

When I'd borrowed the money from Virgil, I'd been upfront about it.

"Not exactly sure when I'll be able to pay you back," I told him. "But it is much appreciated."

He just grinned. "Shoot, boy, that's an afternoon's con. Not even." He tapped out a cigarette. His case was expensive and silver-sheened;

here was a man who spent his money deep, the sort who wouldn't blink at buying a five-dollar hair clip. "Question isn't how you'll pay me back, son, but where you're going to keep all the money you make."

I left Paradise Flats on the very day that Mussolini invaded Albania. The car radio crackled with the news of it, of how King Zog had been forced into exile. Terrific name, that one, like a character in a Flash Gordon movie serial: *"So. We meet again, King Zog!"*

The fascist conquest had been launched with clockwork clarity. They'd bombed the coast, landed troops, seized control of the kingdom. It violated some Anglo–Eye-Tie agreement, but not a peep from the Brits. Tied up with settling the Drake estate, no doubt, and there's Mussolini given a free hand.

Virgil changed stations.

"Enough of that," he said. He found some cowboy blues to cheer us on our way, and the sorrows of King Zog dissolved into the ether. The Ambassador had one of those new Motorola push-button radios, requiring just a press of a finger and a fine-tuning twist to pick up a signal. A real marvel.

And so it was, to washboard rhythms and yodeling wails, we raced across the sunbaked desert. Was one of Slim William's early tunes, I do believe.

"Peckerwood music," said Virgil with a sigh. "No offense, Jack. But Lordy. How do you people listen to that without going mad? A raccoon in a trash bin makes a more melodious racket. Can't wait for jazz to reach these parts. Getting awfully sick of peckerwood."

We passed Consolidated Salt on the way out of town. One truckload of workers was heading in, another one was heading out. Jorge was in the back of one of the trucks. I saw his head bobbing as the pickup ground its way along the ruts. They'd be wondering where I was by now. They'd be tallying my debts. Waiting for me to appear.

Wasn't going to happen.

Once we'd cleared the Flats, I asked Virgil to pull over, and I walked out into the salt-pan desert. I threw that bearskin of mine as far and as high as I could. Someday someone would find it. They'd look at that dusty mound of fur and they would say, "Something died."

I didn't give a damn. When I came back to the Flats it would be in a fresh suit and a Nash Ambassador all my own, and Rebecca's undergarments would melt away.

I was done with penny candies.

TWENTY-THREE

We were heading north now, towards Silver City, driving hard into the gathering dark. The Richardson Range was on our left, closer now, and blanking out the stars halfway up the sky.

The towns we'd passed through had shared an essential *sameness*. A tired Main Street. A mangy main square. False fronts. Empty windows. Filling stations and feedlots. You might see small variations: a town clock that was round instead of square, a water tower that was square instead of round. In one town, the mailboxes were painted in the brightest of colors, mad dabs of red and pink and gold, as though a minor craze had swept through. On other occasions we passed the faded signs of larger failed dreams, in among the soup kitchens and midnight missions: shops with lettering that read SOCIALIST CO-OPERATIVE LOANS, or PLENTY-FOR-ALL stores, a GLOOM CHASERS CLUB, even a UTOPIAN SOCIETY or two, boarded up and long abandoned. Mad dabs and empty plentys aside, it was the sameness of those towns I remembered best. They seemed to roll in towards us as though carried on a conveyor belt.

On the highways, we saw families trundling along, handcarts and baby carriages loaded down with their worldy alls. Some rode in trucks, filing past in caravan, wheels groaning, the sides piled high with furniture and bedding, like armies in retreat, the skillets and water jugs dangling off.

At one point, Virgil stopped at a rail crossing while a stainless-steel, streamlined Zephyr flew past, diesel powered at eighty miles an hour, the crossing bells clanging, the suction of it whooshing through, your heartbeat racing at the sight of it. Men in hats and women likewise, silhouetted in the windows, en route to somewhere else. Once that streak of silver had passed, the boxcars of older trains rolled through, flashing a different sort of silhouette, like the frames in a motion picture: freight-train migrants in open cars, riding the rods, searching like all of us for someplace better.

The sun went down and the darkness swallowed us whole and I fell into a deep slumber, head heavy against the Ambassador's side window. I was roused, not five minutes later, it seemed, on a shove and a whisper from Virgil.

"Wake up, Wheaties. We're here."

Dawn, seeping in. A faint morning chill. Groggy and dry-mouthed, I stumbled from the car like a drunkard. Shivered myself awake. Rose was still sleeping in the back, for real this time, legs up, dress gathered at the top of her thighs.

We were in an alley behind a building. Virgil got out, closed the driver door quietly. Stood, perfectly still. Like he was listening for something. He walked down the alley, looked both ways, first one corner, then the next, did a full walk-around and came back to the car.

"Gimme a hand with the steamer," he said.

He left the walking stick he'd picked up at Tweed's in the car, but everything else had been wedged into a large trunk. We lugged that son of a bitch up a fire escape, two flights of stairs with a narrow turn halfway. I imagine Virgil would normally have made several trips up and down those stairs, but now he had a strong back to help with the heavy lifting.

"Gotta earn your keep," he grunted.

We startled a pair of alleycats on the landing, and they fled in a ripple of fear. The building we'd climbed had a third floor, or rather, a partial third floor, one that was set back and hidden from view from the alley-way below. Virgil and I hauled the trunk across a tar-paper roof to where a pair of doors—1-A and 1-B—faced us.

Virgil stopped. Ran his fingers lightly up and down the length of the door to 1-A, and then, satisfied, took a key from his pocket, slipped it in, turned the lock.

Inside was a kitchenette with a two-pot electrical range, a card table, an old sofa, a couple of chairs, and a Murphy bed folded into one wall. Virgil pulled the bed down, shook the blankets, and opened a window, giving the curtains a shake as well. The place smelled of stale sunlight and old dust. When Virgil went back to wake Rose, I pulled the faded curtains aside and peered out the window. The room was flush with the front of the building, and I had a sniper's vantage point on the street corner below. Every angle was covered. You could see the trolley lines leading one way, the sandstone storefronts leading another, a thin slice of street running between the two. Good place for a last stand.

I hadn't been to Silver since I was a boy. I remembered climbing on the luggage carts at the railroad station while my Da conferred with out-of-state men about things that didn't matter. I'd hung out well over the tracks, looked straight down them like I was peering into a rifle barrel. My Da had promised me a trip on his rail pass, a "grand tour of the known world," as he put it, out to the mango groves of California and east to the wetness of Florida, where the moss hung "right off the trees" and alligators lurked in every pond. My Da had seen it with his own eyes. But that was before the Berton Line closed down and the ledgers burned. Our only hope of making a Grand Tour now lay in a drawer filled with false promises and golden Drake dreams.

Silver City was known far and wide as the "Chemical Capital of the Greater Southwest." It was here in Silver that *anhydrous ammonia,* the liquid fertilizer that'd turned the barren aridity of the West Texas plains into cotton country, was first concocted. Corn had replaced cotton in many of the counties, true, but Silver was still a witch's brew of chemical potions, with the reek of it coming in off the plants, smelling like money.

From the window, I saw a cat's cradle of power lines and the city stretching out beyond, with the higher buildings rising into the haze like mesas. If the towns we'd passed through had been boxes, collapsing in on themselves, then this was the packing crate that contained them all. Silver was a real city.

I had arrived.

Apartment 1-B was beside 1-A, but 1-B didn't really exist. Turns out, 1-B was just a storage room that was connected to Rose and Virgil's apartment. It had a door leading onto the roof as well, but that was about all. Not even a closet to stow any belongings I might accumulate.

Virgil threw some cushions onto the floor of 1-B. "We'll get you a proper cot later," he said.

Rose was sleepwalking through her unpacking behind him. "Home sweet home," she said.

The window in the storage room opened onto a side fire escape, and the ladder led to a sidewalk below. You could enter 1-A, slip over to 1-B, and then disappear down the side even as someone was hammering at the main door. From the outside they looked like two separate apartments, but the inside told a different story. It was like a magic trick.

Twenty-four

The apartment—I should say, apart*ments*—that Virgil and Rose rented were above Wong's Café, and Wong's Café was home to the finest apple pie south of Iowa and west of Missouri. To hear Virgil tell it, anyway.

"Oven-warmed cinnamon-sugar crust with a scoop of whipped and malt on top. That is a work of art, my friend!" Virgil sat, napkin tucked under his chin and fork at the ready, as Charley Wong put the plate down in front of him.

"Hello, Rose," said Charley.

"Charley," she said with a nod, as she lit another cigarette.

He never seemed to ask any questions, Mr. Wong. He never asked who I was or where I came from or why Virgil and Rose paid their rent in cash that day—and not with a check. He was a round man with round features and a round smile. No corners on him to get snagged on. In a rainstorm, water would roll clean off him. As I watched Mr. Wong in the kitchen, peeling the skin off chicken backs, I wondered what his story was. For me, Paradise Flats already felt like the far side of the moon. What must the Orient feel like to him? I wondered if he'd fled Hirohito's armies, been pushed out of his home, or if he'd been pulled instead, if he'd come here like my Da, looking for a larger canvas on which to paint his life.

"We've got to get you out of those overalls," said Virgil as he worked his way through another slice of Charley's pie. We were in the rear booth, beside the kitchen and me with my back to the door. Virgil leaned over, looked at my shoes. "We'll get rid of those canvas sneakers, too. Get you some proper Oxford browns."

Virgil's mustache was so thin it looked like the work of a grease-drawn pencil. His hair was parted clean down the middle and slicked back with brilliantine. My hair, shaggy and refusing to hold a part, would cause Virgil no end of vexation. That first afternoon he gooped on some Vaseline and had me comb it straight back. "There," he said. "A real slick customer. Now all you need is a decent suit, maybe double-breasted, with a watch chain, pegged cuffs, a fedora set at the proper tilt."

I washed the grease out of my hair—didn't like the feel of it—and I never would learn to wear a fedora at the right angle. "Too sinister," he'd say, when I tilted it forward. "Now you look like a goober," he'd say if I tilted it back. "Not like that—don't wear it like some rube. Here."

But he couldn't get it right either, and in the end we went with a straw hay-skimmer instead. Made me look like an Englishman on a Sunday outing, but Virgil said that was the right look for me.

"Adds a jaunty element," he said. "And anyway, it's getting too hot for fedoras." Virgil soon switched to Panamas himself. His summer hats, he called them. He had several, stacked on the dresser. Sometimes he'd pull on a tweed cap, like he'd just got off a golf course or shooting range. That was when he wanted to project a sportier image.

While I was being outfitted by Virgil, Rose stayed the course with long dresses and uneven hems and an array of hats, ones with feathers and flowers and bows, plumes and ribbons. She had her own stack, though not as high as Virgil's. She owned several wigs as well, in browns and black.

Rose could be beautiful when she wanted to. "It's all in the carriage," she'd say. In the confidence you moved with, the cigarette holders you chose, the flair with which you flicked ashes from the end.

I found this out firsthand when we hit the road again, heading north and then west this time, into the valleys beyond the hills. After a week of apple pie and several rounds of tailor-shop measurements for me—"We'll need extra fabric just for the shoulders," one chalk-marker complained—we were ready to head out on another forage, as Virgil referred to the trips we took.

We had one last slice at Charley Wong's, and when we got up to leave, I said to Virgil, "I'll get it." When Charley passed me the change, I said,

"Gee, that's an awful lot of bills. What do you have there? How about I give you four, you give me back a ten, and we'll call it even."

But Virgil cut in. "Boy made a mistake, Charley. He owes you another five-spot. Isn't that right, Jack?"

"Really?" said Charley.

"Really," said Virgil. "Jack, pay the man." And then, under his voice and angry, *"Y'don't shit where you sleep, boy."*

So I tossed back a five and then Virgil said, "Give him another five. As a tip."

I hesitated, then threw in another fin. That was an expensive round of pie.

It was a bit rich of Virgil to take the high ground. Heck, he didn't even buy his own newspapers. "Charley gets the morning *and* afternoon editions. Why should I pay when I can read them for free?" Whole time we were in Silver City, I only ever saw Virgil read a newspaper when we were in Wong's Café, and then usually just to scan the society pages for potential marks. That and his horoscope.

As we left, Virgil touched his brim to Charley, said, "Keep an eye out?"

"Always," said Charley.

Twenty-five

We left Silver City and made a large, looping circuit, picking off towns as we went, with Rose in the back because she liked to stretch out, or up front when she started to feel lonely. We'd work our way up one route and down another, prowling through—and preying upon—each community we entered, big or small. Hundreds of towns were scattered across the Southwest like so much spare change, from Utah to the Texas panhandle, and we plied our trade well. We went on five forages over the next six weeks, and we never ran short of marks.

"It's not like we're knocking over banks or anything," said Virgil. "We don't heel a joint like a pair of grab-and-dash lowlifes. We extract the money, cleanly, in the manner of a parlor trick. We take it right before their eyes, right while they're watching. We don't rob anybody. We're the aristocrats of the criminal set, Jack. And we sure as hell don't plan on having our bullet-riddled Nash end up on display in some cheap, two-bit gawker's gallery, way Bonnie and her beau did."

The trick was finesse.

"You don't take their money," said Virgil. "They should *give* it to you. Willingly. And let me tell you, there is nothing sweeter in this world of ours than when someone happily hands you their money. It's not stealing when they give it to you. Remember that. You outsmarted them, is all. Won that money, plain and simple. It don't count as stealing."

Maybe he was right. Maybe it wasn't theft. Maybe it was actually a contest of wills.

Oftentimes, road signs would count down the miles to a phantom: ghost villages, clusters of farm homes boarded up and abandoned, root cellars caving in. Barns swaybacked, fences sagging. The ribs of mowers, sticking up like the bones of long-forgotten animals. Hayracks and binders. Broken-toothed windmills, turning on the wind. Wagons. Disc-harrows and cultivators, left to fade and fall apart where they lay. Fields unplowed, gardens untended—and you'd think to yourself, *Something died here.* It must be hard leaving a homestead like that, having put ten, twenty, thirty years of your life into it. Must be hard to close down that much of who you are, to walk away as though none of it had ever been. I wondered if someone was keeping a list.

We out-drove more than one storm, the sky turning black behind us, the topsoil climbing into the air like a wall of muddy water, and more than once we veered off our route when clouds started to gather in front of us instead. We would drive and drive until the day gave out and the headlights started picking up jackrabbits and skeletal weeds.

"It spooks me still," said Virgil. "How there's no lights down here once you get past the town limits, how the entire landscape is blacked out like that, how the road just … disappears."

Distant farms flickered past in gaslamp glows, and sometimes not even that. It was deeper than night itself, it seemed, as though a greater darkness had lain itself across the land.

We stayed in small towns, interchangeable, and hotels likewise. Fleabags and flophouses for the most part, with pillows that stank of head sweat and sheets so thin you could've spit through them. "Glamour of the road," Rose would say with a sigh, stringing up a sheet between bed and sofa, giving me half a room to squeeze myself into. Virgil and Miss Rose would sleep on the other side, with Virgil snoring in no time and Miss Rose restless. I would watch her silhouette against the sheet, lit from behind by a nightstand lamp or from light spilling in from a window. I'd watch her shadows ripple as I fell asleep. It was like a movie screen seen from the other side. Sometimes she'd wring out her hosiery and throw it over the sheet to dry, and her stockings were *taupe,* a deep brown like warm clay. It was the kind of color you wanted to touch, and there were times I wanted to pull down that taupe from the line and sleep curled up with it.

When the opportunity arose, we would stay at one of those auto-tourist cabins, feeling very modern. North and then west, farther still, the plains giving way to wider hills, long low rolls in the earth: slow rises and sudden falls, where hidden rivers twisted through equally hidden valleys. Towns were more prosperous up this way—or at least, not so dire.

Mostly we played short cons, or "pocket stings," taking shopkeepers and bystanders for whatever they had on them. We switched a lot of tills, wrote a lot of receipts, and everyone always seemed so eager to hand over their money. It was a test of mettle not to grin sometimes.

Virgil could pick a mark out of a crowd like nobody's business. We'd be in some small town—"Bumfuck, U.S.A.," as Virgil called it—on the stroll and eyeing the streets, and Virgil would suddenly stop and nod at some fellow out front of a barbershop or tilt his head towards a man in an ill-fitting suit crossing the lane with a determined stride. Somehow, he always knew. He'd come over, whisper "Fellow by the druggist's. Can tap him for a C-note. Half a C at the very least." Rose would act as the sounder, feeling them out, and would signal to us if she thought it was worth our time. She'd adjust her hair, tuck it behind her ear, that sort of thing. We weren't picky; if we could clear a man of twenty dollars—well, it was twenty more than we had before.

Virgil had a supply of "magic wallets" on hand as well, billfolds stuffed full of blank paper, with one forged hundred-dollar bill poking out, ready to toss onto the sidewalk for a quick pigeon drop or to use as the country-boy inheritance in a Tennessee Switch. They played out more or less the same, main difference being the Tennessee Switch involved a gullible rube (me), a kindly Samaritan (Virgil), and a passerby (the mark), and usually ended with the mark being sent home for more funds once we got him pinned. A pigeon drop was simpler. Rose would place the wallet and I would spot it, noisily, just as the mark walked by. Virgil would swoop in before either of us could get to it, snatching up the billfold with a hoop and a hidy-ho! An angry exchange would follow, with Virgil and me each accusing the other of cutting in until, well, the only way to settle things was to hand the wallet to the third man, allowing *him* to claim the reward. We'd sell him the wallet, basically. He'd already have calculated that the money inside was worth far more than any finder's fee, and he'd be eager to walk away with it. Heck, we didn't even have to blow the mark off at the end—he blew us off.

"The key is the quality of the arguing," Virgil told me as we were driving away. "They see us in a full-blown spat, they figure we couldn't possibly be in cahoots. Nate Kaplan, out in New York City, they called him 'Kid Dropper.' He could pull it off singlehanded. Argued with himself! No lie. He'd pretend to be rushing to catch a train with no time to reap the reward. Would talk himself into giving up the wallet. It was an art form, the way Kaplan played the pigeon, it truly was."

I had almost ruined it my first time out, calling Virgil by name in the heat of the argument. He recovered fast enough. "*Thought* I knew you!" he roared. "I kicked you out of my store only last week for thieving!" He turned to the mark. "Don't you trust him! If he takes this wallet, he'll pocket the entire amount." We sold that particular billfold for sixty-two dollars. Higher than normal. Some went for as low as ten. True, the wallets only cost us a buck a piece, along with the paper we stuffed them with, but still. Hardly seemed worth the effort to me. Sort of like playing vaudeville to a half-empty hall.

Virgil had purchased a box of surplus barometers from a supply depot in Silver City and had carefully painted u.s. govt. approved on the back of each one with a stencil. These, he declared, were "tornado alarms." He sold them to hospitals, sanatoriums, and warehouses we passed along the way. He'd simply show up with a clipboard, drop the Tornado Alarm off with an invoice, and ask for payment. The price was contingent on payment being made before the end of the month. After that it went up, and Virgil wouldn't be back before then, so ... unless they wanted to explain their budgetary overpayment to head office ...

They usually coughed up the full fifty-five dollars right there. And why not? Who wants to miss a bargain like that? Not when tornado alarms are on sale half-price.

"Fully guaranteed!" Virgil would tell them.

That's right. Tornado tears apart your feedlot or factory, leaves it in ruins, you have only to locate the receipt among the rubble and then track us down, and we will gladly give you a full refund. Prorated, of course.

"This is nothing," Virgil said to me after he sold the last of the alarms. "When Rose and me swung through the Deep South last year, we sold a whole carton of Stonewall Jackson Bibles. One of a kind, they were."

Virgil had picked up a box of old Bibles for free at a church that was being shut down for a lack of sinners, telling the rector he planned to ship them to Africa for "them poor little heathens out there who've been denied access to the Truth." Virgil then carefully removed any pages that might give away the date of publication and signed each Bible with dime-store ink and quill: *To Stonewall, from the boys, at Chancellorsville, 1863.* "It was the very Bible that Stonewall had been carrying when accidentally shot by his own men. Seeing as how in the South the Civil War still hadn't been settled—"They're asking for best two out of three," Virgil said—he and Rose did a roaring trade. Virgil would show up at some local museum or archive, scratching his head and saying he'd been bequeathed this from an elderly aunt who'd passed on, and he was wondering if it was "worth anything."

"Some of the Bibles even had a bullet hole in 'em," said Virgil. "Which added greatly to the value, as you can imagine. Took some doing, as I'm averse to firearms and had to hire a farmer to plug them. Told him these were the last remaining batch of 'wicked Bibles,' ones where a misprint had rendered the Seventh Commandment '*Thou shalt commit adultery.*' Told the fellow I was going to take the Bibles he shot out on a tour, to Sunday schools and such, teaching children to be on guard against Satan's wiles wherever they may crop up. That old farmer had blasted holes through several Good Books before his wife came running out, waving her hands in horror and wanting to see the misprint firsthand before she'd let her husband continue." Virgil looked over at me and grinned. "I beat it out of there double-quick."

Old Stonewall must have been carrying a library with him when he was killed, by the number of Bibles that Virgil and Miss Rose had unloaded.

"We burned through the last of them midsummer," Virgil said. "A schoolteacher in Alabama was the final one to fall for it, as I recall. Gives you a warm feeling, it does, knowing that our genuine Stonewall Jackson Bibles are on display in small towns clean across the South. Sort of like those churches down in Mexico, displaying the body of Christ. Heck, I heard of one church in Mexico had *two:* a big one and a little one. The body of Christ as an adult and one as a child. I wouldn't be surprised if some hickburg museum somewhere don't have two copies of our Stonewall Jackson Bible as well. One with a bullet hole, and one without."

Virgil didn't have any more Bibles, but he did have that walking stick he'd purchased at a profit from Cyrus Tweed back in the Flats. He spent a Sunday afternoon in Silver City laboriously carving an inscription into it: *"To Stonewall from the boys in honor of the First Battle of Bull Run, July 21, 1861."* When he was finished he rubbed dirt into the carved message to give it the appearance of age.

"Letters are a little rough," he admitted as he showed me his handiwork. "But that'll play in our favor. It was wartime, after all."

"Um, Virgil?" I said.

He was rubbing his wrists, sore from the carving. "Yeah?"

"How would they have known it was the *first* Battle of Bull Run? Second battle wasn't till a year later."

Virgil glared at me. Looked back at the inscription. Gnashed his teeth so hard you could almost hear them cracking. *"Goddammit!"* he shouted. "Would've been swell if you could'a mentioned that earlier!"

I didn't see how his poor grasp of Southern history was my fault.

"Hang on a sec," said Virgil. "I've cut the six and the one a bit close, but I think I can still change the '61 into a '64. Ha!" He snatched up his carving knife.

"Um, Virgil?"

"What now, dammit!"

"Stonewall Jackson died in 1863. Remember? The Bibles?"

Virgil made a noise halfway between a sigh and a growl, and then said, "Hell with it. We sell it as is."

He took it as a challenge of sorts; to see if he could convince a museum or an antiquarian to actually take it. And he did. First try. He sold that walking stick to a Civil War memorabilia shop. You'd think that of all people they'd have noticed, but no. They wanted that relic so bad they wouldn't countenance the possibility that it was a fake.

Virgil sold it for eighty dollars—along with a guarantee of authenticity, which he drew up and signed right there in front of the fellow. Provided a receipt as well.

Virgil could turn a profit on an empty bucket. Made me wonder sometimes whether, if he'd gone into a more legitimate line of business, he might not have become a Captain of Industry, a robber baron honored in the highest levels of society, strutting about in top hat and tails. Could have given ol' Rockefeller a run for his money.

Twenty-six

I was soaking it all up, the repertoire of cons Virgil had at his fingertips. One of his favorites was the Coupon Spiel. He owned a leather folder filled with phony paperwork—invoices, work orders, receipts—of a general nature and easily purchased at any stationery shop. However, one item had been printed specially for him: coupons that read "$50 VALUE ON ALL MERCHANDISE. *Price per coupon: $20. Expires* _____." He would scrawl in the day's date whenever he used one.

"A man with a printing press and a bank loan will print just about anything for money," Virgil explained, "and never say boo. Letterhead, stock certificates, lines of credit, calling cards, testimonials assorted and endorsements heartfelt. People figure if they see it in print, it must be true."

Virgil sold coupons mainly in front of department stores, but he hit the bigger agricultural co-ops, too. Ladies' clothing shops worked exceptionally well. I would wait in the Nash—with the motor on idle, in case Virgil came running. Which happened only once, when a butcher gave chase in a stained apron. Virgil dodged him with a dancer's ease. Still. Having stalled the car once, I wasn't planning on getting caught short again. We idled through a lot of gasoline when I was behind the wheel.

Virgil targeted matronly types primarily. "Have your coupon?" he'd ask, and before they could brush past him, Rose would jump in. "I heard about those! Any left?"

"Just a few. Limited number."

The other lady would immediately try to elbow past Rose. "What is that you've got?"

"A coupon. Twenty-dollar price, fifty-dollar value. All you need do is answer a few questions—"

"I'll do it!" said Rose.

And wouldn't that bring out the competitive edge in the other female. "I was here before you," she'd snap, and would insist on going first.

The idea behind the coupons was that whatever store the women were about to enter—be it a Piggly Wiggly or a ladies' boutique—was rewarding customer loyalty. The women had only to answer a few questions, while Virgil acted like he cared, jotting down gibberish in his notebook. "How long have I been shopping here? Well, coming on seven years now—no, wait—I was in Texarkana for two of those, so maybe it's better if we—"

"I'll just put down seven," Virgil would say.

The women would crowd around, pushing in, waving money, one lady even insisting that Virgil sell her *two* coupons. One pair of them bickered away like Myrt and Marge over who had dibs for so long that Virgil had to holler at them, saying they could both of them buy two.

It was a quick con. *"Flim-flam, thank you ma'am,"* as Virgil put it. We would sell off a stack of coupons and then beat it out of there right away quick, before any of the ladies tried to cash them. It was the last scam we played in any town, Hell having no fury like a posse of women cheated out of a bargain.

I took Rose's place a couple of times, just to mix things up. But it didn't work nearly so well. Maybe it came from being trained to defer, but the ladies in question would almost never complain when I cut in. "I believe she was ahead of you, young man," Virgil would say to me, but the lady would reply, "Oh no, you go ahead." We still sold the coupons but not as many, being unable to create the same sense of urgency as when Rose tried to hog in on it. Women, it seemed, weren't nearly as competitive with men as they were with other women.

Rose looked at me when I mentioned this to her. "You only now figured that out?" she said.

On the road after one Piggly Wiggly coupon raid, with Miss Rose at the wheel and Virgil counting out the cash, Virgil suddenly shouted

"Ha!" Someone had shortchanged us a dollar. This pleased him to no end. "What did I say, world is full of crooks."

Virgil's central syllogism, as I figured it, went like this: (a) you can't cheat an honest man and (b) there are no honest men. There weren't very many smart ones, either.

"You know," said Virgil, "I've run this scam from Raleigh, Carolina, to Eugene, Oregon. Up and down these United States, top to bottom and back again, and not once in that time has a single person ever—and I mean *ever*—thought to ask, 'Instead of selling fifty-dollar coupons for twenty, why doesn't the store just hand out thirty-dollar coupons instead? Why are you charging for them? Why does any money need to change hands?'" Virgil had an answer for that too—a vaguely worded excuse about needing to "boost overall sales for inventory purposes"—but hadn't ever had to use it.

"Y'see?" he said. "If you're that stupid, you deserve to be taken."

"There you go again," said Rose. "Blaming the mark."

"Well?" he asked. "Who else you going to blame? *Me?*"

Virgil always liked to swing by the post office when we passed through a town, just for "pie money," he said, though you could buy a lot of pie with what Virgil skimmed.

He would visit the post office so as to mail a birthday card to his favorite nephew. The fact that said nephew didn't exist did nothing to diminish Virgil's enduring affection for the boy. Virgil had a stack of cheap birthday cards, each one addressed to the same fake address.

Virgil would go in with two of these envelopes: a sealed one hidden in his pocket and an open one held in his hand.

"May I borrow a pen?" he'd ask at the counter, the picture of charm and clean living. "Got a nephew heading off to college. My sister's boy. Could use a little encouragement." Virgil would then write *Happy Birthday to my favorite nephew Bucky, from your Uncle Tucker!* in big plain letters. Then, to the clerk: "Say, friend, could I buy a ten-dollar bill, a crisp one if you have it?" "Certainly."

Virgil would hand over a stack of ones, and as soon as the clerk passed him the ten Virgil would slip the bill into the card and quick as lickety

seal the envelope, just in time to hear the clerk say—you guessed it—
"You're a dollar short."

"A dollar? Are you sure? Could you count it again?"

As the post office clerk went through the one-dollar bills again,
counting them out carefully this time, Virgil would rummage around
in his overcoat pocket, muttering, "I know I have another dollar here
somewhere." He'd make the switch in his pocket, leaving the card
containing the bill in there and slipping the other card out. The sealed
one that had exactly zero ten-dollar bills inside.

"Tell you what," said Virgil. "You hang on to this. I'll run to the car."
He'd scoop up the pile of ones, leaving the sealed envelope as collateral,
and hurry off. Perfectly safe, the clerk would figure. He doesn't come
back, I have his money sealed in an envelope.

Except, of course, he didn't.

Virgil said some of the clerks would wait till the very end of the day
before they opened the envelope, expecting to retrieve the ten so they
could cash out. But many wouldn't even do that, knowing as they did
that opening other people's mail was a federal offense.

"That nephew of mine must be rich by now," Virgil said, somewhat
wistfully, as we left yet another post office behind. It wasn't mail fraud,
because the mails had never actually been used. It was a straight-up
countertop switch.

"We can only hope young Bucky is investing it wisely," said Rose.

"In Bibles perhaps," said Virgil.

"Or other such historical memorabilia," said Rose.

And the two of them would laugh, light and free, like the world
consisted only of them, like they were privy to a punchline only they
could understand.

That's how I prefer to remember them, back before things went
wrong and the bodies started to pile up, back before it went off the rails
in Silver City.

TWENTY-SEVEN

Unlike Virgil's imaginary nephew, I really was getting rich. Or as close to it as I'd ever known.

We divided every score three ways, clean, even if Virgil had pulled some of them singlehanded. My roll of bills was growing thicker by the day, so much so I could barely get my fist halfway around it.

On one of our forages, east into Oklahoma, Virgil decided to run a "canister con." He targeted the larger stores in the towns we passed through, leaving behind tin cans labeled for nonexistent charities on our way out: THE GOOD SAMARITANS FOOD FUND or the longer-named CHRISTIAN ASSISTANCE: "CHRISTIANS HELPING CHRISTIANS IN THE NAME OF CHRISTIAN CHARITY" (a stroke of genius that, working the word "Christian" in four times on a single can) as well as the overseas ORPHANS & WIDOWS SOCIETY and the equally charitable BIBLES & BISCUITS FUND.

"Have to be careful using real charities, Red Cross or Sally Ann," he said. "One of their volunteers might notice."

We swung by on our way back to Silver City to gather the cans. Virgil sent me in to collect them. "Look bored," he told me. "Like it's just a job. Anyone asks, you shrug and say, 'Management sent me.' And if they continue to press you—"

That's right. A receipt. Virgil's answer for everything.

No one paid me any heed whatsoever, though. They just assumed I was supposed to be doing that. Still, it was a bit of a bust. In one of the better towns, we netted a grand total of eight dollars in loose change.

"Hardly a slice in it!" Virgil complained. "Let alone a scoop of ice cream. Cheap sons of bitches. What kind of town won't donate more'n eight dollars to charity? Doesn't anybody care about anybody else anymore?"

Virgil was off in his calculations. Eight dollars would buy us twenty-two slices of pie, with a scoop on top and change left over.

"Relax," said Rose. "Not every stream pans out."

"Sure, they'll drop twenty bucks for a fucking coupon, but what about helping their fellow man? What about that? Eight damnable dollars in a town that big? I tell you, it's enough to make you lose your faith in humanity."

Virgil tossed his canisters back in the trunk, but he hadn't given up on them entirely.

"The holidays," he said. "That's when you really clean up. Birth of Our Lord. Spirit of giving and all."

Virgil was always going on about the greed of our victims, but there wasn't any greed at play in a canister con, least none I could spot. But Virgil said, "There's no difference between someone angling for a monetary reward and someone looking to pat themselves on the back. They do it so they can look in the mirror at the end of the day and say, 'I made a difference!' As though throwing a handful of pennies at a problem will make it go away. Like old Rockefeller there, handing out dimes to street urchins. They gathered those dimes back after the photographs were taken, is what I heard."

Really?

"That's what they say."

Who?

"*They.*" And he gave me a look like I wasn't holding up my end of the conversation.

I didn't push the matter further, but I wasn't sure Virgil was right on that count, on it making no difference in the grander scheme.

Made me think again about the ripple effect of things: about how someone might drive across America dropping money into the hands of the broken poor as he went, leaving it almost at random, and the unforeseen effect that might have on people. The lives it might save. The stories it might change. Drop a stone in a lake, and you have no idea how far those waves will roll.

TWENTY-EIGHT

Virgil could read a town simply by the size of its trees. I found this out when we headed west, into deeper hills. The plains had been empty and wide, with nothing to break the wind or slow the dust, and the towns we'd passed through had huddled behind scraggly clusters of trees, scrub-small and ineffectual. The hills out here were bald as well, but beyond them the windbreaks grew larger and leafier.

We were driving slow through the streets of Cuthbert, a red-brick regional supply town lined with overhangs of oak. "Bigger trees here," said Virgil. "Notice that?"

True enough, the ones here were bigger than most. Couldn't see what he was getting at, though.

"Every tree in the Southwest was planted by man. Before settlers came, it was just grasslands and buffalo. Every tree out here was planted. The bigger the trees, the older the town. Older the town, older the money."

"Or more the rain," I said.

"Even better," said Virgil. "More rain, more crops. More crops and there's got to be a higher than usual amount of money sloshing around. For bigger trees, we need a bigger con."

Virgil had noticed something else that was odd. "Only two financial institutions. Did you see that?" He turned the car around, took us through again. Sure enough, there was only a Co-Op Savings and the centerpiece First National, a stately arrangement of brick and ivy. There were a couple of check cashers and a loan office farther down, but no real *bank* banks aside from First National. Nowhere except there where you could let your savings marinate.

"A town this size, only has two banks?"

"That's all Paradise Flats has," I said.

"Really? Shoot, if I'd known that ..."

He circled back, and First National floated by again, with Virgil eyeing it *avariciously.* "All those bank accounts concentrated in one place," he whispered.

"You're not thinking of ..." I said.

Rose and Virgil laughed. Loud. And harshly so. "Thinking of what? Going in guns blazing? Shooting up the place like Clyde Barrow?" Virgil hooted. "What do you figure, Rose, you up for it?"

"I would," she replied. "But I just had my hair done. If I get your brains on my do it'll ruin the curl."

"Ha! Wheaties thinks we're a pair of outlaws, Rose! And here I don't even like shooting Bibles."

And they laughed some more, even though, really, they were. Outlaws, I mean.

Virgil coasted to a stop in front of the town's shaded central park. Heck, the fountain even had water in it. A true sign of wealth, that: the ability to waste things.

Virgil turned to Miss Rose. "What do you think? The bank inspector gig?"

"I don't know, Virg. We usually set up for that one. Don't exactly feel comfortable doing it on the fly."

"Well then," he said. "We'll skip the call-back, just go for a single sting."

"No call-back?" She laughed at this too. "You're getting soft, Virg. Used to be, once you got ahold of them, you wouldn't let up. What happened? Prison spook you?"

The smile dropped clean off Virgil's face. If she was expecting bravado, she got none. "Spooked isn't the word, Rose. I'm not going back to Eastham farm, you know that."

"I know."

"Can't."

"I know."

Rose was feeling bad over how she'd poked fun. You could tell by the way silence filled the car after that. And when she finally did speak it was with a softness I hadn't heard in her before. "That's fine then, Virgil. We'll do it straight up. No call-back."

"You were in Eastham?" I asked. But Virgil ignored the question.

He put the Nash in gear and continued his slow crawl down Main. "Eyes peeled," he said.

"For what?" I asked.

"A steeple. And a phone booth."

We passed a telephone out front of Walt's Malt Shoppe & Druggist's. The steeple we found soon after. It was a Baptist spire, sharpened to a spike with a cross up top so thin it was almost invisible. But Virgil was looking at what was beside it: the minister's residence.

"No flower beds," he said. "That's not good."

Against the front door was a bicycle, leaning sloppily. A man's bicycle, painted a jaunty red with orange trim.

"Let's go." Virgil spun away. "Keep looking," he said.

I had to ask. "Why'd you ..."

"A bachelor is preaching at the Baptist, I'd bet my family Bible on it—with or without a bullet through. He's a young man, too, by the looks of it. Little if any savings. No point pursuing it."

Farther down, above the town's canopy of oak, we spotted a square-crown steeple of the Presbyterians. Bigger church. Bigger residence. Flowers out front, pansies fat and well watered. Lace curtains, drawn in, but with a gap for peering through. There were even some old-lady bloomers on the back line. Hidden behind a discreet wall of bedsheets, true, but visible enough when the winds flapped.

"Jackpot!" said Virgil. He read the name on the church notice board out front. This week's sermon was on sin, original and otherwise, and the minister's name was W. Pegler.

"Reverend Pegler's, please. Knox Presbyterian. Thank you, operator. Yes, I can hold."

We were at the phone booth, and Virgil was being patched through to the Pegler residence. Getting the number was as easy as snapping your fingers. As was what followed.

"Mrs. Pegler, this is Officer Grimes, special detachment, bank fraud. I have some … unsettling news regarding your account at First National. You do have a savings account there, yes? That's the one, ma'am. I think you had better call me back on a secure line. I'm going to hang up now. You call police headquarters, ask for my confidential phone." He gave her a code. "I'll wait for your call."

Mrs. Pegler hung up, but Virgil didn't. He covered the receiver, listened in as the lady picked up and carefully dialed the police, and then handed the receiver over to Miss Rose.

"Cuthbert Police Department," she said. "May I help you? What was the number? But—but that's Officer Grimes's private line! Yes, ma'am! I'll connect you right away!" Rose handed the phone back to Virgil.

"Grimes here. I said to keep this line clear! I don't care what the emergency is, I have an important call coming in regarding First National—Oh. Mrs. Pegler. Is that you? Thank you for getting back to me so quickly. I'll remember that in my report. Now then. Mrs. Pegler? Are you sitting down for this?"

What Virgil spun was a tale of corruption and greed—of sin, if you will—running deep and rampant at First National. An older lady? The wife of a reverend? They look for the worst in people, and they have a habit of finding it.

"I knew it," she gasped over the line. "It's that new manager, isn't it? That Yankee boy."

When they feed you information like that, it doesn't get much easier.

"I'm afraid so," said Virgil. "We believe he's been moving dirty money through your account. Think of the scandal should occur if word gets out. So not a peep to your husband, y'hear. He's a good man, and we don't want him caught up in this. Do you have gloves handy? We have to be careful not to contaminate the evidence. Not when we're dealing with … dirty money."

Beauty of it was, "dirty money" could mean anything from opium to gambling, from brothels to white slavery to Catholic charities. Could mean whatever you wanted it to mean. Virgil left that up to her imagination.

He had banged the gong of fear; now it was time to dangle the lure of reward. "You help us catch this … this northern boy"—he played that phrase thick for her benefit, laying on the contempt with every syllable in *northern boy*—"you help us put that Yankee ne'er-do-well back where he belongs, and I can assure you there will be a citation waiting for you at the town's annual year-end dinner. Plus a spot at the mayor's side." A place at the head table of a date-as-yet-unnamed town dinner! For all to see! How could she say no?

It was fascinating, watching Virgil play people like that, like they were a fiddle and he was a man with twelve fingers. Made me wonder how someone would ever know they were being played. Made me wonder if I would know either.

Mrs. Pegler was a matronly woman of wide berth, who joined us at the park in a frantic whirl, her bosom arriving five beats ahead of the rest of her. She was wearing her white gloves and clutching hard at her pocketbook.

"You have the money?" Virgil asked.

She nodded. Breathless. Vigilant. Ready to do her civic duty.

Virgil (or rather, Officer Grimes) had asked her to clear out her personal savings, more than $500 in all, so that her money could be "dusted for evidence" and then redeposited back into her account along with a twenty percent "federal recognition payment." Somehow—I was never clear on this—by having us dust her money and then redeposit it, we'd be able to nail that northern Yankee once and for all. Dusting? For what? For why? Never was explained.

Virgil introduced me as a junior G-man. "One of the best young minds we have in the field of chemical sodium pollination. If anyone can catch a crooked banker, he can."

I nodded and kept silent, trying to look competent in whatever "chemical sodium pollination" might involve.

"Our boy here will run your money through the lab," Virgil explained, as she handed over an envelope thick with bills.

He took out his notebook. Squinted at her. "Notice anything suspicious while you were in the bank?"

"Yes! When I—when I went to the—to the teller—I , I ..." She was starting to go faint on us.

"Ma'am? You need to take a deep, rejuvenating breath. Ease your fears away. I'm here now. Everything is under control." Virgil was the voice of calm in a crazy world.

"Well," she said. "Well, when I—when I withdrew the money, the clerk, a young man, a Methodist I believe, he asked me, 'Are you okay, Mrs. Pegler?' *Like he knew something was wrong.*"

"Hmm. The bank teller may be in on it, too," said Virgil. "In cahoots with the manager."

"And he asked me to spell my name. Twice!"

"Twice?" Virgil reeled at the news of this. "*Twice,* Mrs. Pegler?"

"Yes! And—and when the manager walked by—oh so innocent, acting like he wasn't up to no good —that teller looked at him. *And they nodded at each other!*"

Virgil snapped his notebook shut. Turned to me. "Did you hear what she just said?"

I frowned in a suitably somber fashion.

"This is worse than we thought," said Virgil. "Ma'am, you go home. Wait by the phone. Our boy here" —he nodded at me—"he'll ring once, and then hang up. Then twice and hang up. Then thrice. You must not answer the phone at any point before then. They may try to get to you, Mrs. Pegler. They may try to buy you off with ... dirty money."

"Never!" she gasped.

"Just wait by the phone, ma'am. Soon as your money is deposited and that northern boy has been cuffed, we'll call you in. And I hope you like lamb, because I do believe that's what's on the menu for this year's town hall dinner."

She nodded, proud of doing her part. She did indeed like lamb.

"Just let me give you a receipt for this money," said Virgil, "and you can be on your way."

And that was that.

We walked off with more than five hundred bucks. Our biggest single haul to date.

We drove back towards Silver. The lights of the city were stuttered like beads on the far side of the sky, and I leaned up from the seat behind and asked Virgil what a "call-back" was.

"A call-back?" he said. "Oh. That? It's when you pick the bones clean and then go for the marrow. You take them for every penny, every dime, every dollar. Suck out every account, every savings plan, every insurance fund they have access to, a line of credit—everything. You keep callin' back, again and again, sending them out for more, upping the ante each time with threats, promises, whatever it takes. You squeeze and keep on squeezing, you squeeze them like you would a day-old lemon, till there's nothing but pulp and rind left, till there's nothing for them to give."

"And then?"

"You discard them."

Twenty-nine

Whenever we returned to Silver City, flush with cash as always, Rose and Virgil would go on a tear, swallowing ten-dollar steaks whole, gargling twenty-dollar wine and over-tipping like mad. They threw their loot around like it was leaves in a cyclone.

The best thing about the end of Prohibition? The surge in the number of nightclubs that followed. Beer and live music were always on tap. Rose and Virgil would sleep late, then hit the dance halls at dusk, dragging me along like an unburst piñata. "You have it in you, boy! I know you do."

"C'mon, Wheaties," Rose would laugh. "Cut loose!"

Silver City had a nightlife that throbbed. Jazz had taken root here, and every hotel ballroom or lounge worth its salt had its own orchestra. Back in Paradise Flats, the chaperones would have soon as died as seen what we got up to, working ourselves into a lather like that, Virgil rolling Rose across his back, shoulders over shoulders, and swinging her between his legs—no easy feat, what with Virgil not much bigger than Rose herself.

It was big-band swing, and as the music blared with trumpets and clarinets rising in turn to stand and play, and with the double bass and drums keeping a swing-time rhythm rolling, Rose and Virgil would break off to hot-shoe some *shim-sham-shammy*, with a stomp, tap, and slide, hands held up like they were surrounded, shaking one leg and then the other as though something were caught on their soles. These were dance steps they tried to teach me, explaining each one in turn. I could break it down into smaller beats and memorize the moves, but stitching them together proved undoable. There were too many variables.

"Point is not to memorize it, point is to live it," Virgil would shout.

Jive and hot jazz. The steps were set, but the dance itself was improvised. Rose and Virgil slid from one pattern to another, on cues unspoken, faces warm and grinning, Rose spinning Virgil and Virgil spinning Rose. Jitterbug and Lindy Hop flowed into each other like liquid poured back and forth. Almost the same, but not quite.

We'd start the night off at one of the city's larger hotels, brightly lit, where a big-band orchestra would lay down an eight-count to rattle your ribs, or slide smoothly into a slower "Stompin' at the Savoy"–style number. But Virgil would soon tire of this. "He's no Benny Goodman," he'd yell. "Let's go," and he'd pull us out into the narrower streets and darker alleys on the far side of the city—"the *wrong side* of the wrong side of the tracks," as Virgil put it.

While the white dance halls might charge fifty cents to enter, or even a dollar, in the colored venues of Silver City you could slip in for a dime, sometimes for free as long as you bought a drink. The music would pound like the blood in your temples. From jazz to fast blues. Music as thick as smoke, warm as sweat. No rules posted here about how far down a lady's back her escort's hand could rest, no warnings about steps that might invite immoral variations. No. Just motion and music, and music in motion, and the taste of rum on your tongue.

I'd watch the Negro man at the piano unroll a boogie-woogie across the keyboard, left hand keeping a steady beat while the right played free and loose. And with the bandleader calling out for couples to come to center floor to "rise and shine," Virgil and Miss Rose would dance the Big Apple with a peck and a pose—elbows out, heads bobbing like chicks feeding off each other's cheeks—and that would turn into a double Charleston or a Suzy-Q, an eggbeater or a sudden spin. They danced like time was running out. Often, they would fall into a Cockney strut, slapping their knees and jerking their thumbs over their shoulders to a cry of "Oi!" It was a dance Virgil said he'd learned on the St. Regis roof in New York City. It was one he'd taught to Rosalind.

"She took to it like a Frenchman to fucking," he said, grinning.

Jive, swing, or jazz: didn't matter what the jangle was, Virgil and Rose were up for it. And if the floor got too crowded, Virgil would pull her in to dance the Balboa, bodies close, chest-to-chest with fast-time footwork: the two of them moving quickly and going nowhere. They'd dance themselves into a sheen of sweat. Dance themselves into joy. Oftentimes we were the only pink faces in the crowd, but Virgil and Rose moved so loose and swell that no one ever gave us any hard looks. The other folks would even egg them on, clapping and cheering as the band tore through "Flat-Foot Floogie with the Floy Floy." They were showboating, Virgil and Rose, and the crowds loved them for it. The bands were primed with verve down there, and when those coal-scuttle blondes took the stage, well, they could sing a hole in your heart.

I hadn't had much contact with the Negro side of life, except in passing. I'd heard they were all hopheads and layabouts, but I never put much stock in that. They'd been hardest hit by the times, no doubt about it. They were moving north now, into New York and other East Coast cities. Heading for the sunnier streets of Harlem. Sharecroppers and tenant farmers, pushed off land they'd worked but never owned. At Southern railyards, Negro workers were regularly killed by Klansmen to open jobs up for whites. Seven were shot dead in Mississippi one year alone. It was like they lived in another America entirely. Died in it, too.

Before we headed out for an evening of jazz, Virgil would plop on a floppy porkpie hat and leave his fedora and Panamas behind. The suit he donned—well, I'd never seen the like. Latest fashion, straight out of New York City, by Virgil's account. A zoot, he called it. "Harlem style," he said. Trousers way up, almost to his armpits, and billowing out like balloons, only to be pegged in at the ankles. Jacket hanging down to the back of his knees, practically. The puffiest of handkerchiefs tucked in, suspenders, a loosely knotted bow-tie and a swing-low key chain completing the ensemble. And all of it in bright stripes and contrasting colors, orange and green and mustard yellow, like a neon sign turned textile. Must have taken acres of fabric to make that suit, which was the point, I suppose. Wearing wealth. It's hard to preen in something like that and not look foolish, but to give Virgil his due, he pulled it off.

And Rose? Well, her dresses never stopped moving, even when she was sitting down. Pastel pinks and pale yellows. Flounces and folds. Hemlines like tattered lace caught on a wind. When she took a turn on the dance floor, her beads and hemline swished and spun. And then a flash of knees, just a glimpse—but enough for a hungry man to dine on for a week.

"She's got some steps would put Gypsy Lee to shame!" Virgil hooted.

With the jazz as smooth as a licorice swirl, Miss Rose and Virgil would be in the groove, moving in a cool calm frenzy, with Virgil bent low in his zoot, fingers snapping, eyes shut, calling out, "Feed it to me, boys! Send me down!" And Rose—well, she really moved when the music cooked. Hips swinging, knees flashing higher, more brazen by the minute, and the colored fellas on the bandstand playing it loud and wheeling free, the air spiced with salt and sugar and mad improvisation until you felt you were drowning in it, deliriously, joyfully, as your senses reeled and you began to think that maybe this is where our salvation might lie, in jazz and swing, in a certain desperate freedom, a thirst.

Oftentimes, I would wonder why Virgil and Rose had taken me on. They needed a point man, true enough. But as I watched them tumble from the dance floor for a gulp of rum, laughing, faces flushed before heading back for more, I thought maybe they just needed someone to watch them dance. Someone who wasn't a stranger.

Thirty

The trick was to stay with the jitterbug till the very end, until you'd exhausted the trumpets and been swept outside with the last tatters of night.

If we timed it right we had only to walk the streets for an hour before the lights of the early-morning diners flickered on, Virgil and Rose having danced away the darkness. Most of these eateries catered to the brown-bag crowd, feeding workers on meal-ticket arrangements. Men would line up for a bit of bellyfare before trudging off to face another honest day's labor. One of our haunts was an establishment at the corner of Devlin and Faust, in an industrial stretch of warehouses and broken-backed factories.

We slumped ourselves into a back booth, with Miss Rose propped against the wall as she finished her last cigarette of the night. (She would immediately reach for another one, marking it as the "first cigarette of the day.") As usual, they had me with my back to the door. "Here, Jack. Have a seat." Don't think I hadn't noticed.

Virgil was digging into a plate of scrambled eggs and dunking his buttered toast into coffee, his porkpie hat so far back on his head it was a wonder it stayed on.

"Are you a gambling man?" he asked me. "Believe in luck?"

"No."

He wedged the last bit of soggy toast into his mouth, nodded approvingly. "Good."

Rose looked at me. "Why not?" she asked. "Every con involves a gamble. Same as card draws, nickel slots, jar games or beano, punch-boards, chain letters, or the Irish Sweepstakes."

"A con is a calculated risk," I said. "Odds are in our favor. But games of chance? You can't outsmart bad odds." It was like trying to beat a carnie at his own game. Like trying to outsmart God.

"True enough," said Virgil. "Gambling is the surest way yet devised for getting nothing for something."

Rose nodded at that for the gospel truth it was.

"Right time, right place, any of us can be played," said Virgil. "Take someone like Yellow Kid Weil. One of the greats. Even he got stung. Soaked for money by a lady in distress onboard a steamship bound for Europe. The fool fell in love and that was the end of that. Once a boy has fallen for a lady, he can be played like a harp. Ain't that right, Rose?"

"Don't I know it," she said.

"Ha! Y'hear that, Jack? She's playing me!"

"Sure," she said, voice flat. "A regular gold-digger, that's me."

"Well, it can't be my good looks and charm."

"No? What else you got?"

Virgil hit a quick eight-time beat on the table, like he was slapping a drum. "I got dreams," he said.

"Well then, you got more than me," said Rose.

A worker tromped by our table, and Virgil fell silent until he'd passed. "In my case," he continued once it was safe to speak, "I started small. I began as a depot worker, playing the con in railroad stations and terminals, bus transfer layovers. Anywhere people were in transit, caught between points of departure and arrival. It's like a gathering spot for marks. Wallets as thick as club sandwiches. Everyone's tired, bored, easily played. Walking piggy banks, and I would merrily rattle the coins free as they passed through. I'd sell wares to salesmen. I'd pander to priests. Cheat the cheats, soak the gullible. It's where I got the suitcase switch down pat."

In among his inventory of props—the charity canisters, the invoices, the endless receipts—Virgil owned three matching suitcases: soft leather valises, green, identical in style, with identical handles and even identical scuff marks (an attention to detail I found wholly admirable). He could switch suitcases right in front of a mark, releasing one handle on the drop, grabbing the other on the rise, and even switching it for a third if he wanted to, as he distracted his target with conversational flattery and flattering conversation. It was a shell game he had so far avoided teaching me.

"I learned from the best," said Virgil. "Suitcase Simpson, outta Omaha. No one could make a switch like he could. He was an artist."

"Suitcase Simpson was an alky with a predilection for young boys," said Rose.

"A *flawed* artist," Virgil amended.

"And a gambler," said Rose.

"True enough," said Virgil. "Suitcase gambled away everything he ever won. Almost like he was trying to lose. But Rose here met him at the end of his game. She never knew him in his prime. Point is, it was while I was working the depot circuit that I first ran up against gamblers. Got set up by a team of cardsharps. It was also when I figured out a way to beat the tear-up. No lie! It happened in New York City—"

"You told me Albany," said Rose.

"Kid don't know where Albany is," Virgil said impatiently. "New York is more impressive."

I didn't know what a tear-up was, or how one went about beating it, but it was clearly a point of pride with Virgil, his having figured it out.

"I'd been passing myself off as a Rockefeller heir," said Virgil. "A distant cousin, but still backed by family wealth. Strutting around like a stall-fed calf. This was in New York—Albany, that is—and I'd been trimming the yokels and city boys alike with tales of a broken-down Rolls and good deeds that would be well remembered and highly rewarded. I was staying at a hotel, and this local businessman—a friendly fellow, full of cheer—he invites me up for a game of poker. Hadn't hardly walked in the door when I recognized it for what it was: a lemon play. An entire game, set up to squeeze a single player dry. Me."

Virgil leaned across, looked at me directly with those strange pupilless eyes of his. "Jack, m'boy, if you ever find yourself in a game, look around the table. If you can't spot the sucker, leave. Because it means you're the sucker." He pushed his porkpie even farther back. "You see, my pal the businessman was a roper, and he and his cohorts had me pegged for a mark. They'd set up a trap to catch me with the tear-up."

"So what is that, exactly?"

"The tear-up? It's when a mark is dealt what looks like a winning hand. The bets go up and up and up, until the mark, giddy at his imminent fortune, writes a large check as collateral. Back of his mind, he's thinking, 'Worse case I can always rush down, first thing in the morning, stop payment.' The stakes get higher and higher, and the mark loses the hand—which increases both his panic and the relief that follows. Because right about then the roper returns from an ice-bucket run, sees what has happened and throws a connip-shit, accusing the other players of trying to con his friend. He insists they give him the check. He rips it to tatters, takes the pieces, flushes them down the john. 'There,' he says. 'We play for nickels and no more!' The mark is reeling with joy at this point. A close call, that one! And for the rest of the night the others ply him with booze and bawdy tales, and they slap his back and take him to his room and they put him to bed. Next morning, he staggers awake in the hotel room, thanking all the stars and saints above. Only later does he discover his check cleared as soon as the banks opened, that it never was torn up, that hundreds, even thousands of dollars have been taken from his account, and all of it through the simplest sleight-of-hand. That's the tear-up."

It was magic, then. Black magic, to be sure, but magic nonetheless.

"I knew they were going to put me in the hot seat," said Virgil. "And sure enough they did. Slipped a cold deck into play and dealt me four aces, straight up. That's a hand you never see outside of crooked card games and Hollywood flicks. Convinced they had me hooked, they bid me up and up and up ... Meanwhile, my roper has slipped away and the stakes have doubled and suddenly they're demanding a check for five grand—as security, y'see. So, what the hell, I wrote them one on Daddy's account. And wouldn't you know it? Someone else had a straight flush. Two of the three highest hands in poker, in the same deal. What're the odds? It's funny, isn't it, how many people think four aces trump all? But aces can be beaten. And beaten they were. Well. In comes my champion, roaring on cue. 'This is just a friendly game!' he yells. So they tear up my check, flush it away—and here's where it gets good. They let me win the next hand because I'd promised to buy a round if I did. They wanted me drunk, so they let me win. That was a couple'a hundred, right there."

Virgil told me how he'd gone to the bathroom, closed the door, and pushed his fingers down his throat until he brought the alcohol back up. "You have to stay sober," he warned. "Never let a mark get you drunk." Hardest thing, he said, was learning how to vomit silently.

"I kept drinking and they kept hooting me on," said Virgil. "I ended the night by borrowing money from them, with stories of having squandered everything and wanting to hire a limousine for the ride home next day. 'I want to avoid the bank lines tomorrow,' I told them. 'I can wire the money that was loaned to me directly back to you.' That was even better, me not going to the bank at all. So they coughed up *another* hundred dollars. And it was right about then I started to complain, said I was feeling woozy and wanted to sleep it off. They took me back to my room, closed me in. I slipped out the window and down the fire escape. Slept in the park, aiming to catch the first Greyhound out. When that check proved entirely fictitious—both in name and number I knew they'd come gunning." He laughed. "Sure enough they did."

"So what happened?"

"Four ribs on this side, two on the other, and a thumb that still don't close right. Morning milk run was delayed, you see, and the next 'hound didn't leave till ten past eight. That would prove a fateful ten minutes. They nabbed me waiting at the bus depot." He was laughing harder now. "The bus depot! Hellzapoppin', boy! What was I thinking? You have to plan your escape, son. Make sure the route out is clear. At the bus depot, mind. *The bus depot!*"

Rose wasn't laughing. Apparently she didn't see the humor in games gone askew and the bone-crunch that followed.

"I learned my lesson in Albany," said Virgil. "I needed my own wheels for future escapades, even if it meant buying a run-down junkbox of an automobile. I purchased a secondhand Bearcat, a real relic, had to crank-start that car an hour before it would cough. Traded it in a couple of years later for a Model A. Pure Niagara Blue, right off the assembly line. Four-cylinder, three-speed roadster. Hell of a bargain, rolling over a flivver like that for a Model A. Figured the dealer I swapped with was a damn fool. Later on, I find out that my particular model of Stutz was highly regarded by collectors overseas. The dealer I'd traded cars with polished my ol' Bearcat up and sold it for a whack of cash to the hoity-toity crowd in Paris. I got taken! Of course, that was back when people had money to squander. I was still driving that Model A years later, when I first met Rose."

"Hated that car," she said. "Nothing but bumps and breakdowns."

"Rose here was the last of the flappers. When we met, her bosoms were still tied down, like they was wild horses trying to escape. Boyish angularity, that's what she was going for."

"The flat look," she said, by way of explanation. "Lots of beads. A bust would have ruined the lines."

"And wasn't the world glad when breasts came back into style!" Virgil hollered.

Rose flicked him one with the back of her hand. Looked towards the other customers in the diner. "People can hear."

"Shoot, Rose. It's only a few hangdog workers clinging to the counter," he said. "Didn't get picked for work detail from the looks of it, could use some cheering. Isn't that right, boys!"

Virgil had called out to the coveralled and workbooted men at the counter, but no one turned. "Aw, to hell with them. Jack, when those new brassieres came in, designed to lift and support rather than flatten and retain, well, let me tell you, they raised up women's bosoms and men's spirits, both. A fine leap forward in human progress the day Maidenform brought out cup sizes, started alphabetizing breasts. I was glad they stopped flattening them down. Mind you, I do miss those flapper hemlines, up where they belonged, so a man could properly admire a girl's knees."

"Wasn't much fun for us, either," said Rose. "Strapped down like that." Then, with a smile: "Specially when you're naturally curvaceous."

"You were a flapper?" I said to Rose. "When you met Virgil?"

"Not a flapper," said Rose. "A former flapper. There's a big difference."

"I met Rose on the con," he said. "Rowena, Texas."

"Beaumont," she said. "Rowena's where I'm from. Get your story straight."

"Beaumont, that's right. At an upscale little speakeasy. I was playing the Murphy game."

"Would have been nice if you'd told me," she said.

Virgil grinned. "Rose here was what you would call an 'unknowing accessory.' Singlehanded cons are hard to play. I was in the bar, mulling this over. Was considering dropping a wallet, when I looked around, saw all these half-cut, horndog men ... and Rose off in one corner, drinking liquor from a teacup, acting demure, looking radiant. A choice bit of calico like that, and all alone? So, I said to myself—"

Rose cut in. "I was waiting on someone, and they hadn't shown," she explained. "I don't want Jack thinking I was in the habit of hanging around bars by myself."

"You were waiting for me, doll! You just didn't know it," said Virgil. "While Rose was sipping her tea, oblivious to what was happening, I started sidling up to the men in the bar, discreetly and one at a time, jerking my jaw in Rose's direction and saying, 'Good-time girl. I'm her minder.' Whatever they wanted, she was up for it. You want to spank her? She's game. Oh, you want her to spank *you*? Not a problem. One fella, I swear, wanted Rose to pee in his hat. 'That's extra,' I told him, 'but it can be arranged.' I worked that room slowly, sent each man across town as far as I could, to an address that didn't exist. Said that Rose would follow once everything was in order. Trick is to demand only a 'portion' up front, saying you'll collect the remainder 'on satisfaction.' Don't that whet the appetite! *On satisfaction*. I dinged some of them ten bucks a pop. Others, depending on the suit they were wearing, as much as fourteen. I slowly cleared that room of chumps, and with the last one, I said, 'When she leaves, wait ten and follow.' Must have been a dozen men wandering the boondocks by then calling out for Rose. I imagine some of them must have bumped into each other. Would have loved to have heard those conversations! Anyway. It was time to scram, so I finally went over to Rose, said—"

"I'll tell you what he said. He said, 'Friend of mine over there has made a bet with me. He figures there's no way I could ever convince a beautiful girl like you to show the slightest bit of interest in a man like me. I'm not imposing on your virtue, ma'am. It's just that my friend's a loudmouth'—and Virgil turned, gave the mark a wave, and the mark, grinning like the lech he was, waved back at us—'and I would dearly like to win his money. Miss, all you need do is give me an innocent kiss on the cheek, maybe a smile and a little wink if you are so inclined. Throw my friend a wave on your way out, and I will happily pick up your tab and then meet you at the diner around the corner in five minutes, where I will just as happily give you a share of the bet and be on my way, with no further bother or ado. Just so long as you don't come back here tonight, to make sure he don't catch on that we're having a laugh on his account.' That was the spiel Virgil gave me."

"And it worked?" I asked.

"It did."

"Kept my word, too," said Virgil. "Met her at the diner, paid out her share. And I ended up leaving with the girl as well! A fine night, all round. *How're you gonna keep her down on the farm, after she's seen Paree?*"

"Never seen Paris," said Rose.

"Sure you have," he said. "Paris, Texas. Just last year, remember?" Then to me, "We've kicked up the dust, Rose and I. Been everywhere and back again. From Paris to the Promised Land."

"The Promised Land?"

"Palestine."

Rose gave a single harsh bark of a laugh. "Palestine, *Texas*."

"That's what I said. Jesus, girl, what's eating you? *Miss!*"

Virgil had been waving for a refill but had been resoundingly ignored—I suspect it was the drape-shaped zoot he was wearing. "I'll just grab the pot," he said. As he slid out of our booth, Rose looked at me.

The silence in Virgil's absence was always thunderous.

"Why'd I join him?" she said after a long pause, answering a question that hadn't been asked. "Why'd I leave everything behind and go? Same reason as you, I imagine. A person looks ahead, sees the life that's coming at them like a line of telephone poles, each one same as the one before. You see that and you ache for a bend in the road." She drew back on her cigarette; the coal glowed like a rivet. She blew the smoke over my head. "Why? Same reason as you."

Virgil appeared with the coffee pot, topping us up, each in turn, throwing a lump of sugar into his, leaving Rose's black.

Her eyes were still on me. "A nurse, a teacher, or a stenographer. Those were my choices."

"Could've been worse," said Virgil, as he filled my mug. "Could've ended up in a brothel."

"Oh. Right," said Rose without a flicker of humor. "A fourth option. Forgot about that."

One thing puzzled me, though. "But—why did *you* go back, Virgil? To the diner, after you ran the con. You could've just kept Rose's share. Why didn't you?"

"Why?" Rose laughed, another single harsh snort. "Because the damn fool was in love with me, that's why. Smitten at first sight. Isn't that right, Virg?"

Virgil grinned. Didn't say anything.

"Here," she said with a laugh, softer now. "I'll take the coffee back."

Virgil watched her go, then leaned in, said with a whisper, "I had to meet up with her. Make sure she didn't return to the bar looking for me. It would've ruined the caper. Needed time to get the dupes out of there, and me on my way. It's why I went back. The con demanded it."

Then Rose returned to our table and Virgil sat up straight, said with a boom in his voice, "There she is! Breasts and all!"

"Shush," she said, "people will stare," and Virgil shot me a glance that said, *You don't say nothing, y'hear?*

I never did. Not then. Not ever.

Back in the storage room that was 1-B, I would open the door to their side just wide enough to catch the light spilling in. I'd watch Rose's shadow as she moved about, readying herself for bed, humming soft, brushing her hair, and I would drift away like that, my ungainly feet hanging over the edge of the cot and Miss Rose in the next room—and in those moments, all was well. Then Virgil's shadow would appear for one last turn and the two of them would dance and Rose would laugh and that was good too.

THIRTY-ONE

Dry heat. Not a whisper of rain. No sooner would we settle into Silver than Virgil would decide to take us out on the road again. We made one forage across state lines, deep into New Mexico. It was a single con, staged for my edification, and far enough from home base that we could exit cleanly if need be. Virgil wanted to teach me something he called the "pedigreed pooch."

"Was one of Yellow Kid Weil's signature pieces," said Virgil, behind the wheel with me in the back and Rose up front as the mesas and flatlands rolled towards us in earthen reds and rusted browns. We were heading for Gran Quivira, where a run of silver ore had purportedly been found. An economic "boomlet," as Virg called it.

"Problem with the pedigreed pooch," said Virgil, "is that it's been entirely too successful, especially down here in the greater Southwest. Yellow Kid and his boys burned through with it. So you have to be careful that the bartenders haven't already been hit—or caught wind. It's why you need a place just starting to boom. One that hasn't been scorched yet." Gran Quivira fit the bill, he explained. "Newcomers pouring in and pouring out, people in transit, hungry for more. The town will be bursting at the seams. It'll have cantinas and taverns, some fine hotels and some big-chested businessmen. Money sluicing through."

Sharing the backseat with me was a box filled with yelps. We'd stopped by the dog pound before we left Silver City. The kennels were in a windowless, cinder-block building out past the tracks, and you could hear the nervous yips and sad low *woofs* as soon as you stepped in. "Reminds me of the Eastham pen," Virgil had whispered. "Smells like it, too."

The lady at the shelter must have figured Virgil was a soft touch, saving an entire litter of puppies like that from a long needle, and we left with a tumble of them in a cardboard carton. The puppies were sandy brown with warm bellies soft as felt, and all of them smelling like pee. Puppy pee. They clambered over each other in the box, nipping and squirming and struggling like they had somewhere important to go. I picked up the biggest one and scritched him behind his floppy-drop ears. He licked my hand and barked, happy to be held.

"Don't get too attached," Virgil said, looking in the rearview mirror. The dogs were a means to an end, as it were.

Torn mountains stretched across the sky. The sun was setting behind them, as though somewhere out there the fields were burning still. Gran Quivira was on the plains just below—out in the open, and the town seemed bigger for it, the buildings crowding in, close together like a clutch of packing crates, sides catching the last of the sun. We rolled in at dusk as the streetlamps flickered on, arc lights crackling white, people laughing their way along the streets. They didn't know it yet, but the carnival had come to town.

"We get in, we get out," explained Virgil. "We take their money, and then we beat it outta here. No overnighter this time. We'll be back in Texas and in our own beds come morning. It's a long drive, but necessary. Don't want to get caught flat-footed in Gran Quivira."

The hotels of Gran Quivira churned with people, with guests arriving and porters pushing mountains of luggage to and fro. We slowed down, rolling past one such establishment to scope it out. Virg parked the Nash and we went inside to prowl the lobby. The place had a slapdash magnificence to it. Chandeliers dripping with cut glass. Towering round columns. I pressed my hand against one. It was wood, painted with green veins to suggest marble—an architectural con known only to the touch. And everywhere, grown children in a swirl, playing at the game of forgetting, recasting themselves as heroines and heroes in tales of their own inventing.

"Still," said Virgil, back outside as we strolled the hubbub on wooden sidewalks, "this boomlet will go bust, too. I've seen it across the

Southwest. Donkey-assed towns that went tits-up, left with nothing but false fronts and empty hotel rooms."

Beyond the cut-glass chandeliers and the painted marble, Gran Quivira was still a Tom Mix sort of town. A few of the older shops still had hitching posts out front.

"Frontier is only a generation or two away," Virgil warned. "So don't be fooled. They aren't drinking sarsparilla out here, I can tell you that. But where there's money, there's greed, and where there's greed there's opportunity."

Back in the Nash, the puppies had clamored themselves into a deep sleep, piling up on top of each other, paws on bellies, jaws on rumps.

"Hand me one, will you?" Virgil asked.

"Which one?"

"Any one."

Evening was still early on, and we went slow through Gran Quivira looking for a quiet bar in which to ply our trade. We found one, and Virgil went in, whistling a how-do-you-do tune with a puppy under his arm.

He'd explained the mechanics of it in the car. Before the barkeep could complain, Virgil would plop the dog on the counter, throw down a ten-dollar bill, and order a glass of tonic.

"Keep the change," he'd say. "Life is good."

The bartender would find a box for the puppy, and Virgil would regale the man with stories. How he'd seen the light and turned his life around, how he'd stopped drinking and stopped gambling, and how he was on his way to Tucumcari to reconcile with his wife and little girl.

Virgil would raise his glass of tonic to the bartender's continued good health and tell him, "I always promised my daughter a dog. But I never lived up to her expectations. Oh, I was a low-down white, I can assure you of that. Blowing my family's rent money on whiskey and foolhardy bookie bets, drinking myself to blindness. And my little angel, she would wait, night after night, for a puppy that never came. Well, sir," and Virgil would beam at him like a searchlight sweeping a prison yard, "I'm finally going to keep that promise."

He had passed a dog shop on the way into town, you see. It was going out of business, and Virgil had purchased this here puppy for a pittance.

"Owner was in tears at having to sell," he said. "Told me it was a rare albino purebred. Well, hell, I know albinos. Does this dog look white-washed and pink-eyed to you?"

Virgil would laugh, and he and the bartender would agree that the pet store owner had been trying to pull a fast one. "Wanted to bid me up," Virgil said. "But I held firm. Say! Can I use your telephone? I was supposed to meet a fella down at the bookie's—there's a race comin' over the wire he wanted to talk to me about—but I'm not going." And it would reappear, that searchlight beam, sweeping the yard. "I've seen the error-filled nature of my ways. I once was lost, now am found."

Oftentimes the bartender would brace for a blast of gospel or a testimonial on the redemption of souls. But none ever came. Virgil would use the phone, speak loudly … and then, in a voice suddenly hushed, "Really? … When? … You're sure? … *Whoooo.*" And he'd puff his cheeks and blow air out of his mouth and push his hat back and smooth his mustache, and by the time he hung up the phone on that imaginary friend, Virgil's entire demeanor would have shifted.

"Got the inside track on a sure thing," he'd say. "My pal caught wind—and it's paying fifty-to-one."

Virgil would let the silence deepen as he tallied the odds, then: "Mister, watch my dog. There's a fin in it for you. I gotta run to the bookie, lay that final bet. All goes well," he said. "I'll be back a rich man, and maybe that fin of yours will become a high C. What say you?"

And before the bartender could reply, Virgil was gone, hurrying out the door.

That was our cue.

Rose and I were parked in the alley, and when Virgil climbed into the Nash, we climbed out.

Miss Rose and I had changed our clothes back at the hotel, inside rest-room stalls. She was draped in satin that shimmered when she moved, and I was wearing my suit and one of Virgil's best ties. Together we looked the picture of wealth. It was my first time to really see Rose in full flight, and it was remarkable. Truly was. She was an actress in her own right, a silver screen diva fallen from grace and trapped in an earthly existence. And me? I just followed along trying not to step on anybody's lines.

The two of us came into the bar in an agitated state of hurry. We were looking for a certain dog breeder's home, had to get there before it was too late. We'd come to Gran Quivira all the way from gay— *"Mon dieu!"* Rose would exclaim, thereby using up her entire French vocabulary in one throw, eyes wide at the sight of the puppy behind the bar.

"Trick is not to speak with an accent," she had told me, "but an attitude. Just a few rounded vowels here and there, and people will hear what they want."

"Mon dieu!" And she would ask to see the puppy and she would hold it up for me to admire. Which I would.

"It is, it is," I would whisper, loudly enough for the barkeep to hear. "I don't believe it."

"An Albanian breeder!" She would turn the puppy this way and that. "Exquisite!"

The bartender would have been hanging on our every word, and when Rose spun her attention onto him, and demanded—with a sniff and a haughty air—to buy the dog, right then and there, he was forced to confess, "It's not mine to sell."

"Oh," said Rose, eyes narrowing. "I see your game. Maurice! The checkbook!"

I would slap it into her hand, and with a determined stroke she would write a check for $1,000.

The sight of that many zeros can pain a man's eyes. "Ma'am," he'd say, "much as I'd love to ..."

"Fine. You Americans. So greedy. Two thousand—and that is our final offer!"

I crossed my arms behind her, looked at him with snotty disdain. "Final," I said, underlining the point.

"You don't understand," the bartender would say, pleading, almost bleating. "I'm only watching the pooch."

Rose would often pause at this point, a cigarette holder held between two fingers contemptuously like she was seriously considering flicking her ash at him. "Fine, we are staying at"—and she'd name the finest hotel in town, the one we'd crawled by earlier, where the monied men were rife—"Executive Suite. Ask for the Chevalier party. Here." She'd scribble down the hotel room number on the back of her check, and would then write VOID across the front. A powerful motivator, holding the promise of a thousand dollars in your hand. "When the owner comes back, you tell this—this fellow of yours that we are willing to part with …" she looked at me, I pursed my lips like I was considering the sum "… two thousand American dollars," she said. "Do that, and we will pay you—how do you say, a *commission*. I trust one hundred dollars will cover your services, yes? Maurice!"

And she'd sweep out of the bar on a swish of satin, with me hurrying to keep up.

A hundred dollars for passing on a message? What could be better than that?

I'll tell you what could be better: dining out on another man's misery. Because didn't ol' Virgil come dragging back in, eyes red from tears (as helped along by a pinch of pepper), and didn't he look shell-shocked and stomach sick, and didn't he speak in a voice that was choked and raw, and didn't he throw a few scrunched-up bills on the counter and say, "Um, here's the five I owe you for … for watching the dog. I'll just take my little girl's puppy and be on my way."

The horse race had been an awful gyp, you see. Oh, the woe of it! A setup most foul, and Virgil taken for everything he had. He couldn't even go to the police, because it was on a supposedly rigged race that he'd been taken. A broken man, he was, and not knowing what he'd tell his wife, or his little girl.

And wouldn't you know it, as Virgil shuffled towards the door the bartender would call out. "Hang on, mister. Maybe I can help you out."

And didn't that bartender graciously offer to buy the dog.

"I'll give you … twenty bucks for the pooch," he'd say. "That should help you get back on your feet. I hate to see a man laid low like that."

Always the height of Christian charity, those bartenders.

But Virgil would clutch at that puppy with both arms. "This puppy is all I've got left."

"Well, let's say fifty."

Virgil would turn to leave and the bartender, seeing easy money slipping away, would almost lunge at him.

"Two-fifty!" one barkeep hollered. "I'll give you two hundred and fifty dollars for the dog."

That was usually as much as the traffic would allow, because they'd often have to raid the safe to get it. Some only had fifty or sixty at their disposal. But others went higher. One fellow, eyes practically ringing up the dollar signs, had gone all the way to three hundred.

And every one of them destined for disappointment.

Rose and I had let them know we'd be out all evening—a stall designed to keep them from immediately ringing the hotel. And when they did? Well, that'd teach 'em.

"Just once," said Virgil, "I would like to have someone say to me, in my downtrodden state, 'Boy! Do I have good news for you. Hurry over to the Grace Hotel. There's a pair of foreigners there that'll buy that puppy for two grand!'" But it never happened.

We beat it out of Gran Quivira free of puppies and moving fast, into a night so dark it felt like we were driving through a tunnel. I was at the wheel now, hunched forward, as the road snaked in towards us in long lazy S's and slow outward curves. Rose was asleep in the back, and our radio was picking up only fragments of voices and static-ridden tunes. Virgil turned it off and let the silence overtake us.

On a few lonely occasions, other headlights would appear, far off, and then be slowly reeled in only to fly by in a sudden burst—passenger buses and interstate freight vans, mainly, or the odd one-eyed rattletrap loaded down with Okies avoiding the heat of day. I hit fifty on the straight stretches, but Virgil found me timid nonetheless.

"Give 'er some gas," he'd say. And I did, but not enough by his measure.

He put his hand on my knee, pressed down hard, forcing my foot deeper onto the accelerator. "Don't be shy," he said.

Comes a moment in every con when the mark *knows*. This was something I'd learned from Virgil. If you're lucky, it's just a flicker, a niggling doubt, there and gone, that the mark will manage to push down. But sometimes they'll look you dead in the eye—*and they will know*. It's the moment when both sides understand what is really going on. It's a moment that every confidence man has to face.

"Your job," said Virgil, "is to stare them down. To look at them without flinching, and to force them to deny what they know inside. You have to throw it right back at them. Your job is to make them *ignore* their instincts. And that takes moxie."

For Virgil, moxie was the highest value: a mix of quick skill, breezy confidence, and brazen charm. Virgil was all moxie. I was only pretending. The goal, I guess, was to get so good you couldn't tell the difference.

Virgil put his hand back on my knee, pushed harder.

THIRTY-TWO

Back in Silver. Next day. Sitting at Wong's Café. Drinking soda and sucking on ice cubes. Rose was sleeping off the Gran Quivira run, so it was "just us fellas," as Virgil said. We'd taken up our customary positions, me with my back exposed.

Charley Wong was in the kitchen, fast-chopping onions for the afternoon's soup, and a waitress we hadn't seen before was running plates and swabbing tables. A curvy girl with peroxide curls and a gum-snapping manner.

"What'll you have?" she asked.

"Pie!" said Virgil. "Biggest slab you've got, with a scoop of whipped and malt on top."

She turned to me. "Are you wanting pie as well?"

Virgil hooted, "Oh, he wants pie, all right! Boy's hungering for it. Think you can help him?"

How Virgil got away with the things he said was a mystery. Instead of dumping the contents of her coffee pot on his head, she just snapped her gum some more and said, with a wry smile, "You two are bad news."

"I'm fine for pie," I said. "Maybe later."

As she went behind the counter to cut a slice for Virgil—and didn't she cut one extra wide for him—he leaned in at me, almost giggling, and said, "How about it, Wheaties? She's got some spark to her. Y'ought to give her a run. Gotta ride a steer someday."

"Odds aren't good," I said. "Of getting out alive."

"What are you talking?"

"Her ring finger," I said. "Has a pale band, where a wedding ring used to be. I see that, I think of a spurned husband lurking in the wings." It brought up memories of Useless Joe, back home, and how, when Henrietta went crying to her Mama's, Joe would stand outside her window all night, wild with caged rage. And how, if a man so much as looked at Henrietta, Joe would pounce.

"You spotted that?" said Virgil. "A missing band?"

The waitress brought over Virgil's pie. Sure enough, the pale mark where a wedding ring had been was faintly visible.

"You've got a good eye, kid," said Virgil after she left. He dug into his slice with the usual gusto. Between mouthfuls he tossed me his hat. "You see that? Panama, right? Top of the line. Cost me twenty bucks because it's hundred percent genuine. Handmade in water for a tighter weave. Check the label inside. See? *Made in Ecuador*. That's how you know it's genuine. Panama hats aren't made in Panama. If a Panama hat is made in Panama it's not a real Panama. Y'see? Nothing in this world is ever straightforward, kid. Everything's played on the angle."

He washed down his pie with coffee, called across to the kitchen.

"Hey, Charley! What's your name?"

Charley stepped away from the cutting board. He was sweating from the heat. Wiped his face with a handkerchief.

"My name's Charley."

"Charley what?"

"Charley Wong. Says so on the sign."

"And that sign was there when I blew through Silver fifteen years ago. Was a different Charley Wong behind the counter at that time. And another one when I returned eight years later. By my calculations, you're the third Charley Wong to operate this café."

Charley looked at Virgil long and hard. "You from the government?"

"Checking papers? Me? Come on, Charley. I've known you for a couple of years now. If I was going to nab you, I'd have done so by now. I just want to know your name, Charley. Your true name."

It was pronounced *Fo' Shing Chao*, or something to that effect. When Virgil asked him for a spelling of it, there was an X, and a Q, but no U.

"See?" said Virgil, turning back to me as Charley resumed his dicing. "Even Charley is playing the con. You take De Valu Amalgamated

Enterprises—big shots out here. Developing chemical compounds, cellulose, plastics, and whatnot. They always set up shop in poorer counties where there's a certain laxness in the application of federal regulations. De Valu pretty much owns the Southwest. Half the filling stations and pharmacies, the petroleum refineries, most of the newspapers, and all the radio relays. It's a shell game, entire thing, under different names, but coming back square on the De Valu family. The Rockefellers, the Morgans, the Cabots and De Valus. Sophisticates of the capitalist class. Except there is no De Valu family. That 'de' is an affectation, pure bunk. They came over as Valutinis. Bunch'a wops out of Philly. They dropped the 'tini,' slapped a 'de' up front for pomp, and *bingo!* You've got yourself an Old Money name. Funny thing is, other Valutinis started doing the same. So you have the De Valus of New York and the De Valus of Baltimore both trying to elbow in on shared glory. Can't tell the real fakes from the phony ones. Ain't that a kick!"

The De Valu corporation operated a plant on the outskirts of town. The very latest in chemical engineering was being brewed right here in Silver, all sorts of new and wonderful products, with names that rolled off the tongue, rich in promise: pyralin and polystyrene and plastecele, the synthetic rubber of duprene, the wonders of vinylite and fabrikoid. It went far beyond the nitrates of old.

"The De Valu plant is run by a grasping Bohunk who thinks he's aligned with the aristocracy," said Virgil. "Ha! He don't even realize he's on the payroll of Eye-Ties barely three generations from Sicilian hardscrabble. They even brought in a heavy from Philly, one Joey Dicannti, a union buster from way back, to keep the local workers in line."

Dicannti had helped smash the picket lines at Republic Steel, Virgil said. Had fought alongside Tom Girdler, cracking bones with the best of them. They called Dicannti "Iron Balls" on account of how he once stared down strikers at a Flint refinery. When one of the workers dropkicked Dicannti in the testicles with a steel-toed boot, Dicannti didn't even flinch. He won the family's loyalty after that.

"Won't be much longer before he adds a 'de' as well," said Virgil. "Starts passing himself off as Lord Joseph Percival de Chanti, or some such."

I'd seen the De Valu plant, the plumes of smoke, the intestinal tubings, the metallic sheen. Word was they were developing chemicals for the military. "Like mustard gas, only better," is how one shopkeeper had put it—and proudly.

"Dazzle and pizzazz, Jack. Where was Bib-Label Lithiated Lemon-Lime Soda going? Nowhere, till they changed the name to 7-Up. It's the fizz that sells the drink, not the lithium." He waved the waitress over. "Miss, may I have a Bib-Label Lithiated Soda, please?"

She looked at him blankly.

"You may know it better as 7-Up."

She snapped her gum. "Wise guy, huh?"

"Just making a point. Where's that accent? Boston?"

"All over," she said.

"All over? Shoot, I've been there."

She threw a smile my way. "You up for some pie now?"

I thought about Useless Joe standing outside in the dark, his fists clenched, and I returned her smile, unopened.

"I'll pass," I said.

THIRTY-THREE

The angle, the pitch, the close, and the blow off.

There was a musical quality to every con, a rhythm that seemed to play itself out. Even the shortest street scams had it. Longer cons were orchestral arrangements, corner hustles were quick little tunes, but every one was musical in nature, whether it was a Big Store swindle or a simple trash-and-dash.

With a Big Store con, you set up an entirely false establishment. "Could be a casino, a bordello, a taproom or a gaffed bookie," said Virgil. "Doesn't matter. The operation is rigged from the ground up."

Virgil and I were sitting at the kitchen card table up in 1-A, with the front windows open, waiting for the night to fall and the heat to seep from the city. He was in his undershorts and sock-garters, fanning himself with a Panama hat while his zoot hung pressed and ready on the door. I was sweating even with my collar open, but it didn't seem right to start stripping down, especially not with Miss Rose in the room. Not that it mattered to her. She moved about in slip and stockings, not the least bit embarrassed. I tried not to look, but my eyes had a mind of their own, especially in such cramped quarters.

If Virgil noticed me stealing glances at Miss Rose in her undergarments, he never let it show. He was too busy carving dreams out of the air.

"If I had enough money," he said, "I'd build a city, out in the desert, with bright lights as far as the eye could see, a sort of permanent carnival, but *classy*. An entire city designed solely for the artful extraction of dollars from dupes. Would be done so deftly they wouldn't hardly notice. They'd come back for more with a smile on their face."

The Big Store was the height of the game, apparently. The trash-and-dash? Well, that was the other side. "A low-end con," said Virgil. "Just an elaborate variation on the common purse-snatch." Virgil dreamed big, but he maintained his appreciation for life's smaller scams.

In a trash-and-dash, grifters would dress as janitors, show up at an office and clean it out of whatever could be smuggled away in trash bins. Petty cash and office equipment was fine, but the real haul was in the checkbooks, blank invoices, ledgers.

"It works because the grifter is disguised as one of the Great Invisibles," said Virgil, his Panama fanning air. "Janitors. Maids. Window washers. Hobos. These are the people that other people look right through. No one sees them. You ever want a quick escape, kid, wear greasy rags underneath. Henry the Horse—so named because of how well-hung he was, he liked to boast, though the gals at Sal's said it was due to his habit of whinnying when he mounted a filly. Others said it was on account of his large yellow teeth. Anyway. Old Henry, he pulled off an impressive trash-and-dash at a jeweler's, emptying an entire display case right under their noses. Unfortunately for Henry, someone noticed the empty trays just as he was leaving. He ran out of there double-time as half the staff gave chase. Henry lost them in an alleyway, pulled off his janitor's uniform and stuffed it into a garbage can. Was wearing hobo clothes underneath. Dumped the jewels into a paper sack and flung himself onto a pile of trash as the cops and clerks ran by, everyone frantic to find him. Henry pretended to be asleep, and no one flickered so much as a look in his direction. Some say Henry even went so far as to shit himself, intentionally, and that he lay there in his own foul reek. That would keep any posse back a few. I ran into Henry in Kansas City, years later, asked him if that was true. He said, 'Hell, no. I wet myself. Didn't take no dump. I have my pride. And anyway, who can shit themselves on cue?'"

"A Prince of Thieves, our Henry," said Rose, as she held up one of her dresses for size, using the window as a mirror. "A real aristocrat."

"The ones who figure they're too clever to be conned, that's who you want to target," said Virgil. "It's a Scandinavian smorgasbord out there,

Jack. You've got your busybodies and your wallflowers, your small-time businessmen dreaming of more and the hausfraus who've settled for less, you've got the greedy and the needy, the upright and the low-down, the stargazers and true believers, the nervous Nellies and the big-bellied risk takers. You have your socialites, your hang-down hoodlums, and your upstanding citizens—with not much separating them at times. And every one of 'em ripe for the picking. You'd think God had set out to create a world of marks, so much blind faith and greed did He inject in people. Everybody has at least one con they can fall for, one con with their name on it."

Even better, Virgil said, was the man who thinks he's got nothing to lose.

"Everyone has something they can lose. We just need to find it. Pride. Possessions. A point of view. Man can lose all three in one swoop. We're educational agents, in our way."

Rose slid a dress over her head and down.

"Educational?" she said.

"Why not?" said Virgil. "We perform a service. We're sessional instructors in the School of Hard Knocks. Greed and need, Jack. That's the hook. They want something—they *need* something—crave it so badly it drives them blind with hunger. We stir up the sediment, rouse their hidden desires. Put some zing in their life. It's promises and coy smiles and flirtatious looks. A burlesque dance, with those ostrich plumes always promising to reveal more than they do. That's the essence of a good con: it's a fan dance."

"Zing," said Rose, buttoning up the front. "Is that what we're calling it now?"

Zing required moxie, and moxie required a certain brashness. But highest on the list of any confidence man's inventory was what Virgil referred to as "a malleable conscience."

"You have to ask yourself who's in charge," said Virgil. "You? Or your conscience? Got to be firm. Show your conscience who's boss. This whole world is crooked, Jack. We're all of us on the take, telling lies. I'm just more honest about it."

Rose tried on one of her hats, tilted it to the side. "More honest?" she said. "You?"

"I am," said Virgil. "I'm honest about my dishonesty."

"Jeez, Virg, you put it like that, they oughta give you a medal."

Virgil slid out his silver cigarette case and opened it with one fluid move, tapped twice for emphasis, and looked at me. "Sincerity. Honesty. Conviction," he said. "If you can fake those, you're on your way. Remember, Jack. A confidence man never meets a stranger." He paused. "Except maybe in his own mirror."

Everyone was a pal, and every pal was a potential mark. That was the trick. To learn to read everyone you met like the potential mark he was.

Virgil lit his cigarette, filled his chest with smoke. "You want to be in the game, you have to study your prey. Every detail. Suspenders? Or belt? Or both? Suit and tie, smartly pressed or wrinkled badly? Tailor-cut or store-bought? And what does he *smell* like? Is he fresh from a shave? Or sporting a week's worth of stubble? Are his nails clean? Or chewed right down? Ear hairs trimmed? That's the best—trimmed ear hairs—that's someone who has money to throw around. And his shoes? A fresh shine? Or a spit-and-buff? You need to catch their rhythm and speak with the same. Does he curse? Or talk proper? Take your cues from your marks. They should find in you a man of kindred tastes. He spits. You spit. He scratches. You scratch. He professes a faith in the Methodist God, by jiminy, you're a Methodist too. He's a Baptist, you're a Baptist. He's a member in good standing at the Anti-Saloon League of America? You bemoan the end of Prohibition and offer a teetotaling smile. He leers at women, you egg him on. He votes Democrat, so do you. He figures Franklin Delano is a Communist and a tyrant, well, dammit, so do you. If you're talking to a machinist waiting on work at a broken-down assembly line, you go Red, let slip how you're a defender of the Proletarian Party and a supporter of Socialist Labor. If you're talking to Henry Ford, you go fascist. You say that someone ought to assassinate Franklin Double-Crossing Roosevelt. You talk about how the 'idle poor' are more to blame than the idle rich, and how we can't coddle the dawdlers, and how the New Deal is being played with marked cards. But if he expresses himself favorably towards FDR? You say, 'Yessir! They ought to put ol' Franklin Delano's face on Rushmore, alongside cousin Teddy's.' Work from the general to specific. Fish for clues. Find out who they need you to be—and then be that person. Give them what they want to hear, you'll extract a price for it later. If you're setting up a small-town businessman, play to the fact he figures the big boys are crooks. You tell him, 'It really gripes my soul to see the little man treated unfairly.'"

Everything griped Virgil's soul; it was a way to get people on board.

"Confirm the universe as they see it," said Virgil, "and in no time they'll be happily allowing you to ransack their wallets. Avoid pipe-smokers. And never—*never*—go up against someone smarter than you."

Pipe smokers?

"They think too much. Last thing you want is a mark that steps back and *thinks*."

Virgil claimed he could read a man by the hat he wore. Homburgs, he said, with their creased crowns and stiff brims, were favored by bankers, lawyers, stockbrokers. Men too clever to be marks, which of course made them excellent marks. Derbys, with their perfectly spherical tops, were different. White derbys signaled buffoons susceptible to puffery, especially if said derbys sported a prominent side-feather. Brown derbys, with stingy saucer-brims and a tighter fit, they were slightly more sinister. Dressy, but not too formal, such derbys were meant to project a halo of respectable jocularity. "But don't be fooled," said Virgil. "I never met a derby wasn't worn by a man with bitter blood."

And Panamas?

"Charm and good looks," he said with a grin. "More so when exchanged for a flat-topped porkpie. Now that *is* jaunty."

Rose had chosen a baby-blue, bell-shaped hat with an enormous bow on one side, like a gift waiting to be unwrapped. She caught me looking at it.

"Poise and grace," she said. "In case you were wondering."

"And a tiger in the sack!" Virgil hooted.

A fellow could read a lot with a single bow.

"Now, we have to work on your smile," Virgil said to me.

"He smiles?" said Rose.

"It's lopsided," said Virgil. "Crooked smiles are fake smiles. They're forced. People know that. You got to learn to smile wide—and with your eyes for it to seem genuine. Practice in front of a mirror if you have to, until faking comes naturally. And don't hold it too long. Real expressions shift all the time. Can't leave a single smile slapped on your face for more than a beat or two. That's a tell as well."

I smiled at Miss Rose, wide as I could.

"There you go," she said with a laugh. "I almost believed you. Still a bit lopsided though."

Virgil crushed his cigarette into a saucer, stood up, and plucked his zoot from the door handle. He smiled. "Time for some jitterbug, kid."

THIRTY-FOUR

It wasn't until I attended a matinee at the Silver City Aztec that I under-stood what was really happening in Nazi Germany. And in Italy. In Russia. In Spain. Japan.

I'd gone to see *Dark Victory* with Bette Davis—that is, she was in it. I went by myself; Rose and Virgil were still tangled up in their Murphy bed. The newsreels at the Aztec featured a parade of Nazi soldiers under a confetti sky worthy of a Lindbergh return. It was Germany withdraw-ing its troops from Spain—General Franco, friend to Adolph and Benito, now being secure in his authority. The soldiers moved past, row after row like wind-up toys, and the Luftwaffe aeroplanes streaked across in perfect formation above.

The bonfires were growing. Books were burning across Europe, and from the burning of books to the burning of bodies seemed like a short step. But books were bad enough. You didn't need to wait for the bodies to pile up; in the fire that illuminated the faces of the crowd, I saw what was happening over there. I knew what was going on. They had invited Dracula into their house. I watched those books burning, and I wondered if Ovid's was among them.

The matinee let out, but I was reluctant to return to 1-A. I'd never overheard Virgil and Miss Rose being intimate; I assumed they waited till I was gone. Some mornings, I didn't bother tiptoeing past their sleep-ing forms at all, but just slipped down the side fire escape instead. I kept my money rolled tight in a tobacco tin, which I used to prop open my window with. Hide in plain sight, I figured, and besides, the storage room I was sleeping in—Apt. 1-B—had grown increasingly sweltered in the heat.

While giving Virgil and Rose the time they needed, I wandered the streets of Silver. Practiced my smile. Trained myself to see people as potential marks and nothing else. I assessed everyone I passed, trying to spot their weaknesses, trying to figure out what I could play them for, what angle I could take. Tried not to think of bodies or books, burning or otherwise.

One thing bothered me, though, in the lessons Virgil gave me. It was something he always seemed to come back to. "I never knew a con man wasn't eventually cheated by his partner," he'd say. "You gotta watch out for tear-off rats, Jack—grifters who prey on their own. This world of man is filled with snoops and finks and chowderheads. But it's the tear-off rats that are the worst. Have to watch your fellow grifters, Jack. Always."

I didn't understand then why Virgil kept bringing up that particular point. Now I think I do. It was like warding off something dark by talking about it, the way widow-peaked Counts are kept at bay with amulets and incantations. Or the way some people believed in luck.

There was no luck involved in what we were doing. A con is crime with intelligence added. You can pull a Dillinger, rob a single bank of $10,000—or you can grift $100 from a hundred different people. The second method takes longer, true, and is less splashy, but you won't end up on anyone's Most Wanted List. No D.A. was going to take on the case of some poor sap who'd been outwitted over a C-note. In the eyes of most prosecutors, what Virgil and Rose and I did wasn't even a criminal offense, I'd learned, but civil. We slipped through the net the law had thrown at us, and we did it with a smile. A practiced smile, in my case.

When I got back to Charley Wong's, Virgil was in the back booth with the afternoon edition open to another tale of gangster-racketeers taken down by a volley of bullets.

"Publicity," Virgil said, barely looking up as I slid in across from him. "Kiss of death."

I waved to the waitress—Susie, was it?—and I asked for coffee. Passed on the pie. Again.

"Once a criminal becomes a star," said Virgil, "they're doomed. Look at Bonnie and Clyde, on the lam but always happy to pose for photos. They were lappin' it up. No wonder they ended their days riddled with holes. Or Dillinger, snubbing his nose at the law, taunting them with phone calls and postcards. A farm boy from Indiana, putting on airs like that? He was askin' for it. Hell, the man even held up a police station at one point. You can't do that. Can't come roaring in like gangbusters, drawing attention, talking loud. Can't skip around singing *'We're in the money!'* either. You don't strut about in diamond scarfpin and bejeweled cufflinks. Save the flash for the dance halls. Dillinger? They killed him outside a movie theater, when his guard was down." Virgil looked at me. "So you be careful."

"Who would want to ambush me?" I said.

"Just be careful, okay? You don't want to end up like Dillinger, your body on display at the morgue, people lining up down the block for a peek. Dillinger's fame didn't fend off the bullets now, did it?"

Virgil took a quick sip of his coffee and fixed me with a stare. "How about you? Ever been hit? By a bullet?"

I was taken aback by this. "Can't say that I have."

"Not something you'd soon forget," he said. "It's a strong man that can take a bullet and not be changed by it."

Rose had joined us at this point for coffee and a cigarette, what Virgil called "a hooker's breakfast." She sighed. "Don't be so morbid, Virg. You'll give the boy the heebies."

"Point is," said Virgil, "life cycle of a bank robber is notoriously short. But con artists have a natural longevity. Take Sigmund Engel. Remember him, Rose?"

"How could I forget," she said. "Man was a walking charm bank."

"Old, bald, and short," said Virgil. "Yet he ran the best sweetheart scam in the country. He married his first gal in 1909 and was still going strong when he tried to make a move on Rose—"

"Damn near worked," she said.

"See, we thought *we* were conning Sigmund. He thought he was conning us. He'd set himself up as a wealthy widower. Rose was passing herself off as a wealthy heiress. All good fun. Shared a laugh over that once we realized."

"The secret was eye contact," said Rose. "*Deep* eye contact. Sigmund would look at the ladies with his big puppy dogs, would hold their gaze just a little too long, and would suddenly gasp and turn away. 'What is it?' they'd ask. 'Nothing. It's just—it's just that you look exactly like my wife … did.'"

"Which was probably true," said Virgil. "Sigmund having been married close to eighty times at last count. Some of them probably did resemble a previous wife. Or three. Now, many of the ladies Sigmund cleaned out were dumber than a barrel of hair, but most were not. He'd target widows, spinsters. Pass himself off as a lonely soul, a widower looking for companionship—and boy! Didn't those ladies need to be needed. He got nabbed once in Iowa, but the woman in question refused to press charges. Even paid his bail. Never saw him again. A strange duck, Sigmund. Always ate at the best restaurants. But he was quiet. Unassuming. He'd gravitate towards social clubs and fundraisers. Would come into town and pore through the obituaries looking for deceased husbands of notable wealth, then arrange an accidental meeting with the grieving widow. Not always grieving, though, as he pointed out. Some looked downright invigorated by their recent loss. Sigmund always carried a book with him. Tucked under his arm. By some Greek poet—"

"Ovid," I said, and I laughed out loud. "Not Greek," I said. "Roman. Book was called *The Art of Love*. Am I right?"

That gave them a start. "I believe so. How did you—"

And I kept on laughing, first time in a long while.

"There!" said Rose. "There's a smile."

"We should set up a sweetheart scam of our own," said Virgil. "What do you think, Rose? Wheaties here runs down a rich man's daughter. Marries her. Cleans out Daddy. Leaves town. Long as you're smart about it, who knows?"

But we knew that wasn't going to happen. I eventually laughed myself clear, and as I wiped my eyes, I said, "*Different hearts require different methods. Some fish are speared, some are caught by line and hook, others are encircled in billowing nets.* That's Ovid." A guide to sussing out marks. That's what it had been all along.

Virgil told me that he and Rose had once worked a Badger game, the difference between a sweetheart scam and a Badger being the difference between sweet-talk and blackmail. In the sweetheart scam you sucked them in slowly, speaking soft in honeysuckle tones. With the Badger game you trapped a man outright. The more respectable, the better. A town councillor or a Chamber of Commerce stalwart on a business trip was ideal, followed closely by a parson (with family) and a parson (without). Rose had the sort of eyes that could draw a man into the open. She would pass herself off as guileless, allow herself to be talked into his hotel room ... only to have Virgil burst in as her overly protective brother, shouting threats and vowing scandal and ruin. Oftentimes, and as extra collateral, Virgil would rush in on a flashbulb pop, as though he'd just snapped a photo—Rose always managed to throw herself across the mark's lap for this. Sometimes Virgil threatened to tell their Pa, who happened to be—well, pick the name of the biggest gangster in the vicinity, and that was their Daddy. Whatever it took to put the fear of God into those poor saps.

Virgil pushed one fellow too far, though. They set out to wring him dry with call-back after call-back, but it turned out the mark had a little *too much* to lose. He tracked Virgil and Rose down, trashed their room while they were out, and had a pair of gorillas stake their car.

"That's how we lost the Model A," said Virgil.

"And not a moment too soon," said Rose. "I *hated* that car."

"Everything we owned was in our room or in that car. Needed to get out fast, and Rose here—well, you tell him."

"I convinced a fella to steal an automobile for me," she said, and she allowed herself a small smile. "Virgil hid and I approached a passerby, tears in my eyes, telling him how I had lost my keys and desperately needed to get home before my husband knew I was out. Gallant to a fault, the fella jimmied the door, hot-started it for me, and then asked for a number he might ring me at. Discreetly, of course. I scribbled something on a rip of paper, borrowed twenty bucks, and then picked up Virg around the corner. Far as I know, that fella never realized he'd been talked into committing a felony. I gave him the Ha! Ha! and away we went."

"It was the end of the Badger for us," said Virgil. "And just as well. Never cared for it. Couldn't handle the blubbering. 'Oh my wife, my kids.' Never seems to bother the womenfolk, though. In a Badger game, it's always the male con who ends up feeling the pangs."

"The pangs?"

"Of guilt. And that's a kiss of death, too, when you're running a scam."

"Serves the bedswervers right," said Rose.

"Oh, we got those bedswervers, though, didn't we!" Virgil hooted. "Got 'em good!"

I threw a glance over my shoulder, even though the place was empty. It made me nervous how loud Virgil could be at times. He was careful enough when customers came in not to talk about business, but still. I signaled for him to lower his voice, but he brushed my jumpy worries aside.

"Relax," he said. "Who's going to hear us? Charley? He's in the kitchen. Now, another version of the Badger, it's quicker and slicker still. Played in brothels and rigged hotel rooms. They call it the 'panel game.' Girl takes a man up to her room. Her confederate enters through a side panel—"

"Hence the name," said Rose.

"Hence the name," said Virgil. "While the sucker is being artfully distracted—or better yet, is snoozing—the pickings are easy. Clothes in a heap, trousers on top, wallet full. Maybe a watch. Even a nice hat. Lila Bauchenmier, she ran a hookshop out of Baton Rouge and she had some fine tricks in her bag. Could outpace a racehorse, our Lila. Always left her men happy—and exhausted. You could've removed their gold fillings and they would've been too deep in snoreland to notice. Was one of the prettiest gals ever to straddle a chamberpot, Lila was. Had long, slender fingers, the sort of which rest naturally in other people's pockets, and her sheets held more secrets than a Catholic confessional. Sex for her was no more serious than a sneeze. You should look her up someday, Jack. Tell ol' Li-Bach that Virgil sent you. She'll know what to do."

I said I would, if ever I found myself in Baton Rouge.

"I only ran the panel with Lila once or twice," said Virgil. "Playing on love like that, didn't seem quite right."

"Love?" said Rose. "Is that what you're calling it?"

And maybe that's all love was, anyway, a mutual con. Rebecca would be getting out of school right about now. It was mid-June, and I'd been gone ten weeks. Who knows? She might be thinking of me right this moment. Or. Maybe not. I looked down at my hand, softer now and free of calluses. The pocket of warmth I'd once felt in my palm was long gone.

"Something wrong?" asked Rose.

I'd been sitting there awhile. Hadn't noticed the conversation lag.

"Lose something?"

I wanted to say, "Yes, I believe so," but all I could manage was a shake of the head, no, and a wide, even smile.

Thirty-five

Virgil decided it was time for me to try tossing the tat. That was crooked dice with a straight throw, or straight dice with a crooked throw.

"Loaded dice only work on rubes," advised Virgil. "Any gamer worth his weight can tell whether a set is gaffed just by the way they feel in his hand—and professional gamblers are not overly forgiving about such matters. Better to learn the toss instead."

To throw a set of dice so that the odds played in your favor required a flat toss. You had to spin them so they'd move only on one plane, without tumbling over. You'd shake your hand like mad but only for show, while gripping the dice in the crook of your finger, with the numbers you wanted facing up. Idea was to skip them low, like a stone, without turning them over. You couldn't pull this on every throw, and not in bright-light casinos. But in a back alley or across a pool table, when the stakes were high enough? A flick of the wrist, a skim of the dice, and bam! Double sixes.

Hard to do.

The idea was simple enough. But throwing tat proved far trickier than tossing hoops over a bottle, and when I finally did get the horizontal spin to work, Virgil groaned. "You might as well have just placed them on the table with the sixes up, it was so obvious. You have to put some *oomph* behind it."

The tat needed faster hands than mine, thinner fingers. Virgil threw five times. Five times lucky. Took me a good thirty throws to produce one decent result, which was about the same odds as if I'd been tossing honest. So what was the point?

We stuck with short cons throughout June, swinging through a town, clearing out quickly. Virgil always worried about staying too long in one place, and overnighting made him antsy. Sometimes we'd clear out in the morning before Rose's stockings were even dry. Bare legs out the back window, dress parachuting out, she would say, "No one's chasing us, Virg. What's the rush?"

County festivities were gearing up by now: bake-offs, hog calling, the celebration of local preserves and public appreciation of pickles, that sort of thing. Men in suspenders and belts heaving iron rings, kids running in and out like alleycats as the women fretted around the tables, hands dusted with flour or sticky with jam. Young lovers would moon about in the prickly dust, dewy-eyed and dumbstruck, pitching woo like it was horseshoes. All very small-scale and innocent. Homely. Which is to say, a perfect place for a scamming. Virgil decided we should hit the fair-grounds around Silver City. "Day trips," he said. "Quick and easy."

Virgil held that you could talk a bored yokel into just about anything, and farm fairs were about as boring a concoction as you could hope for. He'd originally wanted to throw the tat, with me as the shill. But that would have required me to win sometimes, to draw people in. It would have been unladylike for Rose to play, so throwing dice was out.

"We'll go with three-card monte instead," he said. "Here. I'll show you how it works."

In the alley behind Wong's, Virgil upended a wooden crate and laid down three cards, a Queen of Hearts and two aces. Idea was to follow the Queen. Virgil moved the cards, a bit stiffly I thought, in and out, over and around, while keeping a breathless banter going. "Find the lady! Place your bet 'n double your money. Keep your eyes on the Queen. Eyes on the Queen. Always on the Queen. The Queen is king. The Queen is king."

We practiced it, with Rose playing the sap and me acting the shill. My job was to block every attempt she made at picking the correct card.

"The first and foremost rule of three-card monte," said Virgil, "is this: *the sucker never wins*. The shill does, but the sucker, never."

Seemed to me we could have played it straight. Move the cards fast enough, let the bettor take an honest pick, and you'd still have a two-to-one advantage. With odds like that in our favor, we'd come out ahead in the long run. But two-to-one wasn't quite good enough for Virgil. He wanted better odds. "Three-to-zero, preferably."

Monte wasn't like other cons, where you might let a few rounds go to bolster the mark's ego. In poker, for example, if you were playing the lemon, you'd let the mark take a couple of hands: that was the convincer. You gave 'em that to prime the pump, get 'em hooked. That never happened with three-card monte, Virgil explained, because three-card monte was a street-corner swindle, and the mark might simply take his winnings and walk away.

There were any number of strategies to ensure that never happened.

As the shill, I'd pick winning card after winning card. I'd make it look easy, because it was. Virgil's hands would move slow enough for anyone to follow. "Even better," said Virgil, "when someone in a derby and a vest is standing back watching, is to have the shill *lose*. Again and again and again."

The too-clever-to-be-cheated mark then thought, "Can't believe that fellow missed it! I would have won every time." Convinced of his own superiority, he'd finally step up to lay a wager of his own.

And that's when something magical would happen. As soon as the mark placed a bet, Virgil's abilities saw a sudden and marked improvement. Now the cards began to fly. Virgil picked them up and dropped them down, quickly, lightly. The classic move was to pick up two cards with the right hand, one on top of the other, and then—instead of dropping the bottom one first, as you'd expect—make a wide sweep and let the top card fall instead. Simple trick, but it worked. The mark would now be following the wrong card. A sideways slide, where one card went over and the bottom one slid out, was also effective, though Virgil had a bit of trouble with that.

"Monte is not exactly my area of expertise," he confessed. "Haven't played much since my depot days. I'm a bit rusty, but good enough to fool the rubes."

And if by blind luck the mark picked the right card? Well, this was where I came in—and I had to move fast.

The instant a sucker placed a bet on the winning card, whether five dollars or ten, Virgil would throw the money back, yelling, "Twenty dollars minimum!" That was my cue to immediately throw in forty, blocking the bet. Because as soon as I did, Virgil would just as quickly announce, "Forty dollar maximum," and turn over the card.

I would win on the mark's pick, which only fueled his desire. If the mark picked correctly again—and it did happen now and then, Virgil said—I was supposed to push in and jostle the crate, knocking the cards. Virgil would then shout, "Bets are off! New deal."

And if the mark chose correctly a third time? Well. It meant Virgil hadn't done his job. "Cops!" he'd yell. "Burn it!" And we'd scramble, leaving the box behind. Which is why you didn't want to use a formal card stand, in case you had to run.

It never came to that, though, and just as well, because I don't think anyone at those county fairs realized three-card monte was illegal. Hog farmers would belly up to Virgil's wooden crate, push back their caps, watch a bit, and then proceed to lose a week's worth of groceries in two or three rounds. They never once suspected anything, because, Hey! Hadn't that young man earlier won a few? Some fellows would bet more, hoping in vain to "even up," throwing good money after bad with a grim determination until they were cleaned out entirely.

I always won a big round right after that happened, cleaning Virgil out, and I'd swagger away as Virgil slumped down in defeat. Sometimes the person we'd just soaked would commiserate. "Win some, you lose some," they'd tell Virgil.

"Wise words," he'd say. "Wise words."

Monte was just another version of the age-old shell game. "As old as America itself," said Virgil. "The first thimble-rigger arrived with the *Mayflower*. That's a fact. And you can read about shell games being played at Pilgrim church picnics." He spoke about it as though he'd been there firsthand to witness it. "In our way, we're keeping a venerable tradition alive," he said, still angling for that medal Rose figured he was owed.

"Selfless of you," she said.

Three-card monte. Thimble-riggers. The shell game. Or even those three soft green leather suitcases that Virgil owned. All part of that 1-2-3 rhythm. Four was too many. Two not enough. You needed a set of three to hide the truth, whether it was a suitcase switch or the light soft touch of a card falling on a table. "Is the hand quicker than the eye?" Virgil would cry. "Step right up, give it a try." And they did. In droves. Like cattle to a hamburger press.

Rose's job was to hang back, throw us hand signals. She'd scope out the crowd, see who pulled a dollar out of a thick wallet and who didn't. Who checked his watch—had to be going soon, so needed to be fleeced first—and who was on a more leisurely schedule. A tug on her ear meant a cop was coming. A brush of her sleeve meant kill the game. Two fingers to adjust her hat meant double it up. Three fingers meant get away from that mark, take the next one instead. When she checked her powder that meant draw it out. If she adjusted her hair, tucked it behind her ear, say, it usually meant the mark was good for the long run. *"Set him up and take him for all he's worth."*

It went swimmingly well until the fifth fair in as many days. That's when we got into trouble.

We'd had a good run and were ready to leave when Virgil smelled oven-baked pie. Bumbleberry, raisin, rhubarb. "Mmmm-mm. Smell that, will you!"

It was coming from a Knights of Columbus tent, and was indeed so warm and rich you could taste it on your tongue.

Virgil bought a whole entire pie. He went with the bumbleberry.

We sat in the shade of a tent, off to one corner, eating fresh-baked wares with crusts so flaky they might have wafted down from Heaven itself and berries so tart they might have bubbled up from below.

Virgil looked at me. "That tobacco tin of yours must be crammed full. What are you going to do with all that money? Must be over two grand in there by now."

"About that," I said. It was actually a fair bit more than two.

"And you never splurge on clothes or wine," said Virgil.

"Or girls," said Rose.

Virgil wiped his mouth clean of bumbleberry. "What are you saving for, boy? A rainy day? Not going to see much rain around here."

Truth be told, I didn't know that I was saving for anything.

I'd sent my Da a hundred dollars, with a note that read BUY FOOD. But other than that, I hadn't spent much of it at all, especially as how Virgil loved to treat. The rum, the steaks, the jazz, and the early morning breakfasts hadn't cost me hardly a cent.

"Maybe I'll put it in the bank," I said. "Save it for later."

"Got plans, do you?"

"No. Not really."

"Nothing?" said Rose.

"Well, I could run off, I suppose. You know, go north. Sign up with the British Army. Join the fight that everyone says is coming."

Well. Was that the wrong thing to say.

Virgil, it turned out, was no Fayther. "What! Tell me you aren't serious. Jesus H., boy!"

"Virg—" said Rose, but he was in no mood.

"I was there, Jack, in the last one. Oh, in our khaki uniforms, didn't we look swell! Full of that Yankee Doodle-de-dum. Half a million boots, kid. Marching straight into Hell. They never tell you that part, do they? God*dammit*, Jack! I thought you were smarter'n that. Didn't we learn anything from the Great War? We Americans live in a fireproof house, far from flammable materials. What are we doing fighting another man's battles?"

"Virg—"

"You want to be like one of those fools who signed on to fight Franco, joining a volunteer brigade, head stuffed with romantic nonsense? And for what? I'm glad old Franco won and put an end to that sort of silliness. Veterans of Foreign Wars, *ha!* They ought to start a support group for Veterans of Future Wars, that's who's going to need it."

"The boy was just musing," said Rose. "Don't get so wound up over it."

"Neutrality Act? Smartest thing Congress ever passed," said Virgil. "*Making the world safe for democracy.* That's what they told us the war was about. Said it was a crusade. But I ask you, when did we ever agree to be the world's policeman? Huh? You want to see the sign of a sucker? Here. I'll show you."

He popped open his buttons, pulled up his undershirt. Ever since Clark Gable had revealed his bare chest, sales of undershirts had plummeted. Virgil was one of the few fellows I knew who still favored them. Now I had an inkling as to why.

There, in the middle of his chest, just below the heart, was a splayed and puckered scar, about the size of a quarter, like a hole had been punched through and then sewn up. Badly.

"There you go. Kraut bullet, and for what? You weren't even born yet, when we marched away. The War to End All Wars, as I recall. Doughboys on parade, and me running off like I was the Lone Ranger to the rescue. Oh, yes, Uncle Sam rode on in, didn't he? Rode in to the rescue, right at the very end, firing six-guns and spooking the Hun. It wasn't the movies, though, was it? I arrived at the front, saw a balloon mired in the muck. But it wasn't a balloon. It was a Tommy, belly bloated, skin a pallorous gray. They handed me a Lee-Enfield, said 'The Great Adventure has just begun!'"

"Enfields?" I said. "Those are British."

"Exactly! Don't be the fool I was. Here's something maybe you don't know. When they send you into combat? You get hit once, you expect that. Twice? You're in trouble. Three times? It'd take a miracle to get you through. I only ever knew one man big enough to take three bullets and live."

"And?"

"The fourth one killed him. Now me, I only got hit the one time. But once was plenty. Kraut sniper, dead in the chest. Missed my heart by a hair. Was miraculous I ever lived."

"I thought you didn't believe in luck," I said.

"I don't. But I sure as fuck believe in miracles."

He stewed awhile, staring at me with an angry disgust.

"It was just an idea," I said.

"So was the fuckin' Hindenburg! Show some sense, boy. It's a mug's game. What the hell ails you that you can't see that? Listen." He leaned in closer, dropped his voice. "You've got a God-given talent, Jack. You've got the *confidence* in you, I can sense it. Don't squander your life on lost causes. Don't let them play you for a sap."

Confidence? No. It was more a matter of turning off those parts of who you were that might get in the way. It was a matter of deciding what had to be done and then doing it. Wasn't moxie. Moxie was the art of embellishment, of adding on layers like you were icing a cake. What I employed was the art of subtraction.

Rose put her hand on my arm. "Virgil doesn't want to see you go to waste, is all."

Virgil tapped the scar on his chest one final time. "This is what heroics gets you."

I don't know how that bullet missed his heart.

It was while he was buttoning up his shirt that I noticed Virgil looking over my shoulder at something coming our way. He smiled. Wide. Held it just a beat too long.

"Afternoon, officer," he said, and I turned to see a sheriff's badge attached to a great slab of a man. Looked like a bull stuffed into a uniform. His head went from ears to shoulder without the usual interval of neck. Face was sunburned and raw, and it didn't smile.

First rule of three-card monte was that the mark never won. Second rule was that the player and the shill should never be seen together afterwards. If it hadn't been for that pie, we wouldn't have.

The man with the badge said, "I understand you boys have been staging games of chance in my jurisdiction," and Rose was gone.

It was remarkable. I don't know how she did it. One moment she was there and the next moment she wasn't, like a lady vanishing.

"Games of chance?" said Virgil. "But that would be against county bylaw 37-4, which clearly limits private gambling at public venues."

This threw the sheriff for a pause. "Bylaw 37-4?"

"Exactly," said Virgil. "Bans all such games, except of course for charitable purposes. Church bingos. That sort of thing. Now, in our case, we're raising funds for the Knights of Columbus, have you tasted their pies? My, my. They're wonderfully good. Go on, have a slice."

But the sheriff didn't budge. "This is my town. You have to clear things with me first."

Whenever we entered a fairground, Virgil would make a point of stopping by the public address booth to shake hands with the man behind the microphone. *"Dale, is it? Dale Whitlock? A pleasure. Excellent job you're doing. Hardly a crackle of static to it."*

Now I knew why.

"Well, sheriff," said Virgil, leaning in a little, dropping his voice. "If you stop by the announcer's booth and see Mr. Whitlock—You do know Mr. Whitlock?"

"Dale? Sure, I know Dale."

"Well, he has an envelope there for you. Tucked in beneath the table. A token of our appreciation, for the fine job you law enforcement officials are doing. It's our way of saying thank you."

The sheriff nodded. This was what he had come for. And as soon as he turned his back and headed off towards the broadcast booth, Virgil and I ran. Rose was around back, had the motor running, and we dove in. "Get down," said Virgil, and he threw a blanket over us as Rose sped away. He needn't have bothered with the blanket. As we flew by, Rose said the sheriff was standing to one side, waiting patiently for Dale to finish an announcement.

She got us out of there, got us out fast.

And once we were clear, Virgil tossed the blanket back, said in a woeful sad voice, "The shame of it. The shame! Having to leave behind a perfectly good bumbleberry pie like that."

I still don't know how that bullet missed his heart.

Thirty-six

On the way back to Silver City, we passed a carnival.

It was on the tattered hem of a larger town; you could see the silos and water towers trembling in the distant heat, part mirage, part not. The carnival had staked out its real estate, banners fluttering, tents arranged like the larger and more elaborate shell game it was. The sign out front read FAMILY FUN! WHOLESOME ENTERTAINMENT PRODUCTIONS PRESENTS—and there I saw it—THE ROBBINS BROS. CIRCUS & CARNIVAL.

"Pull in," I said. "They owe me a bear."

But Virgil would do no such thing, even though we were talking about the Deluxe XL Bear with Teddy Roosevelt glasses.

"You want to get redlighted?" he asked. "Y'don't pick a fight with carnies, it's like picking a fight with a nest of rattlers. You might get one or two licks in, but either way, you're going to go down, pocked full of tooth marks and sick with venom."

Redlighting, he explained, was the art of throwing people from a train, so named because the last thing you saw as you lay in ruins on the tracks was the red flicker of the caboose as it disappeared into the distance.

"Couple years back, in Mobile, carnies threw several workmen from their circus caboose after the fellas complained about their pay. Two were crippled for life. One died. All of 'em had been redlighted."

I looked at Virgil. "You worked the midway?"

"I did. And I'm not stopping."

He sped past the carnival turnoff without slowing down.

"After the war," he said, "I'd tasted the wares that the world had to offer, both the bitter and the sweet, and I found I couldn't settle down.

Was like having a nervous knee when you're trying to sit through a sermon. Kept bouncing. I was itching to leave. I've got restless bones, Jack. And I ended up on the midway, working the circuit. Among confidence men, who hasn't? It's sorta like jury duty. You do your time, and you try to get out in one piece. Getting in isn't too tricky. It's the leaving that's hard. The carnival either swallows you whole or spits you out—soul-broken and well-chewed."

The carnival was where Virgil had learned his depot tricks, it turned out. It was where he first switched suitcases and where he first learned to play three-card monte, talents that had eventually taken him clean across America.

"What does the chalk mean?" I asked. "In the carnivals. I know mostly it signals a sucker."

Virgil nodded. "Mostly. Pickpockets use them too. Have their advance man mark where the wallet is, using the back of the jacket sort of like a compass, pointing to which pocket. Dead center if it's on a chain. Mid-shoulders if he's already been hit. By the time some of these fellas got to the end of the midway they were marked good and well," said Virgil with a laugh.

"What about red?" I asked.

"Red?"

"Chalk. That's what one of them patted on my shoulder," I said. "Thinking I hadn't noticed."

Virgil looked over at me, *aghast*. "They put red chalk on your shoulder?"

I nodded. "Yes sir. Knew it was a signal," I said. "Figured it meant, 'The boy's on to us, leave him be,' because no one would tout me over after that."

"Not quite," said Virgil. "Not quite. Close, but no. A mark with red chalk means *'This fucker gives you any trouble, redlight him.'* It's an 'All bets are off, take him down if you have to' sort of thing. If you had pushed your luck, had refused to leave or had come back later that night, they'd have invited you onboard their train. Would have plied you with soothing words and backslappery. And as soon as that train started to roll, they would have tossed you from the caboose. Red chalk? You don't know how close you came." Virgil looked across at me. "Still want to go back for that bear?"

I smiled, wide and crooked. "Think I'll pass."

As Robbins Bros. disappeared into dust and distance, Virgil told me not to feel bad about getting taken by carnies. All confidence men got stung at some point.

"That's usually how it starts," he said. "Someone swindles you, knocks you back on your heels, and you decide, in the ledger of life, that you're going to be the duper, not the dup*ee*. The carnie, not the mark. Soapy Smith? He was just a kid out of Georgia, working on a ranch in Texas when he got taken for all his money by a thimble-rigger. Instead of getting angry, Soapy decided to learn the trade himself. Turned up in Alaska at the turn of the century, ended up *owning* Skagway. That's what separates a confidence man from the rest of the crowd. Most men who get burned, they nurse their wounds, whimper a bit. Take their lumps. But some? Some get burned and want to handle the matches themselves. Those born of a bunco soul. They think to themselves, 'How *did* he do that? I want to learn to do that, too.' Anybody can get taken, Jack. Dapper Dan Collins was fleeced by Count Lustig. Count Lustig was taken by Yellow Kid Weil. Happens to the best of us. Think of it as educational, a lesson learned. My case, it was Suitcase Simpson and his three dastardly identical satchels. I tracked Simpson down, but instead of beating the tar out of him, I said, 'Teach me.' Well, soon enough I learned to pull that switch as smoothly as silk from a sow's ass."

There was more than one meaning of the term *switch*, Virgil explained as we drove onward, the sun low across the road. "The switch" also referred to that moment when you shifted responsibility for the scam onto the mark. When you convinced him it was his idea all along.

"When they force the scheme onto you," said Virgil. "When they *make* you take their money. That's a beautiful moment. You tell them, 'No, no, no. I couldn't!' and they say, 'I insist!'" He was smiling wide and free now. "Running the perfect con. Ain't it a kick! Playing a game where the rules are stacked in your favor. *Heads you win, tails they lose.*

Outsmarting the world, that's what this is all about. Me? I moved from the suitcase switch to matchbox shuffles, and from matchboxes to monte, and from monte to Mish roll. And here I am. Still alive."

In the world of Virgil Ray, there were no second-place prizes. Everyone was either a chump or a king. There were no average confidence men either, only artists and masters, greats and all-time greats. So-and-so was the best check kiter, the best advance man, the best roper ever to walk God's green. Someone who earned a living obtaining refunds from large companies for minor purchases—and then erasing the ink and writing in a new amount: he was never simply a check bleacher, he was "the greatest check bleacher that ever was. He should have been working on oil paintings, restoring great works of art, he was that good!"

"Is that what we are?" I asked. "Artists?"

"Oh, more than that," said Virgil, glancing over at me. "The confidence man is the great all-American hero, like Paul Bunyan or Robin Hood."

Robin Hood?

"We traffic in dreams and false hope, Jack. And what could be more American than that? Charley Fisher, up near Passamaquoddy Bay, he started the Electrolytic Marine Salts Company. He sold shares in the ocean. The ocean, mind you! Used his patented 'gold accumulator' to extract tiny amounts of ore from the sea. All true enough. Saltwater does contain traces of gold. But you'd have to strain half the bay for a single fleck. We're talking molecules, here."

Not that Fisher cared. He was in the business of selling shares, and sell he did.

"Took those New England Yankees for a modest fortune. But I went one better. I once sold a pile of dirt seven times, at a thousand bucks a pop. I want that on my headstone—*Here lies Virgil Ray: He sold a pile of dirt, seven times over.* Best thing? It was all legit. Unprocessed tailings from a bona-fide gold mine."

"Unprocessed tailings?" I asked.

"Dirt. They paid me to get rid of it. I decided to sell it instead, to save me the hauling. Paper trail was clean. The tailings did contain gold.

About as much as you'd find in seawater, and if you sifted carefully enough you might pick up a speck or two, like finding a flea in a sandbox. But it was still gold, and gold is like H to the greedy, Jack. The promise of it feeds the habit, makes hopheads out of us all. '*Gold-bearing soil, duly certified as such by the U.S. Assayers Office.*' You've heard of dirt poor? Well, I was dirt rich."

"Come now, Virg," said Rose, stirring in the back. "Why do you have to go and fill the boy's head with stories like that?"

I met Rose's gaze in the rearview mirror.

"I tell no lies," said Virgil. "And I never let facts complicate the truth of a matter."

Rose should have given me more credit. I knew there were gaps in Virgil's tales. I knew there were things he wasn't telling me, details he was trying to fog over. His stories never quite lined up. When he said he'd been selling tailings from a mine in Nevada, he'd also been playing the Badger game in Baton Rouge. He'd given me at least four versions of where he was when the stock market crashed. Virgil would have needed several lifetimes behind him already, would've had to be wandering for several centuries, to have accumulated the experiences he claimed as his own. After a while I stopped keeping track, and I wondered if the day would come when I'd be telling someone younger than me, "Virgil Ray? Hell, I worked with him in '39. The man was an artist. He was one of the greats." I wondered if people would nod and smile and think to themselves, "Yeah, sure you did."

Maybe Virgil was right, though. Maybe America was just one long con, a Ponzi scheme in which the payoff never came and the call-back never ended. Maybe the game was gaffed and the bunco artist was simply a one-eyed man in the land of the blind.

We were part of the next great wave, to hear Virgil tell it. The game had once been limited to railroads and riverboats, which tended to funnel people along similar routes. No sooner had one team of hucksters passed through than another team followed.

"The marks were getting picked clean, and more and more often confidence men found their scams had already been played," said Virgil.

"But the automobile has opened up the greater American heartland to our trade. Once was, you were hostage to a train schedule. Now you can get in and get out quick as a blink. The automobile makes getaways a done deal. Of course," he looked across at me, pointedly, "have to make sure you don't flood the engine."

I let that pass.

"Riverboat artists like Canada Bill opened the way for Count Lustig and Yellow Kid Weil. Just as Weil and Lustig cleared the way for Rose and me. Just as Rose and me are paving the way for you, Jack. Who knows what wonders, what new swindles you'll see in your day! The future just keeps getting brighter and brighter."

We drove past derelict farms and baked fields where crops hadn't grown in years. The sun was swollen on the horizon. Sky was red. Virgil didn't seem the least bit tired, though. He was on a roll and the stories kept coming as surely as the blacktop.

Some of the best confidence men hadn't even been men, he said. Ladies like Cassie Chadwick, who was born on a farm in Canada and drifted south, into New York City, where she tangled herself up in the family tree of Andrew Carnegie. Miss Chadwick, apparently, had passed herself off as the secret daughter and heir apparent to the aging bachelor. She'd parlayed a few well-planted rumors into a sizable fortune.

"That was back at the turn of the century," said Virgil. "She took the banks for twenty million—on little more than gossip."

Then there was Chicago May—undisputed Queen of the Con, according to Virgil.

"When she was thirteen, May stole money from her father's strongbox in Ireland and ran off to a better world in America. Some say she rode with the Dalton gang out west for a while, though I'm not entirely sure on that account. Later, she opened a brothel that was really just a front for a well-oiled Badger game. Ran it like it was a military operation. Had half the police department on her payroll. She specialized in follow-ups. Blackmail, that is. She'd contact the distraught men after the initial payment, saying she was running a little short this month and would they mind helping out. If they balked, she'd ask if she might speak with their wives for a moment. A highly effective call-back, that one."

Later in life, Chicago May claimed she'd gone straight and "seen the light." But Virgil had it on good sources that she'd done no such thing.

"The greats never go clean," he said. "They stay in the game, play it to the end. Anything less would be—well, it'd be sacrilege."

Fred Buckminster? Only the greatest con man that ever lived.

Colonel Jim Porter? Only the same.

"They called Fred Buckminster 'The Deacon,'" said Virgil, "on account of his doleful ways, though he seemed cheerful enough when I worked with him."

"You knew Fred Buckminster?" said Rose from the backseat.

Heck, even I had heard of Fred Buckminster.

"I did," said Virgil. "The Deacon and the Colonel both. The Count, as well. I knew 'em all." Then, with a look and a smile tossed my way, "I even knew Jack McGreary, back when he was young and just starting out."

"Wheaties McGreary?" she said. "You knew him, too?"

"I did," Virgil said. "Knew him well."

"Is it true, then?" Rose asked, "what they say about him? That he was seven feet tall and made of steel?"

Virgil threw back his head and laughed. He floored the Nash and we almost took flight in the gathering dark, heading home. Virgil's eyes shone like polished marbles in the light of the dashboard and the road rushed towards us, coming in as a blur.

That night, while Virgil and Miss Rose slept, I made a list:

Suitcase Simpson
Henry the Horse
Yellow Kid Weil
Canada Bill
Sigmund Engel
Kid Dropper
Soapy Smith
Count Lustig
Charley Fisher

Colonel Jim
The Deacon
Cassie Chadwick
Chicago May
Virgil Ray
Rose Scheible

And at the very bottom I added:

Jack McGreary

And I wondered if that name belonged on that list.

Thirty-seven

During our days in Silver, I'd kick around town a bit, watch the trains pull out. I would drop off my laundry, usually at a cleaners, but sometimes at one of the new washaterias, where you operated your own machines. It was an idea out of Fort Worth that seemed to be catching on, though I don't know why. Saving pennies, but operating your own wringer? Where's the marketability in that? Still, it was nice to be part of something so modern.

Some afternoons I'd soap down the Ambassador in the alley with bucket and sponge, wash the bugs from the grille and the dust from the wheel wells. I'd polish the fenders till that ol' girl gleamed. Other days, I might play the pinball boards in the hotel lobbies and tobacco shops, a nickel a turn to watch marbles cascade down pins. Soon enough, though, I would drift back to my old ways and my old haunt: the library.

The Silver City Library was bigger than the one in Paradise Flats, and it wasn't *archaic,* either. It had new books and current newspapers and a top floor crammed high with archives and assorted documents. I would load up on books using a card issued in the name of "C. Tweed" (I figured if anything went wrong they could shake down Cyrus instead). When Virgil came in to Charley Wong's for a late-afternoon breakfast of pie and pie, scratching himself and yawning still, he'd often find me at the back booth behind a pile of sign-outs—and he'd sigh.

"You and your books," he'd say with a sad little shake of his head. "Nothing worth learning can be found in a book."

This always rankled me. "You wouldn't know, though, would you?" I said. "Not having read any."

Virgil went through the newspaper at Charley Wong's—morning and afternoon editions—mainly to search society page obituaries or to check his horoscope. "All that spiritual hokum," as he said. "Soothsayers and numerologists. Table-tippers and glass-ball gazers. Pure bunk." But there he was anyway, checking the astral predictions of Belle Bart or the algorithmic forecasts of Elaine. And you might find him thumbing through a dimestore Western or a creased copy of *Skullhead the Pirate* someone left behind, but that was about it.

"I've read more'n my share," he said. "I've read plenty. I can pick up any book, read the first two words and learn everything I need to know about it right there. I extrapolate." (He pronounced it *extra-pole-ate*, which I didn't think was entirely right.)

"That's quite the trick," I said, trying to ignore him so I could concentrate on the Plato I'd been plumbing.

"Take a book that's divided into four parts," he said. "Same thing. I can read the first two words at the start of each part, put 'em together, and tell you the moral of the whole entire thing."

"In the," I said.

He looked at me. "In the what?"

"In the."

"What the hell are you—"

"Holy Bible," I said. "First two words. You can extra-pole-ate an entire religion from that, can you?"

"Maybe not," he said. "But I can sum it up in three: *Thou shalt not.* There's your religion in a thimble. Susie!" He waved the waitress over. "I'm thinking blueberry today."

It was the same gum-snapping girl as before, the one with the accent from all over, and friendly as ever.

"For you, anything."

The Silver City Library was a repository of secrets as well as books. I had found this out when I started exploring the darker reaches of the highest floor, which were packed tight with land titles and deeds, with wills and national research reports, with military roll calls.

Among the many and varied schemes of Roosevelt's Works Projects Administration was something called the Historical Records Survey.

The WPA's manual labor projects were a fount of beneficence, true. But not all the unemployed souls out there were fit for digging ditches. Downtrodden authors, not accustomed to carrying anything heavier than a deadline, were put to work compiling roadside travel guides that mapped out America mile by mile—the very same travel guides we'd been using to our advantage when charting our forays. Souls of a more professorial inclination had been sent out to sift through the attics and filing cabinets of America. Teams of researchers cataloged and collated and compiled. They searched through church basements and courthouse cellars, city hall closets and moldering old libraries, archiving newspaper articles, obituaries, and birth notices and culling records both military and judicial. The WPA had even sent men tromping through graveyards, checking the names and dates on headstones. With the wonder of modern microfilm, everything was now being transferred into a permanent photographic record.

Once I got poking around in the library, I found it hard to stop. Virgil would talk about the legendary bunco men, and then I'd sift through the records and find that Canada Bill had died penniless and alone, and that his body had been dumped in a pauper's grave.

Virgil would tell me about the glorious gold-brick swindle, how men like Tom O'Brien and Reed Waddell had refined it, painting lead bricks—but adding a plug of solid gold in the middle, which they would then gouge out and pass to the marks so they could have it evaluated. Virgil would tell these stories, but he'd forget to mention how O'Brien and Reed had had a falling out, as I'd discovered, or how O'Brien had shot and killed his former friend.

Lustig? He was sitting in a prison even as Virgil regaled us with tales of the Count's exploits, doing twenty years' hard time with no chance of parole. And Lustig was not a young man.

Henry the Horse? Drank himself to death. They found him in an alleyway. He was there for three days before anyone noticed the stink.

Suitcase Simpson? He'd died in Sing Sing years ago. He'd had three previous convictions, all minor, but was still given mandatory life as a fourth-time offender.

Cassie Chadwick, the Canadian farm girl who'd passed herself off as a Carnegie? Ten years in the state penitentiary. Died there.

Soapy Smith, up in Skagway? Shot to death by vigilantes.

A high number of Virgil's heroes had ended their lives by their own hand. Like Philip Musica, who pulled off a $21 million pharmaceutical version of three-card monte, moving imaginary inventory back and forth among imaginary warehouses. He kept that particular thimble-rig going right through the Crash of '29 and for several years after that before it finally collapsed. When the federal agents came for him, Musica invited them into his elegant home with good grace, excused himself for a moment, and then stepped inside his bathroom and politely put a bullet through his head.

What of the French con woman, Marthe Hanau, Queen of the Financial Shell Game? Found dead in her prison cell beside a bottle of sleeping pills and a note that read, *"I am the mistress of my fate."*

And what of Chicago May? All I could find on her was a weathered news clipping from 1935, when she'd been arrested at the age of sixty for soliciting men on the street. Her price: two dollars. There were no takers.

It would seem there were fates worse than a bayou ambush and a bullet-riddled automobile.

THIRTY-EIGHT

The only time I ever saw Virgil look truly scared was when he told me about the Travelers.

I first heard about them during a street con in Wichita Falls. We were running a Tennessee Switch when Virgil suddenly called it off. I was at my dumb yokel best, in town with a wallet full of money. "Golly," I said to the fellow Virgil had roped in, a thin smiling man who was all too eager to join us. "If you would hold my winnings for me, I'd sure like a turn on the dance floor with Ella May over at the Rio."

The scam had Virgil cutting in, saying he would hold my money-stuffed wallet instead. "I'll walk it around the block as a test of faith," he'd say, after which I was to declare my mistrust of him and insist that the mark hold it instead. We'd send the mark around the block with my Mish-roll wallet while we held his bankroll as collateral. At which point we would disappear. That was the idea anyway. But when Virgil returned, he grabbed me by the arm without breaking stride and said to me—loudly enough for the mark to hear—"Only safe thing to do is take this money to a bank, young man." Then to the mark, "Good day, sir."

It was only after Rose had whisked us away that Virgil explained what had happened. "I was walking the block," he said, "when I saw a truck filled with children of every size and a lady waiting to one side. The kids looked just like our mark."

"Okies?" I said.

"Too rich for Okies," he said. "This wasn't no barefoot brood turfed from the fields. No. These were Travelers. I'd bet it on a blindfolded toss of the tat."

And though he didn't know what their particular game was, or how they'd go about beating a Tennessee Switch, Virgil wasn't keen to find out. "You always listen to that voice inside you," he said. "When something don't quite seem right—there's usually a reason."

Maybe it was a certain turn of phrase the man had used, or the faint echo of a lilt in what he said, but *something* had set the nape of Virgil's neck to tingling. And spotting that truck with its Catholic-sized family around the corner only confirmed this.

The Travelers were Irish, Virgil said, out of Carolina mainly, though they had also taken root in secretive pockets across the deeper South: Georgia, Alabama, into Mississippi, too. There were some Scottish families as well, and they'd settled in Cincinnati, where they were known as the Terrible Williamsons, on account of the surname of their leading family.

As Rose put gravel between us and Wichita Falls, Virgil filled me in. I leaned up from the backseat.

"They're known as 'tinkers' back in Ireland," Virgil said. "Out here they're simply Travelers. Left their homes during a time of famine. Caused by a potato blight, I believe. Fungus rotted the tubers from the inside out. And much like our own Okies, they found themselves pushed off of land they'd worked but never owned. A good deal came to America. Worked as traveling tinsmiths, peddlers, craftsmen. Moved from town to town. Took to thieving easily enough, and to horse trading and horse stealing, and combinations of the two. They branched out from the tinker trade. Started running fortune-telling tents, targeting true believers and other such members of the easily duped. They specialize in the 'blessing' of money, and the installing and removing of curses, that sort of thing. They say the Travelers can pluck your eye from its socket *and you won't even see them do it.* They belong to clans, speak in code, consider themselves a breed apart. The Toogoods. The Gallaghers. The Carols. Gormans. Reillys. Only a handful of surnames among the lot of them."

Not unlike my ancestral isles of St. Kilda, I thought, and the crofters who had once lived there. *If you don't want to be the horse's hoofprints, you have to be the hoof.* An old saying, that.

Virgil warned that an offshoot of the Carolina Travelers had moved west and taken up camp near Port Connor, down on the Gulf.

"O'Malley Settlement," he said. "A community of caravans and gaudy homes two thousand strong. Religious shrines everywhere. They're devout, you see. And tribal. Have their own laws, their own customs, their own rules of behavior that come complete with hard justice. Worst punishment is exile. Worse even than kneecapping, I'm told, because once you're outside the circle, you're never allowed back in."

Lately, Virgil said, the Travelers had been branching out further: phony home repairs, business stings, and especially blackmail.

Rose turned onto blacktop. Aimed us towards Texas. The hood ornament of the Nash was a compass needle pointing home.

"When they're running a Badger, they don't even bother pleasuring the mark first," said Virgil. "They send in a ten-year-old girl and then immediately barge in, swinging ax handles and roaring how the terrified dupe was trying to defile their virginal lamb. They squeeze that rind dry. One high-level scion of the De Valu family? Out in Baltimore, a man with political aspirations? He's been on the hook to the Travelers for seven years now. He's damn near broke. They say half the homes in O'Malley Settlement were paid for by a single indiscretion on his part."

Rumor was, the Travelers out of O'Malley Settlement were working these parts now, the Toogoods and Murphys, mainly. The crime syndicates gave them a wide berth, even in Kansas City, where the mob owned everything.

"Word is," said Virgil, "Travelers have taken up residence in Fayetteville. Word is, they're aiming to take over the entire Southwest."

You didn't want to cross paths with O'Malley Travelers. Most confidence men eschewed unnecessary violence as unbecoming to the craft, I knew that from Virgil. Travelers were different.

"They'll bring in heavies on the slightest of provocations," said Virgil. "Hell, they even contract out their services. Have a menu of prices available: fifteen dollars will buy you a blackjack to the back of someone's head, twenty-five a sandbag. Five dollars will buy you a straight punch to the face. If the jaw breaks, they tack on an extra two clams."

And if you wanted someone dead, well, that was open to negotiation, too.

"They're born into the life," said Virgil. "Trained for it. Travelers set their sights on you, can't talk your way out of it. All you can do is pay them off and pray you don't offend their Irish sensibilities. They'll kill a man over a card game. They'll kill a man on a point of pride. You steal a penny from a Traveler or a suitcase of fifties, makes no difference, they'll arrange a meeting with your Maker in either case. Those card-sharps I took for the tear-up in Albany? Had they been Travelers out of O'Malley I'd be sitting here dead right now. Hell, they don't even kill a man decently. Make him beg for his life first, just so his last moments on Earth are stripped of any dignity."

Virgil said the Travelers were now buying up carnivals. "To the customer service strategy of redlighting, they've added the Irish art of kneecapping." Hard to imagine how the carnie circuit could have gotten any darker than it already was. But there you go. Things could always get worse.

Thirty-nine

Good as I was getting at playing the angles, my would-be career as a pool-hall hustler was short-lived. Came and went on the same breath of wind.

It started when Virgil tossed me a cue one day and said, "Let's see what you've got."

We were at a tavern in Silver City, escaping the heat and killing time, and I ran the table on him.

"Where'd you learn to do that?"

"Ninth-grade geometry," I said.

Virgil racked the balls for another game, to make sure this was no fluke. I let him break. And then I ran the table. Again.

Virgil played pool as though he could charm the balls into the pockets, as though *wanting* a ball to sink would somehow convince it to do so. But billiards isn't an art, it's a science. No element of jazz involved. No improvised rhythms. Just brute mathematics all the way. I didn't do any of the fancy, behind-my-back, aren't-I-the-clever-one, eyes-closed side shots. But I could work out an angle easily enough, and I could certainly choose the best odds. Didn't take a genius.

After our third straight game and Virgil's third straight loss—and didn't I regret not playing him for money—he said, "You should be hustling games."

Pool halls made Virgil nervous. They were usually on a second floor, up narrow stairs and with limited avenues of escape. You're surrounded by enemies—and they're armed. Armed with sticks. Long, pointy sticks. They even kept a selection of hard round projectiles close at hand. It was dangerous in every way.

"It's difficult getting out with your money and all major bones intact," said Virgil. In spite of that, he decided it was worth the risk. To me.

"Need to get far away from Silver, though," he said. "Someplace big enough to generate real money, but not so big that the halls are rigged."

Next morning, he spread out his WPA guides and filling-station maps and pinpointed the spot: Talmo, Kansas.

"Talmo?" said Miss Rose with a sigh. "Couldn't we go somewhere upscale for a change? Someplace with a proper opera house perhaps? Or at least where the people still have most of their teeth?"

"Talmo it is, then," said Virgil.

It took us a day and into the night to get there. We drove clear across the Oklahoma panhandle, into that sad state and out again, and along the way we passed a remarkable sight. A forest, taking root on the edge of a desert. Small trees, trying to grow. The hills bristled with them. I sat up, took notice.

"What is …"

"Shelterbelt," said Virgil. "A damn fool scheme if ever there was one. Two hundred million trees to be planted, a hundred miles deep, a thousand miles long. Greatest conservation program ever undertaken, that's what they're saying."

A swath of trees that would stretch from Texas to the Canadian border. Had never been anything like it. Idea was to break the winds and stop the erosion, to hold the water in the roots so the roots could retain the soil.

"If God can't make a tree grow out here, how in hell is Roosevelt going to?" asked Virgil. "Nothing more than boondoggling."

Virgil said it couldn't be done. But it was. Right in front of our eyes.

I saw the spindly trees, saw them holding back the winds, and I knew—I knew as sure as anything that it was going to work. We drove alongside it, this Dust Bowl forest, this improbable landscape. It looked like a pincushion turned inside out.

We passed a line of men from the Civilian Conservation Corps planting the trees, backs bent as the dust powdered past them.

"That'll be cottonwood mainly," said Virgil. "With a row of willow and ash, honeylocust or hackberry on either side. Knew a fella worked at one of the nurseries. Foolhardy is what it is. Know how long it takes for a tree to grow out here?" But I was transfixed at the sight of this undertaking, at the scale of it, at the foolish heroics involved, the courage and the naiveness. I knew what they were doing, recognized it for what it was. A wager, made in the face of enormous odds.

Virgil caught me staring out the window as the trees flitted past.

"There's no angle to play," he said. "Trust me, I've tried to come up with one. No money to be had in it."

He hit the accelerator and sped us away. The road arced east and the forest slipped out of sight again, like it had all been a mirage. It got me thinking maybe *we* were the mirage—ghosts passing through, made of equal parts smoke and dust—and it was the forest, struggling and small, that was real.

We arrived in Talmo well after midnight, with Virgil selecting our hotel solely on the basis of the band that was playing: Ronnie and the Rockets, or some such. Didn't matter. It was the sax player/pianist on the marquee outside that had caught Virgil's attention. "Billy Tipton? Goddamn! If I'd known he was playing, would'a left Silver sooner."

Virgil had an affinity for Billy Tipton. "Ought to have his own band," he said as we checked in. "The man plays a mean swing. He takes to hot jazz like no white boy I've ever seen. Sax or piano, makes no never mind. Billy's the best there ever was." Virgil wouldn't even let us drop our bags off, but herded us into the hotel's dance hall instead to catch the last of the licks. Tipton was on stage, blowing hot and cool at the same time, like a man caught between the two, and Virgil and Miss Rose were swept along on it.

Jazz is the art of improvising, same as running a con game: set moves played out in endless variations. *Jazz is art is magic is con.* All aspects of the same.

And yet.

Were times I do confess I yearned for the music I'd left behind—the twang of Slim William, say, or the hurtin' songs of Tom Phillips. I hadn't heard from the Men of Constant Sorrow in a long while, it seemed.

In the Talmo Hotel we had adjoining rooms, so I was spared the shadow play of sheets that night. Even then, I found it hard getting to sleep, the pulse-beat of Billy Tipton still echoing somewhere deep inside, like a secret trying to get out.

We waited till dusk the following day to find a pool hall.

Drove deep into the seedy side of things, past the squalor of tenements—open windows, women with children on hip, the wallpaper water-stained behind them, plaster moldings crumbling, the lights reduced to oil lamps—and I thought, *We have enough money right here, on us right now, to change your life.* And no sooner had the thought formed than another window-side vignette appeared, like photos in a slow-moving slide strip. Fire escapes crawled down the walls in rusted latticework. Some were heavy wrought-iron cages, others looked more like a tangle of mattress springs that had long since sprung. You'd hate to have to navigate an escape along one of those.

Virgil had scoped out a billiard hall that was seedy, but not too. One with a solid enough fire ladder on the side, in case of a quick dash from the second floor. He wouldn't let Rose wait in the car, not at that hour and not in that neighborhood. "Bars on the windows," he said as we drove through. "What does that tell you?"

"Tells me the thieves in Talmo have no style. Tells me they're as unsophisticated as they are ugly." She blew smoke into the air. Glowered at Virgil over being cut from the con.

"Wait for us back at the hotel," he said. And then: "Why are you fretting, anyway? I'll be fine."

"It's not you I worry about," she said.

Rose wouldn't budge on this. Instead of going back to the hotel, she parked in an alley, doors locked, engine idling, as Virgil and I took the stairs.

Just as well.

The room was sparsely populated with the usual assortment of pool-hall rats dressed in loose shirts and floppy hats. Virgil was clearly overdressed, but that was okay. He was the uncle. I was his nephew, and this was my coming-of-age pool-hall lesson. "Boy's first beer!"

Virgil shouted, annoying the room with the loudness of his ways, as was his intent. "Just passing through on our way to someplace better. Which don't exclude a whole lot, huh? Joking, of course. Fine town you have here."

Virgil was loud and drunk. I was big and dumb, always missing my shots—but just barely.

As the room slowly filled up, Virgil picked his mark, a round-bellied man with gold teeth and a chorus of laughers behind him who took everything he said to be the height of hilarity. The type of man with a lot of small-souled pride riding on his friends' opinion of him. The kind you could lock into a death grip. The kind who couldn't turn back once the game had entered the darkness.

Virgil played a round with him and lost. Then, dropping some coins on the table and hollering for more booze, he shouted at me, "You play him this time, Bucky, yer a fine kid."

And I did. Always just missing. Always just losing.

The night ground on. The room was dank with sweat and the smell of salt, as though the very walls were perspiring. I had to chalk my palms after every shot.

We ratcheted the bets upwards, even as we lost, till Virgil suddenly declared it was double-or-nothing, winner take all. "Everything on the boy!" he yelled. He seemed so soused, so pickle-eyed and owl-stewed, that the bartender tried to talk him out of it, but our friend with the belly just waved the bartender away, smiled gold at me, and said, "Time you became a man. Ain't that right, fellas?" They yuckled at this like it was something funny. It reminded me of the gobbling of turkeys.

We were well past the $200 mark by now, and our round friend had to call on his gobblers for money. They threw in the bills, knowing their champion would take this hick and his drunkard of an uncle.

And then, wouldn't you know it, instead of just *missing*, I started just *making* the shots. Balls that had once rolled past the pocket now tipped in. Angles that I couldn't quite get, I now could. Game went back and forth, but didn't I sink that final eight and take a stack of cash?

"If we're gonna pop your cherry, gotta go now," Virgil said, voice slurring. "Best of the bordello will be picked over by the time we get there. Don't want to be stuck with sloppy seconds, Buck." Then, turning to the crowd with a broad smile, "I plan on giving my sister's boy a well-rounded education."

But the man with the golden smile barred our way with his stick. Throwing a comment over his shoulder, he said, "Rack 'em, boys." And then to Virgil. "Another round."

Virgil protested the time. "If I'm going to get the boy's dinky stinky, we have to go right now."

"Rack 'em," said the man with the metallic smile.

So around and around we went.

Three more games, and me winning each one by the thinnest of margins. The man's jocularity had turned to bile. He hit the balls harder than necessary. I kept just tapping them in. Kept just winning. Kept taking the man's cash. He was caught in a spiral at this point, in deep and chasing his own money. He tossed back a chunk of ice from his drink, spit it back into his glass. "Davey," he said. "Give me your watch."

"Jesus, Roland, that's from my—"

"Give me the watch. Y'owe me on that bank loan as it is."

"But Rolly, that's from—"

Rolly glared at him. The watch was tossed onto the table. "Worth a hundred at least," said Rolly.

"I can't take a man's watch," I said. "Let's call it a night, Uncle Tuck."

"Boy's right," said Virgil.

But Rolly with the gold in his mouth wouldn't hear of it. "Last game," he said. "Different cues." As though I had some kind of magical stick that was defeating him.

He handed me the crookedest piece of hickory I'd ever seen. I decided to harp on this, like he was outsmarting me, even though it didn't matter. It was the angle of contact at the end of the cue that mattered. Long as I got that right, I would still win.

"Can't use this stick," I said. "It's shite."

Rolly was chalking his own cue, smiled at this like he'd caught me on something. "Shite?" he said. "*Shite?* Where you from, boy?"

I rolled the cue across the felt, watched it wobble up and down. "My granny's knees are straighter'n this," I said.

"Just play the man, will you?" said Virgil. "So we can getcha to the cat house 'fore last call."

"I asked you a question," said Rolly. "I asked you where you're from."

"Around," I said.

"Around where?"

"Abilene," I lied.

"I mean your people. Where're they from? Originally."

"Cape Breton," I said, and this provoked a bark of laughter from Rolly.

"Cape Whoosit?" He was mugging for the crowd. "Never heard of no Cape Whoosit."

"Breton," I said. "It's an island or a state or something up in Canada. Father came from Scotland. My mother was Scandinavian."

"Scandahoovian?"

"Finnish."

"Scottish *and* Scandahoovian?" And then, grinning in anticipation of the jape he was about to make, he stepped in close enough for me to smell the malt on his breath. "So. You're cheap *and* boring?"

Down he went.

"Don't get up," I said.

He got up.

And down he went. Harder this time. And this time, he didn't get up.

Slowly, I uncurled my right hand. Fist was throbbing. I looked around. No one said a word. "He was baiting me," I said. "You all saw that."

The man was moaning now, like a kitten. His nose was smeared across his face, blood running like it was on tap. That would have been the first blow. The man's jaw looked to be dislocated, or worse. That would have been the second. You could see a nugget or two of gold on the floor, in there among the blood. That would be his teeth.

I picked up the pile of money from the side of the table. Folded it carefully, put it in my pocket, pushed it down deep. I tossed the time-piece back to Davey. "You can have your watch," I said. "It's a piece of shite."

They parted as I moved through them, and Virgil followed, struck mute by what had happened.

I walked down the stairs. Out the door.

On the street, Virgil started to pick up his pace. "Slow down," I said. Sure enough, I heard the door open behind us. "Don't you turn around," I said to Virgil. "Don't be playing the hinge, looking back like that."

It was like with dogs, how if you run that triggers a chase response. Had we fled, they would have come charging. Instead, I came to a stop. Deliberately. I stood under a streetlamp and said to Virgil, "Scold me, like we really are family."

So Virgil wagged a finger at me. I hung my head. We stepped around the corner—and then bolted, into the alley and the waiting arms of an idling Nash Ambassador.

We sped away, with Virgil and me in the backseat. He looked at me, and I could see he was still shaken by what had happened. A long silence passed between us before he spoke.

"Jesus, Jack. You broke that man's face."

"He had it coming," I said.

"I don't know that he did," said Virgil.

"It was shifting," I said. "Couldn't you feel it starting to shift? The mood. The mocking in his voice. I was becoming the target of mirth. Sure enough, mirth will turn to contempt, and contempt will turn to attack. If I hadn't taken him down, we wouldn't have been able to walk out of there. There were five of them. They come at us with pool cues, and what did you plan on doing then? Can you take five men? I can't. They wouldn't have stepped aside for us. They would never have let us go. I could feel the room shifting." I looked at Virgil. "Couldn't you?"

The streetlamps and store lights flickered past. On Virgil's face was a look I hadn't seen before, something that resembled respect, maybe even fear—and aren't those two so often entwined?

Virgil cleared his throat, said, "We'll keep you out of the pool halls from now on, if that's all right."

"Fine with me," I said. "Think I cracked a bone."

Which is to say, I hadn't gotten out of there entirely intact, either.

FORTY

South of Talmo, they were turning back the rivers. Building reservoirs, pooling the water for future fields and orchards as yet unborn. They were folding the creeks in on themselves.

Where once shallow streams had spread out into thinner creeks and the creeks had disappeared into an arid landscape, the flow was being redirected, collected into lakes and ponds, the way a man might cup water in his hands—like it was something precious.

Boondoggling or not, they were building bridges and viaducts, they were draining ditches and tackling typhoid, they were running a million miles of sewerage connections and blacktop highways over and under and through this Great Land and back again, interconnecting us in a web of make-work projects. Forests on the open plains, water in the desert.

On our way back to Silver, with the heat rising in wavering sheets, Virgil pulled over at one such irrigation lock. "We'll take a dip. It's hot as Hades," he said, with the air of a man who's been there.

My fist was still throbbing, even though Rose had bound it in a mummy-wrap of clothes to keep the swelling down. I didn't feel much like a swim, but Virgil went ahead and peeled off his clothes, right down to his BVDs, and then cannonballed in from the highest embankment. Came up in mid-*whoop!* Must have started his holler while he was still underwater.

"Rose! Jack!" He tried to fan water at us, but we were too far away. He plunged in again, came back up like a carburetor gasping for fuel and grinning mad all the while.

Rose gathered her dress up and dangled her legs into the water, but she wasn't inclined for a full-scale plunge into the cold. She had loosened the buttons on her front, had opened it to the air, and was fanning herself now with a newspaper. Beads of sweat were pearled along her collarbone. A trickle slid down her chest, contouring inward and disappearing into cleavage. She fanned herself harder, raising goose bumps as she did. And in the flick of her wrist, I read the headline on the paper.

GERMANY ... MUSSOLINI ... STEEL ...

The newspaper stopped moving, and I saw that Rose was staring at me. She smiled, so faint it might have been a mirage.

"What exactly are you looking at?" she asked.

"Me? That headline. On the newspaper."

"Oh." She continued fanning herself. "And here I thought you were trying to sneak a peek at my bosoms." Then: "Look at you. Blushing like that. Here." She tossed me the paper. "You can read it. I'll just soak in my own sweat."

The headline was several days old. I remembered Virgil buying the paper on one of his change-raising walkabouts, and now it had resurfaced. Like a bad dream.

NAZI GERMANY SIGNS PACT OF STEEL WITH MUSSOLINI. US REASSERTS ITS MORAL NEUTRALITY.

Didn't need to read any more. I could see what was coming.

I handed the paper back. "Hate to see a lady melt like that," I said.

She started fanning the air onto her face and chest again. "Any hotter and I would have had to shed these clothes, I swear."

Virgil pulled himself up onto the bank, refreshed and invigorated. "Ha! You two don't know what you're missing! Take off your clothes, boy. Let's see what you're made of."

When I declined, he turned away from me and began toweling himself off with his undershirt. That was when I saw it: a second wound. Smaller than the first, and this one on his back: a round pucker of skin. A bullet hole.

"I thought you were only ever hit once," I said. He turned from drying his hair and looked back at me.

"I was."

As Virgil continued on his scalp, drying away with vigor, I turned to Rose. Was this true? Could it?

"The bullet passed right through him?" I asked.

"It did," she said. "Like he was hollow."

Virgil scooped up a lump of clay from the swimming hole, came over to us. "Rejuvenating mud!" he said. "Right here. We could sell shares in it."

His hair was still damp, and his clothes too. He picked up a chunk of dried clay now, let it crumble in his hand. "My late Pappie's ashes," he said, as the dust ran through his fingers. "Could very well be. And maybe this was his favorite fishing hole. Can you guard my money—here, I'll wrap it in a handkerchief with yours—so's I can scatter his remains behind that tree? Or maybe this dust is from angels, descended. The ones who fell with Lucifer. Maybe it'll help you cheat death and live forever. Maybe it's powdered luck."

He looked at me. "There's only three ways to draw a line through a man's chest and not hit any bones or vital organs. The bullet that got me followed one of those lines. It passed the heart, missed the vertebrae. Came out in a burst of pulp. Had that bullet been a nudge to the left going in, I would have died. A nudge to the right coming out, I would have been crippled for life. As it was, I bled for days and damn near died anyway. Spent three months in an army hospital, received last rites eight times. And I'm still here! You can't kill Virgil Ray that easily, boy. It'll take more than a long-bore rifle at close range to do that."

Rose stood up, brushed the dust from her dress. "We should be on our way. Silver City's still a long way off."

"The Krauts took the hospital," said Virgil, marble eyes shining now. "I ended up in a prison camp on starvation rations. But a man survives a bullet like that, he figures he can survive anything."

He waited for me to say something. "So what did you—"

"I escaped! Ha! That's what I did. Clean across enemy lines. They pinned a medal on my chest for that one, too."

"Escaped?"

"You can't kill me, Jack. You can cage me, but you can't kill me."

"Come along," said Rose. "Sun's going down, there's a chill setting in."

"I shared a cell with a pair of other officers," said Virgil as we walked down the hill to the car. "A Welshman named Edward Jones, and an Australian airman by the name of Hill—Cedric Hill. Both lieutenants in the British Army. The three of us were determined to get out, and I'd noticed something odd about the angle of the sun. On our afternoon work detail, it shone through the window in the equipment shed directly into the eyes of anyone inspecting it. I figured, if the three of us crouched down in plain sight, just beneath the window, we'd be invisible. And we were. As the other prisoners filed back to the barracks, we hid in the shed. Guard opened the door, stuck his head in, not ten feet in front of us, and then moved on. We ran, and were well in the woods before the camp siren ever went off."

Good story. Only wish it was true.

FORTY-ONE

The next day, as Virgil and Miss Rose were sleeping the light away, I went down to the Silver City Library, started pulling microfilm of U.S. military records. They had entire catalogs of personnel, of awards granted, honors discharged. My right hand was still throbbing, but my left hand was fine, so I scrolled through and made notes with it instead. Ambidextrous. Comes in useful at times.

There was no "V. Ray" listed under any of the roll calls. I went deeper into the archives, sifted through British reports instead, looking for Americans who'd signed up with them. Were a lot of names, but no "V. Rays," American or otherwise. I did find an "E. Jones" and a "C. Hill." There were many of both—apparently every Welshman on earth was named Jones—but there was only one Australian airman named *Cedric* Hill, and I traced him back to a POW camp not in Germany but in Turkey. Now, Cedric, he'd been held at the Yozgat prison, a particularly harsh billet by the sounds of it. Also at the camp? A lieutenant named E. Jones.

Jones and Hill had escaped, all right, that part was true, but not through any trick of sunlight. They had feigned madness and been transferred to a mental hospital in Constantinople along with a junior officer named G. Balsamo. They spent six months there. Jones and Hill were released just a few weeks before the Armistice, and they immediately submitted a report on how they had tricked the Turks with their antics. Jones and Hill, they were hoisted on shoulders and *huzzah*'d with great cheer after their release, and both of them went on to bigger and better things. But not Balsamo.

I went through the records of prisoner releases, week by week, looking for him. I checked the obituaries, too. But no. Balsamo hadn't died, or made the Armistice. Diagnosed with "delusional derangements of the brain," he was kept in the asylum for *another* six months and was released not into military custody but into the care of British doctors. He was quietly discharged a few months later, without any fanfare or final report I could find.

I lost track of him after that. It was as though he'd disappeared.

I left the library, stepping outside into a heat as itchy as dry hay, and made the long walk back to Wong's Café, my head full of questions. I was almost there—was about to cross the street—when I stopped. Looked around. The sidewalks were clear. A few window shoppers went by, wistful and walking slow. A truck rumbled past. A few motorists. Kids chasing a cat down the side of the street. Nothing unusual, but then ...

Kitty-corner from Wong's Café, a dark-green sedan was parked to one side. It was half-hidden behind a vegetable stand, but I'd recognize a 1939 Graham Supercharger anywhere, with its sharp-angled grille, slanted upwards like a shark about to break clear of the water, and those bulging headlights staring hard ahead. I'd seen that car before. Somewhere in Texas, to the south maybe. I walked slowly, under the shadow of an awning. I could see Colorado plates and someone behind the wheel. The motor was running. The Graham Supercharger that I'd seen—in Sweetwater? Plainview?—hadn't had out-of-state plates. I would have remembered that. So it must have been a different Supercharger.

I was getting jittery, I thought, the way Virgil was. There was no shark about to pounce, just a car idling on a street corner, waiting for someone. And I saw how easy it would be to let your nerves undo you, how easy it would be to get spooked.

I knew there was nothing to worry about, but still. Who parks that close to a vegetable stand? And so, to be safe, and knowing full well I was letting my imagination get the better of me, I doubled back, slipped into the alley, and entered the café through the kitchen instead.

Charley was at his cutting board. He looked up as I passed. "Jack," he said with a nod.

"Charley," I replied.

He never did ask questions. Always was one of his finer qualities.

Rose and Virgil were at their posts, a bit more hungover than usual, and I could see a mound of cigarettes in the ashtray.

"Wheaties," Rose said with a smile.

I slid into the booth, considered mentioning the sedan I'd seen outside to Virgil, but rejected the notion. It would only feed the nervousness that already afflicted him, and anyway, I knew there was nothing to it.

Instead, I asked, "Who's Balsamo?"

Virgil looked up from his empty cup. Stared at me, not angrily, though. It was almost like he'd been expecting it. "Balsamo?" he said. "Now, where'd you hear a name like that?"

"I was at the archives. Down at the library. Happened upon some military records."

"Did you?" said Virgil. "How fortuitous."

"So, who is he?"

Virgil lit a cigarette, clouded the air with it. "Balsamo?" he said. "Just somebody I used to know. He died a long time ago."

"Died?"

"In the Great War. Took a bullet. Never recovered."

Rose's smile had vanished. She gave me a look of cold granite. "I think I have a paper cut," she said. "Here on my pinkie. Would you like to put some lemon juice on it, Jack?"

I could have pressed the matter, I suppose—there was no hostility in Virgil's gaze, just a certain weariness, as though a stray dog he'd been trying to lose had shown up once again.

You have to kill a monster three times before it stays down, I'd learned that from Bela Lugosi. How many times do you have to drive a stake through your past before it'd do likewise? Would I ever be able to shed Paradise Flats? Or would Paradise Flats pursue me across the plains as well?

It made me think of some letters I'd seen in Rose's closet, bound up in string, unopened.

I had helped put Rose to bed one drunken night, Virgil snoring on the Murphy bed with his shoes still on, Rose kicking uselessly at her own. I got them off for her and took them to the closet. And there, in the corner, was a faded hatbox, and in that box was a stack of envelopes. I untied the string, rifled through, felt the heft of them in my hand. The letters had all been sent to the same address in Beaumont, Texas, and had come back marked "Return to Sender," c/o Charley Wong's Café. Every one, unopened. But that wasn't Rose's name on the top left-hand corner of the envelopes. And it wasn't to Rose that those letters had been returned. It was Avanna Sherrill. That's who'd been sending letters to Beaumont, and that's who'd been collecting these same letters when they were mailed back.

Virgil Ray and Rose Scheible were made of smoke, it would seem. They didn't exist. Whether G. Balsamo or Avanna Sherrill did was a matter of debate, too, I suppose. It would seem a person could slip into that hovering dusk, caught between evening and nightfall, between pretending and being, and never come out again—the way a man might play at being mad, might play it so well that even he didn't know whether it was real anymore.

FORTY-TWO

One of the first things the Nazis had done when they took power in Germany was to ban jazz.

"And they were right to do it!" said Virgil. "Ol' Adolph was right to fear jazz. Because jazz—it's restless, always shifting, can't be contained. You have to ban it outright if you want people to march like that, as though they had a ramrod up their behinds."

We were walking along the tracks after a late night of swing, with Virgil still wound up and Miss Rose going on ahead, her arms held out for balance, like she was walking the high wire. A cat loped by, limp rat dangling from its mouth. Virgil, his hat pushed back and suspenders dangling, face still sweaty and smiling, started to sing "With Plenty of Money and You" in a key of his own making.

"Hey, Virgil," I said. "How come we never pull our scams in the colored sections of towns?"

He stopped singing, said, "The colored sections?"

"You know," I said. "When we're on the grift. Why don't we ever run swindles on colored folk? They have shops and stores and no shortage of dupes, I imagine, just like anywhere else. Seems to me a pigeon drop or a Tennessee Switch would work well."

Virgil wouldn't even pull a till exchange on a colored man. At one shop, the clerk had said, "I'll need to get Mr. Rawls." Well, out comes Mr. Rawls, smiling in a "What can I do for you, gentlemen?" manner. He's a colored man and he says, "Of course, officer. You go ahead and swap tills." But Virgil couldn't do it. He just stammered and said it'd be fine, no need to remove the money. Back in the Nash on the way out of that town I asked Virgil why he hadn't followed through.

"The man had enough of a hill to climb," Virgil had said. "Don't need us adding to it."

But I couldn't see how that mattered, and I said as much now as we walked along the tracks. A mark was a mark was a mark. What difference did it make if he'd had a hard time of it or not?

Virgil stopped. Rose continued on, arms out and wobbling. He looked at me. "I never pegged you as anti-Negro," he said.

"I'm not," I said. "At least, not so far as I know."

He pushed on ahead.

I caught up. "Seems the only fair thing to do is rob the colored folks same as we would anyone else."

Virgil snapped at that. "We don't rob! How many times I have to tell you? *When they hand you their money, it doesn't count as stealing.*" He stomped on, fuming now.

Thing was, Virgil had no compunction about swindling Chicanos, and it seemed to me they were having a hard time of it, too.

"Yeah, but no one's lynching Chicanos," Virgil said when I brought this up. He stomped on farther ahead along the tracks, his zoot hanging loose on him.

Virgil also drew the line at the very, very poor. And the very, very old, unless they were shamelessly rich—in which case, somehow, they were to blame for their own dupeness. But for the most part, Virgil avoided the toothless, prune-eating set. Which was odd, because they made excellent marks, it seemed to me: they were lonely, getting forgetful, looking for someone to talk to, sitting on savings and overly trusting. And if we did get nabbed?

"Put an old person on a witness stand," Virgil had said himself, "and they get addled and confused."

So why weren't we targeting them as well?

"Because I'm playing the odds, is why. Purgatory, I can get through. I can do a hundred years on my head, if I had to. But wiping out an old lady's life's savings? There's no bargaining down that sentence. It's straight to Hell."

Virgil's own form of Pascal's Wager.

Purgatory was God's anteroom, as I understood it. An in-between world, not quite Hell, but the next thing to it. Sort of a twilight holding pen for lost souls, to see if you were worthy of hellfire. Now, we Calvinists had no need for such a place, preferring instead the stark beauty of Damned or Not Damned. Was no hedging of the bets with us. Robbing a millionaire or robbing a sweet, shawl-wrapped grandmother, frail in her old age, made no never mind.

"Anyway," said Virgil. "It's cowardly, matching wits against someone who's losing theirs."

One of his partners, he told me, had cleaned out the life's savings of an eighty-year-old man who was dying of some sort of cancer. "Took his house. Everything," said Virgil. We walked along a bit and then he said, "It ended our partnership."

"But the man was dying," I said. "He was going anyway."

"That's just it," said Virgil. "He never got a chance to rebuild, to be wiser for it."

It was like trying to catch smoke in a net, pinning Virgil down.

"We're not common thugs and cutpurses," he insisted for the hundredth time, as though repeating something often enough would make it so.

"Sure," Rose said, calling back to us. "Reg'lar Robin Hoods. That's us."

"We are," said Virgil. "'Cept we don't limit ourselves to the rich."

"And instead of giving to the poor we keep it for ourselves," I pointed out.

"Yes, yes—but those details aside," said Virgil, "we're exactly just like Robin Hood."

The tracks snaked through the railyards and loading docks, and we could see the molten glow of distant fires, where the vagabonds and raggedy men were stirring. Men who might yet have wedding bands or pocket-watches hidden away in their tattered bedrolls, men who might have some money still, men we would never target.

Even Virgil had rules. Even Virgil had a code that he followed. It might be contradictory and inconsistent, but it was still a code. And if someone like Virgil couldn't live a life that was amoral, then maybe that was the proof I needed that amoral didn't exist.

The ache had gone from my hand, but I never was able to make a proper fist again.

FORTY-THREE

Geordie Dee was a colored man who'd known his way around a con, Virgil said. "He was from some backwater burg, Asswipe, Kentucky, or Jonesboro, Arkansas, or some such. But the man was an artist."

We were back in our booth at Charley Wong's, planning the future: Rose wreathed in smoke, Virgil with his WPA guides and filling-station maps opened in front of him. We'd returned from sparse hunting along the Canadian River, and Virgil was scouring the map for any oversights on our part. He ticked off the places we'd passed through: Raton, Farmington, Clovis, Lubbock, Hugo, Great Bend, Goodland—an ever-widening arc that circled the borderlands of Texas, of Oklahoma and Kansas, of New Mexico. We'd even gone as far north as Nebraska at one point, hitting McCook on the Republican River. It was taking us longer and longer to reach an area the Nash hadn't swept through already.

"We need to go somewhere better," said Virgil. "I'm tired of dealing with peckerwoods and rubes. No offense, Jack."

"None taken."

"Someplace more urbane," said Miss Rose. "Someplace with a proper opera house."

While we studied our maps, a beggar came into the café. A grubby old rummy, he gave Mr. Wong a sad-eyed what-for and was sent on his way with a few coins and some boiled drumsticks Charley had used in a broth.

Virgil leaned in to us, whispered, "See that? Ol' Charley just got scammed. Vagabond's shoes were tied up with twine. You notice that? But the soles were still good. So why the twine? That was a professional sobber."

Virgil circled a clutch of towns we had missed on an earlier pass through Shawnee, then called for a slice of rhubarb and brown sugar. Susie the waitress brought it over, flirting less now that Rose was with us.

The conversation had drifted from opera houses and the lack thereof to former partners and the lessons they might offer.

"Geordie Dee was the best monte player I ever knew," said Virgil. "Was a privilege working the con with Geordie. Usually he'd deal, but often as not he'd play the shill, winning money so clean and easy it drove the white boys wild with distraction. '*If a Negro can win, then sure as hell I should be able to!*'"

Geordie was credited with inventing a scam, Virgil told us, something that put him in the hallowed company of Count Lustig and Yellow Kid Weil.

"They call it the Texas Twist," said Virgil. "On account of where Geordie perfected it."

The game played on anti-racial feelings, and Texas was never in short supply of those.

"It was a *reverse* monte," explained Virgil. "One Geordie cooked up in Alabama when he noticed how difficult it had become to rope in suckers, what with the number of shell games and card dealers that had burnt so many of the towns. Cops were cracking down on depot workers, and it was getting tough to earn an honest living. So Geordie figures, why not hit the fellows who *know* monte is rigged and think they're too clever to be taken? They always did make the best marks. Throw in an appeal to white bigotry, and hoo-boy! You've got yourself a game!"

As Virgil described it, Geordie would play a loud-talking simpleton, a country rube in bare feet and overalls waving around a fat Mish roll he said he'd scammed from a "white" insurance company. He'd approach the meanest, reddest neck he could find at a filling station or café and ask him if he knew the way to some local arena of ill repute. "Then, as they're talking, I happen by, say, 'Hey, I know the street, but ... not sure if they take to Negroes down there.' Well, Geordie keeps talking, how he's going to get himself a white woman, saying how he prefers white meat on a chicken, how it's more juicier. I throw a glance at the mark. Geordie says, 'Hol' my money, so's I can go'n take me a dump,' playing the Stepin Fetchit for all he was worth. I would hold Georgie's roll of money, mutter darkly to the mark, feel out his sentiments. On rare occasions the fellow would defend Negroes, saying Geordie was just a bad seed and we shouldn't judge them all by that. When that happened we blew the fellow off, went fishing for someone else instead. For the most part, though, the marks seethed at the thought of a colored man with a white girl. 'So why not take this Negro for all his money?' I'd say. 'I've seen games of three-card monte. Why don't we play a twist on it? I'll deal, and throw signals your way.' You see," Virgil said, "a Texas Twist relies on using the mark's knowledge about monte—on turning that knowledge *against the mark*. It's a double dodge, and brilliant."

When Geordie came back, Virgil and the mark would cajole him into a few rounds of monte. Idea was to have the mark intentionally lose big, Virgil said, to encourage Geordie. They'd then take Geordie for his Mish roll, and meet up later to split the winnings. Except, of course, Virgil would never make the rendezvous. Sometimes they'd throw in a reverse Tennessee Switch as well, with Geordie insisting that he and the mark wrap their money in two different handkerchiefs for Virgil to hold. With a wink to the mark, Virgil would switch the packages—with the mark thinking he was coughing up his own money for a bigger roll. The surprise when he unwrapped it later on must have been staggering.

"Geordie was one of the best partners I ever had," said Virgil. "We made a fine marblecake team, the two of us. I loved that man."

"So what happened? You had a falling out?"

Virgil looked off to one side, and far away. "Geordie never cared for jazz. Isn't that funny? Him being from the South and all. Was more of the gospel-choir ilk."

"And?"

"One night, while I was out celebrating, dancing jive, Geordie went looking for a late-night revival hall to sing his sins away in. Always was worried about the sins he'd accumulated. Sins of the flesh. Wanted me to come along and be absolved as well, but I figured I was so long gone by that point it would have taken divine intervention to save me. So Geordie went off alone."

"And?"

Virgil didn't say anything. He was silent so long I thought he'd forgotten what I had asked. When he spoke his voice was distant, like he was clear across the room from me. "Some good old boys caught up to him. They hung poor Geordie from a tree."

After that the silence turned into something deeper. Mourning, maybe. Or something softer still.

The tales of Virgil's former partners always seemed to end in jail, madness, murder, or paupers' graves. And bodies turning on a wind.

Virgil pushed the maps aside. Looked at Rose. "What do you think of Oregon?"

"Not much," she said. "Rains all the time. I'm a child of the Dry Belt. I tend to rust."

"Settled, then," he said. "Oregon it is. We'll make camp in Eugene, play the Pacific coast."

Rose was ticked, but I have to admit I was pleased at the prospect. I'd never seen the ocean, had always wanted to. And maybe it was in contemplating that expanse of water that my scheme was born.

Virgil was back to telling tales of other partners he'd had over the years, tossing the stories around us like so much tickertape. One got caught in my craw, though. Tweaked my interest, as it were. It was the story of a former cohort of Virgil's, a fellow who came up with a simple car swindle.

"This fellow," Virgil said, "he decided to pull a ruse on a pair of car dealers in Missouri using an automobile as collateral. Dressed to the nines, he shows up Friday afternoon, just after the banks are closed. Writes a check for a new Ford. Drives the car across town to another dealer, offers to sell it for half of what he paid. Figures he'll make a quick $600 on a $1,200 car and be well on his way by the time his promissory note bounces back Monday morning. Problem was: for such a scam to work, you need a town small enough to trust a check-writing patron.

Larger cities won't allow a car off the lot till the check has cleared. So a small town it was."

That was the man's downfall.

Small towns are not only more trusting—or gullible, if you prefer. They're also, well, *small*. Everybody knows everybody, and when the second dealer was writing out a bill of sale, he noticed that the vehicle in question had been purchased that same day from Bobby Joe's lot across town. He calls up Bobby Joe, says, "Bobby Joe? Billy Bob here. Did you just sell a Ford to a fellow by the name of—" And that was the end of that.

"They threw my friend in the hoosegow, said, 'Let's just see if that check clears.' When it didn't, friend there got ten months in the county jail. Y'see?" Virgil said to me. Like most of his stories, this one had a moral. "Just because a con sounds good, don't mean it will work." He waved Susie over.

Hmm.

I turned that story around in my head, looked at it from different angles while Rose and Virgil debated the merits of rain versus sunshine, mildew versus dust. And I thought, What if ...

"When we get to Oregon—"

"We're not going to Oregon," said Rose.

"When we get to Oregon ..."

That's the start of any story, isn't it? The question: *What if?* What if Amelia Earhart was still alive? What if she was out there waiting for someone to save her? What if Tom Mix was real? What if Dracula wasn't? And in this case: What if you let the law take its course?

I thought about the scam Virgil's friend had tried to pull, and how easily he'd been nabbed. But what if the checks were only a feint? What if your true intention all along *was to get nabbed?* What if the real con was in getting caught?

What if you set yourself up? On purpose. What if getting arrested was the whole entire point?

Rose swatted Virgil on the arm, gestured my way. "Virg," she said. "Will you look at the lopsided grin on that boy?"

Part Three

CATS AND RATS

FORTY-FOUR

Who I was depended on what the game required. Usually a young rube or a shifty bill passer, but for this one I had to be dripping in wealth. Or the illusion of.

Virgil bought me a shimmering green suit, cut to fit. He loaded my fingers with rings and tucked a heavy whack of a watch into my vest pocket. A gilded tie pin, French cuffs, and a six-dollar shirt with a collar so high I'd have had to climb a stepladder to spit. He even bought me a pair of bright yellow shoes.

He turned to Rose. "What do you think?"

"Well," she said. "He's either the son of wealthy lineage or a swindler on the make."

"Perfect!" said Virgil. It was just what we were going for.

We chose Louisiana as the site of my arrest, reasoning that it was a state crooked enough to fall for our ruse. One where matters were settled locally, without calling in the higher authorities. So we drove east, following abandoned rail line across the plains, past the emptiness and wooden oil derricks of northern Texas. As the sagebrush turned to city lights we swung wide, past Arlington, and pushed on. We crossed the Angelina River, the air growing heavier and more humid the closer we drew to the Gulf. We couldn't see it, or even smell it, but we could feel it, that vast presence of wet, out there in exactly the wrong place, where it wouldn't do the crops of the Southwest any good.

We were looking for the right town, and we found it in Boulaye, just across state lines. We didn't turn in, though, but drove on instead into Shreveport, which was the next stop along the tracks. A sad and wilted sort of place, Shreveport was, and thick with wet greens, looking like a salad bowl had been upended over the place. Shreveport had been selected solely on geographical criteria: it would be our base for the run into Boulaye. Shreveport, you see, offered several avenues of escape. Drive west, and we'd be quickly back in Texas. North, and we'd soon be in Arkansas. East a hard day's drive and we'd be into Mississippi if we had to.

Virgil opened a checking account at the Shreveport State Bank, then drove back to Boulaye on his own to "reconnoiter," as he put it.

"Don't let anybody spot you," Rose said to him as he climbed into the Ambassador.

"Won't leave the comforts of our Nash," he promised.

Rose and I awaited his return in the faded-wallpaper room of a second-floor suite. "Not exactly the Waldorf-Astoria," said Rose. But it would do. Threadbare drapes and a dresser that had long ago lost its luster. A davenport across from it. A love seat beside. Must have been a beautiful room in its day. Outside, the city was growing dark, and shadows were pulling themselves into the room. I sat by the window, keeping watch for what I wasn't sure.

Rose had a long soak. Left the door half-open. Virgil had wanted a cheaper room, one without a private bath, but Rose had nixed that idea. "A girl needs to simmer," she said, "without unwanted interruptions." I couldn't tell if it was the "interruptions" or the "unwanted" that she was emphasizing.

I could hear her ease into the water, could hear her sigh, could hear the occasional small splash—and then her lifting herself out again. Turning from the window, I saw the light from the bathroom flickering as she toweled herself dry. She reappeared soon after in a loose robe, said it had been like a warm, slow baptism. "Left some for you," she said, but I declined. Never was one for sharing someone else's water.

Rose squeezed past me so close I could smell the softness of Camay rising from her. It was her secret scent, one I only ever caught in passing, usually just before it was clouded over with matchsticks and the smell of Virginia tobacco. Cigarettes may have been her chosen perfume, but it was the scent of that soap I always associated with Rose.

She plunked herself down in the love seat, stretched her feet up on a footstool. The upholstery might have been faded. But Rose? She glowed—still pink from the bath, scrubbed down and without the eyeliner or waxy red lips. Looked like she'd just walked off a farm somewhere.

"Nervous?" she said.

"About what?" I asked.

She stretched her arms out, over her head. "Feels like I'm a Belgian waffle," she said. "Warm and syrupy. Can't beat a long bath after a hot day."

Rose lit a cigarette, drew deep and blew long, a cloud of blue that camouflaged the last of the Camay. "Most confidence men spend their lives trying to avoid ending up in jail," she said. "And here you are willingly walking into one."

"Virgil will get me out," I said.

"You think so?"

"That's the way I'm laying the bet," I said.

She laughed, that single harsh snort of hers. "Back on the road," she said, "that first day? When you stalled the Nash? Virgil wanted to leave you there, in that hardwares store. Wanted to drive off and abandon you to your fate. You know that, don't you?"

"I figured as much."

"I talked him out of it."

"I know."

"Said we owed you another chance."

I nodded.

Footsteps, coming up the stairs two at a time, a quick three-four rap on the door, and Virgil was back in among us like a Kansas cyclone. "It's all set!" he said, breathless and beaming. "Boulaye it is. Courtyard and county jail are near the railroad station. Trains come in on the hour. They connect to the northern branch line, so a Washington D.C. arrival is perfectly plausible."

"I thought you weren't going to get out of the Nash," said Rose.

"I absolutely didn't," he said.

"Then how'd you get the train schedule?"

"I asked the station master. I had to get out for *that*. Anyway," he said. "Last train out, heading to D.C., is at four o'clock."

Virgil sketched it out on a piece of paper.

"There's three dealerships. Here. Here, and here. Forget the last one. It's a franchise, factory direct. We'll stick with the independents. This one—" he tapped his finger. "Start here. Then drive across—*here*—to this lot. That's where the shit'll hit. I saw the owner as he was closing up." Virgil grinned. "A fat man."

"A fat man?"

"You want to hit a hothead on the resale. Someone who'll go into a rage and immediately call in the police. You want a fat man for that. Fat is congealed anger. If you hit this chump on the resale, you'll be in the clink, no time."

He pulled out an envelope from his jacket pocket. "I stopped by the station here in Shreveport. Got you a ticket to Boulaye. Leaves first thing tomorrow morning."

He slid it across to me, and I was wondering whether it was a ticket to somewhere else, as well—to glory or to prison. Or maybe to both.

I couldn't get to sleep that night. I turned and twisted, and tried to get comfortable, but my feet kept spilling off the davenport and eventually I kicked the cushions onto the floor all together and laid there instead.

I couldn't sleep, and neither could Rose. I heard her stirring beneath the covers, sighing between Virgil's snores. I pretended it was because she was worried for me.

Forty-five

The man at the first Boulaye dealership was more than happy to take my money.

He was a gaunt fellow of sour means, gator-faced and gloomy, but he forced a smile when I pulled out my checkbook. Money has that effect, even on the most gatored of faces, I've found.

Boulaye was a soggy place. A thick river slid through, so silted and sludgy you could have floated coins on it. Town square was farther down, with a fountain that trickled silted water of its own and a courthouse presiding. It was so muggy the trees seemed to be fanning themselves. As Virgil had promised, the railroad station was but a brisk walk from the courthouse.

The storefronts of Boulaye were a sad lot. The Liberty Bank, now closed. The Hermitage Trust & Loan, same. Everyone moved slower down here, it seemed, like they were half-asleep. The humidity was chaffing at my neck, and my handkerchief could have been wrung for water. No matter. I kept as jaunty a step and as friendly a smile as I could, nodding to everyone I passed.

The Association of Southern Women for the Prevention of Lynching (about as effective a group as the Woman's Christian Temperance Union, I imagine) shared a storefront with the Commission on Interracial Cooperation. That made me nervous. Didn't want too kindhearted a town. We didn't need forgiveness, we needed *umbrage*.

Ah, but good fortune was with me, and farther down I came upon competing doomsdays glowering at each other from across the street: a Moody Bible Institute on one corner and a Millenarianists Society on the other. This raised my spirits considerably—and things got sweeter still. Another street corner and another stalemate: the Church of

Evangelical Reform on one side, the Reformed Evangelical on the other. A town with an argumentative nature, and quick to pass judgment. Just what we were looking for.

I made my way to that first dealership, took a steadying breath, and then, with a wide and symmetrical smile, I strode onto the lot. The owner came out to meet me—I was the only customer there—and I gave him a hearty "Hello, good man, what's the word?"

He shadowed me like an undertaker waiting for the first sign of a cough. I stopped to admire a red La Salle convertible parked out front.

He nodded. "She's a beaut, ain't she?" he said.

I ran a hand along the fender, whistled low. Pushed my hat back, said, "That is one fine automobile. Yessir."

We talked ventilators and radiators (both standard and sloping). Mulled over the benefits of free-wheeling, the pros and cons of hydraulic brakes and hydromatic gears.

"Foot off the throttle, coasting free like that?" I said. "Nothing sweeter, is there?"

He agreed wholeheartedly. "You sure enough know your automobiles," he said, adding extra syllables at no charge: "mo-ah-bee-ulls."

I checked my watch—made a big production of saying, "Hmm. Still ... a bit ... early," then bid him good health and went on my way.

I squandered the day, taking a malted drink at one of the local druggist's followed by a leisurely constitutional around the square. I had a fine pork sandwich at a luncheon counter, finished it off with some Bib Label. Walked the streets of Boulaye all afternoon ... and then returned, in a hurry, to the lot.

It was a Friday. Three o'clock. Banks were just about to close for the weekend and wouldn't be opening again till eight o'clock Monday morning.

The dealer came out to greet me, but this time I was quick about it. No dilly-dally, no chit-chat.

"The Packard," I said. "The silver one out front. I'll take it."

His smile faltered at this. I hadn't even looked at the Packard, and it carried a tag of $1,850. It was the La Salle convertible I'd had my eye on.

I had asked all sorts of questions, mused openly about taking it for a test run, expressed my enthusiasm unequivocally. And here I was, writing a check for a much more expensive automobile, without so much as getting inside or turning the engine.

I'd dropped hints of familial fortune during my earlier visit, and now I added a hundred onto the price "as a tip."

"A tip?"

I smiled at him, broad and even. "For taking the time to make a sale at the end of the day. When the banks are about to close."

Who can say no to a hundred-dollar tip? He telephoned Shreveport to confirm my check was covered. It was, and I filled in the rest of the paperwork and then drove the Packard off the lot. I did a couple of turns around the square to run out the clock, then headed directly to the second dealership.

It was farther out, past the ball field, and marked by a hand-painted sign that read FRENCHIE'S AUTOS. At the sound of the Packard a fat man came out, just as Virgil had promised. He was pink with sweat, and he gave me a fleshy wave as I pulled in.

"What can I do you for?" he asked.

"I need to sell this," I said. "Right away quick. The banks have just closed and I need the money. Have to catch the next train out. Got a—a sick aunt, needs tending. Train leaves in twenty."

He looked at his watch. "Gonna be tight."

"Mister, I'm willing to sell you a Packard Eight for nine hundred cash. All you got to do is get me to the station. I have a train to make."

He didn't like being hurried along, but how could he turn down a bargain like that? "Car looks brand new."

I started to get snippy. "It is, it is. Quit wasting my time. I have a train to catch. Can't wait to get out of here. There isn't a dollybird worth ogling in this entire sad town of yours. Never seen such a collection of knock-kneed, flat-chested girls in all my days. Here's me, a boy from the big city. I can have the pick of the litter, but the litter's not worth picking. I'm not sure how you even manage to procreate down in these parts. Just shut your eyes and hold on tight, I imagine."

The fat man's smile was gone. The pink in his face grew deeper.

Funny, isn't it? The proprietorial pride that people invest in their women. You can insult a region's cuisine, its politics, its weather. But make a crack about how mud-ugly their women are, and you are sure to press some buttons. Don't know if it's chivalry or just a sense of ownership at play, but if you want to get someone good and riled, that's the route to go.

"Let's get your forms sorted, then," said the fat man.

I followed him into his office, tossed the keys to the car onto his desk, told him again to hurry it up. He pulled out the paperwork—and that's when everything blew apart.

"What is this?" he said, looking at the bill of sale. "You just bought this car. Across town and for twice that amount." His piggy eyes narrowed to piggy little slits. "Trying to pull a fast one, are you?"

"I bought the Packard, fair and square," I said. "Now give me my money. Nine hundred. Cash."

"Bought it fair and square, did you?" His face was red now, bordering on purple. He snatched up his telephone receiver, called the operator. "Get me the sheriff's office."

I got up, like I was going to flee. "Give me back my keys."

He refused. He had me now. The fool.

The sheriff arrived in a self-propelled huff. Here was a man apparently made from spare parts: ears from a bat, eyes from a garden mole, neck of a gobbler. He listened to the fat man, and then pulled out the cuffs.

"On what charge?" I demanded to know.

"We'll let the judge decide about that."

The courthouse was flying a state flag and a Confederate cross, though flying wasn't quite the right word. Way they drooped, it looked more like washing, hanging damp on the line. The sheriff and his star witness took me inside, past pillars and through a rotunda. The building had a musty smell, like the mildew itself had seeped into the air.

I had to admit, the case against me looked pretty bad. The sheriff roused the judge, and the judge was none too happy about it. He blustered in, pulling his robes on like an afterthought, and took his perch. From his heights, he glowered down at me. A balding man with white eyebrows, a large voice, and a hammer-of-God demeanor—one I went out of my way to provoke.

"What kind of hillbilly justice is this?" I said. "Release me, *this instant.* I demand it! I've done nothing wrong."

"Nothing wrong?" boomed the judge. He took a moment to wipe a kerchief across his face. "*Nothing wrong?* Writing false promissory notes? Attempting to defraud the hardworking citizens of Boulaye? You have made a grievous and fatal error in judgment, young man."

"You can't do this to me!"

"I can't?" He was roaring now. "*Can't?* Insolence!"

"That check will clear," I said. "The fellow at the dealership called the bank. You got no reason to hold me."

The judge scoffed at this. "Thought you'd pull a fast one, did you?" He turned to his spare-parts lawman. "Sheriff, lock up this ill-mannered boy. Hold him till the banks open Monday morning. We'll just see if that check clears."

The first owner had now arrived, gator-faced and gaunt, and he made a point of thanking the other fellow. "Think nothing of it," said the fat man. "You'd have done the same for me." Small towns. You just can't beat 'em. Well, you could, but it wouldn't do any good.

Oh, they were in high spirits, the bunch of them—the fat man, the dour one, the sheriff, and the thundersome judge—giddy at having nabbed a big-city grifter. A swell day for all involved. Hardest part for me was in the not laughing.

FORTY-SIX

Jail time was different from real time, I discovered. It moved not slower, necessarily, but *thicker*. It didn't tick by when you were sitting behind bars, it oozed and trickled like sludge on a shingle, one dollop at a time.

The jail was attached to the courthouse, and the judge came by to speak with the sheriff afterwards. He peered in at me like I was a caged coyote, shook his head grimly, said, "Let this be a lesson."

The judge had changed out of his robes, was dressed in freshly pressed cotton with a white derby up top and a side feather.

"Nice hat," I said.

"Thank you," he replied, not knowing how to take it. Then, remembering that he was the judge and I was the prisoner, he said with extra gruff in his voice, "I'll see you Monday morning. For sentencing."

He wasn't expecting a lengthy trial, apparently.

Deputies took turns sitting watch over me, in case I pulled a Houdini. I was the only person locked in that weekend, and as I lay on the cot I stretched out both arms and found I couldn't quite reach the walls. Which is to say, my prison cell was bigger than the storage room I called home back in Silver City. More comfortable, too. I slept deep and woke late, the sun slicing through the bars in a jab of harsh stripes. They fed me something gray. Meat, maybe. Along with cornbread and cold coffee.

Sunday morning a local man took over, a skinny fellow who cowered behind a stack of books at the desk across from my cell, scratching notes with a pen.

It was the books that caught my attention. "Hullo!" I called. He pretended not to hear. "Mister!" I said. "What's that you're doing?"

"Lesson plans," he said, trying hard to sound tough. "It's no concern of yours."

He was a schoolteacher, it would appear, moonlighting on Sundays as a deputy jailer for the county. A schoolteacher working on the Sabbath? That told me everything.

"Teach science, do you?"

"Ah, yes. Yes, I do. How did you—"

"I have a cousin," I said. "Up in Tennessee. He taught science, and they arrested him unfairly, too. Just like me."

"Was he a car thief as well?" asked the teacher.

"Nope. He was an educator, same as you." None of which was true, of course, up to and including *I have a cousin*. "They nabbed him for doing his job."

"They arrested him for teaching?" This he found intriguing, in spite of himself.

"That's right. Monkeys and such. Big trial 'n all."

And whoo, boy, didn't that hook him!

"Surely not Scopes?" he said. "Not John Scopes."

"That's the one. He lost the case," I said. "But claimed a moral victory."

The teacher's eyes were saucer-wide now. "You're related to John Scopes?"

"Only through marriage," I said.

"And what would your famous cousin think of you sitting in the clink, awaiting trial?" he asked.

"He'd say, 'falsely accused.' Same as he was, mister. I'm an innocent man, that's the truth. And the truth shall set me free." Then, just casual-like, "You teach mathematics as well?"

He nodded.

"Are you a betting man? Mathematically speaking."

He wasn't sure he'd heard right.

"Up for a friendly wager?" I asked.

"A wager? What kind of wager?"

"Oh, I don't know, anything really. Numbers, say. Why don't you give me an amount, as big as you like, and I'll add it instantly by, say, 98 or 99? You then work it out on a pad and see if I'm right. It would only be nickels and dimes, to pass the time."

He hesitated, and in that moment I knew I had him.

"Are you really John Scopes's cousin?" he asked as he got out a pad and pencil.

FORTY-SEVEN

Sunday was a long time dying, made only slightly less intolerable by the money I'd managed to pluck from that schoolteacher. Credit where due, teacher was a man of his word. He paid.

Monday arrived, and with it came Virgil Ray.

He strode into the sheriff's office, shook the lawman's hand heartily, said with a mighty smile, "Godfrey Tanner. Attorney at law. It's a pleasure."

He handed his card to the sheriff.

The sheriff looked down at it, at the corporate heading above the name. "De Valu?" he said.

"I represent the boy's family."

"He said his name was—"

"It is. His mother was Clarice de Valu, daughter of Vincent. You've heard of him?"

The sheriff's voice wavered, ever so slightly. "Of course."

"Fetch the boy. We'll meet with the judge in his chambers."

Godfrey Tanner had been sent to Boulaye to track down the missing son of Washington high society, he explained to the judge.

"Imagine my shock," said Virgil. "On finding him here."

The judge was sitting behind a wide expanse of desk. The sheriff stood next to him, arms crossed.

"It was all just a misunderstanding, I'm sure," said Virgil. "So. Here is what I propose: fifteen thousand, paid in full, and no one goes to jail."

Judge and the sheriff exchanged looks, barely able to suppress their glee. They hadn't expected to get fifteen grand out of us. If you could've cracked open their heads, you would have heard the Hallelujah chorus.

Didn't last long, though—not when they realized what Virgil was actually proposing.

"Fifteen thousand, plus legal fees. And we will walk away without pressing any charges against you—and you—or the municipality of Boulaye. That is our one and only offer. Pay up, gentlemen, or the De Valu family will take you and this bumfuck, backwater shithole of a town you call home for everything you have. And that includes what you get for renting out your sister on a Saturday night." Virgil sat back, smiled sweetly. "Gentlemen? Any questions?"

The silence was like a bomb going off.

"You ... you want us to pay *you?*"

"False arrest," said Virgil. He slid a slip of paper across the desk. "The check cleared this morning. Young Jonathan here purchased that vehicle legally and with honest intent. He was originally planning to take a couple of days, make the drive back to D.C., arrive in time for a fundraiser at the Rose Garden. Then he found out his great-aunt was dying. That woman was like a mother to him. He absolutely had to get the next train. Banks were closed and he needed cash. But he couldn't get home, could he? And why? Because you stupid fucks had him arrested—illegally and without due process. Unlawful confinement, that's a very serious charge." Virgil turned to me, voice hushed. "Your aunt passed away last night, Jonathan. I'm sorry you couldn't be there. She was asking for you right till the end."

I hung my head low, closed my eyes for a moment.

Virgil looked back at the judge, and his voice had a sudden sharp edge. "By the time I'm done with you, Your Honor, you'll be wrung dry. Mr. De Valu himself has expressed his personal ... outrage over what has happened to his grandson. He wants retribution. Wants blood. So. We can settle this right here, right now, or I can go on a rampage. I won't stop until you've been disbarred and disgraced and your inbred fuck of a sheriff here has been sent to jail." Virgil leaned in. Stared down any doubts they might have had. "Gentlemen," he said. "You have no idea what you're up against ... or maybe you do."

The judge and the sheriff looked as though a shovel had hit them full force on the back of the head. The judge opened his mouth, but only the faintest of squeaks came out. And then—nothing. His thunder was sapped.

"Friends," said Virgil, on a roll now and flying free. "You may try to pull this sort of crude shakedown on the hayseeds out here, but you are now up against the might and fury of the De Valu family fortune. I was at that function at the Rose Garden when they called me away for this. I could've been having tea with the Rockefellers right about now. Instead, I'm down here dealing with the likes of you. I don't plan on negotiating. That's our offer. Fifteen, plus legal. Take it or go fuck yourselves. Either way, I don't care."

Virgil stood, straightened his jacket. "My train leaves in one hour. I will be on it. And if Jonathan here is not, I will initiate proceedings against you and the municipality of Boulaye. Good day." He turned, but then, almost in afterthought, said, "Y'know, in prison they usually separate the crooked cops and judges from the other inmates. So don't worry. You'll probably do just fine. Odds are you won't end up with a shiv between your ribs or a wire around the throat."

Virgil hadn't walked half a block before the sheriff went running out, waving him back in. The sheriff's face was a ghostly shade of pale. Ol' Thunder Judge had to loot the town's discretionary funds to make the payment, but it was on judicial orders, stamped and approved, so it didn't take long. This was Louisiana. They could do that sort of thing. Virgil had chosen well.

We walked out of there, Virgil and me, with $18,000. The check for the car had indeed cleared. So had the refund.

At the Boulaye station, the man behind the booth looked at Virgil and said, "Don't I know you from somewhere?"

"Don't believe so," said Virgil.

"Sure I do," said the man. "You were in last—Thursday, was it? Asking about train schedules. Sure, I remember you."

Virgil said nothing. Just smiled.

"Well," said the station master. "You have yourself a good one." And with that we dodged our last bullet. The station master punched our tickets. "Washington D.C. is it?"

"That's right," said Virgil.

We'd purchased tickets all the way through, but we hopped off the train at Shreveport, where Rose was waiting for us in the Nash. We drove directly to the bank. The Boulaye check was certified, so it went into our account without a hold. We transferred the amount to a bank in Lubbock, Texas, and shut down our Shreveport account. We would cash out when we passed through Lubbock on our way back.

Eighteen grand. At his peak, my Da was making $4,000 a year with Southern Pacific. And it was down to $1,900 at the very end, just before they closed the line. My cut alone was one and a half times his best year, and I'd done it over a single weekend.

"Eighteen thousand dollars in one swoop. Ha!" hollered Virgil as we sped away, with Rose at the wheel and me in the back.

"In actual fact," I said, "it's eighteen thousand … and twelve." I unfolded the bills I'd won. Eight on the betting and four on showing the teacher the trick so he could fool others. His entire pay for watching me gone right there, and then some.

Virgil wasn't sure he'd heard right. "You turned a profit while you were in jail? How do you come out on Monday with more money in your pocket than when you went in Friday?"

When I explained the wager I'd made with the schoolteacher, Virgil set to hooting even more.

"He made money off his jailer! You hear that, Rose?"

"I heard."

"Boy's a pro!"

"I know." She looked at me in the mirror. Like she was disappointed or something.

I didn't understand the look she gave me, not then, but I think I do now. My Louisiana arrest had been all too successful. There was no turning back after that. I'd proven I could do this, could do it well.

FORTY-EIGHT

We beat it across state lines, past Waco and then up, stopping at Lubbock to collect our winnings before heading on to Silver. Drove right through the night, with me and Virgil taking turns at the wheel, stopping only to siphon gas off cars in the towns we rolled through.

Somewhere, in the deepest hours of night, we found ourselves driving alongside a westbound freight that was trailing cinders across the plains. Whenever they stoked the boiler, the smoke glowed red. You could see men sitting on the top, silhouetted and silent, others hanging from the sides or between boxcars just above the spark-flying wheels. We kept time with it awhile until it pulled away and was swallowed up by the darkness.

We arrived in Silver City punch-drunk with joy and just in time for breakfast at Charley Wong's. Tired, but too giddy to sleep, we headed down.

The only spoiler thrown upon our return had been the sight of a certain car with a certain shark-nosed grille and bulging headlights pulling away as we drove up. "I've seen that car before," I'd said. "Graham Supercharger, 1939 sedan. Dark green. Saw it in Kansas, maybe. It turned up here in Silver City just last week. Had Colorado plates at that time." I squinted at the car as it slid away. "Has Texas plates now."

Virgil had looked at me like he was concerned for my sanity. "And here I thought I was jumpy," he said. "That car was dropping someone off. Wasn't exactly skulking around. Graham-Paige sells its automobiles clear across these United States, and that includes the greater Southwest." Then, quieter now. "Is it getting to you? The game?"

"Me? Nah."

"That's how it starts," said Rose as we walked around to Wong's.

"Skin starts twitching. Hair on the back of your neck starts to tingle. You start to see figures in every shadow, shadows in every figure. You start imagining things. Start thinking you're being followed, being watched."

"Been driving too long," I said. "That's all."

"You're probably right," said Virgil, holding the door open for Rose and me. "C'mon. A mess of pottage will do us good." But I couldn't help note how he threw one last look over his shoulder before we entered.

Over breakfast, Virgil tried to talk us into running the car dealership scam in other counties, other states.

"They're just as crooked in Mississippi," he said.

But Rose wouldn't hear of it. "It's dangerous," she said. "Putting Jack behind bars. They ever call our bluff, he's got nowhere to run."

"There's no crime committed," said Virgil. "You can't arrest someone for selling an $1,800 car for $900."

"It's not the selling," she said. "It's the pretending. Passing yourself off as high-society De Valu stock like that. Only takes one local lawman to make a phone call or two, and where's your escape plan then?"

"Fine," said Virgil. "We'll use Jack's real name and hire ourselves a real lawyer, make it legit."

But Rose wouldn't budge, and to tell the truth I wasn't overly keen on making a career out of getting arrested. It's not that I was worried. It was just, well, it seemed the sort of thing might come back to haunt you if you ever decided to go straight.

"C'mon, Rose," he said. "It's a Mill's lock, a sure thing."

"No such thing as a lock, Virg. You know that."

"Aw," Virgil said, voice full of rue, like a fisherman watching a trout slip free from the line. "But that was such a sweet swindle."

"You like it so much, you do the jail time," said Rose—and didn't that slam the door on any further discussions.

I suppose I should have been afraid of prison, too, but I can't say I was. Ten-to-twenty? That was a span of years I couldn't quite grasp, like trying to imagine what the ocean must feel like. Truth be told, the sight of that Graham Supercharger had spooked me more than the imaginary world of hard time.

Virgil was determined to turn our good fortune into something grander, and our weekend windfall had revived that long-held dream of his.

"If we pool our resources," he said, "we'd almost have enough to pull it off."

Pull what off?

"A Big Store. An establishment all our own, where every game is rigged and no one gets out without a fleecing. Music. Girls. Games of chance. A fleet of shills circling the floor."

"Seems I've been listening to your Big Store dreams since before we met," said Rose.

Virgil ignored her. "Y'see, Jack, we're on the grift, now. But I got bigger plans."

"A clip joint," said Rose. "Some dream."

"Yes. A clip joint, but not—not low rent. I'm talking glitz and style. Roulette wheels and chandeliers. A dozen pianos—all grand, all white, and girls in sequins draped over every one of 'em. Would be like an ongoing theatrical production. We'd have fine china and silverware settings with fourteen forks and three kinds of spoon. Doormen in velvet suits. Soft jazz playing in the background, a fellow in a tuxedo tickling ivory in the foyer as you enter. A respectable gig, where we'd set 'em up and knock 'em down. We'd invite 'em in—and then soak 'em dry."

"Soak 'em dry?" said Rose.

"You know what I mean," he said. "We'll skin those suckers so smoothly they won't even realize they've been peeled and sliced. Wheaties here could count cards, work the tables. You could handle the girls. It'd be lavish. That's the word I'm looking for, *lavish*."

"That's a mighty big investment, Virg."

"But see, now we got the means. The money's been washing in. Jack here's our lucky charm." He leaned in on both elbows, spoke like he was trying to sell us something. "I'm thinking Denver," he said. "I'm thinking soon. We start small. Churn our profits back into the Store."

Denver was the con capital of America, according to Virgil. "Home of the Big Store," he called it.

"Or maybe Webb City, Missouri. Or Council Bluffs up in Iowa. Towns known for the pliability of their elected officials. The three of us'll set up shop, settle in. Soon enough, we'll be sitting pretty."

"Thought you had an aversion to long cons," I said. "The law, remember?"

"We play this right, we'll be above the law. You asked me if this is a common clip joint I'm talking about? Answer is no."

Virgil ordered another rasher of bacon and then stretched himself out, arms behind his neck. He had a head full of dreams, but I noticed he'd given me the seat with its back to the door once again. He still didn't trust me to look over his shoulder and make the right assessment.

We slept that day away and crawled back to Charley Wong's in the evening. I was drifting again into their way of doing things, prowling the streets at night, avoiding daylight, growing pale, falling out of step with the rest of the normal world.

"Hardest thing about going out on the road is having to live normal hours," Virgil said. "Always a relief to return home to nocturnal rhythms."

We'd missed the Fourth of July celebrations just a few days earlier; I'd heard the drum and whistles of the parade while I was still in my cot. Sounded like it was a million miles away. Before we went out to the clubs we watched the fireworks from the rooftop behind 1-A: pincushions of red, cymbal crashes of white, the *boom-boom-boom* of blue.

That night we stayed in Charley's café well past closing. Mr. Wong didn't mind us hanging around while he cleaned up. He had an old Silvertone radio he left on most of the time, one of those tombstone tabletop models, six-tube, four knobs, and tricky to tune. It was scuffed up a good bit and the sound was scratchy. But it picked up the major relays, and that's what mattered.

The *Collier Magazine Radio Hour* had been running a serial on Fu Manchu and his "evil machinations."

"Do you suppose Charlie Chan ever went up against Fu Manchu?" Virgil said.

I shrugged. "Don't know."

He mulled this over a bit. "Because you'd figure Chan would be the man for the job. Oriental cunning pitted against Oriental cunning. Wily detective against equally wily villain. Hey Charley!" he called out. "You're a Chinaman, what do you think?"

Mr. Wong stuck his head out of the kitchen. "About what?"

"Fu Manchu versus Charlie Chan. Who would win?"

"Who would win?" said Mr. Wong. "Dick Tracy."

Virgil laughed. "Ha! Spoken like a true American."

Mr. Wong went back to his cleaning and Rose looked down at the tabletop, at the cigarette in her hand. "Chan," she said, mostly to herself.

"Chan?" said Virgil.

"Law always wins in the end, don't it?"

Wasn't really a question, the way she put it.

The debate about Fu Manchu and Charlie Chan might have continued if it hadn't been for a news bulletin that came through. The U.S. government was reviewing its trade pact with the Japanese Empire, the announcer said, threatening to revoke the treaty in protest over Japanese actions in Manchukuo. That was the puppet regime the Japanese had set up in China, or the parts of it they'd occupied, anyway. Hirohito's army was massing along the border of some distant frontier, half a world away.

Charley had come out of the kitchen. He was standing perfectly still, a washcloth in one hand, an empty soup bowl in the other. He seemed very much alone.

When the news report had ended, Virgil gave me a prod. "Change the dials, will you? Find something better."

I looked at Charley.

He nodded. I could change stations if I wanted. He went back to his work, absent-mindedly, cleaning the same bowl a second time and staring into the middle distance.

"That where you're from?" I asked. "Manchuria?"

He shook his head. "Nanking," he said. "My family. Still there."

"Dammit, Jack. Will you find something better?" Virgil was growing antsy. Maybe the announcer's doomful voice had brought back memories of his own, of boots slogging through the muck. Of Kraut snipers. And Turkish prison cells.

FORTY-NINE

Who knows but if I had turned the dials on Mr. Wong's radio the other way that night we might have ended up in Oregon or Denver, the three of us running our Big Store, lighting cigars with hundred-dollar bills and living large. But I didn't. And we didn't.

"Are you a manly man? Full of vigor? Or has your youthful virility begun to flag?"

"Goat Gland Brinkley!" Virgil called from the booth. "Is he still on the air?"

I'd heard about the goat gland man, but had never caught his program before.

"Dr. John Romulus Brinkley," said Virgil. "Greatest snake-oil salesman alive. Greatest that ever lived. Only two others were better than him."

According to Virgil, Brinkley had started out as a "herbologist," selling naturopathic wares, and had later purchased a medical degree from the Eclectic Medical University of Kansas City—"an institution not known for the rigors of its academic standards," as Virgil put it.

Brinkley was a man of no small ambition. He cured cancer, right off the bat, using his patented "electro-magnetic restoration" procedure. Mainly involved the flashing of lights on the afflicted region.

"Problem was," said Virgil, "in spite of being cured, the patients kept dying anyway. Downright inconsiderate of them. Doc Brinkley needed to find a more elusive malady to treat, and he hit upon it almost by happenstance: the aging male and his limp libido."

An elderly farmer in Kansas had been unable to satisfy his wife for sixteen years. He needed to acquire a more animalistic drive. So,

Brinkley figured, why not add the animalistic part directly? Why not transplant animal gonads into the farmer's own? And what could be randier than a rutting billy goat? Brinkley replaced the farmer's "worn-out" testes with those of a young goat. He sliced open the testicular area, inserted goat gonads—and wouldn't you know it, the farmer was rejuvenated. Fathered a son the following year, named him "Billy."

"Are you having troubling fulfilling your husbandly duties?" the announcer asked, voice rich as chocolate. *"Can't get your missus in the family way? What you need is a pair of Dr. Brinkley's sure-fire, goat-gland transplants! Success guaranteed!"*

Dr. Brinkley went on to perform thousands of his patented transplants, even though the regular medical community dismissed it as so much nonsense. Didn't matter. All the scientific refutation in the world couldn't dissuade those whose husbandly duties were flagging. Brinkley's fame spread around the world. A maharaja from India made the pilgrimage to Dr. Brinkley's Kansas clinic, as did a count from Bavaria and even the Bulgarian finance minister. Movie producers and publishers, they all came calling—looking for that goat gland zing. He was charging upwards of $1,500 an operation. If he was a quack, he was a very wealthy one.

"Doc Brinkley was making millions a year at that point," said Virgil. "Even founded his own bank. No lie. Built his own radio transmitter, too, the better to broadcast his down-home Medical Question Box."

That was where people would write in with various problems and he would prescribe cures, potions, and patented compounds—all of which, coincidentally, were available for sale through his mail-order program.

"Wears a little bitty goatee, too," said Virgil. "The man even looks like a goat!"

Brinkley originally broadcast his program at breakfast time, when farmers were most likely to be listening, but then moved it to evenings, the discussion of goat testicles being perhaps not the best choice for early-morning broadcasts.

After a while, the American Medical Association launched a full-scale attack on Goat Gland Brinkley. They pressured the state of Kansas into revoking his medical license and brought Brinkley up on charges of medical malpractice and conduct unbecoming. They forced him to close down his radio station as well. So Goat Gland had moved his operation to Del Rio, Texas, built an even bigger radio station, XER, just across the border in Mexico, and continued to peddle his wares. XER was the most powerful radio transmission in the world, Virgil said, 100,000 watts strong, and it reached clear through to the Canadian border and beyond. It was XER that I'd tuned in to.

"Let Dr. Brinkley get your goat and you'll be Mr. Ram-What-Am with every lamb!"

Not quite the lyrical charms of Ovid, poetry not being the Goat Doctor's strong suit.

Miss Rose snorted with something akin to genuine laughter when the announcer explained how a simple operation could transform a man from "listless to licentious."

"Hey, Virg," she said. "Maybe you could use some of those glands, become a real man, a manly man, a regular ram-a-wham with the lambs!"

"Never cared for lamb," said Virgil. "Too gamey."

Thing was, Dr. Brinkley had reams of testimonials from satisfied patients. Anecdotal evidence is always meaningless, of course, but Brinkley's customers were adamant. The procedure had worked. They swore by it, and I think I knew why. It was the *placebo effect* in action. If you'd decided that testicle transplants would save your marriage, then by gum, save it they would.

"Now you take Roy Wells outta Omaha," said Virgil. "Greatest snake-oil man ever lived. His specialty was Genuine Detoxicolon Treatments. *Of course* it was genuine. He invented it. Was an enema attached to a high-pressure hose, basically. Colonic irrigation: the old raw-liver-juice-and-coffee concoction with a bit more zing. Roy's Detoxicolon treatments were known to uncross eyes and cure narcolepsy, to shake off shingles and clear up everything from piles to poor penmanship. It cured blood pressure—both high and low—and cancer too, I believe. Cleared 'toxins' out of the system, y'see. He'd get his patients to eat

bales of fiber and would then apply his high-pressure Detoxicolon appa-
ratus, and they'd shit themselves into good health. That, or the nearest
emergency ward. His wife, she sold 'magnetized bracelets.' You wore one
on your wrist to cure arthritis and asthma and whatnot. Same slop,
different bucket."

Virgil stopped to savor the sweep of medical quackery, the outlandish
nature of the swindles.

"Whether it's naturopaths or homeopaths," he said, "Royal Jelly or
shark oil, bee pollen, miracle formulas, magical rejuvenating creams, or
musical dynaspheres. Bust developers—for when nature hasn't favored
you as kindly as it might have—and weight reducers for when nature has
favored you all too well. It's part and parcel of the same, boy: the foster-
ing of false hopes. And false hope is a commodity that never decreases in
value. Name an ailment and there's a cure ready for the peddling. Name
a worry and there's a panacea, reasonably priced and in conveniently
packaged supply. Bleeding ulcers, varicose veins, diabetic wasting
disease, chronic hemorrhoidal inflammation. Bunions, baldness, buck
teeth or bowlegs. Deafness or myopia, jug ears or wall eyes. Cancerous
livers and jellied gallbladders, cataracts and consumption. There's a cure
for everything. It's the abracadabra of charlatans and scientific smoke
and mirrors, the likes of which we haven't seen since the days of Count
Caligostro and the Wandering Jew. False hope, Jack. That's the key.
When people want to believe something in the worst way, they will. In
the worst way."

Virgil got a dreamy look in his eyes; it was the kind of look he always
got when contemplating easy money. "I tell you, Wheaties. People will
believe any damn fool thing you tell them, long as you say it with the
right authority and a fulsome and unwavering confidence. Shame we
can't tap into that."

"What's stopping us?" I asked.

"Well," he said, "when it comes to quackery, sexual prowess is defi-
nitely where the money is. But grafting goat glands onto men's gonads?
That's messy."

"Don't need goat glands," I said. "We could sell … aphrodisiacs."

"Aphrodisiacs?"

"Potions," I said. "Mixtures and compounds, to heighten one's desires. To, um, excite sexual feelings."

"What, like oysters?" said Rose.

"I'm not operating no fish stand," said Virgil.

"No, not oysters," I said. "Spanish Fly. Not—not *real* Spanish Fly. That's from a beetle. It's a poison, actually. Makes it burn when you try to pass water. Can get a person terribly sick. It's banned from sale in the States. But—but we could just sell—I don't know, baking soda or something. Maybe sugar pills. And just call it Spanish Fly. They sell everything else through advertisements in the almanacs and magazines. Why not that?"

"Mail fraud," said Virgil. "That's why. It's how they nabbed Charles Ponzi. It's how they got Oscar, too."

"Oscar?"

"Hartzell. Oscar Hartzell. The man behind the Drake swindle. You've heard of it?"

"I have."

"Well, old Oscar was careful. Made his dupes sign confidentiality agreements. Banned all use of the federal mail services. Messages were sent by private telegraph, or through couriers. Payments went directly through the banks or Western Union. Unfortunately, some of his reps weren't as meticulous as they should have been. Several of Drake's saps— what you might call 'investors,' I suppose—sent their money in through conventional mails. *And Oscar's reps accepted it.* That's when the government pounced. Using the U.S. Postal Service to commit fraud? That there's a federal offense, boy. No way to squirm your way out of that jurisdictional snare. You're looking at hard time, in a federal pen. Old Oscar, he ended up doing ten in Leavenworth. Still in there, last I heard."

"He is," I said. "People continue sending him money, though."

"Ha!" said Virgil. "Not surprised, not at all. A fool and his money aren't just easily parted, they're damned lucky to have gotten together in the first place." He took a swig of stale coffee. "Now, the type of cons we're running, they're mostly handled by local police. Forget state lines. Shoot, you beat it across *county* lines and you're as good as gone. Street cons can get you thrown into jail by the local flats, but money will get you just as easily thrown out. Don't know how many cops I've paid off over the years, but you'd think they'd hold a thank-you party for me for all the retirement fund donations I've slipped their way. Even back in Louisiana," he said, "that would have been a municipal matter, county at most. And if they'd cottoned on to what we were doing, that was still a local jail you were sitting in. I could have bribed your way out of there—"

"Not that you would've," I said.

"Not that I would've. But still, we're talking highly regionalized swindles. Soon as we left Louisiana and crossed the state border into Texas we were home free. But mail fraud? That's a whole other animal. Ever since Franklin Delano expanded the Federal Investigations Bureau and gave J. Edgar a greater sweep, it's got so's an honest thief can't catch a break. Hell of a time we're living through."

"But we wouldn't defraud the people who ordered our Spanish Fly," I said. "We'd fill their orders. Every one. It's not like we'd be pocketing the money without providing the merchandise. We'd follow through."

"It doesn't matter," said Virgil. "Can't use the U.S. Postal Service to sell fake goods. In Ponzi's case, it wasn't even money that was going through the mail. It was postcards, notifying investors that their interest payments were ready to be picked up. Based on that alone, he got five years. If we hawk phony medicine through the mails, the FDA would be all over us. In this game, there are two things you don't want to get mixed up in: murder and mail fraud."

By this point, Charley Wong was asleep. Head back and breathing slow, Chinese newspaper open in front of him. The lights in the café were off, except for over our booth. Outside, the swing bands were whispering for us, the jazz was calling, but I couldn't let it go.

"What if it *wasn't* fraud?" I said. "What if we told our customers exactly what we were doing?"

Blank looks from both of them, so I carried on.

"What if we never claimed it was real? Have you heard of the placebo effect? It's a genuine medical occurrence. Scientific fact, measurable, well known among the medical community. It's what you've been saying all along, Virg, about how people decide something is real because they want it to be. About how thinking makes it so. Magnetized bracelets. Naturopathic what have you. Aphrodisiacs, too. They work because people decide they do. It's the power of suggestion, I suppose. People find what they go looking for. *Believing is seeing.*"

Rose was tapping out a back-beat only she could hear, restless to get moving. But Virgil could sort of see where I was going with this. He tilted his head at me, as though he were trying to focus better.

"So what are you saying?"

"Placebos," I said. "We don't sell them medicine. We sell them placebos. 'Genuine 100% Authentic Placebos.' We can even put it in fine print: '*Placebo effect medically proven and fully documented.*'"

All of which was entirely true. Which is how we got even richer and why we stayed on in Silver City

The dog was baying and the moon was spinning.

FIFTY

I spent a few days at the Silver City Library, double-checking federal regulations and FDA guidelines. There'd been talk of making "intent to mislead" a crime, and of adding that to the mail-fraud statutes. But so far, no laws had been passed. Labeling something PLACEBO was perfectly legal.

We rented a post office box and ran advertising notices in several monthly almanacs and regional magazines, and within a week the first orders came in. Virgil looked on, amazed, as I wrapped tablespoons of baking soda in wax paper, sealed them with tape, wrote PLACEBO on the front in big bold letters and then sent them back in the stamped, self-addressed envelopes customers were required to provide, along with our instructions: "Add to liquid of your choice. One TBS, mix well."

Sixteen orders of Spanish fly at $6.50 each came to $104, against the cost of running the advertisements for that week: two dollars per notice, in eight different publications. Plus the cost of the baking soda: twenty-four cents. And five dollars for the post office box rental.

"Why, that's a profit of ..." Virgil tried to work it out in his head. Couldn't.

"Eighty-two dollars, seventy-six cents," I said.

We placed more and more ads, in everything from *Farm & Fireside* to *Southwestern Weekly Review* to *The Protestant Churchman*. We got a number of orders through *Literary Digest* as well, the professorial class being in particular need of a boost, it would seem. Got more orders from that one ad in *Literary Digest* than from three weeks of *True Story*. We started running notices in church bulletins and company newsletters, in national magazines and small journals. Even gag mags like *Ballyhoo,* chock full of jokes and japes, ran ads for our placebos. *Ballyhoo* often published risqué cartoons, so they weren't put off by the wares we were peddling. No one ever challenged us. I guess they were hurting for revenue like everybody else. The only publications we didn't advertise in were *The New England Journal of Medicine, Scientific American,* and the like—just in case, even though we featured some of their names prominently in our ads. (They had indeed published articles on the placebo effect, but, we thought, no point waving a red flag at anyone.) *Popular Science* was fine, though, it being the realm of tinkerers, and Spanish Fly being a way of oiling a squeaky hinge, so to speak.

We toned some of our ads down, leered others up, but the message was more or less the same:

SPANISH FLY
Drives women crazy!
Genuine 100% PLACEBO
Medically proven effect*

*as described in *The New England Journal of Medicine,*
Scientific American,
The Journal of the American Medical Association.
and elsewhere.
Put the passion back in your life.

It was Rose who wrote that last line. Virgil wanted to add "And turn your lamb into a lion! Your ewe into a ram!" but that didn't make any sense, confusing ewes and rams like that. Virgil didn't exactly have a knack for advertising copy, but he did admire the money that came in.

What began as a slow flood turned into a deluge. We spent our evenings stuffing envelopes on the kitchen table in 1-A. We expanded our selection and began offering three different lines of Spanish Fly: *Placebo* (at $6.50, still the mainstream of our orders), plus a higher-end *Spurious Spanish Fly* (in pill form—sugar pill, that is—for easy dissolving, priced at $14 a packet and aimed at our "more discerning customers"), and *Pseudo Spanish Fly* (which we sold in bulk, at a reduced price—but only on minimum orders of $25).

Every package of Spanish Fly we sent came with an "iron-clad" ninety-day guarantee. That's right. If it hadn't worked within ninety days, people had only to send in the original receipt (which we somehow always forgot to include) and within sixty days a full refund would be mailed. *"Couldn't find the receipt? Shame about that."* We got some complaints right away, of course. But not near as many as we expected, which Virgil ascribed to people being too embarrassed to admit they'd failed in whatever seduction they'd been trying to orchestrate. I suspected there was more to it than that. I figured, for a lot of our clients, it *did* work. Maybe spiking their loved one's soda pop with baking soda had given them the confidence they needed to push on.

The money fell upon us in a cloudburst, filling our pockets and wallets like they were rain barrels, open, thirsting for it. I stuffed a second tobacco tin with cash, started on a third. Hid them high in the kitchenette of 1-A now, above the cupboards, under a loose panel. I kept a healthy fold of bills handy—"walking-around money," Virgil called it—even though I scarcely dipped into that either. I didn't have expensive tastes, and Virgil insisted on picking up the tab most places we went.

Wrapped tight with the sweat of however many palms they'd passed through before being plucked free of that mug's game of honest work for honest pay, well, my rolls of money started to stink. It was something I noticed whenever I crammed more bills in. Smelled awfully good to me just the same. Was the sort of stench a fellow could get used to.

FIFTY-ONE

We had become *alchemists,* converting baking soda into gold, turning the foolish and forlorn desire of men—and even a few women, from the orders we got—into U.S. tender. There was no need to go on the forage anymore, and anyhow, we'd raked the surrounding area fairly fine. It was nice to settle in to Silver and just collect the money as it swam upstream towards us.

Virgil, though, was restless as a dog on a short leash. He found it hard stuffing envelopes in the evenings and not pulling cons during the day. Soon enough, he suggested we turn our attention onto our own city. "Can't run street cons or pocket stings in Silver," he said. "The sidewalks wouldn't be safe for us after that. But with our dream"—his dream—"of a Big Store so tantalizingly near, seems a shame not to spend this free time of ours building up more revenue."

It was time, he said, time for biz ops. These "business opportunities" were longer than short cons, but not so long as long cons, if you can follow that.

"We'll set up businesses—home repair, supply companies, investment firms. Go trolling for clients among the entrepreneurial and homeowner set. Instead of conning lowly clerks, we'll hit the owners instead. A little slower, but the rewards reaped are of a higher nature."

Biz op swindles were harder to prove and easier to dodge clear of if you got cornered. Took an investment on our part, though, of time. Money. Had to shed some of our anonymity, too. Virgil found a basement office not five blocks from Charley Wong's, past Temple-Off Drugs and near a tobacco shop and billiard hall, in a walk-down flat that was below street level. We could see someone on the stairs before they

entered. That would give us time to either lock the door or prepare to
dazzle. The office came furnished with a stenographer's desk, some
empty filing cabinets out front, and a second room—the "inter-
sanctum," Virgil insisted on calling it, even after I corrected him—with
a sizable desk and a couple of chairs for clients to park their wallets on
while we decided how much they were worth.

Rose was our receptionist, though her real job was the evaluation of
potential dupes as they came in. The place smelled of old plaster and lost
battles, but Rose stuffed the front room with flowers and went to the
stairwell outside to smoke, so as not to interfere with that burst of fresh
scent that hit you when you entered. She wore shorter skirts now, up to
her knees at times, and took to crossing her legs and batting lashes at the
men who showed up looking for insurance assessments or wholesale
bargains. She could be beautiful. When she wanted to.

"You can smoke inside my office, if you like," Virgil said to her. "It'll
give it a nice manly stench."

He liked to leave a wine-soaked cigar or two smoldering in his
desktop ashtray as well, to add to that aroma of masculinity. It was a
one-two punch, walking through our flowery anteroom into the
"inter-sanctum."

Virgil rented a telephone and paid to have nine different numbers
routed in. The phone company provided a switch box with a line of
lights that lit up depending on which number had been dialed. You
pressed the button below that light, and the call switched over. It was
cheaper than paying for a company switchboard to be installed and
worked just as well. You could hear it clicking over whenever a call
came in.

Virgil assigned different scams to different lines, to make sure
someone calling a phony plumber didn't get, say, a phony electrician
instead. He answered the calls directly. The telephone on Rose's desk
wasn't connected to anything. The first one Virgil gave her was just a
shell that he'd dug out of a trash bin and given a quick wipe.

"I'm not picking that up," Rose said, when Virgil asked her to be "on
the line" whenever a customer came in. "Smells like pee."

"Fine," said Virgil in a huff. He stomped off to a secondhand shop to buy one that didn't carry the markings of an alley cat, or worse.

"Makes me wonder if Henry the Horse has been in town," I said, gingerly lifting up the first telephone for a return to the trash.

We took turns cold-calling clients, whose names we got from the telephone book. Virgil naturally had the best gab, but Rose was just as effective as the secretary of the company president. She started off by *assuming* the sale had been made and said she was calling just to confirm the order. The prices we offered were always unbelievably low. *If it sounds too good to be true, it usually is.* That was the First Almighty Commandment in spotting any swindle. The purchasing agents and businessmen we phoned knew that, we all did. But they fell for it just the same.

Homeowners were no better. Business cons and home repair swindles would set you on the wrong side of the state contracting boards, but, as Virgil noted, the process was gloriously slow. A formal complaint had to go through a review, with lots of follow-up reports and red tape and—more to the point—lots of time to skip town.

"No such thing as sudden arrests for shoddy workmanship," Virgil said with a certain misplaced pride. "Cops'll tell the complainants it's a civil matter, not criminal. The police don't like people using them as a collection agency. Not when they have shakedowns of their own in play."

As long as we fulfilled the basic orders, there wasn't much people could do except stew. What was promised and what was delivered: did the latter live up to the former? There were no laws covering perception. Who was to say whose interpretation of events was the correct one?

"Long as we keep to the letter of the law," said Virgil, "the spirit of the law can go piss up a rope."

Virgil brought some rusted tools and a pickup truck that seemed to be suffering from the DTs. It was a wheezing Ford, barely able to catch low gear.

"Our company fleet," he said.

The first contract we got was to prune trees outside the chemical plant. Didn't bother with a ladder. Virgil just drove the truck out, parked under an overhanging tree. I stood on the roof, wielding the rusty shears and cutting at branches willy-nilly. We then drove the branches I'd cut around to the front of the plant, where we'd been hired to do some land-scaping. We planted the leafy branches into the ground as saplings. They looked like it, too, save for their having no roots. The price Virgil had quoted for the pruning was remarkably low—till they got our bill and found out that the estimate given was per *limb,* not per tree. When challenged, Virgil went indignant: "Who could make a living cutting trees for that?" He threatened lawsuits and thunderbolts, until it became clear that it'd be easier to pay him off than drag it through the courts.

We offered our services as roofers as well. If we got hired by a grain elevator or warehouse to seal their roof against leakage and rot, we'd drive out in our backfiring Ford and slap on a coat of—well, water, really. Water, mixed with aluminum paste for color. Shiny and silver: the height of modernity, a metallic roof like that. It would stop approximately zero percent of the rain, but what did that matter when it looked so pretty?

Driving away from one warehouse, I asked Virgil what would happen if it ever did rain.

"Read the guarantee," he said. He'd had a stack of them printed off. They were clad in iron, every one, and they covered everything "up to and excluding normal wear and tear or Acts of God."

I had to admit, the phrasing "up to and excluding" was a patch of sheer brilliance.

"You could'a been a lawyer," I said admiringly.

"A lawyer?" Virgil replied, appalled at the notion. "Give me some credit, boy."

I figured a law office would have suited Virgil well, though—Swindled, Bilked, Cheated & Conned—especially seeing how smoothly he'd impersonated a member of the bar back in Louisiana.

We sold lightning rods as well. To churches. That was my idea, though in truth they weren't new rods. I'd just scamper up the church ladder—never was afraid of heights—and paint the existing lightning rods with some of our leftover aluminum. Shone pure and silver in the sun after that.

"A newly developed scientific coating," Virgil would explain to the rector. "Doesn't just prevent lightning strikes, but redirects them away."

"Away?" they would ask.

"Yes," he said. "Usually to the next highest steeple."

Well, didn't that seal the deal.

The Catholics paid to have their lightning redirected to the Methodists. The Methodists paid to have theirs directed to the Lutherans. The Lutherans paid to have it sent to the Baptists. And the Baptists sent it back to the papists. The Presbyterians declined, though that was due more to a moratorium on church spending than to any moral compunction on their part. The young Presbyterian minister looked out his window at the Pentecostal spire across the street and sighed, somewhat wistfully, I thought, as he passed on our offer.

Sometimes we simply drove through town trolling for customers. Virgil had recently changed the crankcase oil in the Nash, and he mixed the old oil into a bucket of sand till it became a nice gritty sludge. We'd drive through the wealthier nooks of town and, spotting a driveway with crumbles or cracks, make a swoop.

Virgil could talk a man out of his shadow. He greeted whoever answered the doorbell with a "Howdy, neighbor" and an explanation of how we were on our way back to the plant after finishing up a job and had extra asphalt left and it seemed a shame just to dump it. How about we fix their property up, on the QT? "No receipts, though," Virgil would whisper with a wink and a grin. "Don't want the boss finding out."

Turns out respectable homeowners had no problem paying a company's workers on the sly. I wondered how they'd feel about it when, after boasting to their neighbors about the cunning deal they'd cut, several days had passed and that darn asphalt *still* hadn't dried.

Other times, Virgil would dress up in starched gray and pass himself off as a city inspector. Timed it while the husbands were at work. He'd show up with a smile and a "standard checklist." That, and some five-cent stickers that read CONDEMNED ... plus a small side flask he filled with oil. When the wife was clearing away space in front of the fuse box,

Virgil would squirt some oil under the furnace. And Lordy, wasn't it lucky he'd spotted that—and just in the nick!

"Entire boiler could blow!" he'd say, and he'd slap that sticker on the side of the furnace and tell the lady to turn off all heaters and gas ranges. "You have to get this fixed right away," he'd say. "Otherwise your gas will be shut off permanently." Then, like he was confiding in them, "The red tape involved is a nightmare. Tell you what. I'll hold off on filing my report. But you have to get someone in *immediately*—here's the card of a city-approved repair company; give them a call, ask them to fix the main gasket, tell them it's an emergency. Do that, and I'll waive the injunction."

Back in our basement headquarters, the phone would ring, and Rose could tell from which line was lighting up whether they were wanting a roof sealed or a furnace fixed. She'd answer, saying she was sending someone right away. I was nowhere near the office, of course. I was down the street, waiting in the truck.

Virgil would step outside the house, take off his hat and fan himself with it, a sign that we had the sale. We usually did. Very few failed to fall for it. One lady had a brother-in-law who was a repairman and she phoned him instead. Virgil cleared out of there double-time. Another had a husband at City Hall and wouldn't even open the door. "Furnace inspector? Never heard of such a thing."

On Virgil's signal, I'd wait ten and then drive up in the old Ford. I'd lug a tool bag filled with rocks downstairs—we owned only a wrench and some pruners—and bang around in the back of the furnace for a while, and then wipe up the oil Virgil had squirted and declare the job finished. The woman would be so grateful—and all done before hubby got home, too!—that she'd write a check for just about any amount I quoted. It was an emergency service, after all. And hadn't we saved her from having her home blow up on account of a faulty furnace? You had to give us that.

Sometimes Virgil would squirt water instead, in which case it was the pipes that needed mending and a call to Honest Abe's Plumbing Service that came through. Or, if he spotted a wire that was the least bit frayed, it was The Trustworthy Electrical Company and a repair that mainly involved me wrapping black adhesive tape around the wire and charging extra for "supplies." Or he might toss a bit of sawdust down and discover termites. He could have dropped licorice sprinkles and found mice, but that would have involved providing carcasses at some point. It was easier to wipe up water or mend a wire—though I have to say, the threat of imminent explosion added a sense of excitement to the furnace repairs that was lacking in the possible burst pipes of a water main.

Virgil would come back, soon as I had gone, to "inspect" my handiwork. He'd nod approvingly, say, "They do good work." He'd peel off the CONDEMNED sticker from the furnace and write the homeowner up as "certified and safe." And then he'd charge them a fee for the inspection. They were always so relieved, no one blinked.

They did get a nice certificate, though. And a receipt.

FIFTY-TWO

July spilled into August, and August was lost in endless toil. Morning to dusk some days, and with envelopes still to stuff after dark. We were "busier than a one-armed paper hanger," as Virgil said.

It was hard work, avoiding hard work. There were nights Rose and Virgil were too tired for jitterbug and I was too tired to watch. Our shift to daylight hours had been the toughest part of it—for Rose and Virgil, anyway. Me? I was glad to see the sun again. Had we kept moving, town to town, con to con, we might be on the road today, chasing down the next name on the map, with Rose asleep in the back of the Nash and Virgil talking loud up front. But Virgil's Big Store dreams were taking shape in front of his eyes.

It was a high-wire juggling act at times keeping our many scams on the go. While one con was paying off the next was already being put into motion. It was like the spinning of plates at a circus, or an elaborate game of Chinese checkers, jumping from one position to the next in zigzags and odd angles.

If you've ever seen a pack mule that's been grievously overloaded, you'll know how one frying pan or tin cup too many will buckle the animal's knees and bring things crashing down. For us, that tin cup was Virgil's discovery of a new storefront swindle to ply: the investigation of human infidelity. He stumbled upon it during one of his city inspector scams, when a man opened the door.

"Um, wife in?" Virgil asked.

The man's eyes were raw and red. "Gone," he said. "You're not with the investigation agency, are you?"

"Do you *want* me to be from the investigation agency?" Virgil asked.

Turns out, no.

An investigator had ruined the man's marriage.

You see, divorce required proper grounds. And proper grounds usually required either physical abuse or infidelity. If your better half wasn't outright winging chinaware at you, you needed to prove instead that you were being cuckolded. Divorce laws didn't leave many other avenues. Only other option, really, was to take up residency in Nevada, where no-fault divorce had been introduced just a few years earlier. Had to live there at least six weeks, though, to be considered a resident, and who had time for that? Better to hire an investigator to tail your cheatin' other. This hubby had clearly been on the receiving end of a fateful indiscretion.

When Virgil learned that private eyes take a hefty retainer *up front,* that settled it. We went into the investigation racket as well, naming ourselves in newspapers as "The A-1 Detective Agency! Satisfaction Guaranteed on Completion of Case—or Double Your Money Back!"

Completing a case, of course, wasn't the goal. All we were after was the hundred-dollar retainer. We could drag out the investigation as long as we liked. Even better, it allowed us to hone in on suspected philanderers.

"A wife pays us to gather incriminating evidence on her husband, how much do you figure that same husband will pay us *not* to gather evidence?" Virgil said.

Virgil was already calculating the haul our private eye business would bring in. "I'm tired of cutting tree limbs and painting rooftops," he said, even though I was the one who did the actual work. "We need a bit of fizz. A splash of glamour. Playing flatfoots for hire will give us that."

It was in anticipation of the flood of phone calls we were sure to receive that Virgil went to Silver City's pawnshops and photographic stores, looking for "cameras, Kodaks, and other such picture-making contrivances," as he put it. He came back with a fancy Leica camera, one complete with changeable lenses and a handsome leather case. Finest in German craftsmanship, that camera: nickel plating and a solid die-cast body. Virgil paid top dollar for the kit at a photography shop, and when we got it home he laid out the assorted accessories and lenses on the kitchen table for us to marvel at. When it came to cars and cameras, Virgil had good taste.

He whistled. "Will you look at that. It's beautiful."

A long pause followed.

"Virg?" said Rose. "You know how to use one of these?"

"Nope." He turned to me. "Jack?"

I shook my head.

Idea was, if we had to tail a wandering wife or a philandering husband, we could hide in the shadows and snap photographs of them, which we could then use to up our bounty. The problem, as we'd just discovered, was that none of us knew how to load the film, let alone take a picture.

Rose said, "I used to have a Brownie. Wasn't as complicated as all this."

So I taught myself how. I was up for the challenge, and it wasn't nearly so difficult as you might imagine. The Leica G had any number of ornamental features, but the basic idea—as gleaned from the instruction manual—was straightforward enough. A camera was just a mechanism for burning sunlight onto cellulose. Too much light and the subject would bubble into emptiness. Not enough, and the image would never emerge from the muck. There were only three variables involved, really: the speed of the shutter—whether you opened it for one second or 1/100th of a second; how big you opened the aperture; and the type of film you threaded into it. Some film stock was more sensitive to light, but grainier as a result. Others gave better definition, but required longer exposures. Once you worked out your setting based on a chart they provided, all you had to do was focus and shoot. Simple.

I practiced on Rose, with her staring into the camera, sometimes smiling, usually not, often behind a cloud of smoke that made it almost impossible to focus through. We'd have to develop our own prints, of course; wouldn't want to be running incriminating photographs to a lab. I purchased the necessary chemicals and painted the lightbulb above my cot red, turning 1-B into a darkroom. Was an expensive undertaking. I had to buy an exposure meter, along with an enlarger, which I used to expand the images from the negatives. I projected them onto light-sensitive paper. I went through dozens of those papers trying to get the timing right—overexposing some and underexposing others, dipping them into one bath to call the image forth and another to halt the process. I'd then pin them up on a line to dry: row after row of Rose, like she was caught in a hall of mirrors. Never could get the settings right on the enlarger. No matter how much I fiddled, she never quite came into focus. The smell of chemicals got into my bedsheets and clouded my eyes, giving me headaches and strange dreams for days after. It smelled like Listerine and warm rubber, with a hint of gin.

I spent the better part of a week under a red light, looking at Rose, before I finally gave up. I threw a sheaf of prints on the table at Charley Wong's where Rose and Virgil were relaxing after another hard day of not working.

"Can't do it," I said. The math involved was simple enough, but math wasn't the only thing in play. There was an art to it I couldn't master.

"They're perfect," said Virgil.

"Is that how I look?" Rose said, picking up one of the prints. "Am I that hard?"

"How are these perfect?" I wanted to know. Virgil's optimism, his insistence on seeing the bigger opportunities in everything, could rankle at times. I'd spent night after night trying to get Rose right, and I still couldn't do it.

"Think!" said Virgil. "We're private eyes, not portrait photographers. It's *supposed* to be blurry, it's supposed to be furtive. That's the whole entire point." Then: "Jesus, boy. You smell like you fell into a tub of kerosene. Bad enough you filled our apartment with fumes, can't you take a bath or something? You reek."

Rose held up another print, studied it. "I can't believe how sad I look."

"Camera don't lie!" said Virgil. "You need some rum and a bit of boogie. That'll cheer you up."

"You go," she said, not bothering to look up from the photographs. "I'm too tired."

So off he went.

Miss Rose looked at me. "Is that how I am, Jack? Am I really that hard? I didn't use to be."

I stared into her—the paleness of her eyes, and I said, "No."

She wasn't sure if I was just saying that to make her feel better, and neither was I.

FIFTY-THREE

It would have been impossible to open a bank account for every one of our companies. Dangerous, too, leaving a trail that wide. Last thing we needed was some Treasury T-men showing up, sniffing the air. Better to funnel our checks into a single bank account, without letting the balance get so high as to set off whistles. A little in, a little out. That was the plan. The account was handled by Virgil, which made me nervous, but he always withdrew my share immediately and paid out in cash, which I rolled into my tobacco tins, tighter and tighter. I didn't trust banks anymore. Too easy to swindle.

It wouldn't do to bounce a phony check at our own branch, of course, but a couple of times we'd net a promissory note that was so sloppily written it seemed a shame not to alter the amount. I said to Virgil, "Here's one, he left a gap between the dollar sign and the twenty and didn't even bother to write out the amount properly. Why not slip, say, a six in between, and scrawl in 'six hundred twenty' instead of 'twenty' on the line. See? There's space. Or we could change nines to *ninety*; only need to add a 'ty.' We could then run these checks to a bank in another town."

"First off, you'd have to provide all kinds of I.D.," said Virgil. "Which isn't insurmountable. But any amount worth scamming would be large enough that the bank manager would have to clear it first. It would require his signature. And no bank manager is going to sign off on a stranger's $12,000 check. Twelve dollars, maybe. But that's not enough to make the drive worthwhile."

Virgil was right, but still. I kept turning it around in my head, thinking there must be an angle we were missing.

"Bouncing checks isn't really a scam, anyway," said Virgil. "It's a compulsion. I've known people addicted to writing rubber notes just for the giddy three seconds of joy it brings. They're the dope fiends of the con man set."

With fewer evenings available for jitterbug, Virgil turned to our upstairs flat for entertainment. The money he would have spent at dance halls went into a new radio for the apartment and an electric icebox, too. Crowded us in even more than before, but now we could enjoy a jar of cold beer and listen to music while we filled our orders. I'd prepare the packets of baking soda. Rose would sort through the envelopes, keeping a running tally and making sure we hadn't left any loose threads hanging, threads a federal prosecutor might latch onto.

She was working hard, and Virgil gave her a nod for it. "A regular Tillie the Toiler, our Rose." But he was impatient as well for a bit of foot-work and jazz.

Too tired to hit the dance halls, Rose would wave him off, and he'd go on alone. He was heading out earlier and earlier, it seemed, and staying out later and later. Oftentimes, he'd scram as soon as the day's racket was done, not even staying to help us stuff envelopes, and some nights he wouldn't come stumbling back till the wee hours, slapping at the light switch and singing a mutilated version of "I'm in the Mood for Love" before flopping onto the bed and falling into a deep and snoring slumber.

I kept Miss Rose company while Virgil was out. The two of us would whittle our evenings down playing hearts and listening to the radio.

Virgil had wanted to buy a portable radio, or at the very least a chair-side model, which would have sat nicely to one side, controls on top for easy access, but no doing. Rose wanted a proper cathedral model in that classic church-window shape.

"Why not get a cloth-covered one with a hinged lid and handle instead," Virgil said. "Luggage-style, for easy escape. Doesn't even have to be cloth-covered. Sky Chief makes a nice one in alligator leatherette, with a handle *and* shoulder straps. Could lug that anywhere and on a moment's notice."

Rose wouldn't agree to that, so they compromised on an elegant but compact Audiola with slide-rule dial, mahogany finish, and fluted columns.

It was during those evenings that I first acquired a taste for Southern Comfort. Rose would eat Almond Joys and raisins and suck on ice cubes soaked in Comfort taken straight from the refrigerated hum. The sweat on her forehead formed like condensation on a glass, and when the day had been overly prickly and our skin felt stuccoed with sweat and grit, she would draw an early bath and soak awhile, then come out in a loose robe, smelling as always of Camay, "the mild beauty soap for a smoother complexion."

Once, when she was reaching across the table to choose a card, her robe fell open and her bosom half spilled out in a sudden pillowy whiteness. When she caught me looking, my face went all blushed, and she sat back and lit a cigarette and smiled a crooked smile at me.

She tucked a strand of hair behind one ear. "You tipped your hand, Jack. Gotta watch that." And then, with a blow of smoke my way, "Guess I'd better get dressed. Would hate to lead a young boy astray." She grabbed her silk pajamas, threw them over one shoulder, and headed to the bathroom singing the theme song from *Jack Armstrong, All-American Boy*. Laughter trailed behind her like an invitation. I'd heard that sort of laughter before. It was the laughter of carnies and midway barkers, daring you to call your own bluff.

"Won't you try your Wheaties?
They're the best food known to man."

I could hear her singing softly, the door not quite closed.

"They're crispy and they're crunchy, the whole year through,
Jack Armstrong never tires of them
And neither will you.
So make sure you eat your Wheaties,
The best food in the land.

For if you eat your Wheaties
You'll grow up to be a man."

On Saturday nights we'd tune in to *Hit Parade* and try to guess what
the week's top song would be, whether it was a Maurice Chevalier tune
or (more's the likely) the latest croon from Rudy Vallee. Rose always
guessed wrong because she chose the songs she liked—ones by Skinny
Ennis or Sammy Kaye—not those that were necessarily the most
popular.

Welcome to Hit Parade, brought to you by Lucky Strikes—the only
cigarettes that steady the nerves without hurting one's physical condi-
tion. The preferred cigarettes of many prominent athletes who rely on
them to keep fit and trim. And doctors agree! Light a Lucky and you'll
never miss the sweets that make you fat.

As Rose smoked her Strikes and ate her candy bars, we'd listen to
Glenn Miller and Tommy Dorsey, Duke Ellington, Count Basie, Ella
Fitzgerald. Sometimes we'd catch a comedy show, *Baby Snooks,* maybe,
or *Fibber McGee and Molly,* but mostly Rose preferred continuing
dramas.

She would catch the evening broadcasts of shows like *The Right to*
Happiness, which began with the same announcement every time:
"Happiness is the sum total of many things, of health, security, friends, loved
ones." Rose claimed she was tuning in just to mock them. *"Our Gal*
Sunday! The show that asks the question, Can a girl from a small town in
the American Midwest find happiness as the wife of a wealthy and titled
Englishman?"

"What a dilemma," Rose would say with a snort. And then, to the
radio itself: "Bump the Limey noodle and book a cruise with the insurance money. Jesus, girl."

They always asked questions like that, usually accompanied by the
warbling note of an organ. "Can a woman …?" "Will our heroine …?"
Backstage Wife asked listeners to consider the tribulations of a simple

Iowa girl married to a Broadway matinee idol, "dream sweetheart of a million other women!" *John's Other Wife* was about a man named John Perry and, well, his "other wife." His secretary, in this case. Not to be outdone, a competing network broadcast *Second Husband,* about a woman with two hubbies. Her first husband was already dead, though, so it didn't have quite the shock appeal as John and his secretary. (And they really stacked the deck for him, giving John a shrew of a wife and the gentlest little dove of a stenographer.) On the radio, they always responded to infidelities with organ music. A man found out that his wife was having an affair, and instead of grabbing a gun or an ax he ran for the organ instead, started playing with all his might. Didn't make a lick of sense.

A new soap called *When a Girl Marries* had just started up, and Rose tuned in with a determined religiosity. *"The tender human story of young, married life ... dedicated to everyone who has ever been in love."*

Rose would snort at this, too. "Opposite of love is marriage," she'd say. "Opposite of woman is wife."

She said she listened to her soaps just to laugh at them. But she listened just the same. Maybe it was because, although none of it was true or ever had been, she still couldn't quite bring herself to let go of it, not entirely. Sometimes she'd cry and laugh at the same time, dabbing her eyes with the folded corner of a hankie.

"Look at me," she'd say, "bawling like a schoolgirl."

Virgil came in on this more than once, back from somewhere else to find Rose sitting beside the radio, weeping. He would throw a look my way like I was somehow responsible, and say, "What's this?" And Rose'd laugh at her own tears, and tell him how it was just her being foolish. Virgil would sit beside her and he wouldn't say a thing. He wouldn't roll his eyes at me or wink. He'd just sit there silently, waiting for Rose's program to end and for her to come back to him.

FIFTY-FOUR

If Rose's Audiola was the source of organ music and continuing dramas, Mr. Wong's static-ridden Silvertone was one of news. Most of it bad.

As Susie asked me what type of pie I wanted, and I replied with "the usual"—meaning none—Charley's tombstone radio crackled with news of another pact. Nazi Germany had forged an alliance with Communist Russia. Between them they had agreed to divvy up Europe, that's what was rumored. It was a marriage deemed impossible until it happened— the Marxists and Fascists being foes, supposedly. But truth be told, I couldn't see much difference between Stalin and ol' Adolph other than in the size of their mustaches, and if you squinted at their photographs in the paper long enough the two of them seemed to blur together. They were calling their new alliance the Molotov-Ribbentrop Pact, but I thought of it as "the mustache minuet." And there was Uncle Joe raising a glass to the Führer, saying, "I drink to his health."

In response to Stalin's salutations, Britain and France ordered their troops to mobilize. The very next day Britain signed a pact of its own, with Poland, and the Polish government began calling up reserves. Caught between hammer and anvil, Poland was, but out here, in the southern plains, it barely ruffled the surface of our lives.

In Silver City, the skies were clear and the money was good. People were humming "Happy Days Are Here Again," and not sardonically. It was a song I'd first heard back when my mother took a turn for the worse, and I could never separate it from the sight of blackening skies or the swirl of locust swarms. Until now.

The good times were on us, and with every tree that needed pruning now pruned and every roof that needed sealing sealed, all we had to do was hang back and let the money from our mail-order placebos wash in. No one was calling our detective agency, true, but the Spanish Fly more than made up for that. It was easy money, what every con man dreamed of, as Virgil always said. But Virgil, being Virgil, was already two jumps ahead on the checkerboard.

"Investors," he said over coffee at Charley Wong's. "That's what we need."

"Investors? In what?" I asked.

"Don't matter," he said. "Just so long as they invest. Yellow Kid? He could find a mark anywhere. Shoot, sometimes they came to him. Weil was leaving a hotel lobby in San Francisco once when a fellow asked him for a match. The match cost that fellow $10,000."

Not that we'd be banking on any $10,000 matches. "But still," Virgil said, "we should start lining up some long-term prospects. Start staking out the fraternal orders, businessmen's luncheon clubs, that sort of thing. If we start reeling them in now, we can milk 'em right into the New Year."

"You don't milk fish," I said.

Virgil gave me a "What now?" look.

"You're mixing up your imagery," I said. "You reel in fish. You milk cows. I'm just saying."

"Oh, for Pete's sake. Stop being such a drip. What I'm getting at is, we start laying out our cheese—"

"Now you're talking rats," I said.

He cast a withering stare my way. "We'll catch fish. Skin rats. Milk cows. Don't make no never mind. Point is ..."

I knew what the point was. Money. Same as it always was. I had to give him the full kudos, though. No one knew how to throw down a story like Virgil did.

The De Valu corporation had just announced it was opening a new chemical plant, with dozens of contracts lined up for military research. Iron Balls Dicannti was keeping the unions on a tight leash, and the scientists and administrators were flooding in. Hotels were rife with disoriented newcomers. You could hear the money sloshing around if you listened close enough, and there was Virgil, eyes—as always—on the prize.

He started to prowl the restaurants and tonier taverns, throwing a smile out like a hat into a ring and then following it in, glad-handing all the while with a "How do you do?" and a "Shoot, I've been there!"

He had a trick for that last one, too. No matter what town or city a person was from, Virgil claimed to know it. In fact, he'd almost purchased some property there, "on Cardinal Crescent." Never mind whether such a crescent existed; they always fed him his lines after that. "What, up by the church?" "That's the place!" Or "Is that over by the river?" "Exactly! Cardinal Crescent."

The ice well and truly shattered, Virgil would then let slip something, *oops-a-daisy*, that he wasn't supposed to mention. An investment, sure-fire. As I watched him finagle a deal, I was always impressed with the way he made strategic use of suggestive silence at key moments. He let the mark fill in the blanks, do the work for him. It was a skill I would soon put to good use myself, though I didn't know it at the time.

Virgil's latest scheme involved the selling of spider farms. When he'd first told me about this, I'd assumed he was speaking figuratively, like how a "cat house" doesn't have real cats. Or a "rat race" actual rats. But no. He was really selling spiders. Or rather, their webs. It was a bit like selling the dew off a leaf, but Virgil was up for it.

"Spider farms in France are doing a booming business," Virgil would confide in his mark. "Wine merchants and wealthy *sommeliers*"—I'd looked that word up for him—"they will pay good money to have their wine cellars draped in proper webs. They do it to add the right sense of history to their wares, to fool people into spending more for last month's pressings. You know how gullible people can be."

They always did.

After sharing a chuckle at how easily people—*other* people—could be tricked, Virgil would let his marks in on a little secret. The dry environs of the American Plains were ideal both for the storing of wine— "Something to do with the acidity of the air and the absorptive qualities of the cork," Virgil would say, "though I do confess the science of it is beyond me. As the Great Almighty Satchmo says, *You don't have to go into no rudimentals*"—and for the raising of Mexican spiders, which were known for their unusually high silk-producing abilities. "A single nest can drape a case of wine bottles within a month. The cost? Pennies a nest. The return? Well ..." He'd look at them with his eyebrows raised, let them finish the equation. Virgil was setting up a whole series of spider farms right here in Silver, he told them. The major wine merchants were filling boxcars with crates of vino even now and would be sending them out as soon as the webs were ready.

The spiders were supposed to hatch in sixty-eight days—a number Virgil had pulled out of the air. That was all the time we needed, he figured, to slip away before the imaginary eggs started producing very real nothings.

"And if we're still around when the eggs don't hatch?" I asked him.

He said, "Well, if we can't stall them, we can always pay them off with ten percent of their original money as a 'return on their investment.' Most will plow that right back into their portfolios anyway. Greed has bankrupted more men than bad luck ever has."

Virgil pitched his spiderwebs to several prospective investors and soon managed to hook one: a Silver City dairy tycoon—a "big butter-and-egg man," as Virgil put it. A sprawling unmade bed of a fellow, the locals called him the "fat mahatma." He was known for his cunning nature and canny business acumen. The dairyman chewed unlit cigars till the ends were soggy, and he was famous for writing his checks with a great theatrical flourish.

"We clipped him good and well," said Virgil on the way to the bank. But as we were about to deposit the check we saw that it was made payable to GO FUCK YERSELFS.

"Damn," said Virgil, taking it in stride. "He seen through us."

Virgil moved on to sell cotton futures and tobacco options, which always seemed a bit mystical to me: selling the future like that.

I noticed, too, how often Virgil's investors turned into bullies. How often they thought they could start dictating terms to us. Just part of the eye-gouging, knee-groining nature of business, I suppose. But I suspect there was something more going on, a certain … *presumptuousness* on their part.

Let's say you grow something for a living, cotton or tobacco, or let's say you *create* something—write a book, say. And someone else sells it on your behalf, maybe sells it in countries all over the world. They do a fine job, and you make money and they make money, and everyone is happy, right?

"You would think so," said Virgil. "But that's not how it works."

Sure enough, don't the fellow doing the selling start to take on airs, as though he wrote that book himself or grew that cotton. And don't he start to feel that *you* owe *him*.

"And once that happens, don't they start to figure they own a slice of you too," said Virgil. He smiled. "Always a pleasure to take people like that down a notch."

I saw this in the businessmen we dealt with, how they figured they could buy and sell our futures, could dictate terms to us. They'd demand gratitude, demand loyalty—even while they themselves thought they could pick and choose which of their own commitments they would honor, and which they wouldn't. Funny, isn't it? How the people doing the selling always get an inflated sense of their own importance. How they start to feel more important than the people who grew the actual cotton or wrote the actual books.

"Demanding gratitude from others is never a smart tactic," said Virgil. It was a lesson that some needed to learn, even if it was the hard way.

We wheeled our deals for ranchers and oilmen and other would-be bigwigs, with Virgil trolling the hotel lobbies and luncheon clubs for investors. It was slow going at times, especially with our prospective investors always trying to renegotiate the terms—and then telling us we should be grateful to them for it.

On occasion, while walking into a hotel bar with one investor, Virgil would bump into another. When that happened, he'd whisper to the first man, "Remember Mr. Moneybags? The gentleman I told you about? Well, that's him. And it looks like he's in!" He would then excuse himself and hurry off to tell the other fellow the same exact thing.

With so many schemes in play—investor stings and second-round repair cons and biz op scams—Virgil had assumed an ever-increasing string of fake names: Godfrey Tanner, Eulen Spiegel, Arthur Orton, Nathaniel Pyke, Talbot Green, John Mount, Charley Urschel, John Philip Quinn, and so on. He had name cards printed up, and he hid them in different places on his person—in his jacket, his hip pocket, even a few in his hat brim. He could produce any name instantly, and on demand. Don't know how he kept it all straight, or how he even knew who he was at the end of the day.

"Eulen Spiegel, nice to meet you," and he'd snap out a name card without breaking banter. If he had to be Arthur Orton, same thing: "My card." Each one had a different number, but all of them funneled back into that same bank of telephone lines.

Virgil practiced in front of the mirror, in the manner of a gunfighter. He'd square off with himself—look his reflection dead in the eye—and say "Nathaniel Pyke, inventor-at-large," and whip out the corresponding name card. "Charley Urschel, oilman," or "John Philip Quinn, claims adjuster," or simply "John Mount, Esquire," and *snap!* he'd produce a card—and then check to be sure he'd chosen the right identity.

He always had.

Fifty-five

After spiderwebs and futures failed to catch on, Miss Rose wanted Virgil to give it up. But Virgil—as Virgil was wont to do—switched instead to something even more outlandish: a little something he called "cats and rats."

Normally, in one of our investor scams, my job was to wander by as Virgil was giving a spiel and be instantly captivated. I would ask obvious questions—*"You're saying there's no risk and a guaranteed return?"*—so that Virgil and the mark could share a smile and a look that said, "Youth, how callow. Not as sharp as you or I, eh, friend?"

But with "cats and rats," I was cast as a dullard barely past drooling.

The first mark Virgil cornered was a research scientist at a Sunday luncheon hosted by the Women's Auxiliary Welcome Wagon. Men of science made particularly good marks, because they saw the world in straightforward terms of cause and effect. (The hardest marks to fool? Magicians. "Don't even bother," said Virgil.) This fellow was pale to the point of translucent, with a downy blond mustache and eyes that bulged when he got excited—a tell as large as a man with signal flags.

After much prodding on the part of Bug Eyes, Virgil lowered his voice and shared his wonderful secret. "Cats," he said. "Most ladies can't afford a proper mink stole anymore. But cat fur? It's luxurious."

Never mind that Miss Rose said no lady would ever be caught dead wearing cat. Virgil wasn't pitching to a lady, he was speaking to a pasty fellow whose experiences with women were, I imagined, purely theoretical. Even with my limited encounters, I would wager that I'd probably acquired more empirical evidence than the scientist had in twice the number of years.

"I'm starting a cat farm," said Virgil. "The science of it is fascinating. We start with 5,000 female cats, imported from Mexico. Plus a healthy selection of local toms to use as breeders. Each cat has an average litter of eight kittens. By the year's end, each of those kittens will have kittens. And so on. We skin the first batch. We sell the pelts—they go for two dollars each—so even hiring men to skin the cats at twenty-five cents per, we're still looking at profit of, what, $50,000 after the first year."

"Seventy thousand, actually," said the scientist.

"Well, multiply that by eight with every successive litter."

His eyes bugged. "It would increase exponentially."

Virgil blinked. "Right. Now, what do we feed the cats?"

The bugginess in his eyes receded. He hadn't thought of that.

"Well," said Virgil, voice dropping to a purr. "This is where it gets good. We open a rat ranch—right next door. Rats breed twelve times faster than cats. We feed the rats to the cats. But what do we feed to the rats?"

The scientist leaned in closer still, eyes starting to swell in anticipatory bulge.

"Cat carcasses!" said Virgil. "After we skin the cats, we grind 'em up and feed the bodies back to the rats. We feed the rats to the cats, and the cats to the rats, and we get the skins for free."

Those eyes almost popped out of his head. "Why, it's self-perpetuating," he said, with a faint gasp.

"Exactly!" said Virgil. "A rat-and-cat perpetual-motion money-making machine. It's just a matter of applying proper scientific principles to the world of business. I tell you, if we'd listened to scientists more we wouldn't be in the mess we're in now."

The other fellow bobbed his head in agreement most earnest.

"I'll let you in on a little secret," said Virgil. "Jack here is just about the best rat-catcher in Texas. Aren't you, boy?"

"Yussir," I said, jaw slack, shoulders adroop, eyes slightly unfocused.

"He'll head up our rat ranching operation."

"Captured a high number of rodents?" the man asked.

"Yussir," I said. "Everything what creeps or crawls, from aardvarks to voles. I done caught 'em all."

The scientist, a man of chemical rather than zoological pursuits, was suitably impressed. After all, how many people have even seen an aardvark, let alone captured one?

By the time Virgil was finished, we had ourselves our first—but not our last—investor in the Silver City Cat Farm & Rat Ranching Venture.

Virgil went back to that scientist seven times over the next week, ratcheting things up every time. There were added expenses, unforeseen of course, which would be repaid in full and at a higher return on our friend's future profits. Then there was the added cost of a municipal "livestock fee." Plus fence posts. Chicken wire. There were bylaws that needed bypassing. Palms that needed greasing. And at every stage, Virgil would write him a receipt. Virgil always said, a receipt is like a guarantee from God. It assures you that everything is in its place and all is well. It's not like someone could just go out and buy a stack of receipt books from any office supplier, right?

By the time he'd finished the paperwork, Virgil's hand was starting to cramp. Twenty-one separate receipts, and each one carefully dated, stamped, signed.

"We'll call these 'operating costs,'" he explained to the scientist, with a nod and an obligatory wink, one that said, "We're all of us sharp cookies here."

The other fellow winked back. "I know the score," he said.

A couple of times the scheme almost backfired on Virgil, though. The worst was when he ran into one of his would-be investors at Charley Wong's Café. Charley had added a "Three-Dollar All You Can Eat Lunch," which was proving popular with the businessman set. Virgil and I were going in and the other fellow was at the till. Virgil tried to walk past, and was making a beeline for the back door when the fellow caught sight of him.

"Hello there!" he said, hailing Virgil like a long-lost brother, home with a winning lottery stub in his pocket.

"Davey, old boy, what's the word?" said Virgil, with a pirouette and an arm on the man's elbow, trying to steer the fellow out the door.

"It's Frederick."

"Frederick, of course!" Virgil kept his own names straight; he never bothered with the names of his marks. Sometimes, I swear, he intentionally got them wrong, just to keep the marks off balance and in a slightly inferior position. It's a matter of status, isn't it, who remembers who.

"I'm catching a train," said Freddy. "But I'll be back next week, and I'd like to talk more about your futures."

"Certainly," said Virgil. "The future's always for sale."

Charley handed over the fellow's change, and then, with a nod, said, "Hello, Virgil."

The other man's gaze narrowed. "I thought your name was Godfrey."

Virgil pulled him away from the till. "Poor ol' Charley," he said, voice dropping. "Don't pay any heed. He's been sucking the bamboo pretty hard lately. Hasn't been the same since that bad batch of opium. Easily confused. Y'see, Virgil was the name of his cat." Then, in a louder voice, "Don't know Wong from white, eh, Charley? We all look the same to you, right?"

Frederick grinned. Virgil slapped his back and sent him off. Charley looked on puzzled, not saying anything.

"A long story," said Virgil. "But from now on, let's avoid using names, okay?"

Charley shrugged.

Virgil took a step and then stopped. "I didn't mean it, you know. About the opium or knowing Wong from white and all."

"It's not a problem," said Charley, but I wasn't so sure.

That was the thing about Virgil. He always said the mark should find in you a kindred spirit, but there were times it seemed wrong no matter how you cut it. If one of Virgil's investors started complaining about how the Negroes were ruining America, how they were a stain upon the land, or if someone spoke bitterly about how the darkies had crossed the tracks and were trying to live among respectable citizens, Virgil would nod and say, "I hear you."

One fellow harangued the air for a good half hour about jazz clubs and dance halls. "That jigaboo music—it's voodoo and sin! Voodoo and sin, is what it is."

"Yessir!" said Virgil, acting like a one-man, church-choir chorus. "Them jigs are dancing with the Devil."

I know, I know. If they hate the Democrats, you do too. If they revile the Republican Party, you follow suit. If they're dripping with Christian kindness, well, you better learn to drip as well. Whatever it takes to separate the mark from his money.

"The Micks and the mockies are destroying this country," the mark would sputter, and Virgil would raise hands and testify.

It was all part of the scam. But still. To jitterbug into the night, and then in the morning act like you hadn't? Oftentimes, Virgil would be rubbing shoulders with a Klansman while still warm from last night's turn on the down-heel dance halls where the colored folks played jazz. His loyalties seemed awfully fluid. And once you started lying like that, to yourself as much as to others, I wasn't sure how you'd stop.

Sometimes during a con Virgil would throw me a line about the Hebrews conspiring with the bankers and how ol' Adolf was right to start reining the mockies in. I'd just stare down hard at the tabletop or tavern counter while the dupe went on a rant about the Elders of Zion and how the Jews were to blame for everything up to and including our latest spell of bad weather.

Even in my silence, though, I knew I was just as culpable. Because silence is never really neutral, is it?

Fifty-six

When Miss Rose decided to get dolled up, our pitch-to-success ratio skewered heavily in our favor.

There were days when all she wanted to do was lie in bed, listening to the radio and drinking Comfort, but then suddenly she'd get hopped up on enthusiasm and false gaiety and go on a tear with Virgil, plucking suckers like they were fruit from the vine. And with Rose beside him, who could say no to Virgil?

She had a beautiful black velvet Empress Eugenie hat. It was a lady's derby, essentially, with a partial veil and an ostrich plume on one side. Rose wore it raked down over one eye when she wanted to be mysterious, pulled level when she wanted to be elegant. The look was a few seasons out, she confessed, but still a showstopper in these southwestern states of ours.

With Rose's help we'd sold some more futures, and we were celebrating among the palm fronds and painted marble of the Silver City Regency Hotel. I was admiring Rose's hat and thinking about how Panamas weren't made in Panama and how certain flies were actually beetles. And how the palm fronds were really cut paper. That's the challenge, isn't it? Knowing whether you're a beetle or a fly. Palm frond or cut paper.

"Is that real ostrich?" I asked. "The feather?"

"This?" she said with a laugh. "Oh, it's real. Plucked it myself from Virgil's backside while he was strutting about."

Virgil slapped the table and laughed loud. "A peacock! Me? Aw, Toots, all this time and you still read me wrong."

"Do I?" she said.

"I'm no peacock. I'm a bird of prey." And he cooed low, like a hawk finding its height. I could see his hand slide up her thigh, under the linen tablecloth. She laughed, but she didn't push his hand away. It bothered me, not the way he was squeezing her, but how they didn't even care I was there.

"You been dippin' into the Spanish Fly?" she asked him.

"Been taking it by the truckload," he said. "What do you say, Rose? Hit the clubs with me tonight. It's been awhile."

And his hand slid farther up, started to move like he was kneading dough.

"Did you know," I said, "most of birds of prey? They live on carrion. You can see them circling the town dump outta Paradise Flats, dining on garbage and rotting carcasses."

Virgil stopped his advance, turned his head. "You don't say?"

I nodded. "It's true. They live on refuse, birds of prey. They're garbage eaters."

His eyes narrowed, ever so slightly, like he was trying to read me. "How about that," he said. "The boy's bursting his britches. Wants to pick a fight."

Rose's smile shifted but didn't quite disappear. It was like she was reading me too.

Virgil leaned across the table while a piano trickled its tunes lightly in the distance. "What do you suppose would happen if I knocked Wheaties's hat off? He don't even know enough to remove it when you sit down at a fine dinery like this. What do you say I knock it off for you, boy? What do you suppose would happen then? Think you've got it in you? I know fourteen ways to take a man down. How many you got?"

I felt my jaw tighten, and I cursed the tell. I was trying hard not to be the first to blink.

Rose's smile was gone now, evaporated like the bubbles in the glass she'd been drinking from. The only sound now was the murmur of distant voices, the faint music of the piano, and me—not breathing.

Then, that great crazy laugh of Virgil's and a *"Whoooie!"* so loud that people looked.

"I had you there, didn't I?" he said. "You were expecting a donnybrook, thought I was serious. I got you, kid! Drinks all around." He waved for a waiter at the far side of the room. "You figure they got pie?"

It was only then I exhaled.

I knew I could beat Virgil, could beat him to the ground. But I still wouldn't necessarily win.

Fifty-seven

In the newsreels and radio bulletins the future was coming at us hard and fast. On August 27, the Heinkel 178 turbo-powered jet aeroplane lifted off over the green forests of Germany.

A new generation of flight was what they were saying. The world's first jet aircraft. Instead of propellers egg-beating the air, turbos sucked it through an intake, into a compressor, and then ignited it, hurtling the plane forward. Shiny and swift, with a dashing Luftwaffe pilot at the controls, the Heinkel 178 broke 400 miles an hour on its maiden flight. It was enough to make Flash Gordon weep with joy.

Virgil and Rose and I had been on fire that summer, fueled by money sucked in as surely as air into a turbo. "We're soaring now!" Virgil liked to crow. His dream of a Big Store was in sight—in the fighter-plane crosshairs, so to speak. But then didn't our engine sputter and die, and didn't we go spinning back to Earth. I've never flown in an aeroplane, but I think I know the giddy sensation that must come when one stalls—and then falls.

Back in our booth at Charley Wong's, having an early breakfast of flapjacks and corn syrup, and me with my ever-lovin' back to the door. I was still trying to figure out a way around the bank manager's signature on a phony check. Virgil was considering a glamour scam. "Vanity is always such fertile ground. We could set up a talent agency, peddle young ladies on the possibility of screen tests."

Ever since that ballyhooed "search for Scarlett" the notion of Hollywood agents scouring small-town America for undiscovered stars, peering under bushel baskets for hidden beauty, had taken a firm hold on the popular imagination. And Virgil always was one for peddling the imaginary.

"We'll drop rumors," Virgil said. "Small at first, and then fan it like a fire. Stoke that gossip good and hot, till we have a bevy of girls lined up at our door, checkbooks ready, heads bestirred with dreams of fame and easy fortune. Build a better lie and the world will pound a path to your door. Soon enough, we'll have stage hens aplenty dragging their little girls in, done up in Shirley Temple curls, with dimples to match. Show me a mother doesn't think her little darling is a star! And won't we coo and gush enough to send their hearts spinning with a howdy-hi and a *Hooray for Hollywood!*"

Rose was disdainful of the sort of marks this swindle would net, though. "Starlets. Terrific."

"Or we could run a charity racket," said Virgil, and then quickly, "Not some cheap canister con, but a full-blown fundraiser. Conning the conscience, a con con as they say. We'll ask for company donations to our many, selfless overseas missions. Homes for fallen women. Recovering heathens. Wayward epileptics. Orphanages for blind children with polio. Or leprosy. Or blind orphaned children with polio who also have leprosy—a particularly hard-hit bunch. We'll get Rose here dressed up in a nun's garb."

"A nun?" said Rose. "I'm not dressing up as a nun."

"Do it for the orphans," he said. "If not for me, then do it for them."

"I'll pass," she said. "Collecting for charities, that's just door-to-door begging. I thought you had more pride than that, Virg."

"Okay," he said. "How about a real-estate scam? I buy an old wreck of a house—a real derelict. Plenty of those to choose from. Soon as I take possession, you and Rose come along, a grieving widow and her young son—"

"I'm not playing anybody's mother," Rose said. "How many times do I have to tell you?"

"And isn't that house the spitting image of the one that Wheaties was raised in? You make a hugely inflated bid on the place, and when it burns down before the sale can go through—there you go: *market value.* Insurance company coughs up what it's worth, not what I paid for it." He smiled. "A beautiful thing, market value. It's whatever we agree on."

Rose stared hard at him. "*I said,* I'm not going to play the widow, and I'm not going to be anybody's mother. I wasn't made for that. And I'm sure as sin not going to ride herd on a bunch of Shirley Temple starlets with fame in their eyes."

Virgil mopped up the last of the corn syrup with a wad of flapjacks, said, "So it's settled, then. We'll run a glamour scam. We haven't mined the female mark as well as we should have. Downright unchivalrous, neglecting the ladies like that."

Back in our basement office, Virgil walked us through it.

"We'll slap up a sign—THE 100% TRUTHFUL TALENT AGENCY. Hold 'limited auditions.' Wheaties can be our fashion photographer. He's the only one who knows how to operate the Leica; we'll finally get some use out of that. And Rose will be the girls', I don't know, their 'poise coach.' We'll have them wait out here"—he gestured to the reception room, where Rose's desk was parked—"to build anticipation. We'll get them to fill out some paperwork, we'll gather their checks, and we'll usher them in, one at a time, to meet Mr. Big Time Producer." He walked us into the main office. "That'd be me … Hmm. Have to get a larger desk. Some fatter cigars. Anyways. After every audition, I'll snatch up the phone and say, 'Get me Samuel Goldwyn on the line! I've found us a star!'"

Virgil picked up the phone, was about to shout into it when—

"That's odd," he said. "The line's dead."

FIFTY-EIGHT

Virgil might have been able to read a mark by the hat he wore, but Rose went one better: she spotted the government man based solely on his socks, on a single flash of ankle coming down the stairs.

I'd gone out back of the building, into the alleyway, to try to track down the problem with our telephone line. We'd received several overdue notices, having never paid a single bill, but each time Virgil would sail down to the phone company and sweet-talk his way into a "temporary extension of services." This time there was no warning, though. Phone was dead as dead could be.

I sorted out which line was ours and followed it up the side of the building, saw where it leapt across to the pole. I could see a metal plug wedged up high in some sort of control panel. It was a U-joint, the kind used to separate contacts in a circuit. We used the same thing in the mines when we had to shut down a dragger unit for repair and wanted to make sure no one got crushed in the process. It made sense here; it was a temporary disconnect. Once we paid, the phone company would send someone over to remove it. Way I figured, I had only to climb the pole and yank that plug out and our line would reconnect. The possibility of electrocution was involved, I suppose, but Virgil always said anything was better than the paying of bills for services rendered.

I went back inside to ask Virgil for a boost up. He was still on the line, clicking the receiver up and down like somehow that would fix the problem. And that was when the city inspector—the *real* city inspector—showed up.

Our front window faced low, just about at street level. Rose saw a pair of shoes appear. Stop. And then start their descent. Argyle socks. Brown on brown tartan. Shoes to match.

Virgil and I were in the main office. "Government," Rose whispered. "He's on his way in," and she quickly closed the door on us.

We could see the shadow of the man through the frosted glass while Rose charmed and delayed him. She eventually opened the door and said to Virgil, "Mr. Orton, you have a visitor." Mr. Orton was our plumber.

"Send him in," said Virgil, putting the receiver back to his ear and fixing me with a fierce scowl.

As the man from the city walked in, Virgil began berating me.

"Is this true?" he demanded. "Is it?"

I hung my head. Said nothing, wisely.

Virgil turned his attention back to the phone. "Ma'am, rest assured that here at Honest Abraham's we take customer service very seriously. If you're not satisfied, we're not satisfied. And if our plumber forgot to polish the faucets exactly as asked, we will discount the entire installation. It's our guarantee to you!"

The man from the city walked over, placed a finger on the receiver, ending the call. He was a thin man with long features, and he smiled a bloodless smile at us.

"Telephone's been disconnected," he said. "For nonpayment. I signed the order myself."

Virgil looked at the receiver. "And here I thought it was just a bad connection."

"Mr. … Orton is it?" said the government man, his thin-lipped smile never wavering. "We understand you have been running a plumbing repair service in our fair city."

"Satisfaction guaranteed!" said Virgil.

"And yet, we can find no record of you ever having obtained a valid trade license. Mr. J.J. McCormick also operates a business out of this address." He checked a piece of paper. "The Trustworthy Electrical Company."

"That's right," said Virgil. "J.J. and I share an office. You just missed him. He was here not five minutes ago. A fine man, Mr. McCormick. Upstanding citizen."

"That may well be, but I'm afraid we can find no record of a Mr. McCormick ever having trained as an electrician either, or having received any accreditation whatsoever in his chosen field." The man looked at the various licenses, certificates, and diplomas that were framed in glass behind Virgil's desk. "Which makes me wonder about those."

"Those?" said Virgil. He *pshawed* it away. "Just novelty items, really. Presents from friends. Gag gifts and whatnot."

The government inspector checked his list. "I'm also looking for—a Mr. Weiss, who is a roofer, I believe. And a Mr. Green and a Mr. Leach, contractors both. And Jeeves, the termite inspector."

"Fine gentlemen, every one. I can personally vouch for each and every—"

"Mr. Orton," said the city man as he slid a stack of sealed envelopes from inside his jacket pocket. "I am here to present you and your colleagues with a civic summons." He pulled off a rubber band, began dealing the envelopes onto the desk. "Subpoenas, in effect. You will appear before the licensing department at City Hall first thing Monday morning, with all your supporting documents in order."

"Monday?" Virgil said. "Jeez. Here it is Thursday already. End of August. Tomorrow's the first of the month and we have our payroll to finalize, our monthly reports are due. You're not giving us much time to—"

"Monday, Mr. Orton. First thing."

Virgil rolled his chair back and heaved a noble sigh. "Listen," he said. "I'm just a regular fella, trying to earn an honest day's wage. Just like you." He pulled open the side drawer and took out a thick roll of bills. "Now then, Mr. ... I didn't catch your name," he said.

"Peabody," said the man. "And do put that away. You are in quite enough trouble as it is."

A local man, won't take a bribe? Made me wonder how long they'd been watching us, how many layers of government were involved. Made me wonder whether Mr. Peabody worked for the Post Office or the Federal Bureau of Investigation, and whether he drove a Graham Supercharger with patented shark-nosed grille.

Our visitor gave us a "good day to you" nod. He turned on his heel like a Prussian officer and then left, not forgetting to tip his homburg to Rose on the way out. A gentleman, our Mr. Peabody.

Rose came in, eyes asking "Well?"

Virgil tossed the stack of summons into the trash can, pulled out a cardboard box from beneath his desk, started taking down his framed certificates. "It's been a terrific run, it truly has," he said. "But all good things. What say you two? Colorado or Oregon? Denver or Eugene?"

I voted for Oregon. "I want to see the ocean," I said. I wanted to know what it felt like to plunge headlong into saltwater. Rose voted for a third option: the Corn Belt, Iowa or Indiana.

"So, Denver it is," said Virgil. "We'll have to ship the radio and icebox. And the other clutter we've accumulated in our Silver City stopover. How many radios have we abandoned over the years, eh, Rose? How many sets have we left orphaned when we slipped out in the middle of the night?" He sounded downright nostalgic.

"Will be nice to have time to pack," she said. "And not have to flee with whatever we can snatch up."

"An orderly bug-out," said Virgil. "The best kind. Jack, give the bus company a phone call, will you, and arrange for the shipping."

I looked at him.

"Oh. Right," he said.

In the alleyway, Virgil gave me a boost up—"Goddammit, kid, you got concrete for bones?"—and I pulled myself onto the spikes the phone repairmen had used.

"Try not to get fried" was Virgil's helpful advice, hollered up to me as I pulled myself to the relay box. Took some doing, but I managed to wiggle the metal U-joint free, and when we went back inside, sure enough we had a dial tone. Rose was already boxing up her secretarial props, was already thinking of Iowa.

"I hear they're trusting in Iowa," she said. "Still believe in the goodness of human nature, the farm wives out there and their men."

I was about to dial the operator, get the direct line for a shipping company—I had my hand on the receiver, *on the receiver, mind*—when I suddenly stepped back.

"I've got it," I said. "I know how to beat the bank manager's signature on a forged check."

And that was when the phone rang.

Whenever we had to dial out, we used Line #7, which was the number for our detective agency. We did that because no one ever called that number, and we didn't want to tie up a line that might actually bring in some business. Out of habit, I always pressed #7 to call out. Had I lifted the receiver just moments earlier—heartbeats, even—there would have been a busy signal on that line, and I might be in Denver or Iowa even now.

But the phone rang, and we stopped what we were doing and stared. The light that never blinked was blinking.

It rang, and rang again. Virgil and Rose exchanged looks. She gave him a slight nod and he sat down, cleared his throat, and took the call.

"A-1 Detective Agency," he all but shouted into the receiver. "E.D. Biggers, at your service."

The use of that name for our private eye was an inside ploy, E.D. Biggers being the name of the man who wrote the Charlie Chan stories. Who knows, we'd figured, might bring us some luck. If we believed in luck. Which we didn't.

There are times I wonder, though.

Luck? *You make your own,* as they say. But that's in reference to *good* luck, to *good* fortune. What about the bad? Because the way I see it, bad luck has a way of happening. If I hadn't climbed that pole and reconnected the phone line, and if I hadn't hesitated before picking up the receiver to call the shipping depot, and if that call hadn't come in ...

The voice on the other end was raw and choked. "Like he was trying to hold back a sob," is how Virgil described it.

"I think my wife is having an affair ..."

Fifty-nine

Virgil was on the phone not five minutes, but that was five minutes of plenty. He grabbed his hat and hurried off to meet the man.

"So mousy he smelled of cheese," Virgil reported later. Our new client was a husband tormented by the specter of infidelity, by the shadows that lurked in the human heart. His young wife, the love of his life, had been disappearing in the afternoons when she thought her husband was at work. The man had heard whispers, had seen how his neighbors looked at him.

"He was sore beset. Took to driving by his own home," Virgil told us. "Like he was casing the place. His wife was always out. And he knew—he just knew, deep in his belly, that she was straying from the matrimonial path."

"How's he handling it?" asked Rose.

"Oh, the usual sob stuff. *How can I live without her. She was my everything.* He was pitying himself aplenty. Still weeping when I left."

Which was pennies from Heaven, far as we were concerned.

Virgil pulled out a fold of twenties. "He paid a hundred up front, as a retainer. One hundred more on completion. Plus another hundred if we get photos—more if they'll stand up in court."

We considered just pocketing the money. Today was the 31st, after all. Tomorrow the rent was due. It seemed right to be leaving Silver City as September came in. A hundred dollars from the distraught husband of a wandering young wife? That was like a parting gift from the town.

But the city wouldn't be knocking on our office door till next Monday at the earliest, and they'd have to form a line behind our landlord and the phone company.

"You still have those chemicals?" Virgil asked me. "The ones you use for developing photographic images."

"Under the cot," I said. "Haven't dumped them yet."

"Well, grab the camera, then. We've got some pictures to snap."

We set up across the street and down a bit from our client's house. It was a plain, sun-faded bungalow, out near the edge of town, with a patchy lawn overrun with weeds. Dandelions, already blowing gray. The curtains were pulled tight. We watched as the wife stepped out, looking both ways, furtive, sunglasses on, kerchief over her head, hair so dark it seemed painted on.

"Looks guilty already," said Virgil, scrunched down in the front passenger seat.

Rose was at the wheel, her being the best driver among us—or at least the most discreet. Virgil tended to gun the engine, I tended to grind the gears.

The wife hurried down the sidewalk and then slipped into an alley. Rose eased us into first and we followed her at a distance all the way to the Bluebird Inn. That was damning in and of itself. The hotels down by the tracks dealt with travelers—salesmen, mostly—and ranged from the seedy to the very seedy. In the center of town were some handsome hotels with fine dining rooms, the Regency being a prime example. But out here, on the raggedy side of life? Places like the Bluebird Inn were fit only for "farmers and fornicators," as Virgil put it. She didn't look like no farmer.

A hot day and dusty. When I lowered the back window of the Nash and raised the camera, the air came in hot and awful, like I'd opened an oven door.

Virgil was urging me to be quick as I focused the Leica G on the wife. She was full of fidgets, looking this way and that as I snapped a frame. I caught ROOMS FOR RENT over her shoulder. A man in pale gray approached, collar up and hat down low, walking quickly, like he didn't want to be spotted. He tried to embrace her—I caught that on film—but she pushed him back a step—I missed that. The fellow put his arm around her waist, escorted her towards the door. *Click*-advance-*click*-

advance-*click*. The last one caught them just as they disappeared into the darkness inside.

"Yup," said Virgil. "She's screwin' around. Six ways to Sunday is my guess."

Rose agreed. "She knows her husband's on to her, too. She's afraid. She wasn't brash about it, like she doesn't care if she gets caught. She cares."

"Afraid?" said Virgil. "Of what? Her mouse of a husband?"

"Just afraid," said Rose.

Virgil pushed his Panama back on his head. "Damn shame we have to leave," he said. "A fearful woman like that? We could shake her down good and strong. How much would she pay us to report back to hubby, tell him we found no evidence of any shenanigans whatsoever? A lady of secrets like that, I guarantee you she has some savings her husband don't even know about. A mattress well-stuffed, no doubt. Dang."

Well, we had our pictures. That would jack things up a few more dollars.

Back at our rooftop "liar" (as Virgil pronounced it) I opened my window and closed the door. I then mixed up the chemicals and turned the red light on.

"Jesus, boy," said Virgil, covering his nose with a forearm as he peered in. "Smells worse than a whore after a night of hard loving."

"You get used to it," I said.

I closed myself back in, stuffed cloths around to block the light outside from seeping in, pulled the blinds on the window. That still let some daylight in though, so I hung my blanket up as well.

"What are you doing in there?" yelled Virgil.

"Go down to Charley's," I hollered back. "I'll meet you there."

I ended up with three good prints. The wife alone. Her embracing her beau. And the two of them entering the hotel together. They were barely visible in that one, though, the contrast between the darkness inside and the light outside having been improperly compensated for on my part. The final photo was just a shot of the doorway, like an empty eye socket, and little else.

When I finally made it down to the café, head throbbing from the fumes and prints still damp in my hand, did Virgil greet me with a handshake hearty, and appreciation likewise? He did not. He just bellyached about how long it had taken, and when I handed the prints over, he frowned at them.

"Can't hardly see her face," he said. "Nothing overly incriminating, but still. Worth a C-note, I suppose. A man grieving his marriage like that? He won't haggle over the price."

Our waitress Susie came in, tied on her apron and topped up Virgil's cup, poured me some joe as well. Rose lit a cigarette and I ordered cornmeal and biscuits.

After Susie had left our table, Virgil looked at the photos again, said, "It's a shame we couldn't see her face better. Or maybe have photographed her in the act. I should've sent you up the fire escape. Could've peered through the window, caught her indiscretions as they unfolded. We'd get a lot more money for those."

I stirred milk into my coffee. "Still could," I said.

Virgil laughed. "You figure they're at the Bluebird, still goin' at it? Would take a goodly dose of Spanish Fly for that."

"We don't need to go back to the hotel," I said. "The photographs—they'd be blurry anyway, right?"

"I suppose." Virgil tightened his gaze on me, like a noose. "What are you getting at?"

He knew what I was getting at.

"We could just fake it," I said. "All we need's a pair of naked bodies."

Virgil went quiet. He looked at Rose. And Rose looked at him.

I was thinking art books. Hit the library before it closed. Look for nudes. I was thinking Sabine women, I was thinking Venus on a half-shell. I was thinking books—like the ones I'd left open for Rebecca to find back in the Flats. Or maybe I could take photographs of burlesque playing cards. The lighting of it would be tricky, and I'd have to figure out the enlarger settings for that, but I could have pulled it off.

Virgil and Miss Rose, they were thinking of something else. Something else entirely.

Virgil took a deep breath, said, "Well, Rose, what do you figure?"

"I am about her size," Rose said. "More or less. I've got a black wig. Could trim it to style."

I was about to say something, but they were right. The easiest photos to fake would be ones of Virgil and Miss Rose. Long as I framed them closely, cropped out any telltale features, I could produce murky images of nude bodies that—when placed alongside the ones of his wife going into the hotel—would work perfectly fine. I looked at Rose. "You sure?"

She looked right back at me. Nodded.

Virgil slapped the tabletop and hollered, "*Whoooie!* If she's game for it, so am I!"

Which is how I found myself back up in 1-A, hands shaking so badly I could barely change the lens. My palms were clammy to the point of slipping. Had to remind myself to breathe.

The curtains were closed, and the light was dim. It filtered in, illuminating arbitrary patches of wall. That's from A: *arbitrary*. The way some things just happen and there's no real reason why. The way an aeroplane will disappear into an ocean, or a coin will fall one way and not another. I turned the camera down a stop to create a deeper darkness.

Rose came out from the bathroom in a pair of satin pajamas, the pants loose. It was a pair I'd never seen on her before, barely tied up from the looks of it. Women were wearing pajamas for all occasions these days, at the beach, as eveningwear even. But they were born of the boudoir, and seeing Rose standing there, the satin catching what glimmer there was available, their true purpose was clear. To invite touch. And to fall away.

Rose pulled on the wig. She had cut it to shape and was adjusting its position.

"How do I look?"

"Wonderfully fine," I said.

"Why are you whispering?"

Virgil came out in his BVDs, his voice knocking over furniture practically. "Y'look terrific, Rose! The mirror image. So. You ready, Wheaties?"

I nodded. Virgil kicked off his undershorts, held out his arms, said, "There y' go, Jack. No more secrets. Nothing left to hide, now."

Virgil plopped down on the bed. Rose loosened the drawstrings on her pajama pants, and they fell into a pool at her feet. She stepped out of them like she was stepping out from water. Pulled her top free, and a silence came over us, as though a wind we hadn't noticed had suddenly ceased its blowing. I could hear streetcars rattling past outside, and a voice somewhere calling, but inside our room the air was thick with quiet.

I worked as fast as I could. The *click* and advance seemed unnaturally loud, my hand shaking so much it probably blurred the images right there. I was framing them through the viewfinder, making sure their faces weren't visible. We wanted only limbs and naked bodies, tangled up, pressing hard and sliding against each other.

Rose was under Virgil, her legs wrapped around him, then she was on her side with her back to me, and then she was on top of him and holding his hands down. And then she was dropping her face to his chest, pushing against him, turning to one side, hiding behind the wig she wearing.

They both had wounds that needed hiding, scars that needed covering. Virgil placed Rose's hand on his chest to cover where the bullet had been, and when Virgil turned Rose towards the camera, she pulled a handful of bedsheet up to cover her stomach.

"Not my belly," she said. "Not the stretch marks."

I finished the roll and Rose slipped off of Virgil and disappeared into the bathroom. Virgil looked up at me, grinning. "Well," he said. "What do you figure?"

"You can get dressed," I said. "I have enough to work with." And I began winding the film back into the chamber.

Virgil pulled on his clothes, and then headed out. He would arrange a meeting with the husband for later that night. I went into my room to develop the film. I was bathed in red and rolling the film through the developer when Rose stepped into the doorway.

She was wearing a robe now, but she hadn't bothered to tie it up. It hung open, loose like curtains that didn't quite close. The wig was gone, and an unlit cigarette dangled from her lips. She held a lighter in one hand.

"How are you doing, Mr. De Mille?" she asked.

"It's better you don't," I said, referring to the cigarette. "Could blow us both up."

She shrugged. "Might be fun." But she didn't strike the lighter. She tucked the cigarette behind her ear instead, the way she did that errant strand of hair that was always falling down.

It was hard to concentrate with her watching. I ran the film through, saw negative images form, the darkness and light reversed. Rose's pale body now as dark as an ink spill. The wig stark and white. The darkened bedroom beyond now a milky glow.

I moved the enlarger into place. I'd have to crop out any traces of face, even earlobes. Leave just the wig. And their bodies.

I could feel Rose beside me, peering at the images as they floated to the surface. She watched as I slipped the negatives between the glass plates of the enlarger. They were still wet, but I didn't care if they got scratched. They were meant to look secretive. In the red light of 1-B, the bodies appeared the way memories do, unbidden, taking shape slowly, ineluctably.

"Virgil photographs well," she said.

I nodded.

"He likes you," she said.

"I know."

"Figures you're the next Yellow Kid Weil."

I dipped the first usable print into the stop bath, pulled it up and down. "Well," I said. "I learned from the best."

"Who? Virgil?" she said, and she gave that snort of hers, that carnie laugh halfway between a poke and a jibe. "I wouldn't be too enamored of ol' Virgil if I were you. He's a bottom-feeder. Just like me."

"He paid his debt," I said. "He took a bullet—took it through the center of who he is." I began pegging the prints onto the line. "Way I figure, a man faces something like that, he's cleared the ledger. Doesn't owe any of us anything after that."

She was trying to meet my eye, but I wouldn't let her.

"Where are the medals, Jack?"

"The medals?"

"Long as I've known Virgil, I never seen any medals. Strange, don't you think? Him being a war hero and all?"

I slipped the next print into the tray. "Maybe he hocked them," I said. "Maybe he used them in a scam. Sold them to a chump somewhere. Or left them behind when he had to flee some city."

"Or maybe he never got any."

"I've seen the scars, front and back," I said. "That's worth more than any medal."

"True enough," she said. "Ever notice something about those wounds, though? That scar on Virgil's back—it's smaller than the one in the front. Ever notice that?"

I turned, looked at her.

"What are you saying?"

I knew what she was saying.

"It would be bigger coming out than going in, wouldn't it?" she said.

She was right. I prided myself on seeing things that others missed, but I had missed that. The wound was bigger in the front, where the bullet had come out. Virgil had been shot in the back—and much as I wanted to believe it had been a cowardly sneak attack from behind, I knew what it meant. He'd been running. Away.

"You know how they execute deserters?" Rose asked. "They don't use a proper firing squad. Not out there on the front lines, with mortars falling. No. They just blindfold them. Kneel them at the edge of their own grave—"

"I don't need to hear this," I said. "Because it doesn't matter." But it did. I held up the next print. It was blurred and murky, with no exit wounds or stretch marks in sight.

"They shoot them in the back with a high-powered rifle, let them topple forward into the hole. Saves them the carrying of corpses," she said. "Or so I've heard. Might just be a story they spread to scare soldiers onto the straight and narrow."

I hung the next print up to dry, wiped my hands. When I looked at Rose, her smile, faint to begin with, had faded completely from view. She stared right into me.

"You chose the worst set of footsteps possible to follow. A hollow man and a woman on the run." She tried to laugh, couldn't. "Want to know what happens to a flapper when she grows up? Well, here's your answer."

And then, with a glance towards the photographs I'd pinned along the line, she said, "You'll be needing some solo shots, I imagine. To be safe. Photographs, just of her."

"Perhaps."

She stood there, filling the room with awkwardness for so long I thought she'd changed her mind. But she hadn't. Rose turned, walked away, shedding her robe as she went.

She was waiting for me on the Murphy bed, the light from my makeshift darkroom casting everything in a low glow of pinkish red.

She leaned back on the bed, said, "I won't need the wig if you keep it close."

I nodded. I couldn't say anything, because my voice was stuck halfway down my throat. I picked up the Leica, fumbled with the aperture settings, looked at Rose through that narrow frame of mine, watched her swim in and out of focus as I adjusted the lens. Even though I had no film in the camera, I froze her in time with a series of *clicks*.

"Come closer," she said, and I did.

I snapped several more into an empty chamber, and then she lifted her leg up, caught the back of my knee and drew me in. I dropped the camera onto the bed. She pulled my belt loose and my shirt out—and me onto her, and her lips on mine like she was drowning and the taste of smoke on her tongue and the smell of Camay in her hair and her whispering into my ear, "*Shhh*. Slow down, slow down. We got nothing but time."

And all I could think, as she pulled me in, was "What's her angle? What's the con?"

SIXTY

Outside on a night full of stars.

Virgil was sitting on the fire escape, watching the moon watching him. I'd come onto the roof for a chestful of fresh air and had found him there, his cigarette like a firefly hovering in the dark.

"Rose is asleep," I said, and he nodded.

The glow of streetlights and shop signs formed a soft haze above the city, as though the rooftops themselves were emitting light.

"It's a beautiful sight," said Virgil, looking across. "You could climb a mountain and never get a view like this."

I agreed with him.

He said, "She's really something, isn't she? Our Rose. She'll teach you things you didn't even know you didn't know."

Virgil always said he knew fourteen ways to take a man down. I had a few myself.

"The nuns used to tell us the story of Lucifer," Virgil said. "And how he fell from the sky. You know the story? Why he fell?"

"Pride?" I said.

"Naw," said Virgil. "It was love. Lucifer loved the Lord too much to bow down to man, and he was sent to the underworld for it. That's one version. But there's another. It's one disallowed by the church, but the nuns would whisper it to us nonetheless. Lucifer was an angel, you see, second in beauty and radiance only to God himself. That's what they said."

He drew deep on his cigarette, watched the city glow. "A band of these angels, The Watchers as they were known, were sent down to earth to study man and learn his ways. They were to report back to the Angel

Lucifer and were not to interact with humans. But The Watchers became fascinated by what they saw, the flaws and the foibles of mankind, and they began to share their secrets with the Sons of Adam and the Daughters of Eve—secrets of love and war and other magics. In doing so, they brought down the wrath of God upon them. This elite group of angels had once lived in the Palace of Light, at the right hand of God, and now they were thrown down into the depths of hellfire. Lucifer among them. He had fallen in love with a human, that's what they say. A woman who captured his soul, pinned him through like a butterfly. When God discovered these transgressions, Lucifer was cast out of Heaven. And so he dwells. To this day. Forlorn and exiled. But you know something?" Virgil said with a smile. "When I finally meet him, and I imagine I will, I'm going to ask ol' Scratch if it was worth it. And you know something? I expect he'll say it was."

Virgil took one last draw on his cigarette and then tossed it over the side, watched it tumble down and break into sparks in the alleyway below. The ember flickered and then died.

That was when I saw the Graham Supercharger sedan parked behind the trash bin, hidden in blue shadows, headlights off, but with the motor running.

"Virgil?" I said.

"I see it." He stood up, stretched, and said, "If I'm going to run those photos over, I'd better go now."

SIXTY-ONE

Virgil managed to shake loose whoever it was who was tailing him. Government men, I assumed. "Lost 'em like a cat in a cornfield," Virgil boasted. "And collected a cool two hundred bucks for the photos."

Rose was asleep in the Murphy. I was in my cot, and Virgil had stuck his head in to pass along the good news.

"Hubby looked gut-punched, but he paid," said Virgil. "Just opened his wallet and let me dive in." Then: "How can you sleep with all this stench?"

Even with my side window open, the smell of the chemicals was strong. "You get used to it," I said. "We're leaving tomorrow?"

"We are." He took a step and then came back. "Listen, if you want sleep over here with us …"

"I'm fine," I said, and I stared at the ceiling until he left.

Virgil and Rose were still asleep when the sun hit the rooftops of Silver City. I went for a long walk and then fell back to Charley Wong's. I watched the people come and go. Didn't see a mark among them. Only people. It was past noon when Virgil and Rose finally showed up.

"Heigh-ho!" said Virgil, speaking to that wider audience only he could see. "What's the word?"

I looked across the table at Rose, and she met my gaze without blinking.

"Pie for breakfast!" Virgil shouted. "Apple cinnamon if you've got. Or cinnamon apple if you don't."

Susie snapped her gum and smiled. Slim William was singing sad on the afternoon's broadcast of Grand Ole Opry, and Virgil groaned at the sound of it. "Change the dials, will you, sweetheart? I can't

stand that peckerwood music. No offense, Jack." He looked over at
me. I didn't say anything.

"I'll give the dials a whirl," she said. "See what I find."

I stole glances at Rose, wanting to hold my face to her breasts,
wanting to push as deeply into that softness as possible, but Virgil was
already tearing through another story. "So, I got this crazed hound tryin'
its best to take a chunk outta my leg, and out comes King of the
Crackers, both barrels leveled, and here I'm fighting off Rin-Tin-Tin the
fucking Wonder Dog, and trying to talk my way clear of a chestful of
buckshot, when who rolls in but ..."

As Susie moved the main dial away from music, she picked up a
different signal: a voice, cutting through the static, speaking German in
a way that was no longer comical. The armies of the Fatherland had
invaded Poland. Entire divisions of Panzer tanks were rolling across
borders half a world away.

"Oh, for god's sake," said Virgil, and he got up and changed the dial
back again. "Peckerwood it is, then. Fuckin' Slim William."

Susie brought the slab of apple over. "Just the pie?"

"Just the pie," said Virgil. "We're hitting the road today. Charley!" he
yelled. "We're moving on, this time for good."

Charley came out. "You'll be back."

"No, my friend, I'm afraid not."

We still had a lot to do. We'd already arranged to ship the radio and
icebox COD to a nonexistent address in Denver. Virgil had checked
"Hold at shipping depot" under the Failure of Delivery box. He'd
bounce a check for them when we arrived. We were going to reroute our
mail as well, to some hotel in Denver, where we'd show up at the front
desk as guests to pick up any Spanish Fly money that had come in.

I had a bunch of packing yet to do, and Virgil wanted to get the Nash
tuned up before we hit the blacktop. He rose to shake hands with
Charley and slipped a few high bills to him while doing so.

"You never knew us," Virgil said. Charley nodded. He never knew us.

While Virgil was sharing a final laugh with Mr. Wong, Rose picked
up Virgil's silver cigarette case, lying there on the table, and tapped out

one for herself. I reached out, tried to catch her hand, but she pulled back, gave me a cold look. It was a look that said, "Don't go all wobbly on me. Not now."

Virgil came back to the table and swung his jacket on. "Time for goodbyes."

"You're leaving already?" said Susie, brushing flies away with her hand. "You didn't finish your pie."

"Have to get on the road," Virgil said.

"But Charley said you'd be back." She seemed disappointed. Who knows? Maybe I should have taken a run at her when I had the chance.

"No ma'am," said Virgil. "Gone for good."

Susie went to get our bill. She was chatting to Charley when Virgil suddenly froze. He spun around—and his smile had vanished.

"What did you say?" he asked her.

The waitress looked at him, puzzled.

"Just now," said Virgil. "You were saying something to Charley. Something about the Bluebird Inn."

"Oh, that," she said. "Did'ya hear?"

"Hear what?"

"They found a lady, in one of the rooms."

"A lady?"

"Butchered, alongside her kid brother. With him just out of jail and from outta state, they're figuring it's crime-related. Was horrible from the sounds of it. Guts cut out, throats slit, and them lying there in their own entrails. Here."

She brought the newspaper over, fanning herself stronger now, clearing the air of flies.

She tossed it down in front of us. September 1, 1939. The front page read GERMAN TROOPS MASSING ALONG BORDER: POLAND STANDS READY. WAR IMMINENT.

"Inside," she said. "Under 'Late News.'"

And there it was.

MURDER AT THE BLUEBIRD INN.

"They say the killer wrote a message on the wall with their blood," said Susie, eyes gleaming. She was enjoying this. "They say it was a code or something: *A-1*. That's what they say." Her smile faded a bit at the sight of our silent, God-fearing faces. She must have been wondering why we didn't find the lurid nature of the crime more entertaining.

Then Charley Wong's phone rang.

We probably should have run, right then, right there. But we were sandbagged by the news, and we didn't really know what to do. Even Virgil was at a loss for words. We just stood there, by Charley's till, trying not to let our knees buckle.

But the phone rang and that was that. I don't remember Mr. Wong picking up the receiver, even though it was right beside the till.

"Sorry, wrong number," said Mr. Wong. "No, I'm sure ... Okay, okay ... I'll check, but there's nobody here by that name."

The lunch rush was over, and we'd been on our way out. There was no one else in the place.

Charley cradled the receiver to his chest and asked us, "You know anybody named Giuseppe? Giuseppe Balsamo?"

Part Four

JACK'S WAGER

Sixty-two

Am now a lonesome cowboy,
Am now a falling star,
Am now a heartsick stranger,
Wonderin' where you are ...

As Slim William sang a slow and sorrowful tune, Virgil stood at the counter, looking gut-punched as any husband ever caught on the wrong side of love, with the telephone receiver to his ear and him not saying a word. Silence from Virgil was always unnerving.

Am now a shipwrecked sailor,
On a foreign shore,
Am now a lonesome soldier,
In a lonely war ...

I always did love country music. Drinkin' and cheatin' and runnin' around and not enjoying any of it. It's the white man's blues.

"If they know my name, they know everything," said Virgil.

Up in our apartment holdout above Wong's with the curtains drawn, Virgil was pacing back and forth—or trying to. The confines of our room forced him to take two steps and then turn, like a rat caught in a cage.

He ran his hand through his hair, his eyes filling up with panic and fear.

"I can't go back, Rose."

"No one's saying you will."

"Eastham farm is not the place for a man like me. They can sense it. It's like I was marked with blood or something. I've served three sentences already. Fourth is mandatory life. Look at poor George Parker, all he did was sell the Brooklyn Bridge to some gullible fools, and the judge put'm away for the rest of his natural born. Parker died in Sing Sing, and why? Because he had three minor convictions previous. And they were nothing. What are they going to do to me, mixed up in all this?"

"Mixed up in what?" I wanted to know. "You didn't pull the trigger. None of us did."

"She was killed with an ax," he said, and then: "You don't get it, do you? Aiding and abetting first-degree murder—"

"Unwittingly."

"*Even* unwittingly—that's hard time, boy. Never mind that I'm already in breach of parole. Never mind impersonating a private investigator. Any way you cut, it's murder, and we're involved." He turned to Rose. "They know my name. If they know my name ..." He stopped. "What if they're Travelers, Rose?"

"They're not Travelers."

"They could be."

"Did you hear an accent?" she asked.

"What if they are? What if it's the Toogood clan from O'Malley Settlement? Or the Reillys out of Fayetteville?"

"Did you hear an accent? On the phone. Any kind of accent?"

"They'll kill a man for the coins in his pocket. They'll shoot him in the back even when he's on his knees begging for his life. You know that, Rose. They'll put a bullet clean through and laugh while they're doing it. They'll leave him there t'die."

The origin of scars, an interesting thing.

"Did they have an accent?"

"I can't go up against no Travelers, Rose. I can't. I—I—"

"*Virgil!*" she said. "Get a'hold."

"Can't go back. Not to Eastham. Can't."

"Did they have an accent?"

"No," he said. "They didn't." He grew quieter, reduced his pacing to a single half-step and turn. "You're right. I have to calm down. It's just … I haven't heard that name in a long while."

"Wheaties managed to find it," she said. "How hard do you think that was? Don't prove nothing, Virg. They're just trying to spook you is all."

"Well, it's working," he said.

"So, what do they want?" I asked, though I already knew. Same thing as everyone: money.

"They want $70,000 by tomorrow night, eight o'clock. Seventy G's or they go to the feds."

"The feds?" I said. "Why the feds?"

"Girl's brother was out on parole, so jurisdiction crosses state lines. They want it in cash, tomorrow night. Told me not to get cute. *'Don't try'n palm off any Mish rolls. We're gonna count every bill. Check for phonies.'*"

"They know you well," said Rose, and immediately regretted it.

"That's what I'm saying!" Virgil yelled. "They've got my number— yours too. I'd bet on it."

"Seventy thou," said Rose. "That's some heavy sugar."

"It ain't hay, that's for sure." He ran his hand through his hair again. "They've been watching us. That's what they told me. Watching. Waiting for us to make a mistake. Well, we've done that, haven't we? Done that in spades."

Mail fraud and murder. We'd avoided getting caught up in the former.

Virgil turned to us, his confidence good and shaken. "What do we do?" he asked.

"We run," said Rose. "That's what we do. What we've always done."

"We can't," he said. "Not this time. This isn't some penny-ante swindle we helped bring about. It's cold hard murder. Two bodies. Husband on the loose. You want to be profiled on *Gangbusters*?"

Gangbusters was a weekly recap of the nation's Most Wanted, where listeners would phone in with tips to help collar criminals. Sponsored by Palmolive Shaving Cream. I used to listen to *Gangbusters* every week back in Paradise Flats. Never thought I'd end up on it.

"We're not going down in no blaze of glory," said Virgil. "Not like Bonnie. Not like Clyde. The state undertaker? In the autopsy? He dug twenty-five bullets out of Clyde Barrow. Twenty-three out of Bonnie. Said, 'I think I've found the cause of their deaths.'"

Over the course of their killing spree, Bonnie and Clyde had only ever managed to amass about $20,000—their biggest single score was less than four grand—and they had to rob a lot of banks and take a lot of bullets to get there. I had more'n twenty grand in my tins already, and I hadn't taken any bullets.

Virgil looked at me. "When they killed Bonnie and Clyde, do you know what they found in her hand?"

"A gun?"

"A sandwich. Half-eaten."

"No one's getting shot," said Rose. "We're already pretty much packed. We'll run."

"We can't," he said. "Not from this. Can't take a powder on it, not this time. It's too big."

"Even if we could pay them off," I said, "how do we know they won't keep squeezing us? Or turn us into patsies?"

"They can't," said Virgil. "Once they take our money, they're as complicit as we are. There won't be a second shakedown. They know that, it's why they want so much up front."

I wasn't entirely convinced. I knew how well the British policy of appeasement had gone: the notion that if you kept tossing table scraps to a tiger—a slice of Rhineland here, the whole Czech nation there—it would eat you last. And now the Panzers were rolling into Poland, war was at hand, and all the peace conferences and treaties in the world hadn't prevented it. Paying off Dracula with pints of blood never did strike me as a particularly smart thing to do. It's an appetite that grows with the feeding.

But in this case, Virgil had a point. Seventy thousand was a huge amount by any standard; it was the sign of a single-sting shakedown. Or so we hoped.

Virgil looked at Rose. "How much we got?"

"Not enough," she said.

He turned to me. "They've been following us since Wichita, I figure. Been waiting to pounce. They've got me pegged, and Rose too. But they won't know much about you, Jack. Take your money and run. Go on."

I looked over at Rose. Our eyes met, just for a second, and then fluttered apart.

"Run," said Virgil. "While you still can."

"No," I said. "I'm not running. Not from this."

"You don't want to get caught up in it, Jack."

"I already am," I said.

"No," he said. His voice was firmer now. "We can't ask that of you."

"I insist."

Virgil looked at me with those polished marbles of his. Nodded. "Obliged," he said.

It was what he'd said when we first met, back in Paradise Flats, back when I'd told him that Tweed was worth a fifty. *"Obliged."* That's what he said. He'd meant it then, and I do believe he meant it now.

Rose had cashed out their accounts in advance of the move to Denver, and she tallied it up. Came to just under $31,000 for the both of them. I had a shade over twenty. Which still left us $19,000 short.

"There's no way we can raise that much by tomorrow," said Virgil.

I looked at my watch. It was Friday afternoon and still early.

"I know a way," I said.

SIXTY-THREE

It was my own variation on the suitcase switch, only using checkbooks instead of satchels.

If we hurried, we could make several of the larger banks in Silver City before closing. We'd hit Union Trust, Chase National, and the Guaranty Loan Company. If we had time, we'd go for City Merchant as well.

The trick in beating the bank manager's signature, I'd realized, lay in setting up two parallel stories: one for the teller and one for the manager. Get both of them to assume they knew what the other was doing, and you could cash a very large check based entirely on misdirection.

Virgil went into each bank first to get a money-order form. We then sent Rose in to cash them, one by one, at twelve dollars each. She prattled on about the church bake sale and how they needed change. One teller was so disarmed he almost paid out her order right there at the counter, but Rose, a stickler for rules, insisted he have the manager sign it "to make sure everything is on the up-and-up." One by one, the managers at each branch dutifully signed off on them. She didn't actually cash any of the money orders, though, but slipped out instead with the managers' signatures.

Back in the Nash, she handed me the money order from the first bank. "Wallace," she said. "Ira. Affable chap. Said he'd have to stop by and taste my wares at the bake sale later. Said he was particularly fond of dates."

For each bank, I had prepared two checks, $6,400 each. I took the first pair of checks out now. They were exact duplicates, and I do mean *exact*. Had to be for the scam to work. I'd even added a smudge of ink on one corner of each, the way Virgil had made identical scuff marks on those three green suitcases he owned.

The two checks I held in my hand were completely interchangeable. I then added a key difference. Holding up the money order to the car window, I signed the bank manager's endorsement on one of them. Didn't trace it, exactly; wouldn't do for it to appear tentative or carefully drawn. I used the original signature more as a guide, signing the second name on top of the first.

Next I slid the original twelve-dollar money order into my billfold, along with the signed check for $6,400. I kept the other check, the one without a signature, in my hand, ready.

Union Trust was a heavy big brick of a building. It was a style they called Bank Gothic: solid and heavy, with thick columns crowding the sidewalk and a Roman facade, or maybe Greek. Idea was to call upon the memory of great civilizations, I suppose, to reassure customers that their money was safe, that no one could just walk in and take it. Was just another architectural con, but it worked. Although I didn't trust banks with my money, it always felt like I was entering someplace holy when I went into one. It wasn't the presence of all that cash, it was the certainty. The illusion of it that got to me.

I took a deep, steadying breath, and walked in.

Sun was spilling in from the west, warming the wood panels, giving the interior a honey-like glow. Staff seemed busy enough, it being a Friday afternoon with lots of paperwork to sort through, and I could see the manager's desk, a swath of wide walnut at the back, up on a raised platform, overlooking the entire operation. I chose the farthest wicket and slapped down that enormous unsigned check. I said to the teller, "Contract with De Valu. I was told to come here, cash it out on their account. I'll need a receipt to take back with me."

It was a safe bet that a company as big as De Valu had accounts with every bank in town, either directly or through one of their subsidiaries.

The clerk, a young man with young features, looked up at me and said, "On the Ryder account?"

"That's the one," I said.

"Checking or savings? Checking has a cap."

"Savings."

I wondered if that was how spiritualists worked, by having the mark feed them the information and then acting like they'd provided it. I had no idea what the Ryder account was, nor did I care. I might as well have been contacting the dead. *"I see the letter ... J ... Or maybe a ... K."* "My grandmother! Her name was Catherine! Spelled it with a C, but still."

The clerk turned the check over in his hand. "Our manager, Mr. Wallace, he'll have to look this over, sign for it."

I looked at the check. "Really? Here I thought Ira already had endorsed it. I'll take it over." It was important to keep hold of the check at this point, lest the clerk decide to walk it over himself. The customer would normally meet the manager in person, so he could check I.D. and such, but I didn't want to take any chances.

"You know Mr. Wallace?" the clerk asked.

"Sure. Him and my dad go way back. Won't take but a moment."

So the clerk opened the counter gate and I walked over to the manager's desk. As I did, I slid the unsigned check back into the billfold and withdrew Rose's original twelve-dollar money order instead. "Mr. Wallace!" I hollered, drawing attention from all sides. "How the heck are you?"

He stood, a tad perplexed at my overly familiar manner, and extended a hand. "What can I do for you?"

You can give me money for nothing, is what you can do. "It's my aunty," I said, dropping my voice to normal tones. "She's in a right tizzy." I pulled up a chair and showed the manager the money order, the one Rose had signed not ten minutes earlier. "She was in such a rush to get to the bake sale, she clean forgot about cashing this. She's manning the booth. Said to tell you she's saving a pan of date squares for you, even if she has to fend people off with a fork. Anyway, they need the change over at the church and the teller wasn't sure if I could cash it. Said I should see you to make sure. My aunt signed it over to me and everything."

He smiled. "Of course you may. And do tell your aunt I'll be looking forward to those dates."

I stood up, pumped his hand and said, my voice suddenly loud again, "Terrific! I knew it wouldn't be a problem. Thank you, Ira." And I left him as puzzled as ever over my familiar airs.

As I walked back, I slid the twelve-dollar money order into my bill-fold and slid the other check out. The one we'd put the manager's signature on earlier.

"There you go," I said. "Signed and approved. I knew it wouldn't be a problem."

And it wasn't.

The clerk had seen me walk over to the manager's desk and had seen me walk back. Ira Wallace had even given the clerk a nod of approval when he looked over.

I walked out of there with a fat stack of fifties. The clerk had counted them below the counter and had slid them discreetly into a manila envelope at my request.

"Don't want anyone to see how much money I have on me," I whispered. "There's a lot of crooks out there."

He understood completely and in doing so removed the last chance the bank had of catching me. The manager's desk was across a crowded room. I don't imagine he would have noticed the clerk counting out a pile of bills on a twelve-dollar money order, but you can't take any chances. I hadn't actually thought of that until the clerk was just about to give me the money, but in any con you have to think on your feet. I was in and out of that bank in under twelve minutes. That was faster than most robberies, I figured. I had $6,400 in my pocket and not a single shot fired.

Had Virgil been standing, he would have fallen over. As it was, he was in the backseat of the Nash, and even then he fell backwards into his seat with a whoop. "It's a beautiful thing, Jack! That's some moxie, you got. Some moxie indeed!"

Rose was impressed as well, and she was not an easy soul for impressing. Hell, even I was impressed with what I'd done. The con had gone down as smooth as honey into hot tea. Never mind that what we were doing was now out-and-out criminal. No beating it across county lines on this one.

The next bank went even better. The manager stood up and called across to the clerk, giving him a "go ahead" wave of his hand. His desk was partially blocked by a pillar, so I didn't have to worry about him seeing the clerk counting out a thick stack of bills either.

But at the third bank it fell apart.

It had started off cleanly enough, the clerk sending me over without a hitch. But the manager here was a tyrant in pinstripes, and he didn't much care for the clerk in question, a possibility I hadn't factored in. A stuffy man, with his head perched high atop a starched collar, he looked at me through half-lens glasses and said, "He shouldn't be sending you over for something like that. The boy's incompetent. Of course you may cash this money order, what with your aunt waiting on it and all. My apologies, sir."

And he followed me back to the counter. "I'll come over, set him straight," he said, pushing himself up from his desk.

"No, no, no," I said. "There's no need. Really."

But he persisted, and we walked back to the counter together, where said bank manager barked at the teller, "Give this young man his money and don't bother me again with this sort of triviality."

Two competing storylines had collided headlong. The clerk looked at me and then at that manager, wondering what he'd done wrong. He wavered between confused and intimidated. "But—" he said. "But—it's because of the amount, and bank policy states that—"

"Just do it," said the manager, face full of scowl. "You don't need my clearance for something like that."

"Yes, Mr. Kerr," said the clerk, meek as all get out.

The manager apologized to me again, and was just about to leave—had turned to go, I was *that close* to being clear—when the clerk asked me, "Would you like that in hundreds, sir? Or in fifties?"

And the manager stopped. Turned back, not sure he'd heard right.

How one would be paid in hundreds for a twelve-dollar money order was so paradoxical it set him off kilter for a moment, and that's all the time I needed.

"I better check with my aunt," I said—and I was gone.

They didn't see me for smoke. No sir. I ran out that door, bolted down the street and into the alley. Threw myself into the backseat and under the blanket as Rose slid the car into gear. She drove right past them. They were standing on the corner, the bank clerk and the manager, still baffled by what had happened. They knew they'd thwarted something, but still weren't quite sure *what.*

You'd think Virgil would have given me some credit for raising $12,800 in a single afternoon, but no. We were still more than $6,000 short, and he railed at me for not holding my ground back at the bank.

As Rose drove through side streets, Virgil cursed.

"Dammit, Jack. I've told you. There's always going to be moments when the mark knows. When he looks at you, and he *knows.* And when it happens, your job is to stare the moment down—to look the mark in the eye and force him to believe. You don't panic at the first sign of doubt. *Dammit.*"

"You're welcome," I said. "For the twelve grand and change I just raised."

Virgil muttered. I said nothing more on the matter, just looked out the window at the trimmed lawns that were floating past, under-watered, but well cared for and trying their best to grow. I didn't realize the significance of those at the time, but they were the key to everything. The maintenance of lawns. The life cycle of dandelions. And the flies at Charley Wong's—those not of a Spanish persuasion. The signs were right there in front of me all along, but I didn't know it.

"So what do we do?" said Rose. "It's closing time. We can't hit another bank, and tomorrow's Saturday."

"Can't believe they went off the six-day week," said Virgil. "No work ethic whatsoever in America today. That's the problem with this country. What do we do? I'll tell you what we do. Since Wheaties here fell short, we'll raise that last six grand the old-fashioned way. Street cons and pocket stings. We burn this town like it's never been burned before."

Six grand. That was more than most men made in a year. And we had to come up with it by tomorrow evening.

"Could sell some more puppies," I said.

Rose had taken us back downtown, and had stopped at a traffic signal beside a pawnshop. The shop reminded me of Cyrus Tweed's, back in Paradise Flats. And not in a good way. Forlorn artifacts hung dusty and sun-faded in the window. A tarnished old trombone. A dressing dummy. A typewriter. A violin.

Across the corner was a competing pawnshop, with a similar sad display behind windows barred and streaked. A guitar. Some patterned dresses. Another violin, shabbier than the first.

Did you catch that?

I didn't. But Virgil surely did.

"Wait!" he said when the light switched to green. "Pull over."

Virgil got out, stood on the sidewalk, fists on hips, like a general examining the lay of the land. He looked at one pawnshop and then across the street at the other.

He called me out of the car.

"Take off your jacket," he said. "Roll up your sleeves, punch the crease out of your hat. And try to look weepy."

"Weepy?" I said.

"Who needs pups?" he said. "We're going to sell fiddles. We're going to sell that violin, there, to that pawnshop, over there. And we're going to sell *that* violin, over there, to this pawnshop, over here." Virgil looked at Rose. "Colonel Jim and the Deacon used to run this one. What did they call 'em? Those fancy Eye-Tie fiddles?"

"Stradivariuses," she said. "Made in Cremona, where your people are from."

"Cremona? Is that what I told you? I thought I said Naples. Or was it Palermo? It's all so foggy now."

That always was Virgil's problem. He could keep his short-term stories straight but had trouble with the longer ones. Like who he was, or where he came from.

"Jack, my boy," he said. "You are looking at a pair of rare, hand-crafted Strada …"

"Varius," said Rose.

"... varius violins. And what a shame it is, you being a poverty-stricken young musician, having to pawn off your grandfather's heirlooms like that. Don't you think?"

I agreed. "Very much so."

Virgil went into the first shop and purchased the violin they had in the window for eight dollars. He came out and handed it over to me, and I walked it across the street, where I entered the second shop looking as beaten-down and hangdog as I could. I pawned it off for a four-dollar ticket. "My granddaddy's fiddle," I said. "He brought it over with him from Europe when he came to this New World. Worth at least a hundred." But the mean little man behind the counter wouldn't budge. "You can go across the street if you like," he said. "But the price here is four dollars. You can buy it back for six, long as it's within a week."

I took the ticket and moped my way out of there. Virgil went in, not five minutes later. He poked around a bit and then purchased the violin that was on display in their window. Paid for it with a haughty sniff, saying it was "only good for parts." But then his eyes settled on the violin I had just pawned, lying there on the counter. He lifted it up, held it reverently in his hands, blew the dust from the strings and then, noticing that it was not yet for sale, he proclaimed, "My good man, this is a genuine Stradivarius, all the way from Naples and worth several thousand dollars." He pulled a name card out of his pocket—one that read, simply, *Talbot Green, Esq.* "I'm a dealer of fine antiquities," he explained. And wouldn't you know it, he was staying at the best hotel in town. "Have the fellow who brought this in call me there. I'll pay you a finder's fee—say, fifty dollars. But you must not tell him its true value. I wouldn't want anyone taking advantage of my wealth."

And as soon as Virgil left, didn't I come right back in saying, "Mister, I can't do it. My granddaddy gave me that fiddle. It's all I've got of him. Here's your ticket back, and your money." I threw some coins and crumpled bills on the counter. "That'll make six. Give me back my grandpappy's fiddle."

And lo! but didn't that mean little man offer instead to buy it from me outright, $450 being the going price for family treasures, apparently.

I had to jig him up to that, but he figured on an easy profit of several thousand, so he cleared out his safe. I took his money—with a great reluctance, you understand, that fiddle being a family heirloom, after all.

I did the same thing again, pawning off the second violin at the first shop, with Virgil again following up. In walking an eight-dollar violin across the street and bringing a twelve-dollar violin back, we had, as middlemen—or "brokers," as they're called—made a profit of almost $500 per. That's what you call a "healthy markup."

We were inching our way closer, we were working ourselves free of a shakedown, but Silver City was getting hot. We'd have to leave soon, before our marks started closing in on us. Every time we showed our faces we escalated the risk that somebody would recognize us.

I suppose we should have felt worse about that young wife, butchered in a hotel room like that, and her hapless brother, cut down likewise. But truth be told, we were more worried about her husband, still at large as far as we knew. He was out there somewhere, and we were getting jumpy.

Rose had warned me, had said that the game can get to you. *"You start to see figures in every shadow, shadows in every figure. You start imagining things. Start thinking you're being followed, being watched."* But those fears had proven true. There were indeed figures in the shadows. At times, felt like the entire world was going to be sucked down into that darkness. And maybe that was the real curse of the one-eyed man: to see the world as it was, to see the very darkness that the blind couldn't.

We holed up for the night above Charley Wong's with the radio on, counting and recounting our money as Hitler's armies marched ever onward. Virgil eventually came clean and pulled out another five hundred he had hidden in his jacket lining. Rose did the same from one of her hatboxes. They looked at me, but I had nothing more to give. My tobacco tins contained the sum total of my education so far. It hadn't occurred to me to hold anything back.

The radio was turned low, murmuring soft about Luftwaffe air strikes. Bombs were falling on Warsaw. Outside our window on the street below, a hand organ played a hurdy gurdy tune and the music drifted up. And there's Franklin Delano, over the air, assuring Americans that "the United States will remain a neutral nation."

Virgil looked up. "We're still short," he said.

"We could sell the company fleet," I said, referring to the rattletrap truck parked behind Charley Wong's.

"Good luck," said Virgil. "We'd have to pay someone to take it off our hands."

"How about the Nash, then? We could easily sell it," I said. "Buy something cheaper. Maybe a De Soto, or a Model A. There's a notice posted on the corkboard down at Charley's. A fellow, just outta town, he has a Bantam speedster for sale. Three hundred dollars. New transmission. It would get us away same as the Nash. A little more crowded, but still."

"Can't," said Virgil. "The Ambassador is not mine to sell. I took it as a sort of down payment, shall I say, in a deal that went sour in Arlington. Anyone traces the registration or serial numbers and I'll have a heavy dose of explaining to do." He looked at me. "I didn't steal it, though. Not exactly."

The only reason he would tell me he *didn't* steal it was to make me think that he had. He looked at Rose, only a dart of the eyes, but it was enough. It was a tell, sure as any. I knew he was lying. It was his car; he just didn't want to part with it, was all, had grown attached to it. And I could see that. The Nash Ambassador was a beautiful automobile.

Virgil stretched out a crick in his neck. "Tomorrow," he said. "We'll pull out every stop, you'll see."

It had been a long day. Virgil climbed into bed and was soon snoring.

I would have done the same, had Rose not entered my room, pushing the door aside and sliding in beside me. "I can't sleep," she said.

SIXTY-FOUR

Morning, and the light filled my room.

The window to the side fire-escape was half open and the sounds of the street filtered up, strangely muffled, like voices at the bottom of a well. Dust was suspended in shafts of sun, so much so that the air seemed to sparkle. Made me think of seawater and how they'd tried to harvest gold from the ebb and flow of tides. If real gold could be strained from the sea, why not fool's gold captured in the air? You'd just need a sieve fine enough ...

Virgil popped his head in. "Jack, it's time. We have to get an early start."

Rose was beside me. The two of us were wedged in on that narrow cot. Hard to miss her lying there, but Virgil? He said nothing. Neither did I. It was a situation never covered by Ovid.

Downstairs at Charley Wong's, and the three of us ate fast.

"I told you you'd be back," said Charley with a satisfied smile.

The morning paper held no further news about the double murder at the Bluebird, which we took as a good sign. Maybe it was blowing over. But that was not to be. Luck, if it existed, had shifted against us as surely as any tide.

Our waitress wasn't in today to share the latest lurid rumors of yesterday's massacre. A man at the counter was telling Charley about it, though. The customer had his back to us, but we could catch what he was saying.

"Police have it clamped down. Entire area around the hotel. Spot-checking cars that go near it. A whole team of FBI agents arrived late last night, is what I heard. Not talking to the press or anything. They're on to something, I say."

Charley came over with the coffee pot, but Virgil waved it away.

"Have to go," he said.

"Are you okay?" asked Charley. "You look pale."

We moved through Silver City in a sort of restrained panic, working quickly, hitting one neighborhood at a time. We ran till exchanges mainly. Used them to fob off the last of Virgil's counterfeit bills. We swept through the colored areas as well, and if Virgil felt bad about this, he didn't let it show.

We stopped only for a quick sandwich at a diner—and even then, raised some change on the way out. There was a light-headed exhaustion at play. The kind that comes over you when you try to outrun a dust storm.

Evening settled on the city.

We fell back to our apartment—our liar, as it were—and we counted the day's take. With everything—the violins, the extra money that Virgil and Rose had coughed up, and the till exchanges we'd run—we had made it. But just barely. Once we paid them off we'd have less than a hundred left over. Less than a hundred to start anew with when we got to Colorado.

Britain and France had given the Germans twelve hours to withdraw their troops from Poland or face a declaration of war. I could barely follow the events of that day as they spilled in through the Audiola, so clouded had my head become. We were all of us hollowed out. Rose had shadows under her eyes, Virgil was too tired for his usual tics and chatter, and I couldn't stop yawning.

Virgil wrapped up his and Rose's share, fifty grand, in a large canvas sack. I held onto my twenty, out of habit more than anything. Virgil checked his watch. He was meeting our tormentors face to face at a diner across town. Once he'd paid them off we'd throw the rest of our things into the Nash and hightail it out. If we drove through the night and into the day, we'd make Denver by Monday.

"We'll put it behind us," Virgil promised. "Like a bad dream."

"Are there any other kind?" asked Rose.

We filed out of the apartment, across the roof, Virgil leading the way, me at the rear, my tobacco tins hanging heavy in my pillowcase.

As Virgil started down the stairs to the back alley, Rose hesitated and then said to me, "You could've left. Could've taken your cut and slipped away, could've freed yourself from this. Why didn't you? And don't say it was because of me."

"It wasn't," I said. "Not entirely."

To tell the truth, I wasn't really sure myself why I hadn't slipped out with my share. Maybe because, when everything was said and done, it was only money.

We were halfway down the metal staircase, Rose and I, when a figure slipped out of the shadows below and came in at Virgil.

Virgil was beside the Nash, had the key in the car door, in fact. He never saw it coming. Never felt the swing of the baseball bat until it was too late. It hit him full force on the side of the chest. You could hear the crack of wood on bone up where we were.

"*Virg!*" Rose shouted, but by then he'd gone down. Hard.

I shoved past Rose, taking three steps at a time, my pillowcase swinging wildly in my fist. The man with the bat snatched up Virgil's money and ran. I looked for a loose brick or a rock of some sort I could wing at him, but I didn't trust my aim. Baseball never was my game. I gave chase, fast as I could, but lost him to a side street. I wheeled around, looking in every direction—down the alley, up at the rooftops. I was short of breath, feeling a rage I hadn't known was in me. If I'd caught him, I would have killed him. A yelp, and I turned, but it was just a cat in pursuit of something else. Another sound, and I spun around to face it. Nothing. Just me and my tobacco tins.

I pulled one of them out, opened it up and grabbed a handful of bills.

"You want money?" I yelled. "I have money! Come and get it."

Nothing. Only my voice, echoing into emptiness. No one took me up on my offer.

Back in the alley behind Wong's, Rose was cradling Virgil in her arms. I could hear his breath, wheezing, and what sounded like the gurgle of bubbles.

"*Rosa, Rosa, mi Seraphina ...*"

"Don't talk," she said.

"My mouth," he asked. "Any ... any blood?"

"No," she said, and I could see she was crying.

"So they ... they didn't burst my lung. Good."

We helped Virgil to his feet, and Rose taped him up right there in the alley. She got bandages and gauze out from the glove compartment and worked quickly. Looked like she'd done this sort of thing before.

Virgil winced at it. "Fella said to me ... when he took the money, said the pawnbroker over on Seventh ... sends his regards." He tried to smile, but his face formed a grimace instead. "At least someone'll ... be happy."

True enough: sending a gorilla out to collect on a debt and having the gorilla come back with fifty G? Was a hell of a payoff.

Virgil said, "Jack. Go ... upstairs. Open the trunk. Take out ... everything."

A look came over Rose. "Virgil, no."

"Have him go to the trunk, Rose. Have him ... pull out the bottom."

SIXTY-FIVE

I'm not sure what I expected to find. A gun maybe. Silver bullets. Spanish gold, even.

But not a wooden box and a stack of blank paper, cut to size. Not that. I tumbled the trunk on its end, spilling clothes and stacks of receipts that fanned out across the floor. Hats telescoped outwards and charity tins rolled across the linoleum. I used a kitchen knife to pry the bottom loose, and the box that was hidden below was the size and heft of a large book. It was rosewood, polished to a high shine. There was a hinge on one side and a lock, so it would open like a book as well. Heavy screws on the top and bottom held both sides firmly in place.

Beside the cut paper was a flat metal canister that had the words PROPERTY U.S. MINT stenciled across it. I twisted the top off, gave it a whiff. Smelled like developing fluid.

A counterfeiter's kit, by the look of it. Having never seen one, though, I wasn't a hundred percent sure on that.

"It's a ... money machine," said Virgil when I brought it down.

We were in the Nash, driving towards the rendezvous. His sides were hurting, you could hear it in every bump and turn. He was breathing shallow, like a man with a weight on his chest. "I bought—two of them. Just have ... the one now."

"You need a doctor," said Rose.

"Purchased them ... from Lustig himself. The Count." Virgil's face was sticky with perspired pain. "I'll be—fine. Just need the morphine to kick in."

Miss Rose had been tending to Virgil well while I was upstairs. I could see a small glass vial discarded on the dash. Guess it was part of their standard first-aid.

Rose slowed down, drove past the diner where Virgil was supposed to be meeting our blackmailers. She circled around. "Two men," she said. "Back booth."

I'd thought Virgil was going to try to barter with them. Give them the twenty grand I still had and throw in the money machine for the remainder, but no.

"They won't fall … for that," he said.

"I don't like this," said Rose. "You're in no shape. Do you remember last time? You remember what happened?"

"Find … an alleyway," said Virgil.

She looked in the rearview mirror, and when she was sure no one was following us, she pulled into a back lot a few blocks away, causing the usual ratters to yowl and flee. She killed the lights but kept the motor running, hands tight on the wheel. Virgil asked me to flick on the interior dome.

In the backseat he loosened the wingnuts that held the rosewood box shut. He opened it up. Inside were two metal plates, engraved with the image of a U.S. $100 bill. Top plate was the front of the bill, bottom plate was the back.

The serial number had lines cut around it and in between every character.

"The serial numbers are loose," said Virgil. "You just—rejig them … to match whatever … whatever bill you place inside."

He unscrewed the top of the metal canister, chugged some of the liquid onto his handkerchief. "You swab the plates. Like so. Then put in … a blank … piece of paper."

He laid a single sheet between the engraved plates and then closed the box snug, tightening the screws and locking both sides.

"The chemicals need time … to be absorbed. Has to be pressed in. It gives it—it gives it the texture of a—of a cotton weave. Brings out … the dyes."

"How long does it stay in there?" I asked.

"Six hours. Twelve. Eight. However much time you need … to make a clean getaway."

In this case, he didn't wait at all. He loosened the screws. Unlocked the box and opened it up again. The blank sheet of paper had turned into a $100 bill. I held it up.

"Incredible," I said. "It looks real."

"That's because it is," said Rose.

"The top plate," said Virgil. "Drops down. Real bill ... is hidden behind it. When you ... when you loosen the screws, you'll—you'll hear—you'll hear a—"

"It'll click," said Rose. "You turn it another half-twist and the second plate falls into place. They'll never know."

The second set of plates were engraved same as the first. When the plate dropped, it revealed the bill that had been planted, covering the blank paper at the same time.

"How'd you get the engravings?" I asked. "Steal them from the Mint?"

Virgil tried to laugh, but it turned into a moan.

"Just cheap etchings," said Rose. "Count Lustig traced a $100 bill onto copper sheets. Had someone go over it with an awl."

"When you ... when you plant the bill—dip it in water first. Helps if it comes out ... damp."

"What's in the canister?"

"Rubbing alcohol. A little licorice oil. Some iodine."

Moonshine, basically.

I looked at the dashboard clock. It was getting late. "Why are you telling me this?"

"Because," said Virgil. "You ... my friend ... are going to sell this—this machine—for fifty grand."

"I am?"

Rose was shaking her head. "I don't like this, Virgil. Not at all."

"No choice," said Virgil. "We can't not."

"The money machine can get a man killed," she said. "It's not some pigeon drop or a Bible with a bullet in it. Have you forgotten how they made you kneel? You died on me, Virgil. Remember?"

"I learned—my lesson," he said. "This time, won't sell it ... to no Travelers."

Sixty-six

Travelers, no.

They would track you down across several states if they had to. They would put a hole through you, even if you were a decorated war hero and begging for your life.

Virgil figured we needed to find someone who was shady, but well-established. Not a drifter. Someone with access to real money, who would be up for something so clearly illegal. We needed someone connected, protected. But rough enough to go for it.

In Silver City that meant Iron Balls Dicannti.

A fellow takes a boot to the balls and doesn't blink? A man who busts union heads like they were pistachios? A man overseeing De Valu's sprawling interests out here? A man, in other words, who could have you killed. That's who we were planning to swindle. That's who Virgil was sending me to face.

Virgil had gone to the diner and talked to our blackmailers while Rose and I waited in the car. He'd given them my twenty thousand—everything I'd earned on the grift—as a down payment and convinced them to give us an extension. He could talk his way out of a glue spill, even with his ribs taped up and his lips numb from morphine.

They gave him till midnight to come up with the rest.

"Tell me they weren't Travelers," said Rose when Virgil eased himself back into the Nash.

"Worse," he said. "Cops."

There had been two of them: one beefy and bald in a dark overcoat. Had a glare, Virgil said, that could melt tar off a roof. The other was half the first cop's size, which is to say, still quite large. He'd sucked on a toothpick the whole time, and had eyed Virgil with a contempt he didn't bother to disguise.

The heartbroken husband had committed suicide, it seemed. "We found him," they told Virgil, "behind a shop over on Seventh. Tragic, really."

"Dead?" Virgil asked.

They nodded. "He shot himself in the back. Five times. Sad news for him, but good news for you. With the husband gone, the story ends with us. Pay up, and you're home free. Skip out and we'll find you." One of the men had smiled. "Fourth time at bat, am I right, Giuseppe? I have a cousin at Eastham farm. Works as a guard there. You should look him up next time you're through."

The sun was long gone. Night was upon us. Our only hope now lay in the miraculous money machine I was holding on my lap. Rose drove us across town, past the carnival-like lights and humming transmission wires of the De Valu chemical plant. The place gurgled and blinked like a high school chemistry set. When we'd been pruning the trees and planting branches out there, Virgil had spotted Dicannti's house, beyond the plant, with a gable and a gate and a man out front. We drove there now.

"Remember," said Virgil. "He'll think—the plates are stolen. So he can't—go to the law without—without incriminating himself. That's the block." He took a labored gulp of air. "Don't always work, though —the block. Not when a mark decides to ... to take matters into his own hands. But, you'll be fine. I'd bet on you ... any day."

"We're not sending Jack in alone," said Rose.

"But if something goes wrong—"

"Virgil, no."

"Fine," he said, irked at her concern for me, irked at the worry she was showing. "Give me ... an eight-count. And then follow." It took him a while to get out of the car. We were parked across the street and just out of view. Every movement was cause for a sharp wince on Virgil's part. He stood, swallowed the pain, straightened his shoulders, and then walked towards the gate.

Rose and I followed a moment later. Virgil had pulled on a clean jacket and wiped the sweat from his face and Rose had given his tie a

crisp knot. He was looking every bit the G-man he'd so often impersonated. Tonight we wouldn't be exchanging cash drawer tills, though.
Tonight the stakes were considerably higher.

Virgil strode straight up to the guardhouse, brash as anything, attract-
ing attention as Rose and I slipped by in the shadows. And it seemed to
me that everything I'd done since I first crossed paths with Rose and
Virgil had been leading to this. *"Think of it as your graduation,"* Virgil
had said in the car. And it was, I suppose, though in more ways than one.

The guard never saw us.

"Special agent, FBI," Virgil was saying in a loud voice. He flashed his
badge. "I'll only need a minute of Mr. Dicannti's time."

It wasn't like Dicannti was a Rockefeller or anything, or even a true
member of the De Valu family. But he worked for them, and as such a
certain protocol had to be followed. The guard called down on the short-
wave, got the nod, and sent Virgil in.

Rose and I were against the wall of the house by now, off to one side.
Virgil saw us, said nothing. A cream-colored Lincoln was parked out
front, a Studebaker sedan beside it. Virgil rang the front doorbell, took
one last pain-defying gulp of air.

Mr. Dicannti was surprisingly small for a man of such large repute. I
had expected a shadow to fall across Virgil when Dicannti came to the
door, but no. Just a thin man in a smoking jacket, barely as tall as Virgil.

Dicannti had a man with him, for protection apparently. Too bulky
to be a butler. Rose and I pressed even farther back against the wall.

"You're with the Bureau?" Dicannti said.

"That's correct," said Virgil. "Can we speak a moment—alone?"

Dicannti gave a nod to the fellow beside him. "See that the others are
tended to," he said. Then, turning back to Virgil, voice steely, "What is
this about?" A man with skeletons, clearly, in closets and cellars and
landfills, too, no doubt. Virgil allayed those fears quickly.

"It's nothing, really," he said. "And I'm sorry I had to … to bother you
at home like this. But a pair of plates have gone missing from the U.S.
Mint and we've been contacting men of—of high stature. Just as a—as
a precaution."

"A precaution?" said Dicannti.

"Yes. To warn you against people who may want to sell you a large amount of cash. The plates are for hundred-dollar bills. They aren't counterfeits. They're real. They were filched directly from the U.S. Bureau of Engraving and Printing. So there's—there's no—" Virgil was sweating, trying not show the small agony he was under. "No way for us to identify—any of the bills they produce. No way for us to trace them. Which is why we wanted to—to give you fair warning. They'd be legal tender, you see. But they'd have been *produced* illegally. We'd ask you to call our office if you see any—Here. I've just received a telegram regarding this. It may have a number you can call." He unfolded a paper, looked at it and then said, "Hang on. There was more to it. Turns out they've been spotted in Jersey." He stuffed the paper back into his pocket. "Never mind. False alarm. I'll be on my way."

"Who was spotted in Jersey?" Dicannti wanted to know.

"The perpetrators. Connie Parker and her young lover, a ne'er-do-well by the name of William Daniel Jones. Sounds like we have a fix on them, so I'll—" Virgil stopped, wiped his brow with a handkerchief. "I'll bid you adieu, sir. Nothing more for me to—to do here."

Dicannti nodded. "Good luck, officer, on catching them."

No sooner had Virgil left than Rose and I jumped up, startling Dicannti back a few steps. His hand went to his side, reaching for a gun that wasn't there.

"Please, mister," said Miss Rose in a frantic whisper. "You gotta help us."

"Who the hell? What in God's—"

"Please," said Rose. "Hear us out. We got a proposition for you, don't we, W.D.?"

"We do. Connie ain't lyin' at you, mister. We heard you was a good man. And if you'll just give us five minutes of your time ..."

Dicannti looked past us towards the gatehouse, and for a moment I thought he was going to summon the guard. But no. He was looking to make sure that Virgil had left and no one had seen us.

He stepped to one side. "Get in," he said. "And hurry."

SIXTY-SEVEN

A fine house it was, the Dicannti *abode*. That's from A as well.

He whisked us upstairs to his office, along a sweeping stairway past urns and ferns and other ornaments. "Wait. Right. Here." And from the chill in his voice, I thought, *Yes, this is a man who could take a boot to the balls.*

Dicannti had been entertaining some guests, and he went to clear them out. Rose and I waited in his office, with its lake of a desk, its statuary of Roman maids—reminiscent of Ovid himself, I thought—and the gilded frame and full-length portrait of Mr. Dicannti. As Caesar.

Rose looked around, whispered, "Money. It can buy you anything except taste."

Then, suddenly, she threw herself onto me, pressed her mouth deeply into mine. For one moment I thought she'd been swept away by the danger in what we were trying to do, but it wasn't that. Dicannti was on his way back in, and Rose wanted him to catch us, lips on lips.

Iron Balls cleared his throat, cast a disapproving glance our way. A woman like that, corrupting the morals of American youth? Shameless, is what it was.

"You come barging into my home with an illegal proposition. What do you take me for?"

As much as I can, pal. As much as I can. I should have been afraid, but I wasn't. He wouldn't thump us, not before he'd heard our pitch. He wouldn't be calling the cops, either. Why get tangled up in something, even incidentally? If he didn't take the bait, the worst thing I could see happening was him throwing us out on our ears.

Dicannti looked at the clock on the mantel and said, "Five minutes.

After that, I call the police." But he was bluffing, I could tell. He was a small man of dark doubts, the kind who eyes his reflection with suspicion when he's shaving in the morning. The kind who figures he's too smart to be taken.

I placed the money machine on his desk, said, "Mister. We're on the lam, and we need money. Lots of it and fast."

"Relax," he said, and his lips curled into something that might have been mistaken for a smile. "They think you're in Jersey."

Here, I thought, was a man who liked to have an inside track—to information, tips, schemes, sure bets. Here was a man who couldn't resist playing a winning hand. Here, I thought, was a mark worth clipping. I knew right then, right there, we had him. He didn't know it yet, but we had him. We had his union-busting, Caesar-posing, jacket-smoking, hard-balled self in our back pocket. It was just a matter of letting it play out. Was like a game of billiards: once you have the shot lined up, the balls don't have a choice but to go in.

"Stolen from the U.S. Mint," I said. "We're not talking counterfeits. We're talking legal tender."

I swabbed the engraved plates, slid a blank sheet in, and closed the box. Tightened the screws till I heard a faint click—and then tightened a half-turn more.

"Impossible to trace," I said. "Now that we're off the gold standard."

Mr. Dicannti gave a thoughtful nod to this and a frown of approval, even though the statement made no sense whatsoever. It sounded meaningful, though, and that was the point. It had crossed my mind that with De Valu Enterprises being a chemical plant, trying to bluff our way through with rubbing alcohol and iodine might be a mistake. But Dicannti had been hired because he was a kneecapper, not a chemist. If anything, the alchemy of the factory, with its white-clad scientists and their pungent mixtures, may have played into our hand. Dicannti was probably predisposed to being impressed by the magic of modern chemistry.

Rose was pacing back and forth, looking through the window, smoking furiously. "Trail's hot, W.D.," she said. "We're in deep with the East Coast bunch."

"It'll be fine," I snapped.

"We'll need fifty G's, at least," she said, "just to get us out of this mess."

"Will you calm down," I said, and I gave Mr. Dicannti a roll of the eyes, one that said, "*Wimmin,* what can you do?" He nodded, like he and I were in the same fraternity. We were just a pair of regular fellas, ones who understood that business was business and that some things took time.

I looked at the gilded winged angels on Dicannti's mantel clock. Was a quarter to nine. We needed the longest stall possible, to get as far away as we could before Dicannti discovered the truth.

"It'll take three hours for the dyes to set," I said.

Dicannti phoned one of his moneymen, told him to come by at eleven forty-five. Sharp. "We'll see if that bill passes muster," he said. "This"—he gestured to the money machine—"never leaves my sight. You understand? I go to the bathroom, I take it with me. I go for a smoke, it comes along. I'm not turning my back on this box until I see it opened. In fact, I'll do the opening myself, if that's all right with you."

I nodded. That was fine with us.

"Now then," and his demeanor softened. "What're you drinking? Gin? Tonic?"

"Comfort," I said. "If you have any."

He took a step towards the wet bar and then stopped, smiled a little smile, and took the money machine with him. What he didn't realize was that the switch had already been made, and right under his nose.

"On the rocks?" he asked.

"On the rocks," I said.

We drank to his health and he to ours. Dicannti put his feet up and he held that money machine on his lap and his smile became a grin.

Lest he consider dumping our bodies in a landfill somewhere once our magical money box had proven its worth, Rose made a point of mentioning our confederates several times, who were waiting for us back in town. The nuance being, if we didn't turn up we'd be missed, and the breadcrumbs would lead straight to this house.

Turned out Iron Balls was from Philadelphia. "Fallbrook, actually. Just outside the city."

"Fallbrook?" I said. "Shoot, I've been there. Got an uncle who owns some property up on Cardinal Crescent."

"Well hey!" said Dicannti with a raise of his glass, and we chatted away amiably about Philly and the old neighborhood and how it had changed, and not for the better, and how the problem was all them darkies who were moving in. And I agreed with him every step of the way.

He stopped at one point, like he'd just noticed something about me. "You look familiar," he said. "Your Pappi? Does he work for the railroads?"

Dicannti used to freelance, cracking skulls for Henry Ford, quashing labor disputes for various railroads as well. I do believe that may have included a certain strike on the Southern Pacific.

"Truth is, I don't have a lot of my father in me," I said. "The resemblance isn't there. And you wouldn't know him anyway, my Da."

"What does he do?"

"My Da? He builds houses."

"Oh," said Dicannti with a nod. "Well, you look like someone. Tell me. You heard about the strike up in Flint?"

"I did."

"Well, what you heard is wrong."

He was only too happy to set me straight on whatever it was he thought I didn't know. And so passed the evening, on battle stories and tales of cowed workers. Dicannti took an avuncular interest in my young and wayward ways, warning me that a life of crime was no life at all. He took a decidedly less avuncular interest in Rose. She was able to parlay his every innuendo by fretting over our situation and pretending not to notice. But it irritated me, the way he tried to flirt with her when I was sitting right there. It made me want to take a kick at the can myself, see if I couldn't crack those walnuts. Though in a way I was. Cracking his nuts, that is. He just didn't know it yet.

The moneyman arrived, a stooped fellow with reading glasses and what looked like a medical bag. The sort of man who gets a greasy thumb from counting so much illicit cash. The sort who would gladly doctor the books to hide the flow of certain revenue streams. He didn't notice the polished rosewood box on his boss's desk. Dicannti told him to wait outside.

Dicannti then turned to us. "When I bring him back in, not a word of where this money came from. Total secrecy. Got it?" Rose and I heartily agreed, though for starkly different reasons. Dicannti wanted to keep his golden-egg-laying hen a secret. We didn't want an expert on currency telling him that copper plates and a chemical that changed ordinary paper into cotton weave was pure bunk. So, yes. Secrecy was best for all concerned.

Dicannti loosened the screws one by one. He opened the box and light all but spilled out of it. It was a moment of magic, on every level. Magic in the awestruck sense. Magic in the sleight-of-hand sense, too. And even though I knew what was coming, it was breathtaking just the same, to see that sheet of paper transformed into a $100 bill—still damp, but every bit a picture of perfection. Was enough to bring tears to your eyes.

Dicannti stifled a gasp, held up the bill like the miracle it was. "Remarkable. It's … Maynard!"

He closed the box and slid it to one side as stoop-shouldered Maynard came shuffling back in.

"I suspect this bill is a fake," Dicannti said. "Examine it and give me your verdict."

Well, well. My, my. Ol' Maynard eyeballed that C-note like he was an Amsterdam diamond dealer. He scrutinized it first under a series of magnifying lenses. He held it to the light, scrunched it up in his palm, and then flattened it out. He ran his finger along the edges, examined the weave. He soaked a wad of cotton in a solution of some sort and rubbed it into one corner. He pulled out some fibers with tiny tweezers, soaked them in the solution, examined the results. A cunning man, casting stones. Reading the signs. Finally, and with a bobbley sort of nod, he said, "Genuine U.S. currency."

"Not counterfeit?"

"Not in the least."

Dicannti grinned. He waved Maynard out of the room with a regal toss of his hand, acting very much the Caesar that he aspired to be. He then turned to us, and his grin was gone.

"I'll give you twenty-five," he said.

"Now hang on a second," I said. "The deal was for fifty."

"Twenty-five," he said. "Take it or leave it."

"Fine," I said. "Sixty."

This threw him back. "Sixty?"

"Okay. Sixty-five."

"But, but," he sputtered. "I said twenty-five, dammit, not—"

"Seventy," I said.

"*Seventy!* What the hell are you—"

"Seventy-five," I said. "And that's our final offer."

His face was mottled with splotches of red, two parts Southern Comfort and one part indignation. "Seventy-five?" he roared. "*Seventy-five!*"

"Great. It's a deal, then?"

"*No!* It's not—What are you trying to—"

I leaned in. "Do the math, mister. You sleep, what—seven, eight hours a day? You keep this nearby, feed paper into it when you get the chance, and that's $400 a day, easy. Which is $2,800 a week, and $145,600 a year."

I held up the canister of leftover fluid, gave it a slosh so he could hear it. "A five-year supply of the necessary chemicals, right here. You want the money machine? Cough up seventy-five grand right now. Don't make me go to eighty."

At which point Rose cut in, speaking harshly at me. "W.D., just take the fifty thousand, okay?"

And so, fifty it was. Dicannti smiled, smug and satisfied, liked he'd pulled a number on us, like he'd haggled me over good. Funny how the mind works, isn't it? But you know what's funnier still? Although raising our price just to drop it was something I'd learned from Sukanen's Dry Goods back in Paradise Flats, and I'd done it simply to cut off the price dickering on Dicannti's part, we might have actually gotten seventy-five grand from Caesar there. Should have *started* at seventy-five. Damn.

While Dicannti opened the safe behind his portrait—how long would it have taken a safecracker to find that?—I slipped another blank paper into the machine.

"Just remember to let it sit at least three hours," I said, tightening the screws, listening for that click, and then rolling past it. "Longer is fine, so don't panic if you can't get to it in time. You open it earlier than that, the colors'll fade."

"Can we go already?" Rose said. "We're late."

And we were.

It was coming up fast on midnight and we had a pair of crooked cops to pay off. We bid a farewell, fond and heartfelt, to our generous benefactor, having checked his stacks of hundreds quickly to make sure it was all there. I was nervous. If anything was going to happen, it was going to happen now. We'd soon find out if our fictional confederates waiting back in town were the deterrent we hoped they would be.

Rose and I walked down the sweep of the stairway. Dicannti's bodyguard was sitting in a chair, bored and lethal, beside the front door. We nodded to him as we passed; he didn't deign to respond. If his boss was going to give him a signal, now was the moment. But we went out the door and up the driveway, then past the guardhouse. We were giddy with fear and excitement, me clinging to the bag filled with Dicannti's money, Rose clinging to me. She was breathing hard. My knees were jelly and my head was filled with helium. It was almost—*amorous,* the effect it had on you, pulling a con like that. The rush of blood, the rising tension, the release and the euphoria that followed. That heady, heady joy. All that time, and I'd never once heard Rose and Virgil making love in the next room. Maybe they got their excitement from running the game instead. Like how they'd dance themselves into laughter and sweat and catch their faces reflected in each other's eyes, the effect not unlike a carnival hall of mirrors.

I could taste it on my tongue, the elation. I could see how habit-forming it might become. An appetite that grew with the feeding.

We hurried down the lane beside Dicannti's house, Rose's heels clicking under the streetlamp gloom, our nerves drawn tight as an overwound timepiece. We listened for the crunch of tires behind us or the soft swoosh of a baseball bat, but there was just the dry-blowing wind and the sound of traffic two streets over.

Lights flashed, twice, and Rose broke into a run.

SIXTY-EIGHT

Virgil had been into the morphine, it seemed. His eyes were smiling separately from his mouth, and he had a touch of drool on the sides of his lips. Still, he wasn't babbling to himself or eating dead flies or anything. Not yet, anyway.

"If it's all the same, I'll drive," said Rose.

"No need," said Virgil, as he put the Ambassador into gear and eased us out of the alley. "I've been in worse shape than this. Remember Albany?"

"I wasn't there for that," she said.

"Really?" he said. "I thought you were. I remember you there."

"C'mon," I said. "We're already late."

"I phoned," he said. "While you two were hobnobbing with Mr. Iron Balls. I called our friends, told them we were running behind."

"How'd they take it?" asked Rose.

"Not well."

Rose stacked the fifty grand into one of Virgil's green leather valises. The diner appeared, and I could see two men hunched over in the back booth. But Virgil kept going.

As the late-night eatery slipped past, a small pocket of neon in a much larger night, I said, "What are you doing?"

"I'm taking you back to Charley Wong's. You wait there, by the phone." Virgil looked at me in the mirror as we drove past darkened storefronts and sleeping tenement buildings. "You don't get it, do you, Jack?"

"Get what?"

"Once I pay them off, they have no incentive to keep any of us alive. Do you want to end up like that husband, with five in the back?"

"The man killed his wife," said Rose. "He had it coming."

Never mind that the only reason he killed her was because of the photographs we had provided. The *false* photographs we had provided.

"Meaning?" I said.

"They're ruthless, Jack. These people we're up against. Won't think twice about killing me. Or Rose. Or you."

I was the insurance policy, it turned out. You see, Virgil was going to threaten them with a blackmail of his own. He was going to try to out-bluff death itself. Was going to point out to our crooked cops that he had the dope on them as well. What was the FBI going to say about two local flats shaking down a material witness in a federal murder case? He wasn't going to ask for money, only our lives.

"So we can't have all of us in one place," said Virgil. "We need an outside ace."

The idea was, as long as Virgil returned unharmed, I wouldn't tip off the Bureau. Our blackmailers would go their way, we would go ours, and that would be that. So fixated were we on those two cops waiting on Virgil at that diner, that it hadn't occurred to us there might be other players involved. It was a grave miscalculation on our part.

Virgil pulled up in front of Wong's Café. Another pocket of light in a dark night. I was told to sit tight at Charley's and wait for the all-clear.

"Go in," said Virg. "Have some pie and coffee. And leave a decent tip, will you? Oh," he said. "One more thing." Virgil handed me an envelope.

"What's this?"

"Two twenties," he said. "And a bus ticket."

"A bus ticket?"

While we'd been dealing with Dicannti, Virgil had made a run to the depot. "It's a ticket south," he said. "To Paradise Flats. If I don't return from the rendezvous, get yourself to the Greyhound. There's a late run to Lubbock, leaves at two. Continues on from there, stops at every hiccup along the way, but it'll get you home. If you have to hide, that's where you'll want to be. Among kin. Rose and I will come for you when things are clear. When we make it. *If* we make it." Then, with a smile that was far too wide, far too broad, and far too sincere, he said, "But don't you worry about us. We'll be fine. That bus ticket is just a backup. You always need a plan of escape, Wheaties."

Was I being set up?

As they drove off with the money, leaving me with only a bus ticket and forty dollars to my name, don't think it didn't occur to me. They might just keep on driving all the way to Denver. Or Iowa. Or Someplace Else.

We all of us have our tells. With Virgil it was a twitch of the lips holding back a smile, the dart of an eye. With Rose it was that one strand of hair that never seemed to stay put. That was a tell; it was also a signal, as I'd found out when we were playing monte at the county fairs. When Rose tucked her hair behind her ear it meant, "Take him. Take him for all he's worth."

A signal thrown is intentional. A tell is not. With Rose it was hard to separate the two.

There were a lot of maybes in play. Maybe Virgil had already paid off our blackmailers with the original fifty thou. Maybe he'd never been asked for seventy. Or maybe there'd never been a mugging, not a real one. Maybe the time had simply come to discard me. Maybe all I'd ever done was help them with the seed money for Virgil's Big Store dreams. Those ribs of his were well and truly cracked, though. I had seen the bones move under his skin as Rose taped him up. I could hear his chest rattle and wheeze when he breathed. But that could have been a miscalculation too. Perhaps the assailant they'd hired wasn't supposed to hit Virgil that hard. Maybe the man had gotten caught up in the excitement and had erred on the swing. Maybe it was supposed to be a bruising, not a breaking.

A setup was certainly a possibility. But as I walked into Charley Wong's Café, and as the door swung closed behind me, and as I nodded to Charley and took my seat—back to the wall this time, because Virgil wasn't there to keep watch over me—and as I asked for a cup of coffee and a slice of Charley's best, I knew the real reason that Virgil and Rose weren't going to leave: *they needed me.* They needed me more than I needed them. From the false arrest to the Spanish Fly to the bank manager's signature, I was the one who'd taken the game to its proper heights. They knew it, and so did I. It was a sad and liberating thought, the realization that they had no more lessons left to teach. It was me who had brought in the big money. And though I suppose they needed me in other ways as well, the monetary would always be the deciding factor. It wouldn't be a smart business decision, leaving me behind.

Charley came over, filled my cup, said, "Are you okay?"

"Just tired, is all."

"A young man like you?"

I nodded, and Charley laughed.

"You need some Spanish Fly," he said. And in an instant, my fatigue was gone.

I snapped my attention onto him. "What did you say?"

"I said ... Spanish Fly, that's what you need."

"Spanish Fly? *Spanish Fly?* How'd you know about that?" I asked again, my voice louder than I had intended. "How did you know about that? *How?*" We had never stuffed envelopes in front of him, had never discussed our activities with him.

Charley's smile faltered. "I don't know ... It's just—You looked tired. That's all. I was making a joke. Susie told me about it, she used to tease me, say 'Charley, you need to get some Spanish Fly! It drives women crazy.'"

"Susie?"

"My waitress."

"Oh, right." *Susie.* The girl who snapped her gum, laughed at Virgil's jokes. A good girl, Susie. One of the great invisibles. Janitors. Winos. Waitresses. Even when you noticed them, you didn't. Not really.

"I'm sorry," I said. "Didn't mean to get so uppity. It's just, I'm a little on edge is all, and when you mentioned Spanish—Where is Susie, anyway?"

"She quit," said Charley. "Went home early yesterday, called this morning to say she wasn't coming back."

Fair enough. Even in these depressed times of ours, the turnover was high in the field of food services. I stirred my coffee and stifled a yawn.

"Well, what can you do?" I said.

"She never even came in to pick up her pay."

And didn't that snap me back awake like a wet towel. "*What?* No."

"Her last week's pay," said Charley. "She never came in for it. I still have her wages in the till."

"No," I said. "No, that ain't right, Charley. That ain't right at all. God*dammit.*"

And in that moment, everything clicked into place, sure as tumblers in a lock. The dandelions. The flies. Everything.

"What's the problem?" asked Charley.

"You don't understand," I said. "You pay shit wages, am I right?"

"Hey! I pay proper minimum wage."

"You pay proper minimum shit, Charley. Forty cents an hour, plus any tips they can scrounge. Am I right? Someone trying to live on those wages, they can't afford to *not* pick up their paycheck. You know that. They wait on it, count the days to it. Every penny matters. No. That ain't right—that's—What time does the afternoon edition come out?"

Charley was confused. "Afternoon what?"

"The newspaper. When does the afternoon edition come out?"

"I don't know, after the lunch rush."

"Two o'clock," I said. "That's when it comes out."

"I guess …"

"Yesterday's paper," I asked. "Where is it, Charley? The morning edition."

"I don't know," he said. "In the back, I think. I was cutting fish on it."

I ran to the kitchen, found the paper. Front page had slices in it, and the center was blotted with fish oil, but I turned the pages, found the story. MURDER AT THE BLUEBIRD INN. It was on a page filled with tractor ads and bland stories about farm auctions and 4-H meetings. The page matched the rest of the newspaper in size and feel—but I'd expected as much. They would have had lots of time to get it right. *And a man with a press and a bank loan will print just about anything for money.* What they couldn't have been prepared for, though, was us pulling up stakes and leaving town on the very day they'd planned to set us up. At the top of the page I found what I was looking for: beside the date—September 1,

1939—in small caps was the heading AFTERNOON EDITION. Every other page was marked MORNING, except that one.

"You okay?" said Charley, watching me examine the newspaper.

I turned to him. "A midnight murder makes the morning edition?" I said. "Possible, I suppose. But why risk raising our suspicions unnecessarily? Better to wait on the afternoon edition."

They had planned on slipping that doctored page in then, to let us come upon it on our own.

Charley's puzzled face told me he wasn't in on any of it. And that was good, at least.

It was supposed to have played out in the afternoon, but when Susie heard us telling Charley we were leaving—for good, this time—she panicked. She had to get us that doctored news story right then, right there. She had to improvise, had to slip the page with the murder report into the morning edition instead. And her waving her paper as she came over, waving wide, clearing the air of flies that weren't there. That would have been the signal. Someone in the café, or maybe outside on the sidewalk. That would have been the signal to make the call. There was a booth across the street from Charley's. They must have phoned from there.

The wig and the dark glasses the wife was wearing. She wasn't hiding who she was from her hubby. She was hiding it from us.

It had bothered me in a vague sort of way, the number of weeds in the front lawn of that bungalow. A young couple, husband obviously in love with his wandering bride? A man like that would pull weeds. Virgil had deciphered the front yards at the church residences of Cuthbert, but this time he'd missed it. So had I. With rain so sparse, how long would it take a yard full of dandelions to sprout? Some time, I'm guessing. And hubby never pulled a single one to please his wife?

Why were dandelions growing? Because nobody was living there, that's why. They'd rented it only a few days before, I would guess, and had kept the curtains closed to hide the emptiness inside.

"Charley," I said. "I need to use your phone book."

Sixty-nine

I asked for Giuseppe Balsamo, and when Virgil came to the phone his voice sounded weak.

"Virgil," I said. "It's me. Stay put. I'm coming to get you out of there. Don't turn your back. Don't try to leave. Stall for time. Have them check every bill for counterfeits. Palm a note if you have to, get 'em to do a recount. Tell them it was your 'insurance policy' on the phone and that I'll be calling right back. Whatever it takes, but do not walk out of there, Virgil. I'm coming to get you."

I hung up the receiver … but I didn't bolt. No. I had another call to make, and after that I stood up, threw a couple of bucks on the counter, and bid Charley a good night. I then sauntered away, slowly and full of yawns. But I was walking faster than it seemed.

I could hear the car pull out behind me. Could hear it roll along at a distance, stalking me. I didn't need to turn and look. I knew exactly what make and what year. Heck, I even knew the color. It was a 1939 dark-green Graham Supercharger sedan with shark-nosed grille, and I knew the headlights would be turned off. I even knew who was inside: a waitress who snapped her gum and had an accent from all over. Beside her, a long-lost brother, the one who'd been killed at the Bluebird; a husband, who'd murdered said brother and then been killed by the cops; and a customer who'd sat with his back to us at the café counter and talked loudly about the killings. Comprising, in all, one man.

She might even have her wedding band back on. Wouldn't matter, because she wouldn't be seeing us ever again, not face to face. And that was the key.

I was laying a fateful wager, you see. I was betting that whoever was with Virgil at that diner across town had never gotten a close look at us. No. Our roper was the lady in the Supercharger. It was hubby's job now to make sure I didn't get out of their sight. I was the insurance policy, after all, and if things went askew at the diner, if someone took out Virgil and Rose, they would need to remove me from the equation as well. They'd been watching Virgil for some time, I guessed, waiting for him to get back in the game. They knew he'd been released from Eastham, knew he had three strikes against him. Knew which blade to twist. They had bided their time, waiting for us to build up a bank roll, waiting for the right moment, the right scam. Everybody had one with their name on it. This one was Virgil's. They knew he would cave.

I headed into the alleyway behind Wong's Cafe, heard the tires turn soon after. Those two in the car, *they* knew my face. I was betting heavy that the other two, the ones at the diner with Virgil, wouldn't. Not up close. Not enough to recognize me. Not if I filled myself with confidence first.

I climbed the back stairway to the roof, feet clanging. I heard the car come to a stop in the alley below. I went into Apt. 1-A, threw on the lights, and then dropped to the floor. I belly-crawled into 1-B, grabbed the second green valise case, stuffed it with a sheet to fill it out, and then slid open the side window and slipped free, down the other fire escape and away. I hit the ground running.

I would have taken our company fleet, if it hadn't been parked in the very alleyway that the Supercharger had staked out. Instead, I ran. I ran and I ran, fourteen blocks at least, jumped on a passing streetcar, rattled through the night with it and then leapt off again.

Rose was there, beside the diner, waiting in the Nash with the motor running.

I stopped. Looked at her, almost as though for the first time. The thought hadn't entirely escaped me that I might still be the mark in all of this. I half-expected it, actually. But I don't think even Rose could have faked that look of raw fear. As I drew closer, I could see her hands clenched tight on the steering wheel, and in her face—everything. I could see how much she needed Virgil, how much Virgil needed her. I could see it in the worry, and the aching of it. And though I'm not exactly sure what love is, I do imagine worry is a large part of it. It's the people we worry about who really matter, isn't it? That's what I saw in Rose's eyes. Worry. And I knew right then, I had lost her. Had never really had her. It was Virgil and Rose all along; I was just there for the ride.

I came up on the side of the car, tapped the glass, and she jumped.

"Rose," I whispered.

She rolled down the window. Saw me standing there with the suitcase. "Jack? What are you—"

"I need a vehicle. Fast," I said. "Go to the Regency. Get a driver and a car. Promise them double pay, whatever it takes. The best one they've got. A Lincoln or a Caddy. Send the driver here right away. Do it now."

I told her what I was planning to do, and why, and a look flickered across her face. It wasn't quite worry. But close.

"Toss me your lighter, too," I said. "If you don't mind."

Inside the diner, they were counting the money. Our money.

Entire place seemed gummy, as though covered in a thin film of cold grease. Stools lined up and empty along the counter, their vinyl seats splitting in half, most of them.

Virgil never saw me coming. But they did. "Well, darn it," Virgil was saying. "I could have sworn the entire amount was there."

He had his back to the door. Across the table from him were the two heavies, draped in overcoats, hats pulled down low. They had Virgil's green suitcase open and Virgil was stacking the bills. Again. My original twenty, along with the fifty I'd sold the money machine for.

"Not sure why it would be short," said Virgil. "Say, you fellas ever been to Abilene?"

I headed straight towards them, past the counter clerk and to the back booth. I tossed the suitcase I was carrying onto their table. The two men looked up at me and then at Virgil.

"Who the fuck is this?" they said.

I threw myself down beside Virgil, loosey-limbed and lackadaisical, like I didn't care.

"Which one of you is Giuseppe?" I asked.

They couldn't help it, their eyes darted towards Virgil, and I immediately bounced Virgil's head off the table. *Bam!* He reeled back up, nose bleeding, clutching his face. *"Fuck,"* he said.

The no-neck across from me sputtered, "What the hell?!"

"I want to know," I said, "whose bright idea it was to walk off with $120,000 of my Da's hard-earned money." I opened the valise I had thrown onto the table, and I pulled out a handful of bedsheet. "Big joke, is it? Maybe Giuseppe here can elaborate?"

"I ..." He was still clutching at his nose, trying to sop up the blood with a handkerchief. "I needed the money, I needed to ..."

And *bam!* his head went back down on the table, harder this time. "Christ," he said, reeling to one side, blood everywhere.

The other two had narrowed their gaze on me. They were trying to read me, looking for tells.

"So," I said, and I let the faintest of lilts creep into my voice. It was the sort of accent my Da had brought over with him from St. Kilda. Not quite Irish, but close enough. "Let me see if I understand," I said, speaking to Virgil, but with my eyes locked onto the two men across from me. "You thought, what the feck, I'm in a bit of a bind, I'll just help myself to some of Jimmy Toogood's stash. Is it? Is that what you thought, you dumb fecking wop? Is that it? Is that the shite yer spinnin', Giuseppe? That you were in a bind?"

I took out a cigarette, tapped it on the silver case. "Who the feck are you?" I said to the other two. "And what are you doing sitting there on your fat arses, counting my Da's money like you earned it?"

They were speechless. As well they might be, caught up in something like that.

I flipped open Rose's cigarette lighter, went to flick the flame. Couldn't do it, though. My hands were shaking. And they noticed.

The larger man leaned in, eyes square on mine, staring hard.

"Who," he demanded, "are you?"

And there it was.

The moment. The one Virgil had always warned me about, the moment when they *know.* I finally got a flame going, and I drew in deeply off the coal. Calms the nerves, tobacco does. It's a wonderful thing. I held back a small cough, let the smoke out slowly ... and then flicked my cigarette into the larger man's face. It burst into sparks on impact, and he leapt back, brushing away at it.

"Who am I?" I said. "*Who am I?* I'm the worst fecking day of your life is who I am."

The other man whipped out a badge, flashed it in my face. "Officer Allen," he said. "Silver City P.D."

I plucked it from his hand. "Really?" I said, and then, without even looking at it, "I've seen better tin at a carnival midway." I tossed his badge with a snap of my wrist. It skittled across the floor like a stone over water. The clerk was mopping behind the counter and he looked up— and then immediately down, trying his best to be invisible.

The smaller man leaned in, patted his coat in what he hoped was a menacing manner. Maybe he was packing a persuader—a billy club or a Roscoe, perhaps. I didn't care.

"My Da has the entire feckin' police department in his pocket," I said, "and I've never seen either of your ugly faces before."

I stared down any doubts they had. Stared until they blinked, until their fear began to show.

"We've got your other two friends, that dollybird and her beau, back at the barn," I said. "Oh, she's weeping now. Seen the error of her ways. Spilling the beans, isn't she? 'Cut him down,' she blubbers. 'Oh, please cut him down. I'll tell you where they are.' Women," I said. "So sentimental. Hate to see someone they love in pain like that. So here I am. She ratted you boys out, led me right to this very diner. And what do I see before me? Three cheap grifters who think they can steal from my Da."

"I'm not with them," Virgil stammered, and I hammered his face back onto the table. This time he was able to brace with his hands first.

"Shut the feck up," I said. Virgil flashed me a look. It said, *You didn't have to hit me that hard*—but I did. To flinch was to die. A pulled punch is no punch. And a head banging, well, that's easier to take than the alternative.

"Listen, chump," said one of the men, trying to regain the upper hand, trying still to sound tough. But his voice wavered. Heck of a tell, that one. It was the sort of thing that could get a man killed.

"A cop, are you?" I said. "You're no feckin' cop. You're a street-hustlin' con man who is just one impolite wisecrack away from a slow and certain death. My Da, he sent me in, because I'm the reasonable one. My brother Davey, he wants to remove your fingers one by one. All ten of 'em. But I says, 'Leave them at least one thumb between 'em, so's they can hitch a ride out of town after we're done with 'em.' Reasonable, y'see?"

I needed time for the driver Rose was hiring to arrive. I stacked the bills on the table, did a quick tally, said, "Where's the rest?"

They'd taken Virgil for fifty in the alleyway. There were four of them working us, so that would be twelve grand each, plus change. These two would have had their shares on them. Can never entirely trust your partners, after all.

"Cough up," I said. Sure enough, pasty-faced now, they handed over envelopes with twelve grand each inside. "You're still short," I said.

So they went deeper still, into their own wallets, emptied their billfolds, turned their pockets. I made another grand or so right there. Cleared those fuckers out of every dollar, every dime. They were so thoroughly whipped they even threw in their watches and rings.

I gathered it up and placed it all inside Virgil's original green valise. "Y'know John Connor O'Reilly, yah?" They nodded, mute with fear, even though John Connor O'Reilly was a name I'd pulled out of the air. "Runs with the Williamsons. Works for us, as well. They call him the Surgeon. You know that, right?" They nodded. "Know why?"

They didn't. And I was only too happy to illuminate them on this matter, for I was sailing now, with a chest full of wind, feeling light and invincible, and the lies just spilled out, so true, so clear, I half believed them myself. "Ol' Connor has an inkling for do-it-yourself surgery, y'see. Came over here from Belfast the Beautiful, made his home in these United States and carved out a niche for himself in that most literal of senses. Some called him the Belfast Butcher, but the way I see it, that's an insult to his craft. The man is an artist. One who commands respect.

He's the only person Dillinger ever backed away from. Ah, but you already knew that." And they did. You could see it in their eyes: "*Lord deliver us. We've crossed paths with a man Dillinger was afraid of.*" It was planted in their brains, and once there, they wouldn't be able to shake it.

"You know how they say 'an eye for an eye'? You've heard that, right? In the Holy Book?" I waited till they nodded before I went on. "They call him 'The Eye Doctor' to his face, but when he's not around they whisper a different name. Not Butcher. No, worse than that. They call him Corkscrew. *Corkscrew Connor,* that's what they call him, on account of that being his preferred surgical instrument. Did'ya know, if you work a corkscrew into someone's eye, that eye'll pop clean out, like a plum from a pie? Fascinating, yah?"

I closed the suitcase, looked back over my shoulder as a black sedan pulled up beneath the diner lights outside. A V12 Lincoln K, from the looks of it. A "Sunshine Special," if I wasn't mistaken. Handsome automobile, that one, with its coffin-shaped hood and its curved pontoon fenders. It was a vehicle often used for the parading of presidents and dignitaries and lesser heroes. A driver in a gray uniform and a chauffeur's hat got out.

"Right on time," I said. I slid out from the booth, nodded towards the window as if I was throwing a signal. I picked up the two valises, one in each hand.

"Gentlemen?" I said.

I led them out onto the sidewalk, and once outside I stopped and then threw a curt nod in each direction, as if signaling a fleet of henchmen who were hovering in the shadows.

And that's when I saw the Graham Supercharger drive up.

It pulled over at the end of the block and killed its lights. They must have realized I'd slipped away and had come scrambling here to tell the others that their insurance policy had gone missing. But dollybird and her beau were hooped too. I turned away from them, just to be safe, but even if they had recognized me from down the block, they couldn't have risked rushing over—a husband and wife back from the dead and instantly recognized? Their entire con would have collapsed.

Still. I had to move fast. I hustled our friends into the back of the Lincoln and threw a suitcase up front with the driver. I then said to them, "You two are going to deliver this money to my Da personally. You are going to apologize for the aggravation you have caused him, and you are going to arrange repayment on the amount remaining. With interest, yah? Do that, and the odds are you'll get away with both your eyes. Which is more than dollybird's husband can say. Poor one-eyed fucker."

I turned my hard gaze on Virgil.

"As for you," I said. "You're coming with me."

"No," said Virgil, fearful, almost in tears. He tried to climb into the Lincoln with the others, begging, "Let me talk to Jimmy, I can smooth things out." But the other two pushed him back like he was going to capsize them. I had to pry Virgil forcefully away. "Not to worry, Giuseppe," I said to him. "We'll leave you your thumbs. I'm a reasonable man."

I slipped the driver another hundred, hit the roof of the car twice. As the Lincoln drove away, and before Virgil could grin or do anything stupid, I grabbed him by his velvet collar, pulled him up on his toes, said to him, under my breath, "Don't smile, goddammit. Across the street. Supercharger sedan. When it pulls away, tell me."

I didn't have to wait for a signal from Virgil, though; I heard the tires squeal.

"Gone?" I asked.

He nodded. "They drove away, fast"—and now he *was* grinning—"in the other direction. Ha!"

Partners. Can't trust them.

Rose pulled up in the Nash, her window down. "Are you all right?" Then, seeing Virgil's swollen face and bruised nose, she said, "Who did that to you?"

"That'd be Jack," he said.

She looked at me.

"It's a long story," I said.

"But a good one!" said Virgil. He pulled open the door, we climbed in with the other suitcase, and Rose peeled away.

In the crash of relief that followed, Virgil shouted, *"Whoooooie!"* And then, "Wheaties here was on a roll, Rose, you shoulda seen it! That was some fine jazz you were selling, Jack. Corkscrew Connor? The Eye Doctor? The Belfast Butcher? You were throwing it out there like a toss of the tat. It was beautiful!"

We had to get back to 1-A and clear out. Rose had told the chauffeur that he was driving to a surprise birthday party and that if he didn't let the cat out, there'd be another $200 when he got there.

"Got where?"

"New Mexico," said Rose, and I had to laugh at that.

"Across state lines?"

"Across state lines," she said. "I gave him very detailed directions to nowhere. 'Take the second access road across, follow it up to the third right, take that until the road forks, go north and then turn back west until you come to a large barn. Second farmhouse after that is where the surprise party is. But not a word!'"

"Ha!" said Virgil. "It's the sort of directions I used to give when I was playing the Badger."

Virgil opened the suitcase and hauled out the money I had reclaimed, both ours and theirs. He held up one of the watches the men had surrendered, shook his head in appreciation. "How'd you figure it out?" he asked me.

"It was the Spanish Fly that did it," I said. "That and the dandelions. I'll explain later."

"Was Peabody in on it?"

"Nope," I said. "He had our phones cut off, remember? It was just our bad luck that I figured out how to reconnect the line."

Virgil was getting giddier by the moment, morphine and merriment, equal parts I figured. "Shoulda seen it, Rose! Was a sight to behold. The boy's an artist. Corkscrew Connor, *ha!* I loved it!"

He was laughing now and hooting it out, and I knew that as the years went by and the story took wing I would grow in stature with every telling, that I would live on as Wheaties McGreary from the Dust Bowl or as Scotland Jack outta Paradise Flats. I knew the tale would be told and retold, would be passed along from hand to hand like a coin steeped in good luck, and no matter what happened to me the story would continue, would live on, would never die.

Virgil and Miss Rose and I returned to our rooftop "liar." We packed the trunk, gathered everything up as quick as we could. We took the camera, but left the radio and the icebox, and the photographic enlarger. I filled the remaining green valise with my own belongings, clothes mainly. And when the other two weren't looking, I packed in the blocks of wood I'd used to hold up the enlarger with. It gave the suitcase a certain … heft.

We lugged everything down the stairs, Virgil wincing with every step.

"Have to get you to a doctor," said Rose, but he wouldn't listen.

"Bones set," he said. "It's what they do."

With the Nash loaded up, and me sitting in the back and Rose behind the wheel, we drove out of that alleyway and never cast so much as a glance back at where we'd been.

"Can you stop at the bus depot?" I asked.

"The depot?" said Virgil. "Oh, right. Your ticket. Good point, might as well cash that out. Your bus'll be leaving soon and once it does, won't be able to get a refund."

"I'm not getting a refund," I said, and the car went quiet.

Rose looked at me in the rearview mirror. "What are you saying, Jack?"

She knew exactly what I was saying. So did Virgil.

SEVENTY

The Greyhound Depot was just about the most modern building in Silver City. Newly built and streamlined, with its rounded corners and flat roof, its vertical neon and its blue-and-ivory tiles—it was a work of art, it truly was.

Beneath the stainless-steel canopy, one of the Greyhound Company's coaches was already idling: silver-on-silver and windows tinted, looking every bit like the future that was coming towards us, sleek and smooth and sure. But even with all that modernity on display, it was still a sad pool of light we drove towards. The glare of it formed deep shadows in the loading bays. Is there anything in this world quite so forlorn or lonely as a bus depot at night? Everyone in transit like that?

I climbed out of the Nash, carrying a green valise. Virgil and Miss Rose followed. She stopped me, adjusted my collar like it was the first day of school, and asked, "Are you sure about this?"

I was.

Virgil shook his head in disgust. "Guess I read you wrong all along, kid. You're going back? To what? Some dirtbag town in the middle of nowhere. And you, driving around in a broken-down flivver, a brood of crusty-nosed whelps squawking loud, life pickin' away at who you are. Back to the humdrum and humble. Is that what you want?" He sounded hurt and angry and sad all at the same time. "This really gripes my soul. You had it in you, Jack. You had it in you to become one of the greats."

One of the greats. That's what I was afraid of.

"You're going home?" he said.

"I'm going home."

Rose had tears in her eyes, but she wasn't sad. Not exactly. Strange, that. Those might not have even been tears. Might have just been the lights from the depot reflecting back in the paleness.

I turned to her, said, "I'd like you to have this."

She looked down, turned it over in her hand.

"A hair clip," she said. "It's beautiful, Jack. Must have paid a heavy price for this."

"No," I said. "Not really."

I wanted to hold her one last time, to press myself into her, to close my eyes tight and fill my breath with the smell of cigarettes and Camay. But it was time to go. The driver called out, *"Night run, points south and southwest! Leaving now!"* Virgil lifted up the other valise, as I knew he would, and said, "Hang on, kid. There's still the matter of your cut."

"I don't want it."

"No? Well, at least take a couple of bucks with you. If only to help you get back on your—"

"I can't," I said. "I have to start clean."

And that smallest of tells appeared on Virgil's face. It was the twitch of a mouth holding back—not a smile, or even the shadow of a smile, but the *promise* of one. "Really?" he said. "You don't want any of the money? C'mon. Even a C-note has got to help."

"I don't want any of it," I said. "I'm bowing out of the game."

"Because I can give you whatever you want," he said. "I can open up this suitcase, right now, and reach in and take out some of the money."

"There's no need," I said.

"Ah, but I insist," and his hand was on the clasp. "I'll just open it up and—"

"Night run, final call! All points south and southwest!"

"Let him go," said Rose. "He doesn't want any of it." And she gave me a kiss, not on the lips, but soft nonetheless, and sweet, like water to a thirsty man. I made a point of closing my eyes, of holding her tight. Of catching that final faint scent of Camay.

"Well, son," said Virgil after I'd stepped away from Rose. "If you gotta run, you gotta run. Here. You take your suitcase and I'll take mine. Have a safe journey."

"I'll try," I said. I took the suitcase from Virgil and then hurried around to the other side of the bus to board.

Rose and Virgil watched as the Greyhound pulled away, and once it had Virgil let the smile he was containing run free.

I know that's what he did, because I wasn't on that bus. I was standing in the shadows of the loading bay, off to one side, keeping a close watch.

"You do realize," said Rose, "that Jack just walked off with all our money." She looked at the green valise on the ground at Virgil's side.

"Give me some credit, girl!" said Virgil. "You think Wheaties is going to beat me with a simple suitcase switch? Ha! When you were giving him that kiss, I switched 'em *back*."

Rose looked at Virgil. Didn't say a thing.

"He had it coming," said Virgil. "Trying to play me for a fool like that. He switched them on me, I switched them back."

There was a long pause.

"Maybe he knew that's exactly what you'd do," said Rose. "Maybe Jack let *you* make the switch for him."

Virgil stopped cold. "What are you—"

"I'm just saying. Maybe Jack put down his suitcase and let you do the honors."

Virgil looked at the green valise with the scuff marks and the soft leather sides, looked at it with a sinking feeling in his gut, I imagine.

"Virgil," she said. "I think you better open that case."

He did, pulling out the blocks of wood and the rest of my clothes, throwing them every which way. *"That son of a bitch!"* Wild and raging, he glared at Rose. "Don't laugh. Why are you laughing? That kid just stole all our money."

"He didn't steal it," she said. "You gave it to him."

"Get in the car," he said. "Get in the car now! We'll catch him at the next town."

But there wouldn't be a next town.

You see, that was when everything really did fall apart—for Virgil and Rose, that is. Not for me. I knew where I was going. Knew it for the first time.

Virgil had piled into the Nash and was raring to go. "I'll drive," he said.

And as Rose opened her door, she looked back … and right at me.

That's the thing about shadows. When you're hiding in them, you're never entirely sure whether other people can see you. Did Rose spot me? I honestly don't know. She just tucked a strand of hair back behind her ear, and then got into the Nash.

That was the last I ever saw of Rosalind Scheible and Virgil Ray. Or Giuseppe Balsamo and Avanna Sherrill, or Connie Parker, or whoever it was they really were—and I wonder sometimes if even they knew. I don't imagine Virgil survived the ride, but reemerged in the next town as someone else. Rose too.

I'd like to think she saw me—that our eyes met. But even if I could track her down someday and ask, I'd never know for sure if what she said was true, or just something she thought I needed to hear.

SEVENTY-ONE

It was a long walk out to the edge of the city, to where a cluster of farmhouses lay. I had to check the scrap of paper I'd written the address down on several times before I found it.

A light came on and a rumpled man appeared, wrapping a bathrobe around himself. He smiled at me. "I wasn't sure if you were going to show," he said. "Come. It's around back."

He took me out to where the Bantam was parked and said, "Four-door speedster. Just had her tuned. Got a new transmission in there and a full tank. I'm, ah—I'm asking three hundred."

"Is cash okay?"

"Sure! But—aren't you going to haggle?"

"No," I said. "You look like an honest man."

The name on the mailbox said *Stoffer*.

"Do you have family?" I asked. "To the south? Down in the flats?"

"Did," he said. "Years back. They were the first ones to break sod. The name would have been 'Offern' back then. They added the 'Saint' later. Became 'Stoffer' after that."

"Well, now," I said, and I smiled. "Isn't that something."

I drove away with the windows down and a suitcase full of money on the seat beside me. Well over ninety grand by my count, plus a pair of gold watches and a couple of rings. Virgil always said he never knew a con man who wasn't eventually cheated by his partner. You'd think of all people, he'd have seen it coming.

I passed the De Valu chemical plant on the outskirts of town, shimmering in the predawn glow. The light was on in Dicannti's upstairs office window. He'd be opening his fabulous money machine right about now, eyes shining with wonder at the magic that was about to occur. He would not be disappointed. Not this time, at least. I'd added a second bill when I reset it, and that hundred would buy me another three hours. You have to plan your escape. Can't be caught waiting at a bus depot. If I'd learned anything from Virgil, I'd learned that.

A fellow can put a lot of road behind him with a three-hour head start. I drove hard, through the day and into the night. Slept in the car, siphoned gas, and pushed on. Stopped the following morning to mail some of the money back to my Da—more than ten years' salary right there—along with a note: "I worry about you, Da. And I know you worry about me. But I'll be fine. Here's some funds to help with food and such, just till your ship comes in."

I was about to seal it up, but then stopped and added, "As I know it will someday."

I put my letter in with the stack of bills I was sending, and then took it up to the counter. There was more in that single package to my Da than Bonnie and Clyde had earned in all their killings and robberies combined. A good deal more, in fact, and not a single person had given their life for it. Which was the way it should be, it being only money after all, and not worth the dying.

There was enough in there to take care of my father. Not enough to finish his manor, what with the crystal chandeliers and turrets he kept adding. But that was fine, too, because I knew all along that the house never would get built. And maybe that was the point of it.

Maybe it's not about the winning or the losing, or about stacking the deck in your favor. Maybe it's not about trying to rig the bet or take the next hand. Maybe it's about laying down a wager even when the odds are against you. Maybe it's knowing the game is gaffed, and knowing you can't win, and playing just the same. Maybe that's the only kind of wager worth making.

I had fifty thousand dollars left over for just such a wager, and I drove north across the plains now, along the edge of a shelterbelt forest as sunlight washed across the land, and I could see it, clear as the road unrolling in front of me—could see it in the soup kitchens and the work camps, in the breadlines and midnight missions, wherever the raggedy men and tattered women were huddled. And there's me, Jack McGreary outta Paradise Flats, giving away money that was never mine to start with, giving it back till it was gone, handing it out by the fistful to the down-and-outers and the lost souls, dropping pebbles by the hundreds, dropping them till the sea began to swell in a wave that would carry me northward all the way to the border and the recruitment stations beyond.

HMS HLRY 3rd Div HQ RADIO LOG June 6, 1945

Allied operations at Normandy began 04:00 at Omaha, Utah,
Gold, Sword, and Juno.

Private Jack McGreary, Third Canadian Infantry, landed at
Juno Beach in the first wave. He was hit three times before he
could reach the shore.

Notes from the Author

There were only five surnames in the history of St. Kilda. McGreary was not one of them.

The Fergusons of St. Kilda settled in Glasgow and later shipped to Cape Breton, to work in the coal mines. My grandfather came over as a young man. But after a cave-in at Dominion Mines, he walked away and never returned. Family legend tells us that he flipped a coin on whether to remain on British territory, as Canada was still considered, or go south into the United States.

The coin landed in Canada's favor. He found work on the CNR. He fell in love with my grandmother from the side of a train, and here I am.

I often wonder about that other history, the one that never happened. In previous books I've written about Canada and Japan, but this time out I wanted to look at the American Dream—at the other side of the coin. The toss my grandfather won. Or lost. Depending on your point of view.

Jack McGreary, the narrator in *Spanish Fly*, first appeared in an earlier novel of mine called *Happiness*. I considered rewriting the character's original biography, having him suddenly move to Red Deer, say, in order to make this story more "Canadian." But that seemed awfully self-conscious. In the end I decided simply to get out of the way and let Jack tell his story.

The photograph that appears on the cover of this book is one that helped shape the tone and character of the novel. I kept a copy of it close at hand when I was writing *Spanish Fly*, and I referred to it often. It acted like a window into that world. In my mind, that's Jack McGreary prowling the streets of Silver City, with Miss Rose behind him. Her hair is darker, dyed perhaps, or maybe she's wearing one of her wigs as she

scans the streets for likely marks. Ah! She has just spotted her prey, a
big-chested businessman shouldering past on the other side. But Jack
has caught our eye too, has seen us watching him. He stares hard, right
at us. There is tension in that photograph. The pool hall and Temple
Drugs, the tobacco shop and storefronts: this was the texture I was
trying to capture. The word "liar" is even embedded in the billiard sign
above Jack's shoulder. And what is the world of con men if not the
Temple of Liars?

The actual photograph is of Ralph Olson of Cremona, Alberta, taken
when he was a young man on the streets of Calgary. Some may recognize the columns of the Bay department store behind him. Mr. Olson is
not, I hasten to add, a con man or swindler of any sort. I first came
upon this photograph on the wall of his daughter Kirsten's home and it
captivated me in the way that I hope Jack's tale captivated you. It is used
here courtesy of Mr. Olson. (Ralph also gave me tips on how Jack would
have flooded the Nash at the start of the novel, and how, in his panic,
Jack might have tried to get the car started.)

The other photograph that seemed to capture what I was trying to
get down on paper is the one that appears at the very end of *Spanish
Fly:* the image of a young mother and a boy, caught in a dust storm. I
came across it in a pictorial history of the Great Depression and have
been haunted by it ever since. The story of Jack and his absent mother
grew directly out of that photograph, and *Spanish Fly* closes with this
image because I wanted to bring the story back full circle to Jack as a
boy, lost in a world of sand.

The con games that appear in *Spanish Fly* are real: the Drake swindle,
the pedigreed pooch, the goat glands of Dr. Brinkley. Change raising, the
bank inspector gig, the pigeon drops, the carnie tricks, the Mish rolls and
the fabulous money machine: all date to that era. Adolph Hitler really
was named *Time* magazine's Man of the Year, and Studebaker really did
have a line of luxury sedans named "the Dictator." And no one ever wins
at three-card monte.

The great con men that Virgil talks about are also real, as are their
fates. Suitcase Simpson and Henry the Horse were grifters that my

father, Jack Ferguson outta Radville, Saskatchewan, told me about. Geordie Dee is a composite; no one in fact knows who invented the Texas Twist. But Count Lustig, Yellow Kid Weil, Canada Bill, Chicago May, Charley Fisher, the Deacon, the Colonel, and all the rest are real figures from the Golden Age of the Con. (Though I do confess that Sigmund Engel of the lonely hearts scam didn't carry a copy of Ovid with him, not as far as I know. That was an embellishment on my part.) The insight that fat is congealed anger comes from comedian Ben Stein.

For more on the sources of these classic cons, along with notes on the geography of *Spanish Fly* and the naming of the main characters, visit WWW.WILLFERGUSON.COM and click on "books" and then "Spanish Fly."

Acknowledgments

I would like to thank my agent Carolyn Swayze, editor Barbara Pulling, and everyone at Penguin Canada who was involved in putting *Spanish Fly* together:

Editorial Director, Andrea Magyar
Head Honcho, David Davidar
Managing Editor, Tracy Bordian
Copy Editor, Karen Alliston
Art Director, Mary Opper
Production Coordinator, Chrystal Kocher
Formatter, Christine Gambin
Publicity Manager, David Leonard
Marketing Director, Yvonne Hunter
and National Sales Director—and up-and-coming
     music producer—Don Robinson

It's a great team. Hope I haven't missed anyone.

I would also like to thank Kirsten Olson, Ian Ferguson, and Mark Zuehlke for their astute advice and timely input. A big thank you as well to Tom Phillips and his Men of Constant Sorrow for setting the story of *Spanish Fly* to music—and giving it the proper country twang.